CECIL ROBERTS

A
Terrace
In the Sun

THE BOOK CLUB
121 CHARING CROSS ROAD
LONDON, W.C.2

Printed in Great Britain
by Richard Clay and Company, Ltd.,
Bungay, Suffolk

TO
GIULIETTA ANATRELLA

CONTENTS

PROLOGUE

I

IT was a poor ballet. The heavy young man, representing Icarus in the legend of the golden youth whose wings took him high above the Ægean Sea, flapped his brawny arms and jumped about the stage in a vain effort to portray an adolescent vigour. Perhaps the eye of Stephen May was too critical in normal circumstances. The painter of portraits has his own peculiar standards of beauty. The attenuated limbs of El Greco's saints, the bedizened stockiness of Goya's royalties, the singular lighting of Velasquez's figures—all these have their inspiring individuality. None of the great masters could have found a moment's inspiration in this Icarus. The perspiring young man was as jaded as the audience gathered on this winter's afternoon in the preposterous, rococo theatre of the Casino of Monte Carlo.

It was New Year's Eve, and the directors of the Casino, in a vain effort to give some gaiety to the Principality, had imported a ballet company. Very old ladies and rheumy-eyed gentlemen, heavy with memories of a brighter world in which the grand-dukes and duchesses, princes, statesmen, and an attendant host of jewelled ladies and valet-groomed men had once crowded the brilliant scene, sat gloomily while Icarus jumped and flapped his wings in a vain make-believe.

Stephen May's eyes wandered from the stage. He surveyed the gaudy decorations of this heavily gilded little theatre. In its peculiar style it was a perfect piece of the period. Between youths whose naked limbs of plaster protruded over the cornice there was a mural painting of a scene on Parnassus, chosen with that constant passion of the French for the female form in the utmost nudity. Succulent-bosomed goddesses plucked harps and played viols. Mercury pirouetted with an archness unachieved by Icarus bounding below. A Grace, with a convenient girdle of flowers, bestowed a laurel wreath on a godlike young man. Timeless and fair, they posed inanely above an audience to whom youth was only a dim memory.

In the third row sat Count Ladislaus Vladetsky, his great frame compressed into a narrow stall. He appeared as deflated as his fortune, with the jowls and bloodshot eyes of a Great Dane, balefully surveying the scene before him. Lonely, impoverished, depressed, he lived these days in a dream of the past. What galas he had witnessed here, what lovely women thronging the boxes and the stalls! And now this dowdy world, this pinchbeck performance. He turned a baleful eye on Icarus, who had crashed to earth and was waving two muscular legs with the spasmodic death-throes of a crushed wasp on a picnic plate. The Count grunted, shifted his bulk slightly and lapsed into the prepossessing problem of these uncertain days. Where, in a world which had changed only the name of its nightmare, from the menace of Nazism to the all-pervading tide of Communism, could one take one's money and find respite on a crazy planet? Cuba, Santo Domingo, Brazil—or maybe Peru? Would the hydrogen bomb that could reduce New York to a tangled skeleton penetrate thus far? In a trance of apprehension the Count watched Icarus flutter and wriggle. He felt just like that. When all his possessions were reduced to a bag of diamonds wedged in a fold of his pendulous stomach, who would want to buy them on a devastated earth? That it should have come to this! Habit-stricken, this was his thirtieth season at Monte Carlo. He felt like the keeper of a morgue, he who had been so kind to so many beautiful young creatures, he for whom a vanished generation of famous chefs had striven to titillate his palate, and win the pearl pin that went kitchen-wards to convey his pleasure, in the regal manner of a Bourbon conferring the *Toison d'Or*.

Stephen May moved in his stall in a vain attempt to lessen the pain that tortured his limbs. He too had memories, but there was no uneasiness arising from his recollections, no lamenting for the past, no fear of the future. In another nine hours he would have no problems to solve, no more physical ills. "To cease upon the midnight with no pain." How oddly apposite that line of Keats's now became! He could not bear to look at his twisted hands. He wore gloves most of the time to keep them out of sight, hands that had once been so skilful and had won for him his fame in the past thirty years. How strange was the circle of life! Here, on the Riviera, where he had known the smile of fortune, he had now closed his career.

It had been utterly foolish for him to court the humiliation that had crushed him here in these last two months, but he believed in courage, and he had cherished a hope that his will could impose its purpose upon his racked body. He had come to paint a portrait of the Hereditary Prince of Monaco in celebration of the young man's accession to the throne of this charming little Principality. He had come with one great determination, to defeat the insidious thing that was locking him in a prison-house. He had not touched his palette for two years—two years of wandering from spa to spa, from clinic to clinic, while the grim enemy crept upon him, relentlessly stealthy. It had been a costly illness, and his finances were getting low. Most distressing of all was his physical handicap. He had bought a lot of gloves these last two years, abnormally sensitive to the disfigurement of his hands. This, more than the pain in his limbs, sitting or lying, afflicted him. Why, why, in his rebellious folly, had he imagined he could work again? For five weeks he had stood in front of the canvas on his easel and struggled like a drowning man. His subject, the Prince, was easy and affable, liberal in the matter of sittings. He had been given an agreeable workroom in the palace, overlooking the crescent of mountains with their villa-covered slopes, the small blue harbour below, the promenade of the Condamine, the two harbour-lights on the jetties, the cluster of yachts and boats. Hour by hour the inexorable truth closed upon him. He could achieve no likeness, he had no precise control of the brush. A mental paralysis worse than the physical seized him. He fought on, a desperate creature who knew too well that his will to create was not paramount. After each sitting of one hour's duration he carefully covered the canvas, and affected an easy manner. Then, one morning, the question he had anticipated was put to him.

" Am I to be allowed to see it soon ? " asked the young Prince, affably. " Or do you prefer only a final revelation ? I confess I am dying of curiosity ! "

" If Your Highness doesn't mind—I prefer that you should see only the finished work," he had replied, and, forcing a light note into his voice, added, " You might be really alarmed if you saw it at this stage, and refuse me further sittings."

"Oh, not at all! I'm quite enjoying them. While I'm here I'm not bothered by anything. I only wish I had a talent like yours—it would be nice to really create something, and not be just a recurring decimal."

"A recurring decimal?"

"Yes, just Louis the Second, Florestan the Third—a number somewhere in a century."

The Prince laughed, and took out a cigarette case.

"Do you mind if I smoke—will it trouble you?" he asked.

"Not at all."

"I'm afraid I shall not be here for any more sittings after today, for about a week. I think I told you I'm going to Paris?"

"That's quite all right, the portrait's almost finished," said May.

"Oh, splendid!—I expected quite an ordeal. When Laszlo painted my mother I believe it was a long-drawn-out business. Do you like his portrait?"

There were two Laszlo portraits in the throne-room, one of his mother, one of his grandfather.

"I think they're very refreshing to look at—though they're not my style," answered May, diplomatically. "He always made his subjects scintillate."

He worked in silence for a while. He had not told the Prince of the decision he had made in the last few minutes, that he would never finish the portrait, that it was a terrible performance. He knew now beyond all doubt that he could not paint, that he would never paint again. He had no control over his brush. The eye saw as clearly as ever, but the hand could not obey his will. He cursed himself for the folly that had led him to this desperate attempt. Little by little the prison walls were closing upon him. But he would never be a prisoner. He lacked the fortitude, even if he had the means to support life as a useless object.

When the sitting was concluded and he had covered the canvas, the Prince, rising from his chair, said, "You've worked very hard this morning, Mr May. I'm longing to see the result. It is a little cruel of you to keep me in suspense!"

"Your Highness will know the result very soon. I shall take the canvas away, and work on it while you are in Paris."

They shook hands. He had liked this bright young man.

The Paris visit provided him with the opportunity he sought. He left the Palace with the canvas, went back to his apartment and, opening a penknife, cut it from the stretcher. Then he burnt it in the kitchen stove. Poor Prince Rainier! He had wasted his time and been used for a mad experiment. That evening he wrote him a letter. It was difficult to write, and the floor was covered with repeated attempts. Finally he wrote out what seemed the best version.

> Your Highness will be surprised to hear that I feel I cannot continue with your portrait. The fault is wholly mine. You merit something better than what I have achieved, and since posterity attaches some interest to yourself this libel—for such it is—must not have circulation. The explanation lies not with the subject, for no one could have shown greater consideration, but with myself. I have for some time been in bad health, and it is clear that this indisposition is reflected in my work. For both our sakes this portrait must not be seen. I am very sorry that I should have wasted so much of your time.

Having painfully written out this note, almost illegible in his racked handwriting, he took it along to his bank on the Boulevard des Moulins, where for a few francs a young clerk typed out his correspondence.

" Very confidential, of course," warned May. " Please send it up to the Palace by hand."

" Oh, certainly, M'sieur May. No one shall know ! "

All that was a fortnight ago. A polite and kindly letter of regret came back from the Prince.

> I hope, nevertheless, you will come to see me. I enjoyed our conversation. How well you know the world ! I shall say nothing about our interrupted sittings. I realise how great an ordeal you are facing.

A nice simple young man. He wished him well, for there were rocks ahead ; a growing financial problem in this Principality, where a vanished élite would come no more ; the assertions of France towards her free neighbour in the growing eclipse of European liberty ; the stout contentiousness of the native Monegasques, bewildered and fractious, like a once rich old dowager forced into petty economies by her trustees.

The curtain fell, there was an interval, the audience began to move out into the foyer. The intervals were cunningly prolonged to enable the visitors to go to the tables for a brief session of gambling. Those who went in the opposite direction, towards the bar, seemed to appease their gambling instinct by putting francs into the automatic machines.

May wandered through into the gambling-saloons. How changed it all was since he had first come here! Or was it that the excitement of a new scene in his inexperienced youth had accentuated the degree of his sensation? No, the change was not wholly in himself. Through the passage of years the scene had deteriorated. There was no one in evening dress. In those far-off days no man would have been permitted past the door unless wearing a dress-shirt. They appeared to be for the most part war-rich Genoa and Turin business men with their gaudily dressed womenfolk. The scene was less cosmopolitan: the grand-dukes, the Italian princelings, the English lords, the Austrian aristocrats, the richly-kept demi-mondaines with their silks and pearls—all had gone from the scene; the blend of the well-born, the fashionable and the adventurous had vanished. The women here tonight could not have qualified for any of the old rôles. They were dowdily prosperous, boringly respectable, unexcitingly dressed. The men had thick necks and podgy hands. But they had money; the stakes were high and reckless. In the gambling the Italians led, the Americans followed, the French took a few plunges, the English were no more visible; they and their pounds were forgotten in this Riviera scene.

Stephen May pulled out a thousand-franc note and advanced towards the roulette table. For a man nearing the end of his resources, financial and physical, it was a pathetic gesture. But tomorrow he would have no more need of money. Even if he were in need it would make no difference to him. It was merely in order to repeat a long-forgotten experience, recalling those heady days of his first success, that he now sought the table.

He did not reach it. As he moved forward, even as the bell rang for the beginning of the Second Act, someone checked him.

"Is it Mr Stephen May?" a voice, feminine and pleasant, asked.

He turned, and saw addressing him a woman of about sixty. She was a complete stranger. He stared, a little rudely.

" Of course you don't remember me, I am a wreck ; but you haven't changed—it's quite preposterous ! "

She laughed and held out a gloved hand. She was well-dressed, a woman of assurance and fashion, though quietly attired in dark purple with a small rope of pearls around her wrinkled throat :

" I'm Georgie Thirkell—you remember, Pacco's friend ? We met there, when you were painting his portrait."

His mind raced over the years. Pacco—the Duque d'Alta-vara and a palace at Seville, in the time of the great *Feria*, with splendid horses, bull-fights, the rattle of castanets, the strumming of guitars till dawn, and, over all, the scent of orange-blossom pervading the Moorish patios and the tree-lined *avenidas* ; the Duke of Altavara, the grandee whose portrait he had come to paint, and thereby to be honoured by hanging in a gallery of ancestors to which Velasquez and Goya had contributed. Georgie Thirkell, the wife of Colonel Thirkell, a Gaiety chorus-girl, a great beauty, reckless, who had astonished everyone by divorcing the Duke of Stornaway for penniless ' Pony ' Thirkell. Out of the mist of twenty years she grew clearer to him, shadow that she was of her lovely past.

" Of course ! " he exclaimed. " How could I ever forget you ! "

It was a gallant attempt, fraudulent to both of them. Only the glitter of her eyes, still lovely, remained—that, and the manner, direct and assured, which had always marked her.

" How nice to see you ! And the Colonel ? " he asked, happy to show he could remember there was a colonel, though he barely existed beside her.

" Poor ' Pony ' !—he died ten years ago. How strange to meet you here ! I've not been here for sixteen years. How dreadfully changed it all is—but how dreadfully changed we all are ! " She laughed as she said it, and added, " Do you come here regularly ? "

" No—I haven't been here for many years ; the change shakes one. I've been doing a portrait of the Prince of Monaco," he explained. He was finding something nice in her face as he spoke. She was sympathetic, mellowed with time.

" The Prince ? Oh, how nice—for him ! " she added, with a ripple in her voice. That had not changed, the voice and the light in the eye brought her back to him. " I was always sorry afterwards I didn't snatch at Pacco's suggestion that you should paint me. But I thought more then of whirling around, and it would have been boring to sit—and you weren't so famous then—so I deserve to have nothing to show against the ravages of Time ! "

" Are you staying in Monte Carlo ? "

" We've been here five days. What a shame to have just met you !—we're leaving tomorrow morning at six. I'm on Tony's yacht—we leave for Portofino."

" Tony ? " he asked. Was there another husband ?

" Tony's my son—Stornaway. I'm with his party on the *Lone Star*," she explained. " I would like you to have lunched with us. What ill luck after all these years ! Are you staying long ? "

" No—I leave tomorrow," said May. " I'm here in the Theatre—the show's very poor. Can you sit down a few minutes ? It's so pleasant to see you again."

" So am I, with Tony's party from the yacht. Yes, isn't it a poor show ? But everything's so third-rate these days. Just look at these people ! Where do they buy their clothes ! "

" Where do they find their money ! "

" Indeed. Yes, let's sit down. I don't mind missing part of the ballet."

They went into the bar and sought a table. He ordered drinks. Her son Tony. He had forgotten there was a son of the first marriage. He must be the Duke of Stornaway whose yacht in the harbour had caused so much comment. There were few yachts in the harbour these days, an English one was a rarity. Everyone seeing the Union Jack astern had asked the same question, " How does the Duke do it ? " Those who knew a little of the young Duke's history had an idea. He had married the daughter of an American ten-cent-store magnate, and the *Lone Star* had a good dollar ballast. As they talked, a question arose in his mind. Across the years he had forgotten the ghosts Georgie Thirkell had now evoked with her chatter of ' Pacco ' Altavara. The portrait of him, painted in polo kit, had gone a long way to build his own fame.

" Tell me, you are still Mrs Thirkell ? " asked May.

" Still," she said, smiling. " Funny, isn't it ? I once thought I could never live without a man, and now I feel I couldn't live with one. How little we really know about human nature ! Poor ' Pony ' was a fool—what you'd call an overbred nit-wit. But he made me happy, though he often stripped me to the skin, with his mania for horses. If my son wasn't so generous—which means Julie his wife, really—I'd be quite destitute. But I'd marry that foolish man again—which shows that one fool can find happiness with another, and that we learn nothing, really."

They talked. When a quarter of an hour had gone she said she thought she must rejoin her party. They went back to the theatre. At the entrance they said " Good-bye ".

" It's been so nice seeing you after all this time. I do hope we shall meet again soon. I go back to London in March. I've a little place in Pont Street. Do come and see me."

She opened her bag and took out a card.

" When I come to England, I will," he said, accepting it. " It's been most delightful for me. Good-bye."

He watched her pass through the doors, still a tall, distinguished woman. He would never see her again.

II

The curtain had risen on *Les Sylphides*. It was a tolerable performance of this hackneyed ballet. May tried to recall the places in which he had seen it—London, Paris, Milan, Vienna, Budapest, Dresden, Copenhagen and New York. The familiar music lulled him into a reverie. He scarcely saw the white ballerinas beyond the darkened auditorium. His encounter with Georgie Thirkell had brought back a horde of ghosts who swam into his consciousness like these fluttering Sylphides. There was a sweet sadness in life of which one was only conscious as the pageant drew to a close. His own story had moved from poverty to success, from the constricted life of an English provincial town to the capitals of Europe and the homes of the great, from a hovel in a mining community to a studio in Italy. In its variety, in the whole gamut of life's orchestration, the material was as rich as it was confusing.

Some years ago at Aix-les-Bains, where he had gone for the cure of an illness that had been diagnosed as rheumatism, he had amused himself by writing his life in the form of a novel. To his surprise the story seemed to write itself. He had shown it to an author whose friendship he valued, hoping secretly, as all amateurs do, for praise while asking for criticism. His critic had been unreservedly encouraging. He had gone so far as to offer assistance in its publication. May had demurred, because the story was too autobiographical, involved others too deeply, and in his own free mood he had even used all the proper names, including his own. These could be changed, some episodes too revealing could be omitted or transformed, persisted his friend. Then, suddenly, as often before, the desire to work again in his own medium had seized him. He put the manuscript away, and a few days later was portraying a living subject, at a large fee, in a château near Autun, taken by his American client. Typed, and bound with gay Venetian end-papers, the novel was now in the trunk he had left at the Hotel de Paris when he had moved into the apartment he had rented here for six months. He smiled to think how surprised Georgie Thirkell would be if she knew she had been committed to paper. She had neglected at the height of her beauty to have her portrait in oils, and, unknown to herself, he had done her portrait in words. He felt a passing curiosity in that forgotten manuscript. Well, there was no time now to read it. It should be destroyed, and he must leave a memorandum to his solicitor to that effect. He was grateful to Georgie Thirkell for the reminder.

Stephen May had to move in his seat. In doing so his leg pressed that of the occupant of the next stall. He felt her stiffen and draw abruptly away. He was about to murmur an apology, but caught a glimpse of her disagreeable face contorted with indignation and protest. She was a woman of over sixty, with dyed red hair, and a black velvet band around her scraggy neck. The silly old swan, arched in protection of a virtue no one would assail! Suppressing the apology forming on his lips, he dragged himself up, and hobbled past her to the gangway, leaving a wake of hostility in the stalls about him. Out in the vestibule he stood a few moments while the familiar pain cramped his numbed limbs. Looking up at the clock, he saw it was nearly five. He walked out of the glass doors and paused before undertaking the downward flight of steps. Already the lights were on. On the emerald sward of the palm-garden rising up the hill the artificially lighted flower-beds and bushes turned Nature into a jeweller's window. He would have a cup of tea, with buttered toast, in one of the shops that maintained that hallowed British rite. Tea and toast. He recalled how in his boyhood he had held the toasting-fork before the hob grate in the kitchen until his hand felt burnt, and how the butter, placed on the hob to soften it, had all melted, evoking his mother's protest. The little kitchen in the Nottingham back street.

He pushed open the door and entered the haunt of scones and China or Indian brews. He gave an order to the pretty Monegasque waitress, undisguised by her plaid apron, and picked up a month-old *Tatler* while the resident cat mounted a chair and blinked at him.

During tea he reflected how difficult it was to make a Will, particularly when you had no one dependent upon you. Casting about for a legatee of his few belongings, he realised with a shock how very lonely he was in the world. It seemed that nearly all those he had ever loved had died or passed out of his life. An itinerant career such as his—for he had travelled and worked all over the earth in these last thirty years—had brought him a great circle of acquaintances but no intimate friends. If he had married again, and had had a family, life would have been much different, but not necessarily any less lonely or more happy. Only yesterday he had been startled by a paragraph in the Paris *Daily Mail*. After forty-two years of married life, and having reared five children, Mr and Mrs Chauncey Trafford had decided to part. They had obtained a divorce. He had painted portraits of the Trafford family—Mr Trafford, Mrs Trafford, Eileen their eldest daughter, and Tony their adored grandson. While painting these portraits he had stayed with them three times for lengthy periods in their beautiful Surrey home, and in their villa near Mentone. A more devoted pair or united family he had never seen. And now, after forty years of married life, two persons, each nearly seventy, had separated. Surely for the few remaining years they could have carried on ! How difficult human relationships were ! On the whole perhaps his loneliness had been the least of evils. There had always been his work to engross him.

How strange that in making his Will a few days ago he had

forgotten the trunk deposited at the Hotel de Paris! It contained nothing much of value—some clothes, photographs of persons he had painted, a few miniatures, and the manuscript of his unpublished novel. It would be better to have the trunk along with his other things, and make it simpler for old Fawcett when he came out to wind up his affairs.

It was quite dark when May left. The shops were brightly lit in celebration of New Year's Eve. There was a dinner and dance this evening at the Hotel de Paris, and a number of private dinner-parties, mostly in restaurants, for servant trouble had invaded Monte Carlo. None of the sadly diminished English colony entertained now. Their shrunken capital and the fallen pound kept them severely restricted. "We're too old to move, too poor to go home, and too scared to die," growled old Colonel Storey, without a car, without a valet and without enough whisky in these last ten years.

In the Boulevard des Moulins May found a taxi, and drove to the Hotel de Paris. A few minutes later he had retrieved his small trunk and told the man to drive to his apartment in the Avenue de Grande Bretagne. It was in one of the tall blocks that rose, terrace on terrace, above each other up the mountain-side, so that each apartment had a balcony looking out across the bay. The ground floor on the entrance side was actually on the third or fourth floor of the building. His own apartment was in a block of twenty. He had a sitting-room with two French windows, and a balcony that commanded a superb sweep of the blue bay, from Monaco and its harbour to the long peninsula of Cap Martin, green by day, violet in the evening and jewelled with lights at night. For a neighbour he had on one side the English church. May's bedroom window, on an angle commanding the Avenue, looked on to the red pantiles of its roof. When services were held he could hear the drone of the organ and voices singing, but the church was not near enough to annoy him.

It was in every sense a convenient little apartment. There was a slip of a kitchen, a sitting-room, bedroom, spare room and bath. Across the landing lived a neighbour he had never seen in two months of residence. There was the inevitable inquisitorial concierge on the ground floor. She must have found his life singularly dull, for no one called. The apartment belonged to a French couple who had a house in Paris.

The husband had gone on business for six months to Indo-China and, liking the little place, whose rent was moderate, May had taken it for six months. He had come in mid-October, and it was his until April.

The taxi-man brought up the trunk. May paid him and shut the door. At dusk a daily woman came in, drew the shutters, turned down the bed and took out an empty milk-bottle. She returned in the morning at nine, made his break-fast, dusted, and departed an hour later. For the rest of the day he was quite alone. It was the same kind of service as he had had in his studio at Campden Hill.

He sat down, tired as always these days, for the nights were no longer for sleep, but for torture. Often, restless with pain, he went to the balcony and saw the dawn come over the sea, purple and then violet changing to rose, and suddenly on the rim of the world the flaming sun peered over the threshold of day. It was a recurrent miracle that not even his pain could make commonplace.

As he sat in the chair, the room dimly lit by a single shaded light, since he found the long mirror, the Louis-Seize furniture and the pear-drop chandelier a little cloying, he began to wonder about his Will. At the most he could not have more than a thousand pounds plus his few effects. He had left his old charwoman—a faithful, Fate-battered retainer—two hundred pounds, and to his one old friend, Letty Formby, who, over seventy, was cheerful and spritely in her chaotic bed-sitting-room among the Chelsea chimney-pots, the remainder, for it seemed as if she would live for ever on means so restricted that it had always been a puzzle how she lived at all. It was little enough to leave, for a man who had had much success. He had always lived well, and taken no thought for the morrow. It was only in these last three years, his industry diminished by his growing affliction, that he had begun to observe income and expenditure. Now the income had vanished for ever. As it was, small as was his fortune, he would leave more than his father had left—a thousand pounds and some furniture, as against sixty pounds and nine hundred dog-collars. He looked now at the gold signet ring on his little finger, engraved with a dog-collar. " Is that your crest ? " someone had once asked him. " No—it's the family tragedy," he had replied, and seeing the surprise this remark had evoked, added, " It would take too

long to tell." Nevertheless, he had told the story in the manuscript in the trunk. He began to wonder what else it contained.
It had been left for two years in the Paris studio of a friend who,
on his way south, had asked him to remove it, as he was giving
up the studio. It was three years since he had opened it.

Taking some keys out of his pocket, he unlocked the trunk.
Raising the lid, he was astonished to find how neatly he had
packed it. He was usually untidy. There were two suits,
two fancy waistcoats, a shantung-silk summer coat, some
shirts, all in good condition. He slipped a hand down one
side and raised the clothing. He found some guide-books in
their blue-and-red bindings, and several large envelopes which
he knew held photographs. He drew out one of these packets
and pulled out the contents. There were about a dozen large
glossy prints, photographs of portraits he had painted in
various parts of the world, and as he looked at them, slowly,
with some surprise and pleasure, he realised anew how varied
and interesting his life had been. Here was a portrait of the
Hereditary Prime Minister of Nepal, in full regalia, with the
pear-drop diamond head-dress and the peacock's feather. He
had painted that in far-away Katmandu, under the shadow
of the mighty Kinchinjunga. Here was the Begum of Bhopal,
an astonishing woman who had reigned over thousands. He
had been housed in a pavilion with sixty servants, a bevy of
dancing-girls and a Rolls-Royce car at his disposal. He was
paid five thousand pounds for that portrait, with no income
tax. It was six weeks' work, and every minute enjoyable.
Here was the daughter of Prince Knevetsky, whom he had
painted in a lovely villa on the Riviera. She was his only child,
a beautiful, delicate girl of seventeen. Two days after the
portrait was finished the little Princess was operated upon for
appendicitis and died on the operating-table. Her grief-
stricken father, a widower, had begged him to accompany the
body and the portrait to Cracow. It was carried in the procession to the church, in the wake of the funeral cortège, and
hung in the old Byzantine Russian church amid the ikons and
the incense. Then it was transported back to the palace,
and the next morning the Prince's valet found his master dead
in front of the portrait, with a bullet through his temple. All
that was twenty years ago in a Poland that had vanished.

May put back the photographs. Ghosts that should not be

raised. Under some clothing he felt a bulky packet. He knew what it was, the autobiographical novel, written during his first illness when trying a cure at Aix-les-Bains. It was too intimate for strange eyes, and should be destroyed. Yet he had a liking for it, something achieved in a medium not his. He would defer the decision and let his Executor determine its fate. Pushing it down again under the clothes, he fastened the lid and turned the lock. Then he went to the bureau and wrote Fawcett a note about it. He should consult his friend Shelden, the novelist, and if it was considered worth publication, then the royalties could go to the Artists' Benevolent Fund. In that event all the names must be changed.

Sealing the envelope, he reflected what vanity it was. No publisher would want it. And why should he care about having it in print—a dead author, in both senses of the word?

May was in the bathroom when a few minutes later the bell rang. He could not think of anyone who would call on him. He did not go to the door. But the bell rang persistently. Annoyed, he picked up his sticks and ambled to the door.

" Mr May ? " asked a young man, touching a seaman's cap.
" Yes ? "

He held out an envelope with the Hotel de Paris crest. May took it and opened it. There was a letter inside, written in a large, sprawling hand.

Dear Stephen,
We are having a small New Year's Eve dinner-party on board. Tony would be delighted if you would come. He knows *all* about you, and his wife is dying to meet you—do you know you painted the portrait of her aunt, Mrs Rosenthal, of Grosse Point? She says it is *marvellous*. So you *must* come, we won't take No, and you can leave early, as you are an invalid. I was lucky to get your address from the Hotel de Paris. The Descamps, of the Villa Fleuri, are coming (he owns Lalage, the great scent business), and I have arranged for them to call for you and bring you to the yacht, at eight o'clock. Black tie. A small party. We leave tomorrow at 6 a.m. Tony is always so absurd about leaving early, and there's no excuse about tides here. It will be so good to have a long

talk. It was wonderful to see you again. So *don't* disappoint me.

Affectionately,

Georgie.

P.S. When you do paint again the Descamps are rolling in money, and she's quite pretty—his second and young.

Hang the woman! He felt like writing a reply, "I have arranged not to see the New Year in, anywhere. Goodbye for ever." But it was good-hearted of her to want him at their New Year's party, despite the curiosity of Mrs Rosenthal's niece, the Duchess of Stornaway. Should he go? He might as well eat his last meal in company. He liked Georgie Thirkell, and he could leave early.

"You are from the *Lone Star*?"

"Yes, sir."

"Please tell Mrs Thirkell I shall be coming at eight."

"Very good, thank you, sir. Goodnight, sir!"

"Goodnight."

He closed the door. It was nearly seven. He had ample time to dress. It was a slow and painful business these days.

The Descamps called promptly at eight o'clock. He was an elderly man with a very smart young wife, a French Canadian. They went down the hill to the Condamine and along to the jetty, where five yachts were tied up, the *Lone Star*, a great attraction to loungers, the largest of them. They went on board. It was a warm evening, and cocktails were served under an awning. Monte Carlo lay in a crescent of light around them, the long Palace with its battlements and bastions high on the Monaco rock, the hill down to the Condamine, the terraces in tiers of lights clustered under the great Tête de Chien, the hotels, and the baroque façade of the floodlit casino, with the cliff-face from Mont Agel to Cap Martin, dotted with lights. The twin port beacons of the jetties enfolding the little harbour cast green and red shafts of light over the calm water. Across the smooth Mediterranean the peninsula of Cap Martin lay out seawards, dim in the moonlight. The lighthouse on the Cap shot an intermittent beam into the darkness. It was a world of enchantment to which man had brought the utmost sophistication.

May liked young Stornaway at once, a thin young man with charming manners. He had a sensitive face and had inherited his mother's good looks. The Duchess was a kind, lumpy young woman, fashionably but quietly dressed. It was Georgie Thirkell who dominated the scene, with her lovely hair, blued in the fashion of the day, her creamy complexion, glittering eyes, and animated manner. A rope of fine pearls encircled her neck. She had a massive emerald ring with ear-drops to match. There were nine guests, making a party of a dozen. To May's surprise, there was an Anglican Bishop with his wife. Georgie introduced them to one another.

" Stephen, this is the Bishop of Gibraltar and Mrs—— " She hesitated, seeking a name.

" Mrs Gibraltar will do ! " said the Bishop's wife. " I live in the shadow of the Rock."

It transpired that the Bishop's diocese ran all over the Mediterranean, from Madeira to Turkey.

" I always feel that the Pope should be the Bishop of Gibraltar—if you don't mind my saying so," said Georgie, with her most winning smile.

The Bishop, a picture of well-nurtured amiability, looked a little bewildered.

" And why, may I ask ? "

" Well, didn't Jesus say something about founding His church upon a Rock—the Vatican's really only a hill ! "

The whole company laughed at Georgie's bright comment.

" My mother will disestablish you, sir, if you're not careful."

" Ah, I see Mrs Thirkell's point," said the Bishop, " but, as one of the Pillars of Hercules, I claim to be a rock of the Church, and will take some dislodging."

The company applauded. The Bishop had adroitly matched his adversary.

In about half an hour they went down to the dining-saloon. The table was a bower of flowers. The stewards wore white monkey-jackets, with the Stornaway monogram and coronet. May liked the young Duke and his Duchess. He wondered about Stornaway, Georgie's first husband, and why she had switched to the inane but amiable ' Pony '. The dinner was excellent. With the champagne the conversation grew more animated. The Bishop was an admirable raconteur with a repertoire of excellent stories.

Stephen May was glad he had come. He refused nothing in the gourmet's feast, for, as with a condemned man's last meal, there were no restrictions. A little after eleven it was announced that the Bishop must go. He was conducting a Watch-night Service at the English Church. A car came for him. This gave May his opportunity; the Bishop would give him a lift, since he lived next door to the church. But he felt a certain reluctance in making this good man an accessory to his plan, though unconscious of it.

" Of course, the Bishop will be delighted," cried Georgie. " Darling Stephen, it was sweet of you to come—and brave," she added softly, holding his hands. She turned to Madame Descamps. " I was a great fool. I had a chance of being painted by Stephen, and I didn't take it—at an age when he could have done something with me ! "

Clever Georgie to be so adroit on his behalf, thought May, but quite useless now.

Their host and hostess followed them to the gangway. Suddenly Georgie Thirkell threw her arms around May's neck and gave him a kiss. " You darling ! Stephen, a very happy New Year—and good health ! " she said.

He held her a moment, kissed her and replied quietly, " Thank you, Georgie. It's been good to see you—and may you have every happiness."

Then he ambled awkwardly down the gangway to the car.

Outside the church he took leave of the Bishop and his wife.

" May I, under God's blessing, wish you a rewarding and happy New Year ? " said the Bishop, sincerely and kindly.

May thanked him, shook their hands and entered his door. He switched on the light and got into the elevator. When he arrived at his apartment he entered, and without turning on the lights walked over to the window and looked down. People were arriving for the service. The church was brightly lit. In the cliff-face of apartment houses rising above him Monte Carlo blazed with light; there was not a dark window.

He felt shaken, not in his resolve, but in his emotions. He thought he was beyond any response to human kindness. That good, kind man had really meant his New Year wishes.

He could not know he had expressed them to one who would experience no New Year, who would be free of the hideous shackling of the flesh.

May switched on the light, drew the curtains and went over to the secretaire. From a drawer he took three letters and a small box. He placed the letters in an orderly row on the desk. One was for his solicitor, Fawcett, in England; one for the local notary he had employed, and one for the young clerk at the bank who had acted for him in a secretarial capacity. These covered all emergencies. Leaving the room, he turned off the light. His bedroom, with the adjoining bathroom, was quite bright when he entered. The illumination came from outside. A cross of electric bulbs shone over the portico of the church. Dismayed, he hurried to the curtains and drew them vigorously. The act gave him a spasm of intense pain, but his discomfort was more mental than physical. To have chosen New Year's Eve for his great resolution! Fate was conspiring against him. First Georgie Thirkell coming out of the past, then the dinner-party, the Bishop, and this service in the church!

He switched on the bedside light, and put down the small box of tablets on the table. He began to feel unnerved. For a few moments he stood still, thinking. Those letters were a mistake, despite the trouble they would save people. A man who took an overdose of sleeping pills might die of misadventure, according to a coroner's verdict. The letters would make no such verdict possible.

He went to the sitting-room, tore up the letters, and burnt the pieces in the grate. Going back to his bedroom, he locked the door and began to undress.

He was in the bathroom when he became aware of organ music. It came from the English church directly under his window. The Watch-night Service had begun. A few minutes later, as he came out of the bathroom, the sound of voices, united in hymn-singing, rose in volume, so loud and near that he could distinguish the words:

> As a shadow life is fleeting;
> As a vapour so it flies:
> For the Old Year now retreating
> Pardon grant, and make us wise.

He put down a glass of water on the bedside table with the box of veronal tablets, and stood irresolute, in his pyjamas, listening to the singing outside. This was something he had not foreseen, this choral welcoming in of the New Year by the English community.

He sat down on the side of the bed. The lines of the hymn evoked memories of a distant past, a past still singularly clear. He was a little boy of five standing with his mother in the pew of a Wesleyan Methodist chapel. His mother wore a black-spotted veil and black kid gloves. Between them they held a hymn-book as they sang. He was excited because he had been allowed to stay out of bed so late, and the occasion was momentous because it was a Watch-night Service not only to see in the New Year, but to witness the passing of the Nineteenth and the beginning of the Twentieth Century. He was an imaginative little boy, and as he looked at all the worshippers in the chapel he wondered what this place and the world would be like when another little boy would witness the passing of the Twentieth into the Twenty-first Century—a tremendous speculation, for of course no one in the chapel here would be alive then, not even himself. This service brought him another excitement besides that of sitting late. His father, one of four sidesmen, was up there in the pulpit with the minister. He was both proud of and nervous about his father. He looked the best of all of them, with his smooth hair plastered down, his moustache trimmed out, wearing a high starched collar, ' a chokee ', and a black bow. He was going to be one of the speakers—they had five minutes each—and he would be the best, and certain to take more than five minutes if the Reverend Thomas Wood did not pull him up. Even so, he was nervous about his father's public performance.

There had been a pause in the singing, and now it had started again. Stephen May looked at his watch. It was eighteen minutes to twelve. This would go on for another fifteen minutes, and after a prayerful silence they would start again, more vigorously. He got up from the bed and went across to a chair, and then sat down again. He felt utterly deranged by this unforeseen interruption of his plan. One could not go into eternity, a suicide, to the singing of hymns. A sense of propriety was still strong in him, and the service had

evoked ghosts of the past that were not appropriate company
for this occasion.

> Another year hath fled ; renew,
> Lord, with our days, Thy love !
> Our days are evil here and few ;
> We look to live above.

They sang the words fervently, believers for the most part,
not troubled by any philosophical speculations or obstacles
of logic, and able to associate their lives of gossip, bridge-
playing, gambling and social preoccupations with the ascetic
poverty of the Nazarene to whom they addressed their prayers
in moments of crisis and sorrow.   For them there was nothing
incongruous in this diluted Christianity.   It was the inherited
creed of their parents and grandparents, the mixture as before.

He must not be bitter.   Many of them were good, sincere
people, like the genial Bishop and his wife.   A man sick unto
death, he could claim no normal balance in his judgment of
the human scene.   His usefulness finished, his body twisted
and tortured, his means exhausted, he had neither the con-
tinuing courage nor the philosophy that would enable him to
drag out a wretched and useless life.   Like an ancient Roman,
he had composed himself to slip from mortality.

The singing stopped.   There was a silence.   It was three
minutes to twelve.   He knew the formula.   He could see the
Reverend Thomas Wood, with his reversed white collar, raising
his arm in the pulpit : " Brethren, let us in silent prayer to
God seek His blessing and guidance in the New Year."   And
there was over all the congregation a long silence until the
minister stood up again and said, " Brethren, let me wish you
a very happy and prosperous New Year ! "   Thereupon there
was a commotion as everyone scrambled to his feet and started
hand-shaking and well-wishing with his neighbours.   The
Reverend Thomas Wood, his mother in a black-spotted veil
drawn round a toque with cloth violets, his father, nervously
dignified, stroking his whiskers and trying to appear calm before
his performance, Mrs Popperwell, the grocer's wife, well-to-do
Mr Mosley who kept the grainstore, the two ' wealthy ' Misses
Pearson, who always put gold half-sovereigns on the collection
plate carried round by his father during the hymn after the
sermon—all gone, all beyond their tribulations and triumphs.

The silence in the church was suddenly broken by a crashing joyous burst of the organ. On top of this came a tumultuous peal of bells ringing in the New Year, and then, mingled in this exultation, the uplifted voices of the congregation. Restless, annoyed, the purpose for which his whole day had been planned thrown out of joint, May got up from his chair, took his sticks, went over to the window and opened it. The night was warm and starlit. It was 1950. He thought with some amusement of the controversy that had broken out in *The Times* as to whether the second half of the century began today or had begun on January 1st, 1949.

The windows of all the apartment houses high above him were wide open. Out of them came sounds of wassail. With champagne, feasting and handshaking, the sexagenarians, the septuagenarians and the octogenarians, forgetting their reduced incomes and blocked capital, were joyously hailing a year of increasing taxation and growing war-clouds in which continuously they would lament their existence and damn their Government.

The service in the English church was over. They were coming out and gathering in groups on the porch, while chauffeurs and coachmen hovered near. May switched off his light so as to be unobserved while observing. The organ was hailing the New Year almost riotously, and had gone from Handel to Mendelssohn. It clashed with a bellowing of *Auld Lang Syne* from the apartment of Baron Berneau, born Bernstein, who wore a plaid ulster and claimed Stuart royal descent through a German grandmother. He had the advertising concession for a well-known champagne, so there was no lack of effervescence at his New Year party.

The Bishop and his wife had appeared, accompanied by the resident parson. There was a cordial exchange of greetings. When the organ had finished, the taxis and carriages had gone, and the caretaker had closed the church doors, it was half-past twelve. The Avenue de Grande Bretagne grew deserted, the cats came out in the warm night. But there was no stillness. The New Year festivities were going strong behind the shining windows. At the Hotel de Paris a ball was in progress. In the Casino Restaurant there was a babble of voices, a clatter of dishes, a riot of ribbons and coloured balloons.

He had chosen the wrong night. He could not affront the

Bishop of Gibraltar with his suicide. He would have one more day of life, and then, in a town no longer noisy with festivity, take the road to " the undiscovered country from whose bourn no traveller returns ".

Tired, mentally perturbed, he got into bed, and after some turning and ruminating, he fell asleep.

III

A loud knocking awakened Stephen May from a deep sleep. The room was scarcely light. The sun had not yet come up out of the sea. For a few moments he lay, slightly dazed. The knocking was repeated and almost violent. His woman came at nine, and it was singular that the concierge should have allowed anyone to come into the building, for the hall door was usually locked until eight o'clock.

With great difficulty he got out of bed, drew back the curtains and put on a dressing-gown and slippers. It was seven-thirty by his bedside clock. He went out into the little hall and opened the door. A youth with a white collarless vest and ruffled brown hair stood there, a muscular youth in the early twenties.

" Yes ? "

" You'll excuse me, sir, but you're English, aren't you ? "

" Yes."

" I'm in very great trouble, sir. Mr Leavens has shot himself—I've just found him."

" Mr Leavens ? "

" He's in the flat above you, sir. I'm his manservant. I knew you were English 'cause I've seen *The Times* in your letter-box in the hall. I'm in such a state, I don't know where I am. I hope you don't mind, sir ; I've never had anything like this before ! "

The youth's mouth trembled, and he rubbed his hands together as he spoke. He was a fresh-complexioned, good-looking lad with a Yorkshire accent.

" Come in," said May.

He closed the door and led the way into his sitting-room. The sun had come up over the horizon. It stood on the rim of the sea, a crimson disk that shot its colour over the mauve sheen of the Mediterranean.

B

" Sit down. When did you discover this ? " asked May.

" Just now, sir. Every morning I take Mr Leavens his cup of tea. He likes it at half-past seven, as soon as I'm up. He was always a poor sleeper, with his worries."

" Worries ? "

" He was awful worried, sir—didn't seem to know what he was a-doing sometimes. I sometimes thought I couldn't stand it any more, and then, being sorry for him, I stayed on."

" Where has Mr Leavens shot himself—was it just now ? "

" I don't think so, sir. He's on the floor of his bedroom, in his pyjamas, all over blood. He's a terrible sight. I didn't hear anything. I sleep down the corridor, next the kitchen. His room's on the front; the window was open."

" Have you moved him ? "

The youth looked at May with wide-open eyes.

" Moved him, sir ? Oh, no, sir ! I couldn't ! I did touch his hand, only with a finger—he's quite cold. It's a terrible sight. He's bled awful, all over the marble floor."

" Have you called anyone ? "

" No, sir. I've come straight down to you. I didn't go to the concierge—them Frenchwomen get hysterics."

" We must call the police at once. They will deal with it with a minimum of red-tape. I suppose it is suicide ? Did he gamble heavily ? "

" He never went near the tables, sir. He'd something against gambling, an' when I told him I'd had a flutter one afternoon, he carried on awful—told me I was a great fool to—— "

" Yes—you found a revolver in his hand ? "

" Yes, sir ; that's what's done it."

May reached to the telephone on the desk nearby and dialled for the police. He informed them that a man had been found shot in the apartment. He gave them the required particulars. They would come at once, they said.

" What is your name ? " asked May, turning to the youth before him, still unnerved.

" Groves—Teddy Groves, sir. There won't be any trouble for me, sir ? I've never been in anything like this before, and I don't talk the lingo. They can't lock me up here in a foreign place ? It's a comfort to know you're here, being English, sir."

" There's nothing whatever to worry about, Groves ; you're
not in any way implicated. Mr Leavens could not have chosen
a better place, though he might have chosen a less messy way.
The Monte Carlo authorities have a lot of experience of suicides.
They do everything they can to dispose of them discreetly and
expeditiously. So don't worry. Did you fasten the door ? "

" I shut it, sir ; but it isn't locked."

" No one will be coming ? "

" No, sir."

" Then I think it will be best for us to wait here until the
police arrive, and come up with the concierge. My woman
won't be here for an hour yet. I think we might make ourselves a cup of tea."

May pulled himself to his feet. The irony of it ! The man
upstairs was dead, and he was alive ! Two suicides discovered
on New Year's Day would have shaken the equanimity even of
the Monaco police.

The youth stood up and watched May pick up his sticks.

" Can I help you, sir ? "

" Thank you—I know my way around in the kitchen."

" You'll excuse me saying it, sir—but haven't you got
arthritis ? "

" Yes. What do you know about it ? "

" Quite a lot, sir. My dad was a masseur in the Hydro at
Harrogate. He taught me quite a lot. When I came out of the
Army, after my service, I took it up—I'd been boxing a bit, but
you get too knocked about. So I looked for a job as valet-
masseur—that's how I came to be with Mr Leavens."

" Had he arthritis ? "

" Oh no, sir. He was healthy really—only he had nerves."

They reached the kitchen, where May lit the gas-stove,
while Groves found a kettle and filled it.

" What age was your employer ? " asked May, searching in
the cupboard for the tea-canister.

" Oh, he was quite old, sir—about fifty, I'd say."

May smiled. At fifty-six he did not expect to be considered old ; but to a lad of twenty-four anyone over forty was
nearing the end.

" Alone ? "

" Yes, as far as I know. He seemed to know nobody, and
wanted to be alone. He was a strange gentleman, sir."

" In what way ? "

Groves did not answer at once. Then he looked at May, slightly embarrassed as he spoke.

" I'd only be guessing, sir—so p'rhaps I'd better not say. Is there any milk, sir ? " he asked, opening and peering into the frigidaire.

" I don't think there is. I take tea with lemon."

" That's all right for me, sir."

From the cupboard they took out cups and saucers.

" These are nice flats, sir, aren't they ? " commented Groves. " They're well fitted. I'd like something like this at home, I would."

" Where is your home ? "

" Harrogate, sir. Lovely place, sir. I often wish I was there, sir—even here, nice as it is, with no fog and a blue sea."

Groves made the tea, cut some bread and found a pot of marmalade. He picked up a tray.

" We'll eat here," said May. " We can hear better when they come."

They sat down at the table. Groves refused some bread.

" I don't feel as if I could eat anything, sir. I really don't know what I'd have done all alone here. It's fair shaken me ! I don't know how anyone can commit suicide. I wouldn't have the nerve."

" Circumstances can make many strange things possible," said May, spreading some marmalade. " I can understand it happening."

He wondered what the lad's reaction would be if he told him that he was talking to a prospective suicide. He changed the subject, and looked at Groves' sturdy frame, with his broad shoulders, large biceps and triangular torso, the pectoral muscles firm under the thin vest.

" You don't look a very nervy person," he said.

" I'm not usually—but all that blood, and him dead on the floor and—— "

He did not finish the sentence. They heard footsteps.

" They're here," said May, getting to his feet. " Say as little as possible—I'll translate for you."

As May foresaw, the police made no fuss. Suicide was a common event in this Principality, where men came to gamble and were often unable to bear the consequences of their folly. There was a smooth legal process that involved no inconvenient suspicions. It operated with a minimum of publicity. There was a cemetery, with decent and free interment for those who had died destitute, and free railway tickets to their ultimate destination for any dependants left stranded.

Within ten minutes the interrogation had ended. Within half an hour the body of Mr Leavens had been removed to the mortuary. His next of kin, a brother in Manchester, was informed by telegram. The inquest would be held the next day.

When the police had gone, the grumbling concierge came up with a mop and bucket. She complained bitterly. " They don't mind where they do it, or what mess they make. And do we get anything for all this? No, *m'sieur*—no *pourboire* from the suicides, and relatives keep away from the place. *Quelle vie!* Why don't they drown themselves at sea? It's cleaner and less trouble."

Teddy Groves began to recover his nerve after the body had been taken away.

" I wonder what now, sir. I suppose I'll have to keep on until his brother or someone arrives? " he asked, when later he came down to May's apartment.

" Sit down," said May, who had just finished dressing.

The late Mr Leavens had seriously upset his plans. A second suicide in the same building within twenty-four hours was now impossible. He had no passion for originality, but a mere repetition was ludicrous, the concierge's grievance apart, even if he left her a *pourboire*. Groves, too, might be wholly unhinged by a second shock. He must think of some other place and time. Confound that man Leavens!

" Tell me about your employer. Had he any money? " asked May.

" I don't think he was hard up, sir. He paid me regularly. There was over twelve pounds in his wallet. He used to send me with dollars to the—to see someone who gave us francs."

" A black-market man? "

" Yes, sir. It seemed quite safe, sir."

" Of course it was safe. The black market is the real market. Any bank clerk will give you the telephone number of an operator. How did he get the dollars—wasn't he English? "

"Yes, sir, but he had a dollar letter of credit. He used to draw dollars on it. I think he had some kind of business in America. He'd lived there a lot, and often had letters from America."

"What was he?"

"I never really knew, sir. He never talked about his affairs. He had had some trouble in England; that's why he was here and why we were bolting tomorrow."

"Bolting tomorrow? Why, and where to?"

"Over the border, to Italy, sir—to Rapallo. He was in a terrible state ever since the detectives came to see him and asked for his registration papers."

"I think you had better tell me the whole story, Groves. This may complicate matters."

"I'd like to, sir; it's worrying me awful. I haven't done no wrong myself, but I've never been happy about it, and I'd have gone home, but he was in such a state. He used to cry and say if I left him he'd kill himself. So I kept on."

"How long have you been with him?"

"About three months, sir. A registry office sent me to him. He asked me if I'd be willing to travel abroad—Paris and the Riviera—and if I could go at once. That was just my cup of tea, and I liked him; he was a kind man, sir. So I just packed my bag, and two days later we flew to Paris. It was all so sudden I could hardly believe it, finding myself in Paris, of all places. At first there didn't seem anything for me to do. He asked me if I'd sleep with him, which I thought peculiar, but he said he had nightmares, and as I'd been a boxer and was young and strong, he had engaged me because he felt safe with me. Well, nightmare was the proper word. The first night was all right, except that he was a terrible snorer and roamed all over the bed—he was a big man, as you saw, sir. But the second night was awful. He sat up in the middle of the night and fair hollered. When I turned on the light he was trembling like a leaf, with beads of sweat on his face. He looked as if he'd committed a murder. I got up and made some tea for him——"

"In the hotel?"

"Yes, sir; we had a large bed-sitting-room with a bath-kitchen—very nice. He never lived extravagantly, but always comfortable. Well, after the tea he quieted down, and we got into bed again. He told me this sometimes happened when he dreamed of his wife, who'd been killed in a motor smash. But he had them fits every night. I told him I couldn't stand it and he'd have to sleep by himself. So at the next place— we left for Cannes in a week—we had separate rooms; but I always had to be next door and leave the door open. Sometimes he'd come in, wake me, and sit on my bed, shaking. It was no fun, but I felt sorry for him. When he was all right he was very nice."

" Did he drink ? "

" No, sir, I never saw him the worse for it. He was very simple really. But he had funny whims. He never stopped reading the English newspapers. He'd go over them from cover to cover. At first I thought it was the Stock Exchange quotations ; he'd a lot of investments and property, he told me, that had to be watched, and he often had cables from America about business there."

" What sort of business ? "

" I never quite made out, sir, but it was something to do with promoting companies for property deals. He told me he'd made several fortunes and lost them, but that things had been very difficult lately, with so many new Government regulations. That wasn't his trouble really. It came out one day in Cannes. He'd taken a flat there—a nice little place on the front. One day a man came from the police and asked to see his passport. I never saw a man in such a state in my life. His passport was all right and the man was very polite ; but that day and the next he wouldn't go out, and was all the time at the window, watching. The second night he broke down completely. He made me promise I wouldn't leave him whatever happened. So I promised, for I thought he was a bit funny in the head. Then he told me he could never go back to England, as the police wanted him. He'd been committed to the Assizes on trial for fraud, over some company business. He swore he hadn't been dishonest, but had got mixed up unawares with some crooks. Until the Assizes he was out on bail for five thousand pounds. One day he felt he couldn't stand it any more. So he decided to find someone for company and bolt. That's how I came into the picture, sir. I didn't like it, but I was kind of sorry for him."

" How long was it before you found out the truth ? "

"About six weeks, sir."

"And nothing more happened at Cannes?"

"No, sir; but he was terribly jittery. He would only go out in the evenings, and always wore dark glasses. Nobody bothered us; but after a week he said he didn't like the place, so we went to Nice. We hadn't been there a fortnight when he wanted to move again—to here, where he thought the French police couldn't extradite him. Three days ago the police called here. He talked French beautifully. He said they said they came to make inquiries because of some law here about tenants not sub-letting. But he didn't believe them. He had an awful night that night, and the next day told me to pack, as we were going to Italy, where he would feel safer. The day after—yesterday afternoon—someone called and said that he must go to the Gendarmerie this morning and take his passport. 'They've got me,' he said; 'they'll not let me over the frontier.' I told him it was all nonsense, like before. He seemed calmer after that, but he couldn't eat any dinner, and complained of his head—it often troubled him. He went to bed earlier than usual. I took a walk at eleven o'clock to look at the New Year doings. I came in about half-past twelve and went straight to bed, and heard nothing. I did notice, however, that he'd shut his door, which he seldom did. That's all I know about Mr Leavens, sir. I suppose I should stay on until someone comes out from England. He's got some nice things, sir—clothes, gold cigarette-case and watch and dress-studs. I've locked them up in a drawer. I wouldn't mind if I could get a job here—it is a nice place, and you don't have all them restrictions like at home, and no fogs."

"The law would not allow you to work here—unless, of course, you found an English employer, and, as you know, Groves, the English here haven't the money for valets."

"No, sir. I don't mind much about the wages, as long as it's someone I like. I hope you don't mind me saying so, sir, but is there any chance of me being with you? I can cook, and also, p'rhaps, I could help you a bit, sir, with your arthritis. I'm a good masseur."

"I'm afraid there's no chance of that, thank you, Groves. I'm leaving here almost immediately."

"Very good, sir," said Groves. He stood up. "Well, sir, I think I'll be going. Thank you very much, sir. I don't know what I'd do without you. You won't be leaving for a few days, sir? I'd feel much easier if I knew you were here until all this business is over."

May looked at him. He liked the lad. His eyes were very clear. He had a young, honest face. His appeal evoked in him a response.

" I shall be here until you've no need to worry."

" Thank you, sir," said Groves, smiling, then he left.

When the door closed, May stood still, looking down into the street, but seeing nothing as he contemplated the strange situation. His own tragedy had developed into something of a farce. A man above him had anticipated him in the act of suicide, leaving a servant who now looked to him for help. Almost unwittingly he had committed himself to a few more days of a wretched existence, a postponement that meant a repetition of all he had gone through before arriving at his resolution.

There was a tap on the door.

" *Entrez*," he called, turning. It was the daily woman.

" You said, *m'sieur*, you wouldn't want any food today. I haven't brought any in, *m'sieur*. There's only an egg and a little bit of butter; the bread's finished, too. Will you be wanting anything tomorrow? "

" Tomorrow? " he repeated. " Tomorrow—yes, I shall want something tomorrow. Some bread, butter, cheese, fruit. If you live, you've got to eat."

" *Mais oui, m'sieur!* " agreed the woman, smiling as she withdrew.

May watched her close the door. She could not possibly appreciate the point of his remark. If you live, you've got to eat. And do a lot of other things. Yesterday he had thrown an old razor-blade into the waste-paper basket. This morning he had had to retrieve it, for it had been his last, and he had to shave again. He must go out and buy some blades, and draw some money at the bank for the meals he would have to buy. Suddenly he laughed. The situation was really quite comic.

Towards noon he went out. It was a lovely morning, the first day of the New Year he had not expected to see. He decided to sit in the sun on the terrace of the Casino, listen to the band and have an *aperitif* before lunch.

As he left the house he found a letter in his mail-box. It

looked like a circular re-directed from his club. He put it into the pocket of the light overcoat he was wearing and stepped into the street. He made slow progress on his sticks. Presently he saw someone waving to him and looked up. It was the old Countess de Flauvier, Canadian born.

"A happy New Year to you," she cried. "And quicker progress in every way!"

"Thank you; the same to you, Countess," he answered.

"Ah, but you've a better chance. It's a case of two to one!"

She grinned at him, red-faced and white-haired. Six months ago, after a fall at seventy-two, she had had to have her leg amputated. She was just getting an artificial one.

"Won't you come and lunch with me—it is a lovely morning?" he called up to her.

"Thanks, I can't. I was a naughty girl last night, and was carried home at three o'clock this morning. I'm still unsteady on my dot-and-carry-one!"

She blew him a kiss and disappeared from the window. He ambled onwards towards the terrace of the Casino. There's courage for you, he mused. Life almost done, a shrivelled income, existing in a tiny room, with only one leg. Her chief interest in life now was a small frog that lived in a glass tank on her table. "Like me, she's only one leg—the dead husband bit it off. *Mais la vie est bonne, n'est-ce-pas, ma chère Manette?*" she would cry to it, and explain to her astonished visitors, "Being a Froggie, Manette talks beautiful French."

There was no doubt that it was a lovely morning. The New Year had come in with something like a summer smile. The air was balmy, the sun hot. He called at his bank on the corner of the Boulevard des Moulins and with a shock discovered that it was closed for the New Year's holiday. Fortunately his money was in dollar travellers' cheques. To flourish one anywhere was like throwing corn to pigeons. So he walked down through the ornamental gardens towards the Casino, amid the palms, the flowering bougainvillea, the scarlet cannas and other flowers that paid no attention to the calendar in this winter paradise. May liked this well-kept garden, set out like a confectioner's shop, with its coloured borders. He had two charming friends who were always there, French to the very *bandeaux* they wore below their fringes—

Nina and Mimi, the two donkeys who pulled the children's diminutive carriage with its yellow wheels, red cushions and shining brass lamps. But this morning, alas, he had no biscuits for them, having said Good-bye to them yesterday. He could only rub their long noses and prove a disappointment.

Aching, he sat down for a few minutes on a bench facing the entrance of the Casino. There was a concert this afternoon and an opera in the evening. Quite a number of people were sitting out in the sunshine before the Café de Paris. Presently he saw Louis, owner of a restaurant down the street, who saluted him. May beckoned him over. After an exchange of New Year wishes he asked Louis if he could take fifty dollars.

"*Mais oui, m'sieur*," said Louis with alacrity, pulling out a fat pocket-book. "A hundred dollars if you like, *m'sieur*."

"Fifty will do—the rate?"

"For you, sir, four hundred francs. The official rate's three-forty-five."

May signed his cheque. Louis gave him twenty one-thousand franc notes.

"My first New Year transaction—any time, *m'sieur*," said Louis, putting away the cheque.

"The pound, what's the rate now?" asked May. He had no pounds, but he was always curious.

"*Pas bon*, seven-eighty. No one wants them, *m'sieur*." He shrugged his shoulders. "And once they kept this Riviera going from Cannes to Rapallo. The best people too, reliable, easy with their money, and always so well-bred. And now —— " He spread his hands in a gesture of disgust. "*Canaille, m'sieur*. All the villas falling into ruin. But, *m'sieur*, I will tell you, the pound will come back; one day it will come back and shake hands with the dollar—the English keep accounts, they pay their taxes—*mon Dieu*, what taxes!—they have character."

"Thank you for those kind words," said May, smiling. "The pound may come back, but I fear the same people won't come back with it."

"The people you and I've known will never come back anywhere, *m'sieur*. I'm seventy, and my world's vanished. It's the charabanc rabble, one night here, two nights there. Look at the Casino—women in trousers, men in shorts and open shirts, crap-tables and slot machines! I once saw

King Edward sitting there "—he pointed to the Café de Paris—
" he was then the Prince of Wales, with Baron de Rothschild,
smoking cigars after lunch, in the company of their ladies.
Ladies, I said, *m'sieur*, with an air, with manners and jewels,
beauties well turned out by their maids—no pull-overs, no
hoydens in blue linen pants and their hair dragged up like a
hedgehog. Ladies and gentlemen, *m'sieur*, *le beau monde*. I
was a little *commis* then, in my first black trousers and white
apron. My uncle was a chef there and got me in—I came
down from the family farm at twelve. I'd never worn shoes
before, and I remember now how they burnt my feet—and
how every morning *M'sieur* Fayout would inspect our hands and
nails. Well, I'm glad I'm an old man. When I remember
what life was, I feel sorry for the young."

" You should never be sorry for the young, Louis," said May.
" At twenty, with good health and no memories, everything's
fun. The old have always felt sorry for the young, and the
young have always laughed at the old."

Louis shook his head slowly at this philosophy.

" They need something to make them laugh," he replied.
Then, with an old-world bow, he departed.

As if to mock him, he was almost run down by a young
couple on a motor-cycle. The girl sat astride, clutching the
youth. Her hair was cropped. She wore green linen trousers
turned half-way up her bare legs and a red jersey with *Kiki*
knitted in white letters across it.

May rose and crossed the road, descending by the steps
and the palms towards the wide, balustraded terrace that
looked on to the sea. Behind it was the flamboyant yellow
stucco façade of the Casino, dizzily decorated with nymphs
sprawling voluptuously amid cupids and swags of flowers.
Below, by a flight of steps, an orchestra played. Little tables
with bright covers shone in the noonday sun. At the other
end of the terrace, beyond a cluster of palms, there was a
vista of sea and mountains under a blue sky. It was as fair
a scene as this earth could show, and yet there was a melancholy
pervading it. This evasion of the winter was rather like
the beauty of a woman who had evaded the ravages of Time, an
achievement that was unnatural and gave an effect of isolation
from the common fate. Or did he imagine it, and was the
melancholy in himself ? He was alive and, having said a

farewell to all this, he had a feeling of anticlimax. He had also to face the problem all over again. He must seek a new scene. Mr Leavens had trumped his card.

May ordered a vermouth and listened to the orchestra playing a Strauss waltz. There was a fair number of visitors on the terrace, but nothing like the bright throng of pre-war years. One thing was as before, and caused him the same dull anger. The music was punctuated by the popping of rifles down at the *Tir aux pigeons*. Without looking over the terrace, he knew that miserable little birds were coming out of traps, momentarily bewildered by the light, and then fluttering up to fall dead or winged into the sea beyond. He liked to imagine another world in which these gallant sportsmen came up out of dark manholes to be potted by beaky competitors in the *Tir aux Hommes*. Well, one nation's sport was another's anathema. The massacre on the moors on the Twelfth of August was worse.

He put his hand into his pocket in search of a box of matches. With it he pulled out an envelope. It was the letter he had put there on leaving the apartment. He lit a cigarette and then examined the envelope. He now saw from the stamp that it had come originally from the United States. The postmark was Los Angeles, California. It had been addressed to his club in London, and forwarded.

He could not imagine who could want to write to him from Los Angeles. He had never stayed there, though he had painted in San Francisco and Hollywood. He tore open the envelope and extracted the letter. The paper had the heavy *de luxe* quality, embossed, that characterised much American stationery. It was well typed and spaced. The heading bore the names of Schwartz, Szabo, and Hillman, Counsellers at Law :

My dear Mr May,

We are acting for the Executors of the Will of the late Mrs Cyrus D. Pulmacher, of Ventura Ranch, who died on October 28th. You have been named among the Legatees of her Will, and before communicating with you further we should be glad to hear from you, as we have had some difficulty in ascertaining your address. We have now received your present address from the *Inter-*

national *Who's Who*. We observe that you are Mr Stephen May, R.A., the painter. In her Will dated July 4th, 1945, Mrs Pulmacher made you one of her legatees.

We shall be pleased to receive your early reply confirming the receipt of this letter, whereupon we shall be glad to communicate to you the details of our late client's legacy.

We remain, dear Mr May,
Very cordially,
Glenway P. Szabo.
(Schwartz, Szabo and Hillman.)

May stared at the letter, re-read the envelope, and re-read the letter. He had never in his life known or heard of Mrs Cyrus D. Pulmacher. He had never painted a portrait of Mrs Pulmacher. He could clearly recall the names of all the American women he had painted—Mrs Robertson, the publisher's wife, dead five years ago; Princess Collacollini, the tinplate millionaire's daughter; Mrs Caine, formerly Mrs Meng, then Mrs Schellberger, then Mrs Schwartzkopt, and now the Marchesa Benevita-Alitari, living in Rome; Miss Carlotta P. Trott; the two Schubert sisters—lovely girls in their teens; and the incredible Mrs Bodditon, who had died almost bankrupt, after living the life of a female Maecenas in Paris—that was the lot. Nowhere in his list had there been a Mrs Pulmacher of Ventura Ranch. Was it possible there was another portrait-painter named Stephen May? A Will dated July 4th, 1945. He tried to recall when he had been in the United States. There had been short visits in 1929 and 1932, to New York, Washington and Philadelphia. He had been in San Francisco and Hollywood, painting, in 1939, the portraits of Miss Trott and the Schubert sisters. There was no Mrs Pulmacher anywhere.

What an extraordinary thing! He ordered another vermouth. The band was playing a waltz from *The Dollar Princess*, somewhat appropriately. It recalled Princess Collacollini, George O'Bourke's beautiful and vivacious daughter, now the Countess of Merrington. He had found himself more interested in his subject than any artist had a right to be, and his feeling was reciprocated. There came a moment when the situation was uncomfortable. He liked Mr O'Bourke, a genial soul who collected Papal decorations, at some cost, and lined his study with parchments from the Holy See. He had become a Papal Count. " I don't see why Nellie should get away with it and leave her old dad behind," he said. Prince Collacollini, an elegant young man who had always evaded work, in the way of the Sicilian aristocracy, played polo all day and poker all night. Old George O'Bourke called him " a poodle in leggings ". Like a poodle he pranced, had black curly hair on a head that was a perfect classical cameo, and by his exquisite manners, dress, and tall slim appearance, charmed all the women but loved none, since his affection was exhausted on himself. He called his wife *Carissima*, but she was utterly bored by him, which exactly suited him, for it left him free. He never ceased making fun of the American civilisation on which he floated so luxuriously.

Not liking the situation, May hurriedly finished the portrait and avoided complications. Soon afterwards the Earl of Merrington came along, a puffy young man, renowned in private as a pianist. In the odd way that women have, Princess Nellie adored him, and to make his daughter happy O'Bourke bought off the Prince, who soon found an even richer support.

What histories of human beings had come under his eyes, thought May, as *The Dollar Princess* ended. But nowhere in his life could he fit in Mrs Cyrus D. Pulmacher. A legacy. What kind of a legacy ? A piece of furniture, a picture, a property, or cash ? If money, how much ? A thousand, a hundred thousand, a million dollars ? The letter aroused a maximum of curiosity with a minimum of information. Possibly it was professionally cautious until the right Mr May had been located. Could he be the right Mr May ?

In the bright noon he felt slightly dizzy. It could not be from two vermouths. In the last twelve hours he had run the gamut of emotional experiences. He had been frustrated in suicide by a Watch-night service, involved with a successful suicide before breakfast, and become a legatee of a mysterious woman at noon.

Once more he read the letter. It was eight days old. He put it in his wallet. It was then, for the first time, that he had a sudden consciousness of the hand of Fate taking direction of his life. By a singular chain of events he was alive to receive a letter to a ' dead ' man. At the ballet yesterday afternoon

Georgie Thirkell had hailed him, a ghost from the past. At dinner on the *Lone Star* he had met the Bishop of Gibraltar and driven back with him to the Avenue de Grande Bretagne. His apartment overlooked the English church, where, at the moment chosen for his contemplated act, they had sung the hymns of his boyhood in a sad-sweet past, which had postponed his intention. The next morning an unfortunate man above him had committed suicide. After going to the assistance of young Groves, he had found a letter in his box. And now here he was, possibly the recipient of some kind of legacy. Curiosity, if not a release from impending poverty, would keep him alive, at least until he had written and received a reply from Messrs Schwartz, Szabo and Hillman. He had nearly a thousand pounds blocked in England. He had also some two thousand dollars, and a few Swiss francs, the only free currency these days. Fortunately he was 'resident abroad' or the British Government would have confiscated these. Two thousand dollars at his present rate of living would last him about six months.

It was warm and pleasant sitting in the sun. The music was gay, the scenery spectacular. How good life could be! If only he was not tortured by this remorseless enemy in his bones, and, most unbearable of all, if only he were able again to exercise his skill in the work that dominated his life. Vain regrets. A few days ago he had read about a new drug they had discovered in America, cortisone. Miraculous cures were claimed for it, but he had little faith in these discoveries of unproved worth. Every month they had claimed the discovery of a cure for cancer, and the fell enemy of man marched triumphantly on.

He had pushed himself all over Europe in search of a cure. He knew the tiers of neat brass plates on the polished doors of Harley Street, the nursing-homes for observation, the dark chambers of the X-ray specialists. It seemed that everyone knew some medical miracle-worker by whom he swore. Docile at first, and desperate later, he had run the gamut of these. There followed a pilgrimage to the spas, in France, Germany, Austria, Italy. He had sat in the radio-active water at Bad Gastein, sweated under the hot mud of Abano and Montecatini, drunk the waters of Vichy and Aix, starved at great expense in a nature-cure sanatorium, and absorbed innumerable picures simply or intravenously. All this in vain, while the prison walls closed in upon him. He saw with growing horror his knuckles begin to enlarge, his fingers to twist, his wrists become less flexible in the growth of ulnar deviation. He had to find a new angle to shave by, control diminishing. Getting in and out of his bath was now an ordeal conducive to uncleanliness. A dozen pairs of shoes had been discarded, and in three years he had had five new lasts. He could still continue to cut his own food, but a stall in the theatre became a Bride of Nuremberg before the last curtain.

Yet, despite it all, sitting here in the warm sun, amid the palms along the terrace, with the light music making the morning festive, he had a brief revisitation of happy hours. He had also a sustaining curiosity derived from the extraordinary letter in his pocket. If he found himself a millionaire in the near future it would not avail him anything. There was only one true wealth, without which one was a pauper—health. As for being a millionaire, the legacy might be only a thousand dollars, or a hundred, or a second-best dinner-service.

He paid the bill and rose. Feeling reckless, he decided to have an expensive lunch at the Hotel de Paris, with a *Chateauneuf du Pape*, of the best year. There was nothing like counting your chickens before they were hatched, if you felt pretty certain the eggs were addled.

He lunched well at a small table by the window looking out on to the gardens. The head waiter, who knew him, and that he was painting the Prince of Monaco, came over and spoke to him, and after expressing the usual New Year wishes, inquired when the portrait might be on view to loyal Monegasques.

"I may have to start again. I am not satisfied," replied May, enjoying his lie.

"Ah, *m'sieur*—that is the sign of the great artist!" observed the waiter, then with a courtly bow withdrew.

In the lounge May called for a cigar, and smoked it with great enjoyment. He began to think of what other infraction of the dietary laws he could commit. The comment of the concierge at his apartment came to mind as he puffed his cigar. He saw her with the bucket and mop, staring at the floor. "Why don't they drown themselves at sea! It's cleaner and less trouble." That obnoxious woman was quite right. He would remember her advice.

It was three o'clock when he called for a carriage. He did not go straight home. He told the coachman to drive out along the promenade towards the tennis-courts and the swimming-pool. It was a sunny afternoon, the colours of the sea and mountains under a clear sky were enchanting. He liked to hear the clop-clop of a horse's hooves. After half an hour he ordered the man to return by way of the Boulevard des Moulins. He must buy some razor-blades and a cake of soap.

Coming out of the chemist's shop on the corner he saw, just as he got into the carriage, young Groves, carrying a canvas bag.

" I've been doing my shopping, sir. I was so knocked out this morning I couldn't do a thing," he said.

" Are you finished ? "

" Yes, sir."

" Do you happen to have bread, butter and milk ? "

" Yes, sir. It's milk and bread I've got in here," he answered, raising the bag.

" Get in. I've got a sudden fancy for tea and toast. I'll ask you to make some and join me at tea."

Groves homely face expanded in a grin.

" That would give me a lot of pleasure, thank you, sir," he said, taking the opposite seat.

That evening, after tea, May wrote to Messrs Schwartz, Szabo, and Hillman, informing them that he was Stephen May, R.A., the painter, but that he had no recollection whatsoever of ever having made a portrait of Mrs Pulmacher, or even of having met her. He would be glad to hear in what manner he could be her legatee, and what was the nature of the legacy. He gave the dates of his visits to the United States. When he had written the letter he sent Groves to the post office to despatch it, airmail. While he was gone he checked the amount of dollars at his disposal. On his return he made him a proposal. He would take him on as houseman for a month. By that time the Leavens business would be cleared up, and he could then make his plans. Groves was delighted.

" I hope it won't be for a month, but for a lifetime, sir," he said, beaming.

" A lifetime might be a month," retorted May.

Groves looked at him, uncomprehending. " I don't quite understand, sir ? "

" Don't try to. I think you'd better move in and sleep here tonight."

" Thank you, sir. I will. I don't relish that flat all alone after last night's business," said Groves.

The following morning, soon after eight o'clock, Groves came into May's bedroom, with a bright morning face. He drew the curtains, collected May's suit for pressing and brushing, and returned with a breakfast tray.

" When you're ready, sir, if you'll ring I'll come in and prepare your bath—can I help you with it, sir, and can I suggest you should let me give you a little massage afterwards ? I'd like to try and see how it goes; it might give you some relief, sir."

May looked at the lad, touched by his good nature. A bath was something of an ordeal, the thought of massage was like a threat of torture, but he did not want to discourage this spirit of service.

" Very well, Groves. I'll ring when I'm through, and then you can give me a bath and massage. But I warn you, I'm a difficult patient."

" You'll find me very gentle, sir."

Groves was clad in his collarless white cotton vest, shortsleeved, with blue serge trousers belted on his narrow waist. He looked like a young naval rating. The muscles on his brown arms and chest were formidable. He was a human nutcracker.

" You don't look exactly gentle," retorted May, looking enviously at the young Hercules before him. " How did you get that way ? "

" I do a spot of weight-lifting, sir."

" Here, in the house ? "

" Oh, no, sir—I couldn't carry bar bells around ! I go to a Gym down by the Condamine. They're very nice fellows, sir—you get soft here very quickly if you don't look out, and it helps me to pick up a bit of the lingo. I'm in their swimming club as well. If I could ski I'd go with them up into the mountains on Sundays. I hear it's marvellous."

" Can't you learn ? "

" I could, sir, but there were difficulties about leaving Mr Leavens—and all the traps are expensive, specially boots and things. If I was staying I'd think about it."

" You should learn to ski, Groves ; it's the nearest experience you'll have of flying in heaven."

" Did you ski, sir ? "

" I loved it. I used to go to St Moritz and Mürren, and a marvellous little place in Austria—Obergurgle."

He fell silent. He used to ski. Once he could fly through the air, over the snowy fields of heaven. Now he could hardly shuffle across the bedroom floor.

Possibly Groves read what was in his mind, for he gave him a smile, straightened his pillow and said, " I've boiled the eggs soft, sir ; p'r'aps you like them hard ? "

" No, soft, thank you," said May, cracking one. " Just right."

The lad went out. May began his breakfast. It was a beautiful cloudless morning. Down the avenue he could see, high above the apartment houses, the sun-kissed peak of a villa-dotted mountain, with the Grand Corniche cutting its face. On to one of the balconies of the tall white apartment house across the road a white-haired Englishman came out with his terrier dog and sunned himself. He had such regularity of habit in this morning custom that May could set his watch by him. He smoked one cigarette, and then disappeared inside. Carpets were hung over other rails, and mops were shaken by maids doing the morning dusting. He could just see the long narrow window above the steps where the old Countess with her white cropped hair and red face dispensed cheerfulness from a chair in her one-legged world.

Breakfast over, he rang for Groves, who filled the bath, stripped him, and lifted him into it like a baby. Afterwards he dried him down, and when he had regained his bed, began to massage him. Strong hands slowly kneaded him with infinite gentleness.

" This lad's a find," reflected May, under the soothing massage. " I'm deeply indebted to that poor Leavens."

When it was over Groves wrapped him up, insisting on an hour of rest, " For it does take it out of you, sir, however gently you go at it."

May asked him to open the trunk standing in the corner of the room. "There's some clothes in it; they'd better be aired."

Groves took out the clothes.

"And what about all the books and papers, sir? It's full of 'em, all over the place."

"I'll deal with those later," said May.

"I'll tidy 'em a bit, sir," said Groves, putting the clothes on a chair, and then kneeling by the trunk. "You'll excuse me saying so, sir—but what a lot of lovely ladies!" He held up some photographs.

"Those are photos of various portraits I painted."

Groves sat back on his heels and stared at May.

"You did these, sir—you're a painter!"

"Yes."

"I've been wondering what you did, sir, or if you didn't do anything at all—like most of 'em here. Fancy being able to paint!" He held up a portrait. "I'd give my right hand to do anything like this!"

"My right hand can't do anything any more like that," said May, with sudden bitterness.

There was silence in the room. Groves put back the photographs.

"There's a manuscript book in a Venetian binding: will you give it to me," said May, "and get me another pillow? I'm going to read a bit."

Groves placed a pillow behind him and brought the book.

"Comfortable, sir?"

"Very, thank you, Groves."

The lad picked up the suits off the chair. At the door he paused, and looked at May.

"You know, sir, it'll be all right again, I'm sure it will. An' I like to see you smile. You've got a very nice smile, sir," he said, and then closed the door gently after him.

May lay still for a few moments, thinking. Then he took up the bound volume of typescript. It was some years since he had finished it. He wondered how it would read now. He turned over the title-page, *Portrait* by Stephen May, and began to read.

THE PORTRAIT

CHAPTER I

A BOY THERE WAS

I

THE Trent, where it flows by Nottingham, is a pleasant smooth river. From the bridge, connecting the city with the road that leads southwards to the Quorn country and London, one can look downstream and upstream. Downstream, beyond the railway bridge that spans the river, rise the thick woods of Colwick Park. In the closing years of Queen Victoria's reign steamers departed from Trent Bridge on a threepenny return trip to the Park, some two miles distant, where the excursionist walked up a landing-board and through woods by a lake to a Georgian mansion converted into a restaurant and dance-hall. In its decay the place was still beautiful and with some interest for those who followed the story of the handsome Lord Byron. One who had entranced the poet's youth had lived here, the Mary Chaworth of his first love-poems. He had often ridden over from his semi-ruinous seat, Newstead Abbey, to Annesley Hall to proclaim an adolescent passion for the pretty daughter of Squire Chaworth. His elder, she had treated his declarations with amusement, and married hard-drinking, foxhunting Squire Musters, who took her to his seat, Colwick Park.

For young Stephen May and other children of his age the ride on the steamer down the river was the height of romance. On the deck of the *Empress* a man with a harp and another with a fiddle made music as soon as the boat's engines began to beat. The Union Jack floated bravely astern, and over the rails, hung with lifebuoys, one could watch the swirling wake. On the approach to The Park the white swans glided away over the dark water by the landing-stage. Even at seven years of age a sense of deep beauty and dark mystery filled the heart of Stephen May. Dressed in a striped print blouse, with white sailor collar, held in at the waist by an elastic tape, with knickers

to match, and long black stockings and strapover shoes, Stephen
was consumed with excitement on the too-rare occasions when
his mother took him to Colwick Park. It was not often he
could go. His father liked to find his mother at home when he
came back from the pit, and the excursion was costly also :
fivepence for the fares, threepence for an adult, twopence for
children under twelve. Also it cost fourpence for two cups of
tea; so often they took their own, with some buns, in a little
two-lidded fishing-basket belonging to his father.

The Trent itself offered endless diversions. Upstream
rose what seemed to Stephen's young eyes a mountain whose
wooded side fell steeply to the swift current. Here the water,
driven into channels by gravel islands, raced furiously along.
The crest of the high wood had a path with greensward at each
side. Its branches almost met overhead, and sometimes the
way was like a cathedral nave. At the top the grove was fenced
off by the squire of all this domain, the lord of stately Clifton
Hall, whose gardens fell in terraces to the river. Its lawns
were swept by peacocks that screeched in the still sylvan
scene. The Hall itself was almost hidden from view, and for
Stephen it was inhabited by a race of demi-gods. Once he had
seen the squire, Sir Hervey Bruce, with his wife, go to church.
Although a private gate in the churchyard wall opened into the
Hall grounds, Sir Hervey came to church in a carriage and pair,
a smart young footman, with glossy cockaded hat and top boots,
in attendance on the box seat. The distance was only five
hundred yards, but he was gouty. Every Sunday morning he
came, not so much to hear his cousin, Dr Rosslyn Bruce—a big,
bluff, fox-hunting parson—preach, but to set an example to the
assembled villagers.

Sir Hervey owned the village. As a special concession he
allowed his tenants to sell teas to the townspeople who walked
out from Nottingham, across the Trent and up the Grove,
where they arrived tired and thirsty. In fine weather the
visitors took tea in the gardens at long wooden tables with
benches. A notice on the cottages said, " Teas 6*d*. Hot
Water 2*d*." Some of the visitors brought their teas. For
twopence they had their tea made in a pot, teacups and saucers
supplied. Tea with bread-and-jam and a slice of home-made
cake was sixpence. It included a chat with the cunning old
grandad who sat toothless in a Windsor chair by the door.

Clifton was a rural village, with one church school and a maypole on the Green, used on May day. No scandal touched the place. If a girl ' fell ' she was sent away. It voted safely Conservative at all elections. The church was small, with an ivy-clad tower, and a churchyard beautifully kept.

When Stephen's mother read Gray's ' Elegy ' to him for the first time he was certain that this was the churchyard where " some mute inglorious Milton " lay. After his first visit to Clifton Grove he had made a drawing, with a twopenny box of crayons, which brought him some renown. The local grocer, who was Stephen's friend, put it in the shop window, and everybody knew it was Clifton Grove. He was seven when he had this first exhibition. It brought him such praise that he was asked by the well-to-do Misses Pearson to do a border for the notice of the Watch-night Service at the Wesleyan Methodist Chapel. He drew Jesus on a Cross at the top and Queen Victoria on a throne at the bottom. Miss Mary Pearson said the likeness was remarkable. He received two shillings for this, which his mother put into the bank. The bank was a small scarlet pillar-box with VR—Victoria Regina—on it, and a white COLLECTIONS notice on the front. In the slot where the letters were supposed to be posted one put in coins. The pillar-box was made of tin, was four inches high, and designed for pennies. It stood on the mantelpiece. The pennies went towards the summer's holiday. Very occasionally it was raided. The top would not come off, and the only way to extract coins was to put in the blade of a knife, invert the box, and carefully extract the coin balanced on the blade. This was sometimes done when the gaslight began to grow dim and the meter needed a penny in the slot.

The Trent seemed to flow through every place of Stephen's boyhood. He lived so near to it that every day he took Ruff, the Skye terrier, for a walk along the bank. The part of the river near which he lived flowed by level fields. Across the river there was a beautiful view much sketched by artists for its rural setting. The tower of Wilford church, square-topped, rose on the opposite bank amid elm trees that led from the gate to the church porch. The old churchyard was bounded by a wall on the river-side, with a green bank below. The roof of the high Georgian rectory with its attic windows could just be seen. The village of Wilford lay beyond. The road from

Nottingham to Clifton Grove ran through it, but the main traffic went over the open Trent Bridge, the Wilford Bridge having a halfpenny toll.

On Stephen's side of the river a high embankment had been built. Here, until he reached the river meadows upstream towards the Clifton woods and Beeston, the landscape had a dreadful scar. The Clifton Colliery raised its gaunt winding-derricks and chimney against the sky. On the apex of the derricks revolved, contrariwise, two pairs of wheels when the cages were going down or coming up. Stephen often watched the wire spokes of these great wheels shuttering the light as they revolved, for he knew they took his father down and brought him up from that grim underworld. He worked a ten-hour shift, and came home tired and covered with coal-grime. In the scullery there was a large tin bath, and out of the boiler on one side of the kitchen grate Mrs May ladled a large canister of scalding water. The colliers got a free ration of coal, so fires were the one thing that was plentiful in this mining district. The coal-fields lay mostly to the north, around Hucknall Torkard and Ilkeston. Nottingham, which prided itself on being a clean city, since its chief industry was lace-making and hosiery, regarded the colliery on its southern boundary as a blot on its fair character. The people who lived in the brick tenements near the pit were pariahs. Anyone living in this low-lying quarter west of the long, dreary road leading to the Wilford Bridge, with its mean shops, cobbles and clanking horse-trams, was an outcast. There were slums at Sneinton, where General William Booth of the Salvation Army had been born, but, although not slums, the neighbourhood of the Clifton Colliery was sniffed at by working-class people living in the other section of the level district known as The Meadows. The dividing line was a wide dreary avenue, called Queen's Walk, with tired trees and bare grass plots, that ran from the Midland Station Bridge down to the Wilford Bridge. No queen had ever walked there. It took its name from the Jubilee of Queen Victoria. There was a frightful statue, at the beginning of the Walk, of Sir Robert Clifton, a mid-nineteenth century buck who had lived at Clifton Hall, the stately mansion above the Trent. Having squandered his wealth on the Turf, he had opened the Clifton Colliery in the hope of re-covering his fortune. The statue showed the one-time member of Parliament for Nottingham in a cut-away morning coat and monstrous baggy trousers. His hands were so large that they could not possibly have gone into the pockets, which would have been fortunate in real life, considering his profligate career. The statue was the work of a local sculptor. No one but the birds paid any attention to Sir Robert, thus memorialised for his public services and for having brought a new industry to disfigure this part of the Trent side. He died soon after the first mining venture had been abandoned in 1869. At the other end of the Walk, adjacent to a waste plot used for gypsies' caravans and an occasional Fair, stood the *Cremorne* public-house, much frequented by miners from the pit, for whom it opened as early as six in the morning and closed at eleven at night.

The Mays lived in a long street in a congeries of mean dwellings that seemed to have come out of a mould. All over England, with the growth of the industrial era in the time of Victoria and Albert, these breeding-boxes were planted in deadening monotony. The wealth created by the workpeople dwelling in such districts was expressed in more grandiose style in the equally monotonous acreage of South Kensington, West Kensington and Earl's Court, into which London expanded. But the London houses, while all in a row, or in courts, squares and crescents, had impressive porticoes over steps mounting to heavy doors, and areas with basement kitchens, where the servants dwelt in everlasting gloom. In high attics these servants slept amid chimney-pot views. Unpredictable and unimaginable was the era eight decades later when the grown-up grandchildren of those proud and prosperous Victorians would be living, at fabulous rents, in the converted basement kitchens, attics, and mews, cunningly transformed, of their grandfathers' stable-hands. The brick tenements of the colliery district were incapable of any such transformation at the hand of Time. Mean in their conception, they remained mean.

Adelaide Row—it was believed it was named for Sir Robert's mother, who cannot have felt complimented—consisted of two rows of houses, identical with other rows of equal length. This geometrical arrangement effected a great saving of space where space, taken from green meadows near the colliery, was ample. The backs of Adelaide Row looked on to the backs of Charlotte Row, identical in every depressing detail. In

Cremorne Row, considered ' superior ' because the rents were sixpence a week higher, there were gardens, and each house had ten yards of hen-scratched soil with the ' privy ' at the end. Adelaide Row had no such amenities. Across the bottom of twelve feet of cobbled yard stretched a line of ' privies ' and coal-houses. These backed on to the privies and coal-houses of Charlotte Row. The water-closet being a costly and exclusive appurtenance attached only to houses of a higher social grade, the ' privies ' of Adelaide Row had round wooden tubs under wooden seats. These were collected once a week by sturdy fellows with insensitive noses who hoisted the heavy tubs on to their shoulders and took them down the yards into the street, where the contents were deposited into a horse-drawn vehicle. These officers of sanitation were fancifully called ' night-soil men ', because they once worked at night, though soil was not what they collected. In summer and autumn they toiled in a halo of flies. They were in the lowest social grade, a little below the miners, and, doing the worst work, they were the worst paid.

But did they do the worst work ? At least they laboured in light and air, far from danger. They had not a crouching three miles to go to the coal-face along dripping tunnels and caverns supported by pit-props, an underworld where it was always dreadful night relieved only by swinging Davy oil-lamps, a world of rumbling ' tubs ' carrying coal to the shafts, pushed by half-naked youths, the sweat making white channels down their coal-grimed torsoes. Some of these were mere boys of twelve. In the heat of the lower galleries they often removed their trousers, and their shirt-tails flapped about their naked buttocks. Others were door-trappers or pony boys, imps in whom the spirit of mischief had not yet been stifled, nor their physical grace contorted by crouching and twisting while working at the coal-face. Unlike the boys who tended them, the ponies had no respite. The long darkness having almost blinded them to the light of day, they were stabled underground. Death from accidents to these boys engaged in haulage was second only to those from fallings of roof in mining operations.

Stephen had been taken down the mine by his father. He had sat in a stall looking at these muscular men with magnificent shoulders and arms swinging their picks as they crouched or lay on their backs or sides. His father had his own stall—he was a " butty ", and paid the four men who worked with him; this was the height of their calling, unless they became shot-firers or overmen. The average wage for a sixty-hour week was twenty-five shillings. On this they kept families, whippets and got drunk on Saturday nights. The wise wives met their husbands at the pit-head on pay day and extracted all they could before the men went off to the ' pub ', where they would stay till closing time. At eleven o'clock at night outside the *Crocus* and the *Cremorne* when the ' chucker-out '—the toughest of the barmen—shut down the pub, the night became vociferous with the brawling of drunken men and their maudlin female companions. Arguments often developed into street fights, in which the women joined with hair-pulling, shrieks and blasphemy. On a street corner, under a gas-lamp, a Salvation Army captain, in a blood-red jersey, with his bonneted wife and attendant lasses, besought sinners to come to Jesus. After an exhortation they broke into a hymn ' Washed in the Blood of the Lamb ', accompanied by four men in peak caps who played the cornet, the trombone, the oboe and the bassoon. Two ' sisters ' rattled tambourines, one beat the drum. A pale, bespectacled youth held a banner inscribed ' BLOOD AND FIRE '. The quarrels, the fights, the wanton singing of music-hall choruses swirled around them as they pulled an odd sinner from the burning, but they went unscathed. The most brutal scoffer refrained from physical assault, conscious that these ardent servants of the Lord got down to the job in a deserted wilderness of depravity.

The local chapels—Wesleyan Methodist, Primitive Methodist, Baptist, and Congregational—made a less direct campaign against sin. They preached vigorously, sang lustily, and had annual ' missions ', when a revivalist preacher was hired for a course of services. The most potent of these was an eloquent old gypsy with a musical voice who roused almost hysteria in his emotional congregation. The Established Church did nothing. Sin had to come to it and be admonished with dignity. The annual bazaar at St Jude's was always opened on the first day by a titled person who received ' purses ' from the children, and was expected to spend at least fifty pounds when going around the stalls. The lady in most request was the gracious Countess of Shelley. It was appropriate for her to show an interest in the mining community. The Earl drew a royalty of one shilling a ton for coal mined on his estate and a toll of sixpence a load for every truck running on a railway line laid through one end of his five-thousand-acre park as compensation for disturbing his birds.

Politics divided Church and Chapel. People with social pretensions attended the former, the common herd went to the latter. All the churchgoers voted Conservative for a candidate who was often a peer's son. It was not a peer's son, but a duke's half-brother, who represented the local Parliamentary Division in the House of Commons. Lord Henry Bentinck was the epitome of an English aristocrat; handsome, charming and a great gentleman, with a beautiful wife. He was a poor speaker, and his eloquent Liberal opponents wiped the floor with him. He infuriated his own party by seeing two sides of a question, and he could never disguise his true sympathy with the depressed classes. He was frequently returned to Parliament, and held in deep affection. To Stephen, he remained one of his idols until he died, white-haired and venerable. All the chapel-goers voted Liberal for a well-to-do commercial magnate. A ranting Labour candidate got nowhere at all. "We don't hold with them there Socialists," said Mrs Pieman, who went charring and lived in sin with a one-legged night-watchman. They were the most vocal pair when the *Crocus* turned out its customers.

In such a world of grimy men tramping home in hobnailed boots, of drunkards singing long after midnight, of fights, Salvation meetings, shrieking children playing in the streets, miners in clean shirts squatting on their haunches outside their houses on Sunday mornings or taking out their lean whippets or bringing back giant dahlias, cabbages and marrows from the allotment gardens, of chapel-going, night-soil collecting, and the yearly week's holiday at Skegness or Mablethorpe, picnicking at Colwick Park, Clifton Grove or along the Trent bankside, in this lusty world of the closing 'Nineties was Stephen May born.

His home had nothing to distinguish it from all the others in the Row. It had the same Nottingham lace curtains, the same aspidistra on a bamboo stand, the same china ornaments on the red plush-fringed parlour mantelpiece. The same dolly-tubs were brought in from the outhouse and put out in the

scullery on Monday mornings, the same garments were hung
out to dry on the line in the communal back-yard. The parlour
was used solely on Sundays. Only ignorant people knocked
on the front door on week-days, opened with suspicion or
annoyance after the housewife had crossed the parlour floor
on a drugget of newspapers spread to save the polished linoleum.
All business and social affairs were transacted at the kitchen
door. In this room, with its snippet-rug and steel fender
before a grate with a cooking-oven on one side, a hot-water
boiler on the other, each topped by a flat hob, a chandelier
with an incandescent gas mantle—the latest thing—a couch, a
high chair, a table, a sideboard and, if 'comfortably off', a
Singer sewing-machine in the corner, the family lived, ate,
bathed on Saturday night, when the fire was kept up to heat the
water for the bathtub, and faced the problems of life. Some of
the miners bathed in the Trent, particularly in summer on
Saturday half-days, when they wanted to go to the cricket
match at Trent Bridge. Sunday saw a migration into the front
parlour. In thrifty homes there was usually a saddlebag suite
and a piano acquired through years of instalments. Only the
menfolk of 'common' people sat there in their shirt-sleeves or
in slippers. When the daughter's young man came, the family
retreated to the kitchen. This withdrawal implied respect,
trust and hopefulness. The young man, when he knocked at
the front door, was always received with glad surprise by the
parents and coy pleasure by the daughter. He always left at
ten o'clock.

Mrs May was respected by some of her neighbours and disliked by others, who said she was 'stuck up'. She had never
been seen in a public-house, nor had her husband, a teetotaller,
a Sunday School teacher and a leader in the Band of Hope—a
society that made war on inebriation and sang hymns that
lauded the virtues of clear water and denounced the perils of
strong drink. Mrs May was not really 'Chapel'. She had
been brought up 'Church of England', a head-gamekeeper's
daughter on the Earl of Westwater's Bedfordshire estate.
She was married in the church of her native village, but in
deference to Richard May's connections with the Wesleyan
Chapel she attended with him, although she disliked 'ranters'
and found the Church service more dignified. She did not
like women in the choir; she liked to see choirboys and clergy-

men in surplices. This set Mrs May apart, and in many small ways she was different from her husband. She was quiet and reserved; he was active and genial. " My missus looks every inch a lady," he would say, proudly. He would have spent his last penny dressing her, for he was as lavish as she was thrifty. There was one other noticeable difference: she spoke without any grammatical errors. She had been a schoolteacher in a village school, having lived for some four years, while in her teens, after her mother's death, with an aunt who was housekeeper at Lenton Abbey. In this way she learned correct speech, good manners and a ' lady-like ' carriage. In this way also she met young Richard May, a fresh-com-plexioned, handsome young man, who worshipped her. To her aunt's dismay, she went courting with him. " She can do much better for herself than marry a miner," complained her aunt, when she went back to her village to teach. She hoped distance would end the affair, but after a year of heartbreak and brief encounters, despite her father's and aunt's disapproval, she married Richard May and went with her husband to live in Nottingham.

She was sorely tried by her surroundings, mean, rough and dreary after the quiet village and a gamekeeper's cottage. Whatever she suffered she never complained. They were in love with each other, and it was a happy home. The first child was stillborn, the second died of whooping-cough at two. Then after an interval of seven years Stephen was born. From the very beginning he adored his father, and Mrs May had a long battle to preserve the child from being utterly spoilt by her husband. As the boy grew up, Richard May's pride in him became ' sommat sinful ', as a Chapel friend said. He was certainly an unusual child. He had big brown eyes that observed everything, he began to talk early, he had a beautiful sturdy young body and was good-tempered. His mother made all his clothes.

II

At five Stephen was sent to school in the Infants Department of a school that was attached to the Wesleyan Chapel. At eight he was moved to a larger Board School, where the boys were segregated from the girls and had male teachers. He was in a class of forty boys. In two things he showed precocity: in geography and drawing, for which his marks were often one hundred per cent. The first time he was given a brush and some water-colours and told to copy and paint a flower, he was in heaven. He produced so perfect a copy the first day that his astonished teacher asked him where he had learnt to draw and paint. From that day on his master passion was drawing. He drew everything—animals, buildings, country scenes, statues and portraits of his schoolfellows. He neglected his other schoolwork and was often in trouble. One other thing set him apart from his fellows. He detested games. Half-way through the morning all the boys, hooligans at large, were sent into the yard to play for fifteen minutes. They played leapfrog, hop-scotch and rounders in the walled-in asphalted yard. He firmly refused to join in, and stood lonely and shivering on winter mornings, until the school bell sent all the boys lining up and they marched, class by class, into school again. Real trouble began for him when they were taken to the cricket or football field to play in organised games. He showed no team spirit and was openly rebellious. Often he was punished for his recalcitrance, but it effected no change. There was a day when, the ball coming near him, he deliberately kicked it into his own goal. After that he was outside the pale. No side would take him. He enjoyed his subsequent ostracism. The news of this coming to his father, he remonstrated with him.

" How can they be so silly running about after a bag of wind ? " said Stephen.

" You must be like other boys and play games."

" But, Daddy, you aren't like other men ; you don't get drunk."

" That's different."

" How ? "

" Well, it is. You must grow up a strong boy."

" I am a strong boy. I can climb the rope in the gym faster than any of them."

" Stephen, you must not be conceited," said Mrs May, looking up from her sewing. " Your father is right, you should play games like the other boys."

" Well, if the bairn doesn't want to, why should he ? " asked Mr May, with a twinkle in his eye.

" Richard, you're worse than he is—you're a weathercock," said Mrs May severely, biting the thread of her sewing. " You'll be the ruin of the boy ! "

Stephen bounced himself on to his father's knees, put an arm round his neck and gave him a kiss in return for a friendly slap on his thigh. Between them they always defeated Mrs May.

In one thing the boy recovered standing among his fellows. In summer he went down to the river-bank just above the Colliery, where the meadows were full of buttercups and daisies. At twelve he was a fearless swimmer, and among the crowd of naked boys that splashed and swam there he had no equal. Twice a week the boys were marched to the public swimming-baths. He always won the high dive and the hundred yards for boys of his age. At this stage, vivacious and tall for his years, with a crown of blond hair and a sensitive face, his school world, hitherto hateful, was made pleasant by a sympathetic young master who nicknamed him ' Pan ' and showed him real affection. For one marvellous week-end, with the consent of Stephen's parents, he took him to London and showed him the Elgin Marbles in the British Museum, a revelation of paradise. When this young master left, to take a position in Canada, Stephen was inconsolable. He never forgot him.

Drawing was ever his master passion. One Christmas, when he was seven, he found in his stocking a complete box of water-colours with fine brushes, and porcelain mixing-tray. They came from the Misses Pearson, the two spinsters who kept a confectioner's shop in Wilford Road. They liked having Stephen to tea, where they let him wind an artificial bird that sang in a cage. Then one day they crowned their kindness to him. At a house in Clarendon Street, facing the General Cemetery, there was a drawing and painting class held once a week. Some twenty children sat down two sides of a long table on which there were pots of paints. They were given various sketches to copy and objects to paint. Two elderly ladies—sisters, with kind voices—went from one pupil to another giving instructions. It was one hour a week of sheer heaven, and cost two shillings, which the Misses Pearson paid.

The children who attended this painting class came from a

different part of Nottingham. They were mostly from a district near the Forest and The Park. The Forest was not a forest at all, though in the distant past it had been a part of the Sherwood Forest renowned for the exploits of Robin Hood, who was such a thorn in the flesh of the Sheriff of Nottingham. The Forest was now a long stretch of railed-in park with a race-course, some recreation fields, and a few knots of trees. Along the south side of this park there was a row of houses, some large, and all of them of some dignity, divided towards the centre by the High School, the city's ancient private educational establishment, distinguished by the fact that the masters had degrees and wore gowns, and the headmaster was usually a doctor of science or literature. The row of houses and the towered school faced the open park. It was a refined quarter only a little lower in distinction than a private residential quarter, that could be closed in by gates, known as The Park. This lay mostly behind the Castle high on its rock, where in 1212 King John had hanged twenty-eight boys of twelve to fourteen years of age held as hostages for the good conduct of the Welsh Prince Llewellyn, who revolted. Down its internal rock staircase Roger Mortimer, the paramour of Queen Isabella, King Edward III's mother, had been apprehended in an attempt to escape, which ill fortune led him to the gallows. The houses of The Park were built on a steep amphitheatre terminating in the Castle rock, which faced the valley of the Trent. From this eminence above the winding river, a silver vein in the green landscape, there was a beautiful panorama of the Charnwood Forest, a long line of violet-coloured uplands.

The Park, thus descending from a high ridge down to the valley, in which tennis-grounds and archery ranges were pleasantly situated, was divided into terraces, crescents, drives and circuses, all well-wooded and of dignified breadth. The houses themselves might for the most part have been called mansions. They had high walls, impressive pillared gates, heavy porticos and large gardens. The rooms within were spacious. In the servants' quarters lived two to five maids, as well as a cook. Some of the houses were dignified by butlers, and two or three maintained a footman or a valet as well as a coachman, who later was converted into a chauffeur, just as the stable was converted into a garage. The people who lived in The Park, while not aristocrats, being for the most part successful industrialists, were considered to be in a privileged class. The Park belonged to the Dukes of Newcastle, whose line had long ceased to live in the massive double-winged mansion called the Castle—by virtue of its site on the high rock. Since the landlord of all these houses in his Park was a duke, the houses derived some reflected exclusiveness from the ducal coronet. An address in The Park extracted immediate deference from the town tradespeople, and from the railway porters, who knew that residents therein always travelled first-class and tipped well.

Most of the children attending the Misses Woodward's painting class came from the houses about the Forest. A few came from The Park. They were well-dressed and well-spoken. A carriage came for two of the little girls.

The house in which the lessons were given seemed enormous to Stephen May. It had a hall so large that his home in Adelaide Row could almost have gone into it. The main door was approached by steps guarded by two stone lions, and the door itself, of formidable proportions, with gothic panels of stained glass, led into an inner hall which had two bells, on either side, one labelled VISITORS, the other SERVANTS. Inside the hall there was a wide staircase with a bronze statue of a lady holding a lamp. The stairs were covered with a heavy crimson carpet. The hall floor was of black-and-white marble. Immediately off the hall Stephen entered the room in which was held the painting class. It had two large windows, one french, which opened on to a garden. There was a white marble mantelpiece carved with intaglios of Greek heroes, all naked and very natural. Never before had Stephen seen inside such a house. It was worth the two shillings to see it; but he felt terribly shy, and was afraid he might slip on the polished wood floor. Later he learned that the two Misses Woodward had once been well-to-do but now they had to keep a girls' day school for a living. His greatest impression came on the second visit, when he had to ask to leave the room. A maid in cap and apron took him upstairs to the lavatory at the end of a wide carpeted landing. Inside, he was stunned. The seat was made of shining mahogany. There was a brass rod with a white porcelain handle which was pulled to flush the pan. In an embroidered box hung on the wall there were sheets of fine tissue paper. He had never before seen anything but news-paper which his mother made him cut up into squares, pierce with a bradawl, and hang on a nail. Now, greatly daring, he took four pieces of the tissue paper and placed them in his pocket for a souvenir to show them at home. Coming out of the lavatory he peeped in through a door ajar, and again was overwhelmed. There was a large white bath, with shining brass taps and a mahogany surround. The big towels on a rail had initials embroidered on them. There was a thick white towel over a cork mat on the floor, and a tray across the bath had a large sponge and three different-coloured cakes of soap. But what really astonished him was a large jar half-full of little pink crystals. Even more than the tissue paper, he found the contents of the glass jar overwhelming. To be rich enough to suck cachous while you were having a bath ! For a moment he hesitated and then, facing the dreadful disgrace of being found out, he entered the bathroom, raised the lid of the glass jar and took some of the cachous. Placing them in his pocket, he left the bathroom and went carefully down the wide staircase, his heart pounding from his adventure.

He liked the children around him in the painting class. They were well-dressed, pleasant to look at and had nice voices. Their speech was very ' refined ', they had not the rasping accent he was accustomed to. The little girl next to him, about the same age, was friendly, and showed him how to mix yellow ochre with ultramarine blue to obtain a nice green for the meadow in his design, and when she saw his work her eyes shone with admiration. She had chestnut-brown hair tied up on her head with a red ribbon.

" What's your name ? " she asked.

" Stephen May. What's yours ? "

" Helen Watmough. Do you like this ? "

" Ever so much. Have you been here often ? "

" Six times. I like to come. My brother doesn't. He says it's stupid, but mother makes him. He goes to school next term. That's my brother Eric."

She pointed to a boy on the other side of the table, older than she. He had a thin, sharp face, the same hair and eyes. He wore a Norfolk jacket with a belt.

" Why doesn't your brother go to school ? I do," said Stephen.

"You silly, he does go to school, but he goes to a boarding-school next term."

"Oh!" said Stephen. He looked with wondering eyes at the boy named Eric. Very recently he had begun to read a weekly journal called *The Boys' Own Paper*. It had an exciting story about boys at a school called St Ermine's College. They had wonderful pranks in a dormitory every night. The ringleader was the Hon. Montmorency D'Arcy, nicknamed Monty. All the boys wore Eton jackets and long trousers. This boy Eric was the first he had seen who was going to a boarding-school. How wonderful it must be! For two months now he had had a secret longing for an Eton suit and a mortar-board with a tassel. The town boys shouted rude things at the boys of St Ermine's, and one day the Hon. Monty had given a street-boy a thrashing. He was a fighter as well as elegant, which was proper in a Field-marshal's son.

"Is your dad a soldier?" asked Stephen, turning from the fortunate Eric to his sister.

"Yes. How did you know? My daddy's just come back from the Boer War. He's a captain with two medals."

Just then Miss Woodward came to them and looked at their work. "Isn't he clever?" said Helen to their teacher.

Miss Woodward bent over them and looked from Helen's painting to Stephen's.

"How old are you, Stephen?"

"Eight, miss."

"How long have you been painting?"

"Almost three months, since I'd a box of paints for Christmas, but I've been drawing all my life."

"Then you like it," said Miss Woodward, picking up a brush and dipping it in some paint. "Look, dear, you wash in the sky like this—see?"

He watched her quick brushwork, and how she ran the colours over the wet paper.

"It looks easy when you do it, miss," he said, admiringly.

"Call me Miss Woodward, Stephen," she said, smiling, giving him back his brush. She looked at a watch pinned on her bodice. "We've five more minutes, children. Don't forget to clean your mixing-trays and brushes."

Stephen heard with dismay that this enchanting hour had drawn to a close. It had seemed only a few minutes.

" You'll come again next week ? " asked Helen.

" Oh yes ! "

" Then let's sit together. I like you," said Helen.

" Let's. Where do you live ? "

" Clumber Crescent."

" Where's that ? " asked Stephen.

" In The Park. Where do you live, Stephen ? "

" I live—I live down in the—— " He hesitated, desperate, aware for the first time that he was at a disadvantage, that he was not going to a boarding-school next term, that he was wearing a print blouse and knickers made by his mother, and not a man's Norfolk suit, and that he lived in the depressed Meadows. " I don't really live anywhere," he said desperately.

" Oh, how funny ! You mean you're a gypsy ? "

" Not exactly."

The pupils were rising. The Misses Woodward were collecting the paintings.

" Next week we shall have a competition for the best painting of a set subject, and the prize will be a pencil case," announced the elder Miss Woodward, as they reached the hall. " Goodnight, darlings ! "

" Goodnight, Miss Woodward," chorused the children.

Outside they went away in twos and threes. Stephen was alone. He was very much alone, and vaguely disquieted. Helen Watmough went off with her brother. She lived where the nobs lived, in The Park. She must never know where he lived.

He started down the street. He had a lot to tell his mother ; the class, the little girl whose brother Eric was going to boarding-school, whose father was a captain back from the war and who lived in The Park, the wonderful lavatory with the mahogany seat, the tissue paper, the bathroom and the cachous out of the glass jar that he was taking to her.

He put his hand in his pocket and felt them, drawing out two, nicely scented, and put them in his mouth. Immediately he had a surprise. They were horrid and tasted of soda. He spat them out, greatly puzzled and disappointed.

Supper was ready when he got home. His father came out of the scullery with only his trousers on, drying himself after washing at the sink. Stephen eagerly told them of his wonderful painting class. When he produced the tissue paper his father roared with laughter and felt the paper.

" Ay, they've got soft backsides all right ! " he said.

Mrs May looked at her husband reproachfully.

" Don't be so coarse," she said, severely.

Stephen told them about the cachous in the glass jar.

" You took some ! Stephen, that was naughty of you ! They were not yours, and you mustn't walk into people's rooms," said Mrs May.

" But, Mom, I wanted to bring you some ! " he replied. " Look—but they taste horrid ! "

He put half a handful on the table. Mrs May picked up a few of the cachous, smelt them, and burst into laughter. She laughed and laughed until there were tears in her eyes.

" What's got you, lass ? " asked Mr May, as they looked at her in bewilderment.

Mrs May pointed to the table and struggled to speak.

" They're not cachous ! They're bath crystals ! "

" And what's bath crystals ? " asked Mr May, picking up one.

" They're what you put in your bath to scent the water and make it soft."

" Did you ever ! " exclaimed Mr May, looking at his son. Then he turned to his wife—" And how do you know that ? "

" They used them at Lenton Abbey. Aunt Edith once put some into my bath," explained Mrs May, brushing the crystals into her hand.

" Well, don't you put 'em in mine. I don't want to go smelling like a scent factory," warned Mr May.

" You needn't worry, I'll keep them for mine," said Mrs May, putting them in a tin on the mantelpiece.

All that week Stephen lived with one idea. He was going to shine at the painting class. He was going to win the prize for the best painting. Then Helen Watmough would want to sit next to him always, and he would be friends with Eric, and Eric would write to him from his boarding-school. Perhaps he would give him a photograph of himself wearing an Eton suit. Perhaps Helen would ask him to tea one day and he would take all his drawings to their beautiful house in The Park.

On Sunday, following the Bible Class, he walked up into The Park and, after a long time—for it was all very involved—he found Clumber Crescent. It was a long crescent, and he was confused by the fact that there was Clumber Crescent North and Clumber Crescent South. He walked along both, looking for the name of Watmough on the door, but many doors had no name-plates. All the houses were very big and tall, with high walled-in gardens. They must be very rich people. He got home tired and disappointed. At supper, seeing he was very tired, his mother asked him where he had been.

" In The Park," he answered.

" The Park—whatever did you go there for ? " asked Mrs May.

" That's where the nobs live—been calling on someone ? " asked his father, facetiously.

" Don't tease the boy, Richard—and ' nobs ' is a horrid slang word," said Mrs May, reprovingly.

" Well, that's what they are—our Manager lives there. The rents are something ! "

" They're beautiful houses. We ought to live there," said Stephen, looking up from his plate. " One day I shall."

" Oh, ay ! " exclaimed Mr May, chuckling. " An' you'll be taking Belvoir Castle for a country place ? Well, don't forget to ask your old dad and mum."

" I'm sure he would," said Mrs May ; " and there's nothing like hoping ! "

The great evening of the painting class arrived. He wore his Sunday blue suit, a starched Eton collar and his best black stockings and shoes. His mother plastered down his blond hair with some pomade. He set off to conquer. Helen was there. She had saved the seat next to her. Her brother was on the other side. She gave Stephen a bright smile.

" You do look nice," she said admiringly.

The subject of the competition was a vase of irises. They would have fifty minutes to paint it, when they must hand in their paintings. A silence of intense effort fell upon the room. After some thirty minutes Stephen stopped painting.

" I've done," he whispered to Helen.

She looked at his work with open mouth.

" It's beautiful—it's the most beautiful ever ! "

" If you've done, don't talk. Write your name on the back of the painting and bring it, face down, to me," called the elder Miss Woodward from her desk.

Stephen carefully wrote his name on the back of his paper, then he went up to the desk. Miss Woodward looked at him with surprise.

" Are you sure you have finished, Stephen ? "

" Yes, Miss Woodward," he replied, handing in his painting.

" Very well, go back to your seat, and you can do what you like now."

Stephen returned to his seat. Twenty minutes later the younger Miss Woodward rang a handbell and asked them to bring their paintings to the desk. There was a long examination of their entries by the two sisters, then the bell rang again for silence. Miss Woodward stood up with a painting in her hand.

" The prize has been won by Stephen May," she announced. " Stand up, Stephen, please."

Stephen stood up, very self-conscious. Miss Woodward pinned up his work on the blackboard.

" I think we should all give Stephen a good clap," she said.

There was a burst of applause. Stephen, very self-conscious, blushed crimson. He was then called to the desk, where the Misses Woodward shook hands with him. The prize had a long sliding lid with flowers painted on it. There were five pencils inside. Before he left the desk Miss Woodward stooped and kissed him on the cheek. When he got back to his seat Helen was the first to see the pencil-box. She squeezed Stephen's hand as the other children stood round them.

That evening he left, dizzily triumphant. He had won the prize. He had been applauded, and kissed by Miss Woodward. It was his first public success. He held the pencil-box in his hand as he went down the steps with the other children. Helen was standing by the gate with her brother and another boy. The stranger, a fat boy with freckles and red hair, when he saw Stephen talking to Helen, came to him aggressively.

" Hey, where do you live ? " demanded the boy.

" I live with my dad and mum," replied Stephen evasively.

"What's your dad?"

"He's—he's—he's a miner," said Stephen doggedly.

"A coal-miner—down a pit!"

"Yes."

Stephen turned to Helen. She smiled at him, holding her brother's hand.

"You mean your dad has a black face like a nigger minstrel?" cried the freckled boy.

"Ough—are you a collier's brat?" exclaimed Eric Watmough, joining in.

"My dad's as good as yours!" retorted Stephen, his face reddening from shame and anger. Helen was looking at him wide-eyed.

"I thought you'd come out of a coal-hole!" cried the freckled boy, with a leer.

Smarting under this insult, Stephen gave the boy a swift bang on the nose with his pencil-box. The victim gave a loud yelp. Eric Watmough dropped his sister's hand and tried to hit Stephen, who was too quick for him. Taking him by the shoulders, Stephen shook his older adversary with sudden fury, so hard that the other boy's head violently hit the garden wall behind him. Eric Watmough, scared as well as bruised, began to cry, whereupon little Helen stepped between them and turned to Stephen, angrily.

"You horrid, common boy—leave my brother alone!" she cried tearfully.

Stephen stared at her, a little frightened by his own violence. His prize had fallen on the pavement. Before he could pick it up the freckled boy had seized it and thrown it over the cemetery wall and then run off. Helen and her brother, still howling, walked away. Then slowly, alone, stunned, Stephen went down the street, half blinded with tears and anger. "*A black face like a nigger minstrel. A collier's brat come out of a coal-hole.*" All his life he never forgot those searing insults.

Stephen's mother and father saw in a glance at his face that he was troubled and had been crying.

"Eh, boy, what's up?" asked Mr May.

Stephen looked at his father, his eyes suddenly swimming with tears.

"Daddy, they called you—they called you——" he began,

and then, his body racked with sobbing, he flung himself down on his mother's lap.

He never went to the painting class again. Nothing would induce him to go, neither the kind Misses Pearson's entreaties nor a letter from the Misses Woodward to Mrs May saying Stephen was their brightest pupil and they had the greatest hopes for him.

III

Queen Victoria died. The school was closed for a day, the shops kept up their shutters, the newspapers had broad black edgings. Emperors, kings, princes and generals came from all over the world to walk in the dead Queen's funeral procession. Then, soon afterwards, preparations began to be made for King Edward's coronation. Suddenly, like a thunderbolt, came alarming news and all preparations were cancelled. The King was dangerously ill with appendicitis. The British Empire held its breath until the royal surgeons' bulletins pronounced His Majesty out of danger.

Stephen was playing by the river when he learnt there was to be no Coronation, as the King was perhaps dying. They had built a wide embankment, with concrete steps going down to the water. This embankment, with trees, wide grass plots and a carriage road, followed the half-circle of the river between the Trent Bridge and Wilford Bridge; beyond lay Clifton Colliery and Stephen's home. As with all improvements that involve innovations, there was much criticism of the Embankment. The river no longer ran waywardly between the banks whose meadows were covered with buttercups and daisies, and, in Spring, with blue and yellow crocuses that the children went to gather. Moreover, new houses began to eat up the fields, and the memory of the flowers was preserved only by this district called The Meadows, a hideous travesty of the name, wrought by the speculator's greed and lack of public enterprise. The dreary streets ate up the meadows, the mean terraces and rows filled the air with smoke in the shade of the gaunt colliery.

One institution remained, and it seemed as if it would go on for ever—the renowned Goose Fair. Once upon a time, long forgotten, there had been a real goose fair held in the big market square in the centre of the town, the largest open square in England; but in time its utility gave place to amusement only. Early in October every year there converged upon Nottingham from all over England all the travelling shows and hucksters. For three days before the Fair opened, there was a tremendous bustling, a hammering, a pulling, by steam traction engines, of great lorries and mysterious vans. By day and by night into the market square came great round-abouts with gaily painted horses, lions and roosters that re-volved round blaring organs decorated with gilt-breasted nymphs. There came breath-taking switchbacks that carried car-loads of screaming passengers up and down an alarming track; helter-skelters like windmills on whose winding slope people seated on mats were chuted down; shows with strong men, midgets, freaks and fat ladies; booths with prize-fighters who challenged all comers, shooting alleys whose celluloid balls bounced on water-jets; coconut shies, with prizes displayed, mystery mazes, haunted castles, flying machines, revolving wheels and breath-taking swings. All these ingenious amusements were erected with furious activity. The last to move in, the most exciting of all, was Bostock and Womb-well's Menagerie, with its cages of lions, tigers, hyenas, monkeys, zebras and wolves. Part of the menagerie could not be hidden from view and gave the excited schoolchildren a free show as it came in, too large for the lorries—the slow, benign elephants and gloomy camels. Outside the show, under a terrifying painting of snarling lions, there was a plat-form, whereon, as a foretaste and attraction, the lion-tamer, in frogged coat, white kid riding-breeches and top boots, would bring out a panther and make it stand on a tub, while a brass band seated along the front played lively tunes.

By Thursday morning all was ready for the opening of the Fair. Presently out of the Exchange fronting the market square came a solemn procession, prefaced by policemen on horseback clearing the way; the Beadle with the Town Mace, the Town Clerk in a wig and gown, and the Mayor, wearing his fur-tipped gown, gold chain of office and tricorne hat, supported by the Aldermen and Councillors. The procession solemnly mounted a special platform, the Beadle called *Oyez! Oyez! Oyez!*, the Town Clerk read the Proclamation and the Mayor then solemnly declared the ancient Goose Fair open. Immediately there was a great blast from the sirens of the round-abouts, the showmen clanged their big brass bells, the organs brayed, the horses, lions, ostriches and roosters began to revolve around their tented canopies, the swings shot up into the air, the screaming passengers came down the switchback, and general pandemonium shook the windows of the shops sur-rounding the square. In the spirit of things, the Mayor and Corporation sampled the Fair. They rode on the roundabouts, went into the shows and were presented with bags of Grantham gingerbread and coloured sugar-sticks of Nottingham rock. After that they adjourned to the Exchange, where they ate a large lunch and made speeches telling one another what good fellows they were.

The Fair began at noon each day. The afternoons were patronised chiefly by children and their mothers. It was at night that the Fair really got going. The spirit of good-natured rowdiness ran loose. The men bought coloured ' ticklers '—soft fibre tufts on wire handles—with which they tickled all the girls in the face and neck, who wildly shrieked and flung confetti at their aggressors. There were other kinds of ticklers : rolled-up coloured papers that had squeakers for mouth-pieces, and when blown into shot out an air-filled tube with an insect on the end. The crowd became greatest towards midnight as all the roundabouts blared and whirled, and people swung in the air, or slid screaming down the chutes and helter-skelters. Then human snakes began to evolve, consisting of long lines of young people, their hands on one another's shoulders, playing follow-my-leader. They wound up and down Beastmarket Hill, King Street and Long Row, indulging in horse-play that never quite degenerated into dangerous crushes, for patient policemen were on the watch for hooliganism. In the midst of all the noise, amid the howling of wild beasts in Bostock and Wombwell's, the sirens, the bells, and the light of the flares on hucksters' stalls, the still white figure of a portly woman wearing a crown, sceptre in hand, standing on a pedestal, gazed serenely across the Fair towards the Exchange and its clock, whose hands drew near to mid-night, when sanity and quiet would return. It was the new memorial statue of Queen Victoria, who, on calmer days, presided over a pot market and two ice-cream stalls kept by Mrs Solari.

The Fair lasted three days, and with the approach of midnight on Saturday frenzy took possession of the square. All day people poured into Nottingham from the surrounding places, brought by special excursion trains. On the last night it was almost a matter of fighting one's way into the packed mass that swayed and circulated in the Fair. There were sudden eddies and crushes that became a near panic, in which a rougher element delighted. Women were bruised, their clothes torn, sometimes good nature became overstrained and an ugly temper began to rear its head. The public-houses were crammed and people struggled for drinks at the bars. There were some arrests of ' drunks ' and obstreperous challengers of the Law. As the hour of midnight approached, the roundabouts and shows doubled their prices, and the crowd, in a reckless mood, under a luridly lit sky, fought to get on the roundabouts, swings and helter-skelters. Then, inexorably, the illuminated clock over the Exchange pointed to twelve and a bell struck midnight. Like a pricked balloon King Pandemonium sank in darkness and silence. The Goose Fair was over. When, the next morning, the solemn church- and chapel-goers crossed the square to the morning service the great space was completely empty. It was as if a magic wand had been passed over that crowded assembly of shows, roundabouts and booths, and they had all instantly vanished. Once more on Wednesdays and Saturdays the square was covered with tented stalls where the housewives did their weekly shopping.

For a week before the Fair, Stephen, like all the other children, was in a state of mounting excitement. They watched for the vans coming, the gypsy caravans that began to squat in open places, the heavy lorries that rumbled in, pulled by traction engines. It was a matter of honour not to miss Bostock and Wombwell's, always the last coming over the Trent Bridge, with elephants and camels in full view. And when the Fair had gone, fortunate children had souvenirs that lasted for some weeks or months, toys that had been bought for them, in a fabulous shop called Beecrofts that stood at a corner of the Exchange and had a permanent fringe of young faces pressed against the plate-glass windows. The favourite gifts for little girls were dressable dolls, with flexible limbs and rolling eyes, that miraculously squeaked when laid down or picked up. The choice for little boys lay between red-jacketed lead soldiers who stood on the ramparts of a fort with a drawbridge, and vertical steam engines, that sometimes worked when the methylated-spirit lamp was lit under the boilers. There were also clockwork trains that rushed round a circular track laid on the floor. Stephen liked these best until, one Goose Fair, he found a fabulous box of oil-paints in the window. It cost seven shillings, and after much hesitation over such an expenditure his parents bought it for him.

CHAPTER II

THE EARLY BUD

I

THE Goose Fair was not the only high spot in Stephen's life.
He was nearly twelve when for the first time he was taken
to the Empire Music-hall. There was a solemn debate over
this, in which his mother was opposed to his father, who was in
favour of his going.

"He's too young—and I never feel quite easy about going
there myself—we shouldn't really," said Mrs May, knowing
how the Chapel frowned on theatres and music-halls, the latter
being an even more sinful adventure.

"Oh, come on—let the kid enjoy himself!" cried Mr May.
"And it's Vesta Tilley!"

He knew her weak spot. Mrs May loved Vesta Tilley. She
was always refined, and never indulged in doubtful jokes. At
that moment of the debate in came cheerful Mrs Popperwell,
who kept the grocery store on the corner. She was the
mother of nine children, an indefatigable worker, with a
dyspeptic and tyrannical husband.

"Why don't you take him?" urged Mrs Popperwell. "The
lad's growing up. For myself I don't hold with keeping 'em
ignorant. He'll soon know what's what—it's amazing what
kids do know these days! I enjoy a bit of fun—in moderation
it doesn't do nobody any harm. And Vesta Tilley—you
couldn't want anything more refined than her!"

So Stephen went to his first music-hall. They sat up in
' the gods ', having stood in a queue for an hour, saving a place
for Dad, who just had time to wash and join them. After paying
sixpence, fourpence for Stephen, they scampered up and up
the steps to get a place in the first row, so that the brass rail
would not obstruct the view. Stephen looked down into a
yawning chasm with tiers of seats and gold lamp-brackets.
The stalls had red plush seats and were still empty. "Reserved

for the nobs," said Stephen's father. As for the boxes, with gold plush curtains, it seemed likely that only dukes and colliery managers would sit in those. The whole front of the wide stage was a sheet of advertisements, but presently, when the orchestra had come in and sat down under little spots of light, the sheet of advertisements rose, revealing two enormous crimson plush curtains quite twenty feet high. Then, as the conductor tapped on his stand, a number shone in two panels, on each side of the stage, the music struck up and the great curtains parted and rose. They did not buy programmes.

" Is it Vesta Tilley ? " whispered Stephen.

" No—she's almost last. The opening turn's generally a dud. The nobs haven't come yet," said his father, pointing to the half-empty stalls.

The opening turn was two girls who sang a song and step-danced. They finished with tepid applause. The next turn was trick cyclists, six in all, who could do everything with their cycles but eat them. They took them to pieces, cycling on one wheel ; they made a pyramid and went round the stage on two wheels, finally on one, whereupon the band gave a triumphant blast and the curtains fell. No. 8 said the side panels.

" Ah, bottom of the bill," said a woman behind, peeling an orange. " ' 'E's good, 'e is ! "

The comedian wore wide trousers, elastic-side boots, and couldn't get rid of his white cotton gloves that always flew back at him. Then he began to sing a song about his landlady. There was a chorus after each verse that ran, " She was cruel and she hit him with the cruet ". He made the audience sing the refrain, which had a lilt. Then he began to talk, very rapidly. Stephen couldn't understand much of it, but it must have been very funny. When he raised two thumbs they rocked with laughter. Mr May roared. Mrs May laughed, but she tried not to.

" What did he say, Mom ? " he asked.

" Nothing you'd understand."

" Why ? "

" Ssh ! " said his mother reprovingly.

" He's a fair knock-out," observed Mr May, wiping his eyes as the curtain fell.

Soon there was an interval. The woman behind had peeled another orange. The odour surrounded them. She leaned over and offered Stephen a slice. He accepted it shyly.

" What nice 'air ! " she said, addressing Mrs May. " 'Ow old is 'e ? "

" Eleven."

" Got one mysen—twelve, but 'e's in 'ospital with tonsils. Always got summat, kids 'as—I've nursed three back from the grave ; but I'd do it again—and I'm expecting another."

" Oh yes," said Mrs May. " Richard—shall we go out a bit ? "

Her husband followed her out with Stephen.

" Stuck up ! " commented the orange-sucker to a friend. " Who does she think she is ? Nice little boy—did you see his eyes ? Takes after his Dad, like my 'erbert."

They were back just in time. There were three more turns, including a ventriloquist with a goggle-eyed sailor boy whose mouth he kept smothering. Finally the rude little boy sang while the ventriloquist smoked. It brought the house down.

And then Vesta Tilley. She didn't come on at once. The band began to play a lively air. Everybody seemed to know it, for they all began humming. Then smartly out of the wings marched a young soldier, dressed in a tight-fitting scarlet uniform, blue piped trousers, a forage cap stuck jauntily on his sleek head, a short cane under one arm. A great burst of applause greeted the figure that came sharply to attention and saluted. Some youth in the gallery whistled.

" Ain't she dainty ? I just love her ! " said someone.

" Ssh ! Ssh ! " cried voices reprovingly, for Vesta Tilley had begun to sing.

" Is she a real soldier ? " whispered Stephen.

" No—she's a lady," replied his father.

She sang brightly, walked jauntily and then came to the chorus that went with a swing. " Jolly Good Luck to the Girl who loves a Soldier." The audience took up the refrain and swayed with the soldier on the stage. Then she was gone. There came two more songs, " The Midnight Sun " and " Burlington Bertie." Then there was a pause, and when the orchestra began to play again the people in the gallery said " Oh ! "

" I love this," said Mrs May.

The next moment a figure came out of the wings that made Stephen's heart jump. It was a schoolboy wearing an Eton suit and a top hat, exactly like the Honourable Montmorency D'Arcy in the *Boys' Own Paper*. He began to sing a song about his father. After each verse there was a chorus, " I'm following in father's footsteps, I'm following the dear old Dad." The audience knew every line of it; they chanted the chorus deliriously while the Eton boy marched round the stage. Stephen followed every step. More than ever he wanted an Eton suit and to go to boarding-school. The last verse was about a dinner at which he drank. He took a cigar out of his pocket, smoked it and began to grow dizzy, staggering about the stage, perhaps also somewhat drunk.

" I don't know where he's going, when he gets there I'll be glad,
   I'm following in father's footsteps, following the dear old Dad."

The final curtain fell to a storm of applause. Vesta Tilley came on and bowed, went off, came on, went off, came on. Then the curtain fell and her number went off the panels. The last number went up.

" I 'oped she'd give us an encore ! " said someone.

" She's tired, poor dear ! This is her third performance today—don't know how she keeps so bright and thin. They say she's forty ! "

Like everyone else, Stephen loved her. She magnetised her audience. He could not know that some twenty years later he would be taken to lunch at a house on the French Riviera and discover that his petite, charming hostess was Lady de Freece, alias Vesta Tilley, now retired.

In the tram going home people were humming her songs. It had been the most wonderful evening of Stephen's life.

" Dad, can we go every week ? " he asked.

" Every week—do you think we're millionaires ? And Vesta Tilley only comes once a year."

It was gone eleven o'clock—long past his bedtime—when they got home.

" Now, drink that cocoa, and hurry off to bed," said his mother, coming out of the scullery with a tray, " and don't talk about tonight at Sunday School. Folks might get wrong ideas."

In bed he wondered how much an Eton suit cost, and what the boys would say if he went out also in a top hat. Then he fell asleep.

The theatre was considered superior, morally and intellectually, to the music-hall. There were some Chapel people who permitted themselves to go to the theatre to see special plays such as *The Sign of the Cross*, in which Wilson Barrett as Marcus Superbus was considered a stirring example of a noble convert to Christianity in pagan Rome. The pagan profligate and the pious virgin, assisted by the ferocious lions of the arena, stimulated a missionary zeal. The Rev. Walter Pooley of the Primitive Methodist Connexion preached a stirring sermon on the subject of the play when it came on a return visit to the Theatre Royal. But the most revered of all the recurrent actors to Nottingham was Martin Harvey, the possessor of a beautiful head and voice, and a splendid product of the Lyceum Theatre school of Sir Henry Irving, under whom he had received his training. He was a sincere orthodox actor, somewhat sniffed at in London when he put on new productions financed by the profits of tried favourites in the faithful provinces. He had three sure theatre-packers on his provincial tours. " The Breed of the Treshams," " The Cigarette-Maker's Romance " and " The Only Way." The last marked Stephen's first introduction to the wonders of the theatre.

Stephen was entranced by the scenery. He was spellbound by Martin Harvey's beautiful voice, and he shed tears at Sydney Carton's noble renunciation of life on behalf of the young lovers caught in the storm of the French Revolution. " It is a far far better thing I do than I have ever done. It is a far far better rest I go to than I have ever known. It is the only way." The curtain came down to tumultuous applause and a sea of handkerchiefs mopping misty eyes.

" He's so Christlike—it's better than a sermon," said Mrs Popperwell, who had accompanied them. " I don't care for her—she's not much to look at, and she's not an actress who'd set you on fire, but she's his wife, so he gives her the nice lines—and faithfulness to your wife isn't usual among theatricals. I've a sister in Sheffield lets lodgings to them, and you should hear her stories ! "

" It's a funny name—N. da Silva. It can't be her real name," said Mrs May as she adjusted her veil to hide the traces of crying.

" Oh yes, it is—she's Portuguese parents or something like

that; an' my sister, who knows her dresser, says she's a very sweet lady and Martin Harvey adores her. They're a happy pair!" said Mrs Popperwell, sniffing, and still dabbing her eyes. "Did you have a good cry, dearie?" she asked, turning to Stephen. "It does you good to let yourself go, I says."

That night, before his mirror, Stephen tried voice and gesture. "It is a far far better thing I do than I have ever done." He repeated it three times, louder each time, feeling very noble.

There was a thudding on the wall from the room next door. "Put out that light and go to sleep!" commanded his father's voice.

II

One clear sunny day in May Stephen was taken by his father on a miners' Hospital Club outing to Belvoir Castle. About fifty miners, their wives and some children made two brake parties. They drove from Nottingham through beautiful woods to the ducal village at the foot of the great wooded hill on which Belvoir Castle so nobly rose. They ate their lunch and walked up the great drive to the Castle. Never had Stephen seen such a place. With its round keep, its rows of windows, its countless chimneys, immense and built of stone, it seemed to have come straight out of Hans Andersen's *Fairy Tales*. He did not know, nor did any of those with him, that the Duke of Rutland's castle was an eighteenth-century building on the site of a former Norman castle. It commanded a wide prospect. Nearer, the hill on which it stood was clothed in noble woods and landscaped with terraced gardens. By the Duke's kindness the Castle was on view once a week, in summer. A man-servant took parties on a conducted tour.

They waited for some time outside the great doors of the entrance. Presently they were opened, and they entered, shuffling and subdued, in the wake of the man-servant. They passed through a high flagged hall, with old banners, men in armour and stacks of halberds and pikes, up wide stone steps.

"Please keep on the drugget," said the man-servant.

Stephen was fascinated by this guide. He wore a light blue cutaway coat with brass buttons on the front and tails.

He had cream-coloured trousers, a stiff collar with a white bow-tie and a waistcoat with salmon pink stripes.

" Is he the Duke's son, Mom ? " asked Stephen.

His father laughed. " Him ! Why he's only a poor nib ! He's a Duke's flunkey," he said.

" Richard—don't be vulgar ! He's human like we are," retorted Mrs May. " That's the Duke's livery, Stephen."

They trailed after the footman, their shoes squeaking as they came into a long corridor. Here a lady dressed in black, with a little lace cap on her grey hair, took charge.

" The Duchess ? " whispered Stephen.

" A housekeeper," answered his knowledgeable mother.

They passed through state drawing-rooms and before full-length oil paintings of dukes, duchesses, marquises, marchionesses, admirals, generals and lovely ladies. They were all very important or beautiful, and the gentlemen, in armour or out of it, always held out one hand imperiously, while behind them rose a great column, the fold of a vast curtain, and, beyond, a landscape seen without any obstructing window. The ladies had feathers, fans, jewels, and generally a sweet smile. They ranged from the time of Queen Elizabeth down to the present day. There were portraits of the present Duke and Duchess. The Duke had no column, no curtain, no scroll in his hand. Instead he wore shooting leggings, and had a gun under his arm.

" His Grace, the eighth Duke," said the housekeeper.

" Caught poaching," said a wag in the company, that laughed.

The housekeeper gave him a stony look, paused significantly, and pointing with a cane she carried to the portrait of the Duchess, said, " Her Grace the Duchess of Rutland, wife of the eighth Duke."

They moved on to admire a Buhl cabinet, a set of Beauvais tapestries, some statuary, an Aubusson carpet of great size, round which they were led. Room opened into room, with panelled walls, decorated plaster ceilings and ornate marble fireplaces.

" Don't see any slippers around—don't they live here ? " asked the irrepressible wag.

" The private apartments are not shown ! " replied the housekeeper, icily.

They came to the library. There were wide views from the windows of all the rooms, for the Castle stood on an isolated hill, but the prospect from the library windows surpassed all the others. They looked down upon a flat plain, a crosswork of fields, scattered villages and church spires.

" On the horizon you will discern the towers of Lincoln cathedral, which is twenty-five miles distant as the crow flies," said their guide.

A few more rooms and the tour came to an end. A large portrait of a youth in hunting kit faced the staircase.

" The present Marquis of Granby, heir to the dukedom," said the housekeeper.

They were led into the hall, and just at that moment a side door opened and a lady with two girls, in walking costume, crossed the hall. The crowd drew aside for them. The housekeeper curtsied. As she passed, the lady turned her face and smiled at the company. Stephen, who was near, saw she was very beautiful. The younger of the girls looked at Stephen. She had the same clear beautiful eyes. Then they were gone.

" That was 'er ! " cried a woman's voice. " Ain't she just beautiful ! Every inch a duchess, I'd say."

" That was the Duchess," said the housekeeper, " with her two daughters, Lady Violet and Lady Diana. The tour is now concluded."

They were out again. " Very nice, but give me Pegg Terrace, I say ! I'd get tired going up to bed," said the wag.

" Never showed us the bedrooms," complained a woman with a curled feather on her hat, " nor the dining-room. They have to sleep and eat like us ! "

" We haven't seen half, but I think it's very kind of 'em to let us see what we have. If I'd a place like this I wouldn't want folks tramping all over it," said Richard May.

" How did they get it anyhow—mostly pinched, I'd say," croaked a fat little man with a hoarse voice, who hadn't taken his cap off all the time. " One day it'll all come to an end, you see if it don't ! "

" Mr Smith, you talk like a Socialist. I don't hold with such nonsense ! They're kind, and I bet they've their troubles like anybody else," said the pale little wife of Jimmy Harris, a deputy in the mine.

" 'ear ! 'ear ! " said the company in agreement. Henry Smith spat and gave his neck muffler a tug.

Stephen remembered the Duchess of Rutland very clearly. Her beautiful face and smile had etched themselves on his mind. Moreover, she was an excellent artist. The housekeeper had pointed out some water-colours and two pastel portraits, the work of the Duchess.

That evening when he got home he took out his sketching-pad and drew from memory her portrait. He added one of the many columns, curtains, and landscapes as seen in the Rutland portraits. Borrowing an idea from an oil painting called " Coronation of the Virgin," he added a cherub, in flight, holding a crown over the Duchess's head. He showed the sketch to his father and mother.

" That's her ! By gum, you've got her, kid ! " exclaimed Richard May. " It's her to the life ! You're a fair genius ; you ought to send that to the Chapel Bazaar ; it's worth at least five bob ! "

Mrs May examined the sketch. She had a fear of Stephen becoming conceited and always kept a low key of praise.

" It's nice—the Church Bazaar would be a better place for this sort of thing, if anybody cared to buy it," said Mrs May, adding, as she glanced at the clock, " It's time you went to bed, Stephen. No drawing in bed."

" No, Mom," Stephen said. He kissed them goodnight and took the drawing with him upstairs.

When he had gone Mrs May turned to her husband.

" Richard, I keep telling you, don't praise Stephen like that, calling him a genius ! He'll get a swollen head. Children so easily get wrong ideas about themselves."

" You can say what you like, my lass, the boy's a genius, and I'm proud of him ! " retorted Mr May, doggedly.

" Genius is a word that can be used very seldom. Michelangelo was a genius. Stephen shows promise, that's all."

" Promise ! My eye ! I know nothing about Michelangelo, but if he drew as well as that his Dad would have been proud of him, as I am of my boy." Richard May bit at his pipe and puffed out a defiant cloud of smoke. " You can't tell me he hasn't got the Duchess to a T ? "

" It's clever for a little boy—but it's never good for little boys to know they're clever. It'll be a long time before we can be sure that he really has a gift."

" I know one thing now about him," said her husband, taking off his boots and getting into carpet slippers. " That boy's not going down any coal mine. I'd blow the pit up first ! "

" You know I think exactly the same—but he must have an education." Mrs May went over to the mantelpiece and opened an old coffee tin in which she kept her odd bits and pieces. She took out a cutting from the *Nottingham Evening Post*. " Look at that," she said. " That's his chance, not drawing duchesses."

Stephen's chance was the announcement of a competitive examination to be held for scholarships founded by a local merchant's Will, for the Nottingham High School. When Richard May had read the piece of paper he passed it to his wife.

" You were always a long-headed woman, lass—I've always wondered why you married me," he said quietly.

Mrs May put the cutting back into the tin on the mantel-piece. Then she turned and planted a kiss on the bald patch beginning to spread on her husband's head.

" I married you because I knew a good man when I saw one," she retorted, gently. Then she picked up his boots and carried them into the scullery.

Sunday had its ritual. The Mays went to Chapel in the evening. They lay late in bed on Sunday mornings. It was the one day Richard May could really get sufficient rest. When they came down they were astonished to meet Stephen in his nightgown coming up the stairs, with an inkpot and paper in his hand.

" Now what are you up to ? " asked his father playfully, collarless, being on his way to wash at the sink.

" Nothing ! " said Stephen, scampering by.

" Nothing ! " repeated his mother. " There's something up ! "

Stephen gained his room. There was something up. He had wakened that morning with a tremendous idea. He put it into execution. He wrote three drafts of a letter; the last satisfied him.

Dear Madam, your grace the duchess of Rutland,

Yesterday I saw you in your hall going across and you were so beautiful I drew you which I send. My father says it's you to the life. I hope you think so, dear Madam your grace.

Respectfully with compliments,
Stephen May.

He had a large envelope that had come with a circular. He crossed out the address and wrote over it the Duchess's. Then he dressed and went downstairs. At breakfast he was secretive when his mother asked him what he was doing with the inkpot. Fortunately he had a penny for a stamp, for he received threepence every Friday and he had not yet spent it. At eleven o'clock he went to Mrs Popperwell, who always had stamps.

Every morning he waited for the postman. A whole week went by. There was no answer. Perhaps she was not a nice duchess, haughty. Perhaps she thought him cheeky. Then one evening, when he came in with his father, having been to meet him at the pit, his mother took an envelope off the mantelpiece.

" This came for you just after you went out," she said, giving Stephen an envelope. " It's got a coronet on the back."

Mrs May and her husband looked at each other while Stephen held the envelope, afraid to open it, his heart beating wildly. Master Stephen May, 17, Adelaide Row, Nottingham, he read on the envelope. The handwriting was bold. On the back of the glossy envelope there was a black embossed coronet with little leaves on it. Trembling in excitement, he handed the envelope to his mother.

" You open it, Mom," he said.

She opened the envelope and drew out a sheet, with an embossed heading, that was covered in a bold handwriting. She read the letter aloud.

Belvoir Castle.

Dear Stephen,

I have been away for a few days, and on my return here I found your very kind gift. Your father is right, it is very life-like, and all my family agree. As one artist to another—for I love drawing, particularly portraits —I congratulate you and wish you much success.   I shall treasure your gift.

Yours sincerely,
Violet Rutland.

" Well, I'm blessed ! It's from the Duchess herself ! " exclaimed Richard May.   " So that was what you were doing with the inkpot !   If you aren't a knock-out ! "

" As one artist to another—well, that's very sweet of her," commented Mrs May, reading the letter again.   She passed it to Stephen, who held it in his hand, but he could not read it, for his eyes were so blurred.

" I knew she was a nice lady," he said quietly.

The next day Richard May borrowed the letter.   He wanted to show it to his mates.   Mrs May took it off the mantelpiece, where it was proudly displayed in its envelope.   All the neighbours had been in to see it.

" Don't let them dirty it," she said, as he put it in his pocket.

CHAPTER III

AMBITION

ONE morning about eleven o'clock Mrs May put on her best dress and hat. Her husband was down the pit, Stephen was at school. She had an air of secrecy, and as she went past Mrs Popperwell's she was hailed by her. She stayed for only a few words. A few minutes later she rang the bell at St Jude's Vicarage. It was not a proper vicarage, but a double bay-windowed house that had been purchased for a vicarage when the new parish had grown up in the mining settlement. The living was poor, the Custs were poor, although Mr Cust's uncle was a peer. Mrs May knew they had a struggle, for Mrs Pieman, from their Chapel, went in as a daily help, since the vicar's wife was an invalid.

It was Mrs Pieman who opened the door. She was surprised to find Mrs May there, asking for the vicar. "Yes, he's in; just wait a moment," she said, and left her standing at the door.

A little later Mrs Pieman ushered her into the vicar's study, a pleasant room that looked on to a garden at the back of the house. The vicar rose from his desk as she entered. He was a ruddy-faced, middle-aged man.

"Ah, Mrs May! Haven't I seen you sometimes in my church?" he asked pleasantly. "Do sit down."

"Thank you, sir; yes, I have been occasionally. I like the service; I was brought up Church of England, and married in church, but as my husband's Chapel, I go with him most Sundays. He's a sidesman."

"Naturally, naturally. Our Father's mansion has many rooms," said the vicar, smiling.

"Well, sir, I've come about my boy, Stephen; he's just twelve and everyone considers him very bright."

"He draws, doesn't he? I saw a work of his in Mrs Popperwell's shop window."

"Yes, that was his. The other day we went to Belvoir Castle, a miners' outing. For a few moments we saw the Duchess of Rutland, and Stephen drew her from memory. Unbeknown to us, he sent it to her and he got this letter back."

Mrs May passed the envelope to the vicar. He extracted the letter and read it.

"How amusing! And how like the Duchess! 'Fellow artist'!" He gave the letter back to her. "I would like to see some of your boy's work. Only twelve, eh? Naturally gifted, obviously."

"I think so, sir, though it's early yet to say if it'll grow to anything. But he's very ambitious in many ways. And so I've come to you, sir."

"I should be very glad to help you in any way I can."

"I know that. Everyone says you're always ready to help," said Mrs May. She opened her bag and drew out a paper, which she passed to the vicar. "That's an announcement I cut out of the *Post*. It's about the scholarships to the High School. Yesterday I went to see the Headmaster. He was very helpful; he says Stephen's plenty of time to prepare. But there's one difficulty, sir. There are five subjects for the examination, and one's Latin. They don't teach Latin at the Board School, and I don't know any, although I taught for five years in a village school. That's my difficulty. So I wondered if you knew anybody who would give Stephen Latin lessons. We could pay a little, and he'd have to do it as homework."

The Reverend Stuart Cust looked at Mrs May. He liked her at sight, she had a refined face, exceptional in a miner's wife. He liked still more her ambition for her boy.

"Well, now. I shall have to think about it, Mrs May. We should be able to get over that difficulty. It's Latin for the entrance examination—very elementary, of course. How long is it before he must sit?"

"About nine months. He might, if he's clever enough, even get a scholarship to the University, the Headmaster told me, sir."

"Mathematics, English Essay, Geography, Latin, Scripture," read the vicar from the paper in his hand.

"He's all right in the other subjects. He's sixth in his class of forty boys," said Mrs May.

" I think, Mrs May, I'll see Stephen, and then I'll have a better idea.   Can you send him along ?   The best time would be about five, when he's out of school.   Tomorrow ? "

" Tomorrow would be quite all right, thank you, sir."

Mr Cust stood up, shook hands with his visitor and escorted her to the front door.   Mrs Pieman, observing from the kitchen, was filled with curiosity.   What was up ?   Was she leaving the Chapel ?   She'd always given herself airs, and it wouldn't be surprising.

At five o'clock the next day Stephen presented himself at the Vicarage.   He was not in his detested print blouse, but wore his dark coat and shorts, and his wide, starched Eton collar with a black bow.   He had washed his hands and knees under his mother's inspection.   He knew the vicar well by sight.   In Stephen's eyes he was distinguished above all the other reverends.   The Wesleyan, Baptist and Primitive Methodist ministers seldom had M.A. or B.A. or B.D. after their names. An odd one or two were distinguished with F.R.G.S.'s, which looked impressive on the notice-board outside the chapel announcing the subject of next Sunday's sermon.   These notices were sometimes startling, such as " Are you booked First Class to Heaven ? "   " Can you call Jesus your Friend ? " " Free Rides to Hell, with no return," etc.   The Congregational ministers were considered ' intellectual ', and the word implied too much mental and too little spiritual endowment. These ministers often had B.A. or B.D. degrees, but again there was a difference.   The vicars got theirs at Oxford or Cambridge, the others at London or provincial universities. " They haven't the tone," said Mr Willis, of the Prudential Assurance Company, who came to collect the payments on Mr May's Life Policy with Profits.   Mr Willis was a district superintendent.   He was handsome, with grey hair and had gold pince-nez which hung on a broad ribbon.   He was debonair, and in summer always wore white spats and carried a brown attaché case.   Sometimes he gave Stephen a penny after ' chucking ' him under the chin.   " A fine boy !   A fine boy ! " he would say.   Mr Willis was a deacon at St Mary's, the leading church in Nottingham.   The Mays regarded Mr Willis as a social figure and listened to him with great respect.   They always inquired about Mrs Willis, a solicitor's daughter, an

D

invalid. "Mrs Willis is better, thank you—but, like me, she begins to feel her years." Mr Willis could not feel his years much, thought Stephen. He was the epitome of health and bustle.

Mr Willis was right, thought Stephen. The ministers hadn't the tone of clergymen, nor the degrees, although they wore their collars back to front, preached and prayed longer, and collected their own incomes and kept their chapels solvent by immense effort. There was a difference, too, in speech and manners. The minister spoke of the Sunday class, the clergyman called it a Sunday clahss, and he said whethah for weather, and God the Farthah for God the Father. Also, while the congregation sang a goodnight prayer, with eyes closed, he did not come out of the pulpit and tip-toe down the aisle in order to stand at the door and shake hands with everybody coming out. The church service was more complicated, with less gusto in the singing and sermons, but, he felt, more solemn. The Church of England was not so familiar with Jesus, and talked less of being Washed in the Blood of the Lamb, which seemed to him a little frightening. He had never been to a Roman Catholic service, but Mr Popperwell, whom his father called a 'ranter', said they did not give Jesus a look-in, and gave the whole show to the Virgin Mary, while the priest bobbed about, tinkled a bell and muttered in a swirl of incense, taking no notice of the congregation. He said other violent things about 'confession' and monks and nuns, and the Pope, until his mother said one day, "Mr Popperwell, I don't like blasphemy, please!" an accusation which so astonished Mr Popperwell that for a month he never spoke to them, although he was a sidesman who waited for the plate opposite to his father. Stephen's only knowledge of Catholics was confined to Danny O'Neale in his class at school, a jolly, witty boy, and Father Flaherty, who went about in a black skirt with a rope round his big belly, but was jolly and brave, for he once thrashed a miner who insulted him.

Mrs Pieman opened the Vicarage door when Stephen rang.

"Oh, come in, dearie," she said, wiping her hands on an apron. "The vicar told me you was coming. He's had to go out, but he won't be long, and he says you've to wait."

She showed him into the study, and closed the door. A french window opened into the garden, but it was the study that held Stephen's eyes. He had never before seen anything so cosy. There were two deep red-leather armchairs before the fireplace, which was of heavy white marble with a long frieze of classical figures, rather naked for a vicar to have. The floor was covered with a beautiful soft carpet into which his feet sank. There were two mahogany glass-fronted bookcases filled with books in leather bindings, and on a writing-desk with a red leather top lay a silver inkstand and tray. There was a crest and an inscription on the front of it: *Stuart Cust, with the Best Wishes of his Friends. Trinity College, Camb. June 4, 1878.* Stephen wondered what had happened in 1878. And it was strange, for everyone thought Mr Cust was an Oxford man, and went to a proper university. Where was Camb.?

The study did not look as if Mr Cust was poor, but he was certainly untidy. There were papers everywhere, and pipes, including a rack with five of them. You never saw those in the Wesleyan minister's study. There was always a suggestion of sin about smoking. Mr Popperwell forbade it in his home and had had a dreadful scene with his elder son, who had called him " a narrow-minded hymn-croaker ". For this he had been locked out of the house and had had to sleep at his aunt's for a week until he had asked his father's pardon and been prayed for by all the family. Nor had the minister a carpet like this. Wesleyan ministers had to change their chapels every three years, and the houses they lived in were provided and furnished for them, very meagrely.

Stephen began to examine the pictures. There were photographs, some of Mr Cust and his wife, and some perhaps of his brothers and sisters. But excitement smote him when he saw the drawings and paintings. There were two large engravings, of wonderful ruins, arches and temples, out of which grew plants and tufts of grass, with small figures standing beside enormous blocks of stone, fallen from the ruins. Some stones had words carved on them.

Stephen could not understand a word of the letterpress under the pictures. *Veduta del Terme di Caracalla.* In the corner of each picture there was the same name, G. B. Piranesi. It must be the name of the artist. The drawings were so wonderful that he felt a little dizzy. Would he ever be able to draw like that? Then his eyes fell on an oil painting, quite small. It showed a large building with pointed arches and columns, and two enormous single columns with something on top of them.   In front there was water on which there were boats with vividly coloured sails.   The sky was blue, such as one saw once or twice on a very hot summer's day, and the water was even bluer.   On the bottom of the gilt frame there was a little name-strip with black letters.   There was a long boat with a serrated prow, propelled by a man standing up at the other end.   He knew that it was a gondola.   It was exactly like the boat painted on the front of Mrs Solari's ice-cream barrow in the Market Square.   Mrs Solari went once a year to Italy, her home.   She had earrings and a coloured shawl, and sat behind her barrow under a striped awning.   Stephen liked Mrs Solari. He did not like her daughter so well because when she gave you a penny cornet of ice-cream she did not make it curl up as high, and she did not talk as much.   All that Stephen knew of Italy he had learned from Mrs Solari.   It was always sunny and warm there, and you could pick grapes from an awning called a pergola.   Mrs Solari came from Padua.   " Where Portia, in Shakespeare, came from, *caro*."   It was Mrs Solari who told him that the long boat was a gondola, " Not gon-doh-la— gun-dolah, *caro*."   So he recognised this boat in the painting that was labelled *Antonio Canaletto*.   1697–1768.

The next object to attract Stephen's attention was a picture near the fireplace.   It was a water-colour in a white frame. Its bright colours showed the terrace of a villa with large green shutters folded back on the white walls.   The wavy tiles were a russet red.   At the far end of the terrace, on a mountain-side, stood a pair of thick dark trees, very straight, and tapering to a point against the vivid blue of the sky.   The terrace itself had a low balustraded wall with six large ornamental urns, from which trailed pelargoniums, white and red.   Across the end of the terrace there was Mrs Solari's pergola, exactly as she had described it—a shady awning made by a leafy vine from which hung bunches of grapes.   The rest of the terrace was ablaze in the sun.   On it stood terra-cotta vases with vivid crimson flowers.   The white-faced villa had four long french windows, all open.   There were basket chairs with bright cushions on the terrace.   On a lower level, down a flight of stone steps, there was a large basin in the centre of which a dolphin spouted a shining jet of water.   The painting was lightly done with washed-in colours, but as Stephen looked at it he seemed to feel the hot sunshine fall upon him, and was dazzled by the light of another day in a world of intoxicating beauty. He knew, without being told, that it was a villa in Italy, a terrace in the sun, under a sky so blue that it made the heart dance.

He was drinking in colour and light when the door opened and the clergyman entered.

" Oh, here you are—I'm sorry I'm late," said Mr Cust, genially, putting out his hand. " So you're our young artist ? "

He was a grey-haired man, robust, of about fifty. Stephen had often seen him in the street and two or three times in a white surplice in the pulpit when he had gone to church with his mother. The reference to him as " our young artist " put him at ease at once.

" Sit down, Stephen," said Mr Cust, relaxing into one of the big leather armchairs. He took a jar off a small side table and began to fill a pipe from it. " How old are you, exactly ? "

" Twelve, sir."

" As you know, your mother came to see me about your entering for a High School Scholarship. How do you feel about it ? " asked Mr Cust, striking a match and lighting his pipe.

Stephen hesitated a moment. Mr Cust wore grey flannel trousers with his black jacket and clerical collar. The Chapel minister never wore grey trousers. But then, he never smoked, nor had a large red-leather easy-chair nor a marble mantelpiece with naked dancing youths and girls on it, nor a flat-topped desk with a silver ink-tray, inscribed with his name and college. " The living's a very poor one ; they've quite a struggle," someone had said, but to Stephen this seemed a very nice ' living ', such as no Wesleyan minister could hope to have. It was so cosy compared with the Reverend William Carter's study, which was bleak and dreary. Mr Cust seemed very happy with his pipe, his nice chairs and his bright rug. Was it all because he had an M.A., and the Reverend Mr Carter had F.R.G.S. after his name ? Once every three years the minister, as a Fellow of the Royal Geographical Society, with no fear of foreign places, conducted a group from his congregation on a tour of the Holy Land. It cost a lot of money. The Misses Pearson, Mr and Mrs Collis, who kept a first-class boot-and-shoe shop, and the Colliery Manager and his wife, not Wesleyans, had made the wonderful trip. Mr Carter on his return gave a lecture illustrated with coloured lantern-slides, a lecture he knew off by heart, for he had made five journeys to the Holy Land. Stephen was thrilled by the slides. They showed such lovely places, with the sun always shining. Because of his travels, Mr Carter always had some interesting scenic tit-bits in his sermons. Somehow, no matter what the subject of his sermon was, he would always contrive to insert a reminiscence of the Holy Land. "When I was in Jerusalem——" or "When I walked down a narrow street in Nazareth, just as when Our Lord trod there——" or "The Sea of Galilee can be very stormy. I was once in a boat——" Some of his congregation looked at each other and smiled, because they had been waiting for this moment in the sermon, but Stephen liked to hear anything about foreign places, only he did wish Mr Carter had gone to Rome. But perhaps he kept away because the Pope lived there.

The question Mr Cust asked him about winning a scholarship seemed to be involved with all these things. If you were an F.R.G.S. you went to Palestine, but if you were an M.A. you had a nice room like this and went to Italy.

"I want to become an M.A., sir, and perhaps then I could go to Italy," said Stephen at last.

Mr Cust took his pipe out of his mouth, looked at the small boy in the chair before him, and suppressed a smile. For a collier's boy it was a singular ambition.

"An M.A.? Well, that is rather a long way off, and means a lot of work, Stephen. And why do you want to go to Italy?" he asked.

"It looks nice. Mrs Solari said all artists love Italy. Richard Parkes Bonington went there—he was a Nottingham boy. Is that a house in Italy, sir?" asked Stephen, pointing to the water-colour.

"Yes, it's a villa at Fiesole, near Florence. My married sister lives there; she painted that."

"Oh, sir, it's wonderful! Is she a great artist?"

"I wouldn't say that—but she's pretty good for an amateur. Now, if you're interested in pictures, I have a very good one—only one, alas!—which my grandfather bought, and we treasure. Come over here," said Mr Cust, rising.

Stephen followed him across the room.

" Now look at that—that's a real Canaletto, a little gem."

" It's Italy ? "

" Yes, of course. He's famous for his Venetian scenes. He was born in Venice, and his real name was Antonio Canale, very appropriately for someone in a city famous for the Grand Canal. So they dubbed him *Il Canaletto*—they liked to do that. There was Andrea del Sarto, for instance, another painter. His name was Andrea Vanucchi, but he was the son of a tailor, *sarto* in Italian means tailor, so they called him Andrea del Sarto—Andrea, the tailor's son. If you'd lived then and become famous you'd probably be known as Stefano del Minatore—Stephen, the miner's son."

" What a beautiful name ! Stefano del Minatore ! " cried Stephen.

" It's a beautiful language."

" Is that Venice ? "

" Yes—the Doge's Palace. Look at these jolly little waves on the canal—little flecks of light," said Mr Cust.

" Stippled," suggested Stephen.

" Stippled ? Oh, yes, of course," agreed the vicar.

" And is the mantelpiece Italian ? " asked Stephen.

" Well, in a way I suppose it is. It's the only good thing belonging to the Vicarage, and should be in the drawing-room, but the last vicar put it here, and left it as a gift to the Ecclesiastical Commissioners. It's Carrara marble, by the Adam Brothers, and since Robert Adam studied in Italy, we can very well say it's Italian."

Mr Cust put his hand on the boy's shoulder. He noticed his vivid eyes, full of light and intelligence.

" You're tall for your age, Stephen."

" Yes, sir ; Mother says I grow out of everything ! "

" Well, to come down to business. You know no Latin ? "

" No, sir."

" Well, that's an essential subject for the examination. I don't see why, with nine months to go, you can't jump that barrier. So I'll consider what we can do. Tell your mother I'll be letting her know."

" Thank you, sir," said Stephen, picking up his cap. " Can I ask you something, sir ? "

" Yes ? "

" That inkstand, sir, with your name on it—what is Camb ? "

Mr Cust laughed and pulled Stephen's ear.

"Camb's a contraction for Cambridge—I went to Cambridge University," he answered.

"Is it as good as Oxford?"

"Oh! oh! oh!" almost shouted the vicar, delightedly. "I would say it's a jolly sight better, my boy!"

He escorted Stephen to the door, and as he left, put his hand under the boy's chin and raised his face.

"Just you remember—if you win that scholarship and others, it's Cambridge you'll select."

"Yes, sir. Thank you, sir."

Stephen left treading on air. He liked the Vicarage, he liked the pictures, above all he liked Mr Cust, and particularly the way he said "A jolly sight bettah, my boy!"

Back home, he excitedly rushed into the kitchen. His father was in from the pit and was having a high tea. Mr and Mrs May listened without interruption. "And when I asked him if Cambridge was as good as Oxford, Mr Cust said, 'It's a jolly sight bettah, my boy!' Just like that, Mom—'It's a jolly sight bettah, my boy!'"

"Now, don't you go mimicking Mr Cust," said his mother.

"The parson can't help talking like that, any more than we can help talking like we do—it's what you're born to," said Mr May, spreading some jam on a thick piece of bread.

"I'm not mimicking him—I like Mr Cust, I like him terribly," declared Stephen.

"I wonder what he's going to say in his letter," said Mrs May. "I think——"

She was interrupted by the sound of voices. They were heard through the wall, from the house next door—a man's voice and then a woman's, quarrelling. Suddenly there was a boy's voice screaming.

"He's drunk again," said Mrs May, pouring out tea.

The boy's screams grew louder. Mrs May looked at her husband.

"He's beating that boy again. I sometimes think we ought to tell the R.S.P.C.C. inspector. That poor boy!" she said.

Mr May got out of his chair to go to the door, but his wife was there first, barring the way.

"Richard, you're not to go out—it'll only make things worse."

" I can't sit here and hear him knock the kid about," replied her husband.

At that moment they heard voices in the back yard. A small boy, clad only in his short vest, had run madly towards their door, screaming " Mrs May ! Mrs May ! " A little man in his shirt-sleeves, a heavy leather belt in his hand, came staggering out into the yard, a woman with dishevelled hair pulling at him.

" You little bleeder—I'll learn you ! " he shouted.

Mr May opened the back door, stepped out, caught hold of the boy, brought him into the house and turned the lock. The next moment there was a savage kick at the door and a voice shouted, " Come out and fight, you white-livered bastard ! You keep your b—— hands off my boy ! You snivelling Jesus-lover ! Just you come out ! "

The drunken miner kicked savagely at the door again. Then he took hold of his wife and threw her across the yard. She got up, her head bleeding from a cut, and went towards him again, screaming abuse. Seeing a clothes-line prop, she seized it, and before he could guard himself she brought it down on his head with all her force. He collapsed to the ground, whereupon she kicked him in the stomach, swearing at him. A minute later she went in and slammed the door, leaving him moaning on the backyard flags.

Indoors Mrs May had drawn the crying boy to her, trying to soothe him. His undershirt did not cover his belly. Across his bare buttocks there were angry weals left by the blows of a belt.

" Richard, get out the bath-tin and fill it. Now, Freddy, don't cry, you're safe here," she said, addressing the shaking boy and wiping his face. " You're going to stay here tonight till your dad's sober."

" I can't ! I can't ! He'll kill me if I don't go home ! " cried the boy.

" Oh no, he won't, son. We'll see to that ! " said Mr May, bringing in the bath-tin, and putting it in front of the fire. He looked at the weals across the boy's bottom and thighs. " I'd like to thrash that brute within an inch of his life—and her too ; she's just as bad," he said.

He began to ladle water from the boiler into the tin bath. Mrs May pulled off the boy's vest. He was twelve, but stunted and skinny. The Fosters had lost three children. The home was a pigsty; when the father was not drunk the mother was. On pay-night they were drunk together. This was pay-night. When Foster was sober he was a weak little man, but in drink he became a roaring lion.

"Stephen, go upstairs and bring me a clean nightshirt. Freddy's going to sleep in your room," said Mrs May. "Now, Freddy, get into the bath—it's not too hot?"

"No, Mrs May," said the boy, dipping a foot. Then he got into the tin bath. He sat down.

"Now, in a few minutes you'll feel better. Then Mr May'll bath you. Do you like cocoa?"

"And what about a bit of Wiltshire ham, my boy?" asked Mr May, cheerfully.

"Yes, please," said Freddy Foster. "I don't like fat."

"Then you shan't have fat. Fair spoiled some kids are," commented Mr May, cheerfully, going to the pantry door. "My dad made us eat fat, but my dad knew how to bring up kids."

Stephen appeared with a nightgown. Mrs May shook it out. Freddy looked at it, while soaping his arms.

"I've never had one of them," he said. "I allus sleep in me shirt."

"There's a lot of things you've never had, and I guess a bit of care and affection are some of them," replied Mrs May, putting the nightshirt on a chair-back to air.

CHAPTER IV

A LITTLE LATIN

I

It was at this time that Richard May was nourishing an ambition for his own improvement. For a few years he had raced whippets against other miners, but as this was usually a Sunday morning pastime, he had given it up. He still maintained an interest in the dogs. There were occasions, of which he was deeply ashamed, when he could not resist putting a bit on some dog, always with the greatest secrecy, and he suffered contrition rather than elation when he won. It did not go with the proper conduct of a steward at the Chapel. There had come to his mind, which had an ingenious turn, the idea of a special metal catch on a dog-collar which should be adjustable and easily detachable. By an ingenius double catch, working in a ratchet, the collar came off instantly, or expanded and contracted as required. Some of the miners were loud in its praise, and he began to think of a wider sale. Accordingly, he ordered some collars with his attachment to be made. After consulting a patent agent and settling specifications, a patent was applied for. The next thing was to get the collar distributed to the saddlery and hound trade. He had no time in which to canvass for orders. He had circulars printed and sent out to the trade, and to induce orders he distributed samples widely. From time to time he made excursions to neighbouring towns—Ilkeston, Mansfield, Hucknall Torkard, Derby, Chesterfield and Leicester. He invariably took Stephen with him on these outings. Once he went as far afield as London, trying to persuade a well-known distributor to take the ' Mayway Collar ', as it was called. He also advertised in the trade papers. All this took a large part of his small savings—how much, he never divulged to Mrs May, who was very sceptical about the whole thing. But Richard May was an obstinate man. For three years he laboured to promote the sale of his invention. A day came when he had to admit defeat. A local manufacturer, tired of housing the unsold dog-collars, asked Mr May to remove them. One day a van drew up in Adelaide Row, and delivered what appeared to be an endless series of cardboard boxes, parcelled in dozens. All these Stephen and Mrs May helped to carry up to the attic, which they half filled.

"Why, there's enough dog-collars to fit all the dogs in Nottingham!" exclaimed Mrs May, aghast. "Richard, just how much money have you sunk in them?"

"Don't you worry your head; they'll all be gone in time."

"Perhaps if we give them away they will!" retorted Mrs May, exasperated. These dog-collars had brought about the only acrimonious moments of their married life. The sight of them seemed to embitter Mrs May. "You've made a proper fool of yourself," she said.

"I shall do what I like, and you needn't share in any of the profits if you don't want to. But I bet you will," declared Mr May.

"Profits!—the money would be better spent on Stephen. He'll be wanting proper clothes soon—I can't go on making his suits for ever."

"That'll be good news for Stephen!"

"So there's all the thanks I get," cried Mrs May.

She went into the scullery and slammed the door. It was wash-Monday. The communal backyard contained every conceivable article of underwear. Mrs May picked up the dolly-pegs and started churning, working off her anger.

When her husband came into the scullery, holding his lunch-tin, on his way to the shift, he came up to kiss her as usual, but she kept her head down over the washboard and snubbed him.

"Well, if that's how it is——" he said, and went out.

But he had not got down the entry into the street before she ran after him. Hearing her, he halted, and she flung an arm round his neck and kissed him.

"Richard, you do make me mad at times," she said with a smile, as he held her. "Mind you come home safe!"

Mind you come home safe. There was always that thought in her mind, and in the minds of other women down the Row.

Little by little the dog-collars diminished in quantity. The Chapel bazaars, and the Church, were certain to have a pile of Mayways. Ruff, of course, had one, and for a time Stephen had the idea of sending fifty to the Duke of Rutland for the Belvoir Hunt, but Mrs May vetoed it. "We don't want to seem imposing on them just because the Duchess wrote you such a nice letter." So the Belvoir Hunt never knew the Mayway. Sir Hervey Bruce, at Clifton Hall, took two sent on approval, and with his cheque came a letter praising them. Later he gave May permission to use it as a testimonial. But slowly the dust gathered on the boxes in the attic.

The question of a suit for Stephen began to be pressing. If he won the High School Scholarship a new suit would be essential, but that was problematical and a long way off. Stephen had transferred his allegiance from the weekly *Boys' Own Paper* to a monthly called *The Captain*. It cost sixpence, which in a lump seemed ruinous, but it was a monthly expenditure. *The Captain* was printed on good glossy paper. What Stephen particularly liked was the fact that it called itself a magazine for public-school boys—boys who, like Mr Cust, certainly said "A jolly sight bettah!" There was a serial in it about an inimitable young gentleman who was very much an improvement on the Hon. Montmorency D'Arcy. It was by an author called P. G. Wodehouse, and illustrated by an artist called H. M. Brock. He drew with a fine black line, and all his boys had handsome, sharp features. They were very attractive on the football field, in their shorts and striped stockings, but they were even more attractive in their Eton suits, always smartly cut, with well-creased long trousers. More than ever Stephen set his heart on an Eton suit. It was a bitter disappointment that the High School boys did not wear them. But he felt there was no reason why, when he went there, he should not start a fashion.

To his surprise, when the subject of a new Sunday suit came up, the opposition was not so strong as he expected. Again his father was his ally, and seemed rather amused at the idea.

"Eton suits are only for boys of well-to-do parents," said Mrs May. "He'd have all the boys shouting at him."

"That's his funeral. After all, it isn't every boy as has duchesses writing to him. If he wants to be following the dear old dad, I'll accept the compliment," said Mr May, winking at Stephen.

" Well, I warn you, you'll be called Vesta Tilley ! " said Mrs May.

" I don't want a top hat and I shan't smoke," replied Stephen.

" Besides, I don't know whether Brown's have got Eton suits—it's very unlikely. And if they had to make one, it'd cost a lot more," said Mrs May.

" Then go somewhere else," said Mr May.

" We can't, we'd have to go to Spender's or Mason's, and they're not as good."

" I've seen an Eton suit in Hope Brothers', Mom," said Stephen eagerly.

" They're not on the Club ticket."

Stephen's face fell. He went to get his drawing-book and pencils from the sideboard.

" No drawing now. It's gone bedtime. Perhaps we'll get your suit somehow," said Mrs May.

Stephen kissed them goodnight, hope rising within him.

When he had gone upstairs Mrs May turned to her husband.

" I can't think what's put that idea into his head. An Eton suit—why, it's for rich boys who go to Eton ! "

" That's probably why—that boy won't be happy till he gets into the House of Lords. Well, he may. Look at Jesse Boot ; he's well on his way ! " said her husband.

All Nottingham knew and took a pride in Jesse Boot. He had started, keeping his mother, in a little herbalist's shop in Goose Gate. Now, although an invalid, he owned hundreds of shops.

" If it had been because Stephen saw Vesta Tilley, I could have understood it better," ruminated Mrs May, giving the fire a poke, " but he began about the suit long before that. I wonder what it'll cost. We never seem to be done paying off the Club ticket. And I've set my heart on a piano. I want Stephen to learn it."

The purchasing of things at a big price was done by most of their neighbours through the Nottingham Buyers Club. The members were allowed a credit of twenty shillings for every five shillings they had paid in. They could obtain an eight-pound article for two pounds, and pay the remainder by instalments. They were limited to the firms registered with the Club. There was a firm conviction among the members that when the shop-keeper knew they were ' on the Club ' and it was an instalment purchase he put up the price.

" You 'as to be artful," said Mrs Pieman ; " don't show your Club ticket till you've done your buying.   Then bring it out.   My, you can see their faces fall ! "

" I don't see why the boy can't have his suit, and you your piano.   I'll be thinking what I want," said Mr May with a grin, taking his boots off, and holding a foot up to the fire.

" You look very tired—are you all right ? " asked Mrs May, thinking her husband looked pinched in the face.

" Right ?   Of course I am ! " declared Mr May.

" Oh, Richard, you've pushed your toe through again ! It must be a May failing !   Stephen's just the same, and you're both always in the same place ! " protested Mrs May.

" Yes, the boy does take after me, Mrs May," he said, catching her by the hand and pulling her to him.   " And I hope he'll be like his Dad when it comes to wife-picking."

II

June the tenth.   Stephen would never forget the date. He was informed of two momentous steps forward into the better life.   He was to have an Eton suit for Sundays, with short jacket and long trousers, and the Reverend Cust had called to see his mother and told her that he would be very pleased to coach him in Latin.   He was to go three evenings a week at six o'clock.   There would be nothing to pay, and no text-books to provide.   It transpired that for three years before he was ordained, Mr Cust had taught at Winchester College.

" Talk about a golden spoon in your mouth—it must have been a tablespoon," said Stephen's father, that evening.

So he began to go to the Vicarage and acquire the rudiments of Latin.   After every visit he brought back the homework for the next day.   The visits were heaven.   Mr Cust became his God.   They often had the lessons over tea, with Jack, the mastiff, wearing a Mayway collar, on the rug.   Mr Cust was very patient, but exacting.   He would let nothing slip.   He mixed the lesson with little bits of history, and one evening Stephen stayed to hear a poem from the *Lays of Ancient Rome* by Macaulay.   It was about how Horatius kept the bridge in the brave days of old. For a week Stephen went about declaiming:

> And how can man die better
> Than facing fearful odds
> For the ashes of his fathers,
> And the temples of his Gods ...

For a time the excitement of a new world seemed to eclipse his passion for painting. Also, he had made a new friend. Mrs Cust seldom came downstairs. She lived in a bed-sitting room, mostly on a couch by the window. Mr Cust carried in their meals on a tray after Mrs Pieman had cooked them, and ate with his wife at a small round table. Every week-end their daughter came home. She was studying art at the Slade School in London. When she saw Stephen's drawings she took an immediate interest in him and gave him some hints for his work. He heard for the first time all about a life-class and that Italians were the best models. A wonderful people. They also made the best ice-cream and were the best singers. "And the best artists—Bellini, Raphael, da Vinci, Titian, Botticelli, Michelangelo," said Miss Cust.

"All those?" asked Stephen, overwhelmed.

"And hundreds more," answered Miss Cust.

The third week-end she brought him a gift that left him speechless. It was a book, *Fifty Italian Pictures*. It had fifty colour plates, on art paper with tissue covers. Never, never, had he seen anything so beautiful. He put the book under his pillow, and woke early each morning to study it. Raphael had painted *The Wedding* (*Il Sposalizio*) when he was twenty-one! Would he paint like that at twenty-one? It seemed quite impossible.

A week after he had been measured for his Eton suit at Brown's—for they had none in stock and had never had an order for one—he went to have a fitting. Even in that stage of basting, chalking and thread-pulling, he knew one of the great thrills of life, standing in front of the pier glass, with his mother looking anxiously over his shoulder as he was fitted with his first long trousers. Another week, and a flat brown box arrived at Adelaide Row.

"It's come," said his mother. "You can go and look at it, but don't touch it. We'll put it on for your father."

He went into the parlour, where the brown box lay on the sofa. Mrs May turned up the gas in a bracket over the mantel-piece. Stephen took off the lid, and his mother unwrapped the tissue paper. There it lay, with long grey trousers, and a black jacket with two wide lapels, the sleeves folded over, the V of the coat showing below. Mrs May covered it up.

" Well, now I hope you're happy," she said, smiling.

He reached up and put his arms round her neck and kissed her.

" I'm the luckiest boy alive, Mom," he said.

Stephen was impatient to break the news to his father. He went to meet him at the pit-head, and when he saw him come out of the cage he rushed up and cried, " Dad—it's come, the suit ! "

" Well, if that isn't news ! " exclaimed Mr May, grinning, his teeth and eyeballs very white in his black face. He carried his dinner tin, and the pots rattled in it, louder than his heavy hob-nailed boots. His shirt was unbuttoned at the neck, and he wore a black muffler. There was another miner with him—their neighbour, Jim Foster, sober and meek now.

" His first long pants," explained May to his companion, as they walked down Colliery Road.

" S'pose he'll soon be courtin' now," said Foster, grinning. " The girls can't leave trousers alone ! "

They parted by their doors. Young Freddy Foster shouted, " Hello, Mr May ! Hello, Stevie ! "

" Hello, Freddy ! " answered May. The door closed.

It seemed a terrible long time before his father had washed and they had had their supper.

" Can I now, Mom ? " asked Stephen as his mother began to clear the table.

" Well, you might give your mother a hand," said Mr May, lighting his pipe with a spill of paper.

" Yes, Dad," answered Stephen, obediently.

He helped to carry the pots into the scullery. Then he picked up a tea-cloth on its hook.

" You needn't bother today," said his mother, washing up. " Take the box upstairs, and come down when you've changed."

Stephen rushed off into the parlour and carried the precious box upstairs.

A few minutes later Mr May heard his son calling " Dad ! "

He got up and went to the foot of the stairs. On the landing, Stephen stood in his shirt.

"Dad, I haven't any braces to hold up the trousers!"

"Good Lord! do you mean to say we've forgotten the braces?"

He mounted the stairs and went into his bedroom.

"Here—you'll have to shorten 'em a lot, but I think they'll do," said Mr May, handing him his Sunday braces. Then he went downstairs again.

They were sitting by the fire when the door opened and Stephen stood there, hesitating. He was wearing his starched collar, a black tie, and the Eton jacket and vest with long striped trousers.

"Good Lord, if it isn't the Earl of Clifton!" cried Mr May, affecting great surprise. He got up, and bowed. "Come in, your Lordship!"

But Stephen did not advance. The great moment had come, but he had none of the *sangfroid* of the Honourable Montmorency D'Arcy, his first hero.

"You look very nice, Stephen," said Mrs May encouragingly.

"It's a bit of a bum-freezer!" commented Mr May, taking a back view.

"Richard! Stephen, turn round," said Mrs May. "Yes, it's a very good fit. You really look like a young gentleman."

"Despite your dad's braces. I shall want 'em back on Sunday," said Mr May.

"Can I wear it tomorrow?" asked Stephen.

"Tomorrow? But it's only for Sundays," said Mrs May.

"I'd like Mr Cust to see me, when I go tomorrow."

"You'd jolly well bettah, my boy!" cried his father, convulsed with laughter, and giving him a spank on the backside.

CHAPTER V

THE HOLIDAY

ONCE a year the Mays had a holiday. In the months of August and September Nottingham and its oncoming rival, Leicester, together with their satellite towns, made a general migration to the East Coast. Skegness and Mablethorpe were the prime favourites. People who went farther afield when these could be reached by a journey of only some eighty miles were considered peculiar, or else they were charged with trying to " swank ", as the vernacular put it. A young couple, engaged, who went to the Isle of Man were suspect in Adelaide Row. They could only want to go so far, a sea journey at that, because there was something they wished to hide.

Skegness and Mablethorpe had leapt up from insignificant fishing villages, known to the boy Tennyson, into sprawling prosperous holiday resorts. They had one great attraction in common—a long expanse of sands with a shallow sea coming in with the Wash on one hand, and a low line of sand dunes dividing the shore from the flat Lincolnshire fens on the other. The air was magnificent and health-giving. A railway company put out an advertisement that had a touch of genius. It was the first railway poster, by Hassall, and showed an elderly salt, all belly and braces, skipping along the wide sands. Underneath ran the legend, " Skegness is so bracing ! "

The place was familiar to Stephen from infancy. He never forgot his first long train journey of some two hours, across the fenland under its great sky, and the arrival at a clean little town that smelt of the sea. There was a wide road that went straight down from the glass-roofed station to the beach. On either side of Drummond Road, well set back, there were shops. Under built-out arcades they displayed their wares, always of attractive colours. There were shops with red buckets and the tin spades for the children who built castles and made pies all day long. There were souvenirs with views of the beach, the pier, and Skegness's one notable feature, the Queen Victoria Memorial Clock, a brick-and-stone tower that stood at the end of Drummond Road, bisecting the promenade. Beyond the clock, down on the sands, stood the donkeys for hire, a threepenny jolting ride to the pier and back. There were also the bathing-vans, large wooden boxes, windowless, that stood on high wheels. As the sea went a long way out, a horse drew them down to the water, and when the sea came in, the horse drew them up the sands. These blue-and-white vans were used only by the well-to-do. Most families undressed surreptitiously in the sand dunes. Stephen had a long-unsatisfied ambition to have a van, but such expensive bathing was quite beyond his parents' means. He fulfilled his curiosity twenty years later at Boulogne, when he hired one. Its whitewashed walls were covered with the erotic scribblings of French bathers.

The annual holiday at Skegness was a matter of carefully planned reckoning for the Mays, and every detail that might reduce the cost was carefully attended to. They did not go to a boarding-house; they took lodgings in a small street behind Drummond Road. The lodgings, kept by a fishmonger's widow, recommended because she was a Wesleyan of good character and allowed no disreputable people in her house, cost one shilling per night per person; Stephen was lodged in a box-room, with an attic light, and for this they paid sixpence. The price included access to the kitchen for making tea, and light cooking. For heavier cooking threepence an hour was paid for gas. In the cost of the lodgings a free cruet was included and, of course, hot water for washing.

The Mays arrived always in the first week of August for one week. They brought with them, put into the luggage-van and taken on a truck to their lodgings for a charge of sixpence, a tin trunk. This held a large assortment of food for the week— a baked ham, cold pressed beef and brawn, and half-a-dozen large fruit pies, cooked in Adelaide Row. There was always considerable concern that the trunk should not be turned on its side, lest the juice ran out of the pies, which were all wrapped in lard-paper. Mr May indulged in a little deception. He plastered over the lid of the trunk a large warning notice, *Glass With Care. Keep This Way Up.* All his life, on the platforms of various stations in England and abroad, Stephen

May never read *Glass With Care* without recalling the annual excursion to Skegness and a fond memory of his mother's excellent gooseberry, blackcurrant, apple and plum pies.

Among many things arousing Stephen's excitement was the singular fact that the departure for Skegness was unlike all other railway departures. The train went from a station built on a high viaduct, and not from the ground level, as at the Great Central and Midland Railway stations. It always puzzled young Stephen why this station to Skegness was called the High Level. " How can it be high if it is level ? " he asked his father, and he received no satisfactory answer.

There was connected with this trip some anxiety. Mr May had certain incurable peccadilloes. He had a passion for taking off his shoes and going to sleep in the armchair with his feet on the hob. As he also had a constitutional habit of always pushing his toes through his socks, despite the fact that his despairing wife kept his big-toe nails cut down almost to the quick, the exposed feet invariably had large holes in the toes. There was a humiliating occasion when the Reverend William Carter, calling to see him, had been shown through the parlour into the kitchen, and had surprised his steward fast asleep with his feet on the hob, two big toes protruding. Mrs May never recovered from her embarrassment. She would bring up this incident against him whenever she had occasion to reproach him. Mr Carter was the embodiment of tact. " Do you know, I love to put my feet up on the mantelpiece, to Mrs Carter's despair," he said, as Mrs May made profuse apologies.

Another failing of Richard May's, quite incurable, was a passion for looking in people's windows. He could not go down a street without peering in between the parlour lace curtains. It was not that he was interested in anything he might see inside, for he was never a gossip, but for some inexplicable reason any aperture drew his eye and had to be examined. " It's a habit I got in the pit ; you have to watch everything," he would say, lamely. There was one occasion when the irate occupant of a parlour in Briar Street, into which he had peered, came out and soundly abused him, to Mrs May's shame.

But the failing that most distressed young Stephen was of a quite different character ; foot-resting and window-peering were merely idiosyncrasies. His father's other peculiarity took on the nature of torture for young Stephen. Mr May would never hurry, for any reason whatsoever. He walked at a slow, dignified pace, and he calculated everything to such a nicety that he never missed a train, often to Mrs May's annoyance, for she would have welcomed his defeat as a reproof to his exasperating procrastination. Stephen and his mother would be dressed and ready almost an hour before the train was scheduled to leave. Not so Mr May. He would decide to change his suit, to wash and to shave, so that the family watched the clock with agonising anxiety. He would arrive at the ticket-office just as the signal for the incoming train fell, and, even then, he would deliberately go over to the bookstall and buy a paper, while the porters were slamming the carriage doors. As his father had the tickets, Stephen suffered agony, certain that the train would depart, leaving his father behind, and themselves without tickets. Exasperatingly, this ever-threatened disaster never occurred. Mrs May would wipe her face, and Stephen have a dry mouth as Mr May calmly seated himself at the penultimate moment.

There was also Mr May's conduct in a railway carriage. The presence of a baby reduced him to a state bordering on lunacy in Mrs May's opinion. He would talk gibberish to the infant, roll his eyes, make popping sounds with a finger in his cheek, pull out his watch and hold it to the infant's ear, fold his handkerchief in the form of a rabbit and make it shoot up his arm. Finally he achieved his purpose. The infant, hypnotised, would be borrowed from its trusting mother. He would dangle it on his knee, encouraging it to pull his hair and whiskers. The fact that sometimes he was wetted never cured him of this frightful affability. Mrs May sat with a sickly smile through all this, while Stephen tried to look as though he was in no way related to the baby-seducer.

Thus with alarums and excursions they arrived at Skegness. It was in Stephen's twelfth year that an appalling disaster overtook them. With a great effort throughout the preceding twelve months they had amassed sufficient money to take a holiday of two weeks. It involved a double expense, for not only was there the cost of the lodgings, but Richard May lost two weeks' earnings besides. Mrs May made the effort feeling that her husband required a longer respite from his exhausting labour in the stall. The first week of the holiday passed without incident. On the Sunday they went to a Revival Meeting held in a large tent put up in a field behind the sand-dunes. The seats were comfortable, there was a portable organ, well-played, and they were received with the greatest affability by smiling young men dressed in frock-coats. It was only when the sermon began, preached with great eloquence by a venerable bearded Elder, that they discovered, as others, that they had been trapped This was no ordinary appeal for salvation. It was a mission of the Latter-Day Saints, who were appealing for recruits to go out to Salt Lake City, where there was a marvellous temple, a gigantic organ and a white-robed choir, a thousand strong. The preacher and the bland young men in frock-coats were Mormon missionaries. They were regarded in Nonconformist circles as the very children of Beelzebub. It was a well-established fact, said everyone around Adelaide Row, that these polygamists captured suscep-tible young women with their smooth stories of conjugal felicity and smuggled them out to the harems of Salt Lake City, in far-away Utah, whence they never returned.

Half-way through the sermon in the Revivalists' tent it was Mrs May who took firm action. She rose, saying in a loud, clear voice, " I don't hold with this heathenish talk ! " and majestically walked out, followed by her family. This act gave courage to about a hundred others, who felt trapped, and a general exodus began, despite the appeal of the preacher to stay and listen. The meeting was wrecked.

It may have been this experience that resulted in Richard May's loss of balance. Half-way down Drummond Road there was an auction-room kept by two Hebrew gentlemen. At five and at nine o'clock they held a public auction. The front window and the interior, prior to the auction, were filled with alluring articles. There were bronze statues of gods and goddesses, almost indecent, but saved by a fortuitous wind that blew a discreet drapery over the unmentionable parts. There were Olympian black-marble clocks with gilt cornices and Westminster chimes, Turkish carpets of oriental lavishness, gilt mirrors, Corinthian pillared lamps with pleated silk shades, young heroes in bronze holding wild horses in check, a Venus in white Carrara marble, plush-lined boxes of cutlery, pearl-handled fish-knives and silver-plated epergnes.

But it was none of these that fascinated Stephen beyond even the lure of Clement's Concert Party on the sands. On the raised platform by the auctioneer's rostrum at the end of the room there was an easel with a blank canvas on it. Every evening, half-way through the auction, an artist appeared who, with incredible speed, painted in oils a landscape on the canvas. Even while the painting proceeded the picture was put up for auction, including a gilt frame. Since the bidders did not see the completed picture they might obtain, there was a sporting interest added to the auction. The landscapes as they rapidly came all wet and shining from the easel were romantic, rich in colour and not ill-painted. They were the work of a perspiring young Italian, handsome, with an open Apollonian neck and masses of black wavy hair—Signor Andrea del Sole. As an inducement to bidders there were bonuses given to those who bought a picture, taken from among the array of articles around the room. Thus the successful bidder for a shining canvas would find himself, at the close of the evening, presented with a marble clock, an epergne, or a set of fish-knives, according to the sum paid.

In a manner it was Stephen who contributed to his father's downfall. This auction-room, with the lightning artist at work on the easel, was the most exciting thing in all Skegness. It surpassed even a high tide that sent the phrenologist, with tent and platform, floating up the beach towards the Marine Gardens. Stephen never went to Drummond Road without stopping to look in the auction-room, for even if there was no auction, the pictures painted by the Italian master were on view. He passionately longed to speak to Signor Andrea del Sole, but that god shone so high above him that he would have been dizzy in his presence. To handle a palette, oils and brushes in that sweeping manner seemed the divinest of gifts. The highly popular comedian in Clement's Concert Party could not compete with such a genius in Stephen's eyes.

There was an evening when Mr and Mrs May, with Stephen, were returning from a long day on the beach. The light was fading and Mrs May was going to their lodgings to prepare the evening meal. Seeing an auction proceeding, Stephen begged to be allowed to watch for a while. Thus it was that Mrs May went on to the lodgings, leaving her husband and son behind. Stephen's delight in the auction-room was also felt by his father; there was excitement in the air. The gentleman on the rostrum was a wit. He kept his audience amused by his genial intelligence upon every subject under the sun.

"This is no ordinary clock which I am about to offer, ladies and gentlemen. You have enough artistic as well as chronological acumen to see that while *Tempus fugit*, as we all learned at school, *vita brevis, ars longa*, life is short but art is long, as the Latin poet says. Here we have a unique combination of time and art. A magnificent, ten-jewelled-movement eight-day clock, in a marble case with twelve Corinthian columns, indicative of the twelve months of the calendar. Observe, ladies and gentlemen, the superb craftsmanship in this piece of sculpture which frames the clock. It is of the same marble from which the great Michelangelo carved his masterpiece *Moses*—which to see once is never to forget, as I was fortunate to see while pursuing my studies in Rome; for I was not destined to be an auctioneer, ladies and gentlemen. I once had the same ambition, but, alas, not the genius of Signor Andrea del Sole there, now completing his superb picture. Ladies and gentlemen, it is Signor del Sole's birthday! This young man of genius is twenty-seven years old to-day, at the very peak, my friends, of his formidable virility in life and art. To mark this occasion I shall auction off his picture, the one he is now completing. To the successful bidder, as a memento of this great occasion, I shall present—give—gratis, believe me—this magnificent clock. Now, ladies and gentlemen, what is the first offer? What shall we say—ten pounds?"

No one said anything. All eyes went from the clock to the artist, whose canvas shook under his spirited attack.

"I am astonished—perhaps you are overcome by the proposition, perhaps——"

"Five shillings!" said a voice.

The auctioneer looked down the room in pained silence.

"I have been many years in this business, my good friends, but I have never heard such an offer as this—five shillings! But I am a sportsman—let us proceed from absurdity to reason. Five shillings—five shillings——"

"Six!" said another voice, a man's.

"Seven!" said a woman.

"Eight!"

The price rose. At fourteen shillings, Mr May, catching

the current excitement, came in. He offered fifteen, but it was at once capped by sixteen. What exactly happened he was never quite sure. Stephen, standing beside his father, was lost in admiration of his doggedness. His father would not let himself be defeated. He was now in competition with a ridiculous little woman in a large straw hat covered with poppies, and a tall lean man with no chin and an enormous nose. At thirty-eight shillings the male competitor fell out, but the possessor of the poppies hung on, and Mr May became heated and annoyed. Finally, to show that he was determined to be master of the field and keep a woman in her place, he jumped the bidding five shillings.

"Forty-eight shillings! Forty-eight shillings! Forty-eight shillings for a masterpiece achieved under your eyes—and a Carrara marble clock Michelangelo would have been proud of. Forty-eight shillings—forty-eight shillings! Going—going—ladies and gentlemen, I cannot believe it!" cried the auctioneer in distress. He looked down the room. There was silence. The hammer fell. Richard May possessed the painting and the clock for forty-eight shillings.

The tension ended, the auctioneer's clerk approached the successful bidder. It was at this moment, after the heat of battle, that Richard May realised what he had done. In his pocket there were fifty-two shillings—the holiday chest of the family. There was one more week to be paid for, and he knew that, with the strictest economy, forty shillings would be required.

He paid the money with all the fortitude he could summon. Stephen proudly volunteered to carry the painting, still wet from the artist's brush. Mr May carried the marble clock, which was surprisingly light, being marble only in front. They were a quarter of an hour late for supper; they tramped back in the dusk.

"What on earth——" began Mrs May as the procession entered the room.

"Mom, isn't it lovely!" cried Stephen, propping up the picture on the sofa. "We got it in the auction!"

Mr May put the clock on the table. Then he sat down, tired by the excitement of the auction-room.

"Hope you like it, lass. I won it," he said, simply.

Mrs May looked at the clock and looked at the picture.

Even before she voiced the question she seemed to comprehend the whole situation.

" How much did it cost ? " she asked, quietly.

" Forty-eight shillings."

There was a silence. Mrs May sat down, her hands resting on her apron.

" The rent will be a pound—and I've things I must buy—it can't be done. I suppose you never thought of that. Some folk never grow up," said Mrs May.

She stood up, and without one look at the picture and the clock, went out of the room. They heard her go upstairs.

Richard May sat for a few moments, then he nervously felt in his pocket for his pipe, which he could not find. He rose and lifted the clock from the table to the sideboard, crossed towards the sofa, picked up the picture and placed it face towards the wall.

"Won't get so much dust—it's still wet," he said to his son, then—" Go upstairs to your mother ; I guess she's having a good cry."

The next afternoon they left for Nottingham, the marble clock in the trunk with the remains of their food. The painting by Andrea del Sole, of a crimson sunset over the pines of Rome, was still wet. It would not go up on the luggage-rack, and was a source of embarrassment.

CHAPTER VI

A LARGE COMMISSION

THAT summer was notable for another event. Greatly daring, the Mays took on what they called 'an overload'. To the instalments for Stephen's suit they added those for a piano. "I think we're losing our heads," said Mrs May, "but you go on hoping for things until you get old, and then it's too late to enjoy yourself. I want Stephen to learn while he's young."

So in September the piano came from Foulds'. It cost twenty-eight pounds—a prodigious sum—and would take four years to pay off. To meet the overload May put in some extra shifts, against his wife's wishes, for he came home terribly tired. There was one morning he could not go to the pit, he felt so exhausted. Despite his protest, Mrs May called in Dr Bentley, who examined him and found nothing wrong.

"You're just tired—can't you give yourself a week's rest?" asked the doctor.

"A week, doctor! Why, this is the first day I've been off for seven years. I told her I was as sound as a bell, but my missus wouldn't listen. I'll be at the pit tomorrow."

"Well, you don't lack spirit," said Dr Bentley. "How old are you?"

"Forty-seven."

"After forty-five we can't drive ourselves any more, May."

"And what about you, doctor!" asked Mrs May. "You're always on the run!"

Dr Bentley was sixty-four. He smiled at Mrs May.

"Doctors are so busy seeing sick people they've no time to be sick themselves," he said, with a laugh. "How's that bright boy of yours? Mr Cust tells me he's giving him Latin lessons. I saw him last Sunday on the way to Sunday school. Quite a masher, eh?"

"There's never a week passes but what he's some new idea

in his head," said May, proudly. "I don't know what we'll make of him."

"I wouldn't worry, he'll make his own way. When you sent him to me some time ago for that bit of constipation trouble, and I tried to impress on him that regularity was everything, what do you think he said to me—' I'll try, doctor, but it's very difficult with the artistic temperament.' I had a good laugh to myself!"

"I know where he got that, doctor," said Mrs May. "It's straight from Miss Cust. They're a pair of artists, and as thick as thieves."

"Well, this won't do; I must push on. Now, May, two or three days in bed. You've exhausted yourself, that's all," said Dr Bentley.

Mrs May followed him to the door. "He is all right, doctor?"

"Absolutely. Now don't you worry. Keep him in bed for four days. Send Stephen round to the dispensary for a tonic."

The piano necessitated a further expenditure. Stephen's lessons had to be paid for. He was lukewarm about practising, and from the start there was a battle to make him go into the parlour to do half an hour's work every day. He had an excellent teacher—Miss Hooley, who lived in Goodhead Street. She charged sixpence for half an hour's lesson and came to the house. Mrs May put the sixpence on the black ledge at the end of the keyboard. There was an initial expenditure for a copy of *Czerny's Hundred and One Exercises*.

Miss Hooley was forty, one of three spinster sisters who lived in a little two-bedroomed house. They were 'superior', and ardent Chapel supporters. They dressed alike in tight-fitting black bodices and skirts, collars with lace frills and high boots. They walked very fast, two abreast and one behind, and they all sang in the choir. The only variation was in their hats. Julia, the eldest, wore a black curled ostrich feather; Millie, the music teacher, had the same-shaped hat but two white roses in place of the feather; Mabel, the youngest, wore a tight-fitting velvet cap embroidered with sequins. Mabel would have been pretty but for her high-powered spectacles. The eldest sister kept house and made blouses to order, Millie gave music lessons mostly in her pupils' homes. She had a

little lung trouble, and took Scott's Cod-liver Oil Emulsion—
" It gives me new life when colds get hold of me." Mabel
worked in an office in the Lace Market. They kept themselves
very much to themselves and were patterns of industry,
modesty and thrift. Miss Millie was punctuality itself; she
arrived and departed on the minute, timing herself by a little
gold watch, on a long chain, tucked in her waistband. When
the lesson began she detached the watch, hanging it by a small
loop on the piano candle-bracket. Her pupils' eyes often
anxiously looked to see if the ordeal was over. She was a kind
but firm teacher. " Your mother is paying me to teach you,
and I expect you to profit by her sacrifice," she would say.
No one would call her pretty, but her smile was a burst of
sunshine. Sometimes, by way of reward, she produced a
sweet. She found favour in Stephen's eyes not because she
knew music—Mrs Starbuck, a viper in a skirt, said no one had
ever heard her play because she didn't know how—but because
she had a vocabulary of Italian words, and could, most surprisingly, talk a little Italian, so that he learned to say *rallen-
tando*, *sostenuto*, *con fuoco*, *da capo*, and *allegro non troppo*.
Although it was outside the music lesson and she was wary of
his avoiding the lesson by side-tracking her, she taught him a
few little phrases, such as *Lasciate ogni speranza*, *voi ch'entrate*,
" Abandon hope ye who enter here," which she told him
was what Dante saw written over the portal of Hell, and, *E la
sua volontate é nostra pace*, " In His Will is our peace," which
was in the *Paradiso* and much better worth remembering.

It was only years later that Stephen learned how Miss Hooley
had gained her little Italian. As a young woman she had been
courted by a young Italian, very handsome and fascinating,
who had come to Nottingham to learn lace-machine building.
They became engaged, but Millie Hooley had great misgivings
because he told her that they would have to be married in a
Roman Catholic church and the children would be brought up
in that Faith, for his well-to-do father was a very strict Catholic.
He returned to Milan, and they corresponded, frequently at
first, then one day he wrote and said that only if she agreed to
be received into the Church would his parents consent to the
marriage. Millie was deeply in love, and had a terrible
struggle with herself before she broke off the engagement.
Her best friend told her it was God's punishment for having

thought of marrying a Catholic and a foreigner. After a month's illness, spent with her aunt in Wolverhampton, Millie Hooley returned to her music-teaching.

Richard May usually reached home before Miss Hooley had finished teaching in the parlour. In winter Mrs May lit a fire for her, despite her protests. " Poor Miss Hooley! she has such a hacking cough—I really don't like it," she would say, carrying in sticks and coal from the outhouse to the parlour grate. Her husband liked to chat with her, and if Miss Hooley had not to leave immediately for the next lesson they would ask her into the kitchen for a cup of tea. She came in, her hands blue with cold, always protesting. " Well, really, it's too kind of you—I must go in just ten minutes," she would say, looking at her watch, and returning it to her waist-band.

The Chapel was rehearsing an oratorio, Handel's *Messiah*. Once a year there was a choir festival, and Mr Pennyfeather, the organist and choirmaster, lived in a state of feverish industry, rehearsing twice a week for six weeks and then, in a final burst, for four nights in the last week. Stephen enjoyed the choir festival because it cut short the sermon and transformed the chapel. A huge stand, covered in green felt, was built over the square mahogany pulpit and ran from the organ and the two rows of choir-seats down to the pews. On these occasions the Communion table and the two front rows of pews were buried under a platform which held the conductor and the four hired principal singers. Two of these, stout ladies, were always called Madame—Madame Colebrook and Madame Blancly— in the fashion of Madame Albani, the favourite of the late Queen. On the platform the augmented choir also sang. To cover the cost of all this, heavy in spite of a packed chapel, there was a silver collection. No one dared to put a copper on the plate. As a steward, Richard May helped to count the money in the vestry, wondering if it would achieve a record.

" As exciting as an election! By gum, we've done it! Did you say you've got six pounds twelve-and-four in your pile, Mr May? " asked Mr Craik, perspiring over the count.

" Yes, including a five-pound note."

" Ah, that's the Misses Pearson; they allus come in with a wallop, they do! Forty-six pounds ten-and-nine, an' six pounds twelve-and-four," said Mr Craik, wetting his pencil and figuring on a slip of paper, " That's fifty-three pounds

three-and-a-penny. That's a record by over six pounds!
And we've beaten the Baptists! They took forty-eight pounds
summat with *The Creation* last week!"

"The Lord be praised!" boomed Mr Jones.

"Amen," chorused the ten sidesmen.

Ambitious, they were now rehearsing Mendelssohn's *Elijah*.
A more expensive contralto had been hired and the orchestra
augmented. The overhead expenses alarmed the Rev. William
Carter. If the festival fell on a wet night, ruin would over-
take them. It was Richard May who had a brain-wave. Why
not repeat the performance on Monday night? The singers
and orchestra could be engaged at a reduced rate for two performances, since the same railway fare would bring them and
take them away.

"But will folks give the same collection two nights running,
and shall we be able to fill the chapel?" asked Miss Hooley,
anxiously, a cup of tea in her hands, as they discussed the
matter. She was always very lady-like, and sat stiffly upright
on her chair. She had a habit of wearing high button boots
which fascinated Stephen.

"It's taking a risk," said Mrs May.

"No risk at all!" declared May. "To begin with,
Monday's a miserable night, with all the damp washing hanging
about the home. Last year all the folks that wanted to come
couldn't get in. We've only to take half on the second night
what we take on the first to split the cost of the performances.
So I'm not worried."

It was a prophecy fulfilled. When the performance took
place the following week the crowd on the second night was
almost as large as on the first. "It's probably because there
was no sermon the second night," declared Mrs Starbuck when
she heard the result. If words could have assassinated the
minister, on the strength of Mrs Starbuck's tongue he was a
corpse. She had never forgiven him for pinning her down
in a vile slander.

All through that winter Stephen tackled three tasks, one a
pleasure, one a duty and one essential for his future: painting,
music, and Latin. Music suffered. Poor Miss Hooley kept
her temper. "Your dear mother is making a great sacrifice,
and unless you practise, and mind your 'time', Stephen, I
cannot continue to take her money on the pretence of teaching

you," she said severely one day, discovering he had only prac- tised once, half an hour before the weekly lesson. Contrite and alarmed, he promised to mend. At the end of four months he had advanced from Czerny to Clementi and the easier pieces in Mendelssohn's *Songs Without Words*. One evening, as a reward, Miss Hooley, having received two tickets for a recital at the Mechanics' Hall, took him to hear a pianist called Harold Bauer. The hall was only half-filled, but it was a revelation to Stephen, and the music entranced him. It was all by a composer named Beethoven. So delighted was he that he clapped vigorously and kept the applause from petering out. He was in the front row, and the pianist gave him a special bow. He was a very young man, and Stephen had a sub- conscious sympathy for anyone artistic.

"Does he make a lot of money?" asked Stephen, waiting for the Wilford Road tram after the performance.

"I shouldn't think so yet; but he will, for he's a very fine artist," answered Miss Hooley.

In an odd fashion Harold Bauer was the cause of the first money Stephen earned with his pencil. That night he drew the pianist from the programme photograph, with a little longer hair and one hand a little higher above the piano than in real life. Under it he printed in German Gothic letters, because the pianist was a German, *Harold Bauer—appassionata*, a name he copied from the programme, and which he liked because it was Italian. When his father, studying the drawing, asked him what the word meant he replied: "With a terrible lot of passion."

"Sounds like a love-piece—I wish I'd heard him," com- mented Mr May, with slippers off, warming his feet on the hob.

The next evening when Miss Hooley came Stephen showed her the drawing. She seemed greatly impressed, and asked if she might borrow it. Two days later she left word at the Mays saying Mr Foulds, owner of the music-shop near the Market, would like to see him.

It was all very mysterious, but it was obviously an occasion for putting on his Eton suit.

A young woman behind the counter asked Stephen what he wanted.

"Mr Foulds wishes to see me," he said.

E

"Oh, yes—what name shall I say?"

"Mr Stephen May—artist."

She repressed a smile, seeing the serious face before her. She returned and escorted him to an office at the end of the shop. Mr Foulds, seated at a roll-top desk, rose as he entered.

"Ah, Mr May—how d'you do," he said. He was a tall, good-looking man with a pleasant voice. "Sit down."

He took Stephen's drawing off his desk.

"Our friend Miss Hooley showed me this. We all think it's very good. It's given me an idea. I wonder if from photographs I will give you you could do a series, say six—Paderewski, Kubelik, von Pachmann, Clara Butt, and Melba—including Bauer? I will frame them and put them in our window, and later use them in our concert announcements. What do you think of the idea?"

"I'd love it!" replied Stephen, his head swimming.

"Good. And what about your fee?" asked Mr Foulds, with a twinkle. The shining young face above the schoolboy's collar and the immaculate Eton suit gave him pleasure mingled with amusement.

Fee? Stephen thought rapidly. If he put the price too high he might lose this tremendous opportunity, on the other hand, if it was too low he might lose Mr Foulds' respect.

"Would—would one shilling one penny each be right for you, sir?" asked Stephen.

Mr Foulds looked surprised.

"One shilling one penny?" he repeated.

Stephen's heart sank. He had asked too much, but before he could lower the sum Mr Foulds asked him a question.

"Why a penny, my boy?"

"When Mrs Cust had a consultation," said Stephen, remembering a bill he had seen on the vicar's desk, "the specialist charged one pound one shilling, so I thought one shilling one penny."

"I see," said Mr Foulds. "Yes, you are quite right—that is the correct professional way; but as I've had a consultation, as it were, suppose you charge me one pound, one shilling each? That sounds fair to me!"

Stephen swallowed, and with a great effort said, "Of course—thank you, sir."

"Splendid! Can you do them in a month?"

" Oh, in a week, I'm sure," asserted Stephen, eagerly.

" Well, there's not that hurry. Now let me pay you for this, as it's here," said Mr Foulds, pulling a sovereign and a shilling out of his pocket, and giving them to Stephen.

" Oh, thank you very much, sir—very much indeed," said Stephen.

Mr Foulds shook him by the hand again and bade him goodbye.

All the way home Stephen was planning what he would do with his fortune. Six pounds, six shillings. Never had he thought to earn such a sum. Two pounds to his mother, for the piano instalments, ten shillings for a pair of slippers for his father, two shillings for a bottle of scent for Miss Hooley, and the rest for a larger palette, more brushes and canvases.

He seemed home before he knew it. Somehow he felt the Eton suit had helped. A sixth-form dandy in *The Captain* serial had said dress was all-important in tackling the important.

He opened the door and was glad to find his parents there. Good news could not be kept.

CHAPTER VII

THE HARD YEARS

I

THE following March Stephen sat for the scholarship examination. Two anxious weeks passed, and then came the news that he had won a scholarship to the High School, tenable for five years, beginning in the autumn term. There was great rejoicing in the Cust household as well as in Adelaide Row. It was Mrs May who kept the general elation within bounds.

" There's nothing that boy won't do, you'll see ! " exclaimed Richard May.

" Don't get so puffed up. There were ten scholarships, and it's Mr Cust we have to thank," said Mrs May, reprovingly. " And don't let Stephen hear you talking like that, or he'll have a swollen head."

" I suppose, Mrs May, you're not in any way delighted ? " asked her husband, satirically, and then planted a kiss on her neck as she stooped over the ironing-board. With that he went upstairs with a bottle of stain to join his son in the attic, for another of Stephen's ambitions was being fulfilled at last. All true artists painted on easels, and now that he had progressed to oil-painting, an easel was the proper thing. Signor del Sole painted on an easel. Since there was nothing his father could not do with a saw and chisel, he gave him no peace until the easel was made, from an old clothes-line prop and pieces of a crate bought for sixpence at Mrs Popperwell's.

The finished article looked very professional, and when the staining was finished Stephen could hardly wait for the easel to dry before putting up his canvas.

The next day, shortly after six o'clock, he rushed home from Mr Cust's in a state of great excitement. To celebrate his success the vicar had given him a fountain pen.

" Look, Mom, isn't it a beauty ! " he cried, in ecstasy. He

glanced at the table laid for tea, awaiting his father's return from the pit. " Where's Dad ? " he asked.

" He's late," replied Mrs May, looking at Stephen's pen. " You certainly are a lucky boy ! "

There was a tap at the back door. She went to it, and found there Fred Emmet and Henry Dyson, two miners who worked with her husband. They were old friends of Richard's, and at once Mrs May asked them in.

" He hasn't come back yet—but he'll be back any minute now. Do sit down," she said.

They did not sit down, and it was then, in the light as they entered the kitchen, that she saw they had all the grime of the pit on them. Her heart gave a leap, but she said, quite calmly, as they stood awkwardly before her, " What is it ? "

" Mrs May, we've bad news for you," said the elder man, Fred Emmet. " It's about Dick."

He hesitated and looked from Mrs May to his companion, as if hoping he would become the spokesman.

" There's been an accident ? " asked Mrs May.

" No, not an accident. About ten minutes before we were knocking off I was coming out of the gallery when I suddenly found someone in a heap at my feet. I stooped down. It was Dick. I couldn't get a word from him—he was on his face when I found him—and I tried to lift him up, but he was so limp I put him down again and called for the boys. It wasn't any use, Mrs May, he'd gone. We brought him up, and the doctor looked at him—he was dead. He must have just dropped—gone in a second, the doctor said. So they've taken him to the mortuary, and we've come—— "

" The mortuary—why haven't you brought him home ? " demanded Mrs May, her face white and strained.

" He has to go to the mortuary—there'll be an inquest. Seems it has to be done that way. That's the law, Mrs May. The Manager asked us to come and tell you—you'll be wanting to go and see him ? We're terribly sorry, Mrs May. We all liked Dick. And he never seemed ill, he got tired like— we all do, and get over it."

" They want me now ? Can you go with me ? "

" Of course—someone had to come and tell you."

" It's kind of you. Then there wasn't an accident, an explosion ? No one was killed—I'm glad of that."

" No."

" I'll get my hat. Won't you sit down a minute ? " she said, and as Stephen rushed to her, in tears, she put her hand on his head, saying gently, " If you come with me, you must be brave."

Stephen nodded, as he pressed against her. She released him, went upstairs, and soon returned, ready for the street. She picked up Stephen's school cap and put it on his head. Then she stirred the fire and added some coal.

" Let us go," she said, turning to the two miners awkwardly standing before her, their caps in their hands. " I hope I shan't do anything silly, like fainting."

She took Stephen's hand and led the way out of the room.

II

The days following his father's death were indelibly etched on Stephen May's memory. Throughout all his varied later life he could vividly recall each detail. At the grim mortuary, with its barren whitewashed walls, they were taken by the police superintendent into a room with a large marble slab. On this lay a shrouded form. The tarpaulin on the body was not quite long enough, and the first things the boy saw were his father's heavy nailed boots. Then the superintendent drew back the sheet, revealing a waxen mask in the calmness of death. Richard May lay there in all the grime of his work, his hair dishevelled, his shirt open at the neck. There were blotches of coal dust on the white face, giving it a strange puppet appearance. His eyelids, drawn down, were strangely clean in contrast with the rest of the face.

Mrs May looked at the body of her husband. She was very calm, and quite unlike any other women who came on similar tragic missions. Her dignity impressed the three men, one of whom—Emmet—was in tears. He wiped his cheeks with a coal-grimy hand and unknowingly transformed himself into a comic figure.

Mrs May leaned forward, kissed the brow of her husband and then addressed the superintendent.

" Yes—that's him. How long must he be here ? "

" Till the inquest's over—tomorrow, Mrs May."

The superintendent knew her and her husband. He some-

times went to their chapel. He liked the Mays. He slowly
drew down the shroud and escorted them out of the cold room
into his office. Here he handed over to Mrs May a wallet,
tobacco pouch, pipe, and some money found in the dead man's
pocket. For these she signed a receipt.

"I cannot tell you how grieved I am by this, Mrs May,"
said the superintendent. "We all liked Mr May." He
placed a hand kindly on Stephen's shoulder. "He was very
proud of you, and now you'll have to look after your mother,"
he added.

Out in the street it was raining, and the little party got wet
waiting for the Wilford Road tram.

At the inquest the next morning the proceedings were very
brief. It was found that Richard May had died of heart
failure due to a sub-acute rheumatic mitral condition. The
rheumatic heart condition would be such that it would not
produce symptoms sufficiently severe for May to report sick.

III

The morning after the verdict Richard May was brought
home. His coffin awaited him, and he was placed in it in the
darkened parlour. He lay there while the neighbours came to
bid him farewell, some silent and dignified, some lachrymose
and emotional. The first caller was the Rev. William Carter.
He was visibly distressed, and while trying to comfort Mrs May
his voice broke. "Let us kneel and pray," he said, and as he
knelt Stephen noticed how worn down were the good little man's
heels, and that one trouser leg was frayed and needed mending.
"Thou hast, O Lord, seen fit to take thy servant Richard May,
but in Thine infinite wisdom Thou wilt not be unmindful of
his sorrowing wife and young son. Thou wilt cherish and
protect them. Thy will be done."

Stephen wondered about the cherishing and protecting.
Why, at forty-eight, should a father he loved be snatched
away? It could not possibly benefit God, and it was a disastrous
blow to his mother and himself. But he revealed nothing of
these questionings to Mr Carter, who departed after his mission
of comfort.

On the morning of the funeral Stephen ventured alone into
the darkened room where his father lay. The smell of the

new varnish pervaded the place. His father lay there in a white frilled shirt that increased the pallor of his chiselled face. Stephen saw how his father's hands were still stained from the mahogany varnish he had used for the new easel. For some reason this unnerved him more than the sight of his father's set face, and he burst into a paroxysm of sobbing. Mrs May, hearing him in the kitchen, came out and led him away.

"Now, now, you've been very brave, and I'll need all your help," she said, wiping his face. But the tears fell from her own eyes, and they held each other, crying for a little while. A few minutes later they heard the sound of horses and a tap on the front door. It was the undertaker and his men. Two neighbours came in, and the last wreath—an enormous one that must have cost a great deal of money—was brought in by their neighbours, Mr and Mrs Foster. "I allus said he was a real gentleman," said Foster, awkwardly. "An' I never meant 'im or you any 'arm."

It was a small, lonely funeral, and singular in that it lacked relatives among the mourners, for Richard May had no living brothers or sisters, and Alice May also had been an only child. On their return from the cemetery, accompanied by the Rev. Carter and Richard May's fellow-sidesmen at the chapel, they entered the kitchen where Mrs May offered them tea, but they declined. When the escort had departed Mrs May got out the tea-things. The house seemed terribly empty, and they ate in silence.

They were washing up in the kitchen when they heard a tap on the front door. Mrs May looked at Stephen. "Now who can that be?" she asked, wiping her hands. Then she went into the parlour, whose blinds were now raised, and opened the door. It was Mr Willis, of the Prudential Assurance Company, as dapper as ever with his white vest-slip, his spats, gloves, and pince-nez on a gold chain.

"My poor dear Mrs May! I only got your letter this morning. Mrs Willis and I have been away at Harrogate; it does her so much good. Dear me, what a terrible business! The Lord giveth and the Lord taketh away. I am distressed beyond words!"

He came in, carrying his little black bag, and they went through into the kitchen, where he greeted Stephen. "Ah, my good little fellow—you will now be your mother's sole support ! " he said, putting on his pince-nez and regarding Stephen benignly.

Mr Willis placed his bag on the table and opened it.

" I'm afraid you've been needing money—but I have brought it, so that there will be no delay. Ah, here is the policy. How I wish that I had succeeded in persuading you and Mr May to double it. Well, well. Now, with profits, you receive fifty-four pounds four shillings and sixpence."

" Fifty-four pounds four and sixpence ? " repeated Mrs May, surprised. " That can't be right, surely, Mr Willis ? I always understood it was about ninety pounds. Fifty on the policy and about forty on the accumulated bonuses."

Mr Willis took off his pince-nez, a little ruffled.

" Ah, then, my dear Mrs May, you did not know ? I had often wondered," he said solemnly.

" Know what ? "

" Two years ago your husband cashed his bonuses. I gather he was a little pressed for money in connection with his invention, the dog-collars. He asked me not to say anything to you, should the occasion arise, as he did not want you to worry. It is very sad, very sad. Who could believe he would be taken so suddenly, and so young ? "

Mrs May stared as Mr Willis, almost shamefacedly, explained. Her heart seemed to miss a beat. It was plain now how her husband had found the money to finance his invention. He was always so confident the dog-collars would bring him a fortune, and he had eaten into their savings, afraid to tell her what he had done.

" Now, here is the money. I'm sure you will be requiring some of it at once, so I drew it," said Mr Willis, counting out the five-pound notes. " And here's the receipt, which I will ask you to sign. This is a sad day for you and for me. I had a very deep affection for Mr May, a very deep affection."

Mr Willis adjusted his pince-nez, looked over the receipt and passed it to Mrs May. She signed it.

" There, that formality's over. Now, may I be personal ? What are you going to do, Mrs May ? Will the Company help you ? "

" The Company ? No, I'd have got some compensation if he'd been killed; but it was a natural death, and so I get nothing."

"Ah, that is a great pity. I hoped there might be something for you. If you won't think me too inquisitive—but as an old friend, of course, how will you manage?" asked Mr Willis.

Mrs May looked at him, more than ever aware of the unction in his manner. He had conspired with Richard to keep her ignorant of the cashed bonuses. His sympathy seemed a little hollow.

"I haven't thought yet how I shall manage, Mr Willis. I haven't had time to think. But I've no doubt I shall manage," said Mrs May, calmly.

"Yes, yes. Indeed you will. I am sure you will, and our loving Father will reward your efforts—and not forget the fatherless," observed Mr Willis, peering at Stephen, fascinated by the five-pound notes, crisp white paper he had never seen before. He put out a hand and held Stephen under the chin. "You will take your father's place very worthily, my boy, I am quite sure."

Mr Willis rose, adjusted his waistcoat and slip, and put his pince-nez into their leather case. Then he gathered together his papers and shut them in the small bag. He held out his hand.

"Dear Mrs May—there's no need for me to express my sympathy; I am sure you know how deeply I feel for you. At any time, remember, I am at your service. In those sentiments I know I speak for my dear wife also."

He shook her hand, patted Stephen on the cheek, and let Mrs May usher him to the door.

When she returned she picked up the fifty-four pounds on the table. There was an undertaker's bill for seventeen, and other oddments. The breadwinner gone, they were facing life on a total capital of some thirty pounds, and nine hundred unsaleable dog-collars.

IV

On one ambition the door was closed. There could now be no question of the High School scholarship. In a month Stephen was thirteen. He must leave school and begin work. Even had he failed in the scholarship examination there was the possibility of a scholarship to a local secondary school on the condition that he remained at school until he was fifteen. That alternative could not be considered now.

Mrs May fell back on the usual resource of the impoverished. She would let lodgings. By moving Stephen up into the attic and surrendering the parlour, she would have two rooms for letting. If fortunate, she might get as much as eight shillings for each room. The rent was seven shillings a week; this would leave her a balance of nine shillings. Stephen might earn five. Thus rent free, with fourteen shillings in hand, and a little taken from capital, she might somehow continue. She was not the first to face such a problem.

That evening Stephen's gift was put to a new use. On an oblong piece of cardboard obtained from Mrs Popperwell, whose shop had infallible resources, he designed a bold but artistic sign LODGINGS. His mother looked at it before he inked it in.

" No," she said, " I don't like the word—it sounds common. Put *Room Vacant*."

" But we've two rooms, Mom."

" Yes, but it'll do. Maybe I shall make a bed-sitting-room of the parlour and get ten shillings."

The next morning, between the lace curtains over the aspidistra standing on a bamboo table that had been obtained free by saving coupons from the purchase of tea at " The Bazaar Tea Stores Ltd.", hung a sign, *Room Vacant*. Like bait on a fishing line, it hung waiting for a nibble.

Stephen broke the news to Mr Cust. It caused general dismay in the vicar's household. They regarded Stephen as Turf followers regard a promising horse, and they had never doubted the scholarship would be his.

" Such a bright boy, and such a little gentleman ! " said Mrs Pieman, in Mrs Popperwell's shop. " I've taken quite a fancy to 'im, I 'ave, an' Miss Cust, if she wasn't getting on for twenty-five, I'd say she was in love with 'im ! "

Mr Cust was surprised by one request from his pupil, and most readily agreed to it. Stephen asked if he might continue to have Latin lessons.

" Why, certainly, Stephen. Now, I think that's very sensible. You can never learn too much," said Mr Cust, delighted by his pupil's thirst for knowledge.

But it was not knowledge or Latin that Stephen had in mind. He could not bear the thought of not coming to the Vicarage, with its gay Turkish carpet, its bright fire under the Adam mantelpiece in winter, the water-colour painting of the villa at Florence, the Canaletto, and Mr Cust's pleasant voice and accent: " —a jolly sight bettah, my boy!" Also he did not want to miss Miss Cust at the week-ends with her art gossip from the Slade School.

So this kindness continued, and help came, unexpectedly. Richard May's pals at the colliery made a collection, and the Union, of which he was a member, voted a small grant, to which the management added a sum. In all it came to sixty pounds. The outlook became less black. Within one week the parlour, converted into a bed-sitting-room, had been taken by a young hairdresser and his girl wife. A few days later the upstairs room was taken by a middle-aged bachelor. " Quite a gentleman," said Mrs May. " In a way it's rather a drawback, for he doesn't seem to have any work, which means he's always in. But you can't have everything, and he's very well-behaved."

The downstairs couple were not so well-behaved. They played a tinny gramophone until after midnight. Mr Connington in the upstairs room complained. Then one Saturday night they came home very late and began quarrelling, so that Mrs May had to get up and knock on their door. They were very rude, obviously somewhat drunk. The next morning the young couple seemed ashamed of themselves, and promised it should not happen again.

In his attic Stephen made himself very comfortable. Happily, the sloping attic window had a north aspect, which was perfect for his drawing and painting. He had a table under the window, and the easel, his father's last work, faced the skylight. It was his own domain. On the wall hung a lovely reproduction of Botticelli's *Primavera*, brought back from Italy for him by Miss Cust on her summer holiday.

In July the school closed, and after a week's holiday, Stephen, in a new pair of long flannel trousers, began the life of a man. He went to work each morning at eight o'clock. The position had been obtained for him by Mr Cust, who had a friend, an architect, with offices in a little court with a large plane tree off Wheeler Gate. Here, at five shillings a week, he became an office-boy. The work was congenial, for he was in an atmosphere of drawing-boards and tracings. His own tasks did not take him to any drawing-desk. He delivered plans and parcels, copied letters in an old-fashioned press, answered the telephone and stamped and entered letters for the post. At half-past four each day he took two cups of tea and a plate of biscuits up to the room in which the two partners, Mr Dane and Mr Playfair, worked. The office closed at six o'clock, and at one on Saturdays. Stephen liked the work, but loathed the head clerk, who bullied him. Mr Dane was kind, and playfully pulled his ear. He lived in a large house in the Park, to which Stephen was once sent for an attaché case. A maid kept him standing in the hall, and he could see into the study. It was hung with large engravings of the ruins of Rome. While he was peering into the room a handsome boy of about fifteen in brief shorts came bounding down the staircase.

" Hullo, who are you ? " he asked, smiling.

" I've come for Mr Dane's attaché case. Please, may I look at those engravings ? " asked Stephen, pointing into the room.

" Come in," said the boy.

Stephen examined the pictures. " They're Piranesis," he said, eagerly. " How wonderful ! "

" Wonderful ? I think they're awful ! You can't really like them ! "

" But I do ! " said Stephen, emphatically.

At that moment a girl of about sixteen came into the room. By her eyes and hair she was clearly the boy's sister.

" Mabel, he's from the office. He thinks these pictures are wonderful."

The girl looked at Stephen, and then at the pictures.

" So do I," she said, after a pause.

Her brother gave a derisive laugh. " You old fraud, you think they're awful, really ! "

The girl blushed. At that moment the maid came in with the attaché case. " Tea's ready, Master Frank," she said to the boy.

" Come and have some with us—it's on the lawn," said young Dane to Stephen.

" Master Frank, he's from the office, and your father—— " began the disapproving maid.

" That's all right, Annie. Dad won't mind. He'll be tickled to death somebody likes his old engravings."

So Stephen had tea on the lawn with Frank Dane and his

sister Mabel.   It was the first time he had ever been inside a house in The Park, in a house where tea was served by a maid in a white cap and apron.   Mabel was shy and said very little, but smiled at Stephen.   Frank did most of the talking.   He was at school at Rugby.   He was tall, strong and assured in manner. He was the embodiment of the boys Stephen had met in *The Captain*.   Despite the fact that he disliked the Piranesi engravings, Stephen found in him all that he could wish to be. His heart went out to him in a surge of hero-worship.   To live in this manner, with such people, with a maid carrying a silver teapot across a lawn, a stand with tiers of bread-and-butter and cakes, to be a handsome assured lad in a blazer with a school crest on it, and to possess a sister who was gentle and pretty—aware of all this, he was aware also of how much he was missing in a world that could be wonderful.   Not even the disapproval of the maid who showed him out could cloud the happiness of that experience.

CHAPTER VIII

ADOLESCENCE

I

SOMEHOW they managed, and if poverty often sat on the frontier of their domain, the Mays never conceded one inch of their proud independence. In the next five years young Stephen made friends, and a little money. To his wages, now sixteen shillings a week, of which he gave fourteen to his mother, he added small sums earned by his drawing and painting. They had been enabled to get rid of a succession of nuisances in the bed-sitting-room. One day the hairdresser was missing and his wife loudly proclaimed desertion, but when someone took up her case it was discovered that she was not his wife. Mrs May felt that this was a terrible blot on her house. The next couple were quiet and respectable, but they produced a baby, which annoyed Mr Connington upstairs, and as he was now considered a permanency, whose respectability was beyond question, the family below had to depart. Their successors monopolised the kitchen and had washing hanging up even on Sundays. After them came the nicest couple of all. Young, very much in love, quiet in manners and regular in their payments, Mrs May felt that at last she had found the ideal lodgers. But one dreadful day two plain-clothes detectives came to Adelaide Row, interviewed the young wife and waited until the husband returned, when they arrested him and took him away. The young husband, a collector for an instalment-plan furnishing company, had misappropriated twenty-two pounds of his employer's money. For a whole month, until the trial came on, Mrs May kept the penniless young wife. Her husband received a sentence of one year's imprisonment. Mrs May felt it was almost a stain on her own character, but, nevertheless, she went with the young wife, who had gone to her parents in Leeds, to meet the young man when he came out of prison. " I liked the lad, he was kind and gentle and a good husband. They never paid him enough and so drove him to dishonesty," said Mrs May.

Their upstairs tenant was mysterious. Apparently he had a private income, but it was very irregular. There were times when his rent was two months overdue and Mrs May would have been desperate but that she knew, from past experience, that Mr Connington would eventually settle up. He dressed neatly. One of his few belongings was a trouser-press, a heavy oak contrivance with four thumbscrews. In this Mr Connington always kept a spare pair of trousers. He was partial to white chamois leather gloves. He owned three pairs, and had them washed in rotation by Mrs May. The only food he was supplied with was breakfast. He 'dined out', he explained. The Mays were convinced he never dined, but drank. He had been seen coming out of the *Cremorne*, and though on occasions he was often fiery in the face he could never be called intoxicated. And nothing impaired his exquisite manners. In after-life when Stephen May was complimented on his manners he would recall gratefully Mr Connington, on whom he had modelled himself, even more than on Mr Cust, who lacked his air of aristocratic aloofness.

There were mysterious periods when Mr Connington went away to visit his brother in Rutland. He always returned very exhausted and with his hands roughened by the labour of gardening. "The gardens are too extensive for only two gardeners," he explained, "with the result that I work like a nigger trying to pull the place round." Mr Connington was a truthful man, but on this occasion he was prevaricating. Twenty years later—long after Mr Connington had gone to his fathers—Stephen learned, while painting a portrait of a Stamford county magnate, that the Conningtons had no gardeners at all on their broken-down domain, a small manor house in which Mr Connington's bachelor brother lived in genteel poverty, served only by a charwoman from the village. Mr Connington himself existed on an annuity of one hundred pounds provided by a generous American who had married his sister, now dead. The American travelled a great deal, and sometimes forgot to despatch the remittance, which in turn embarrassed both Mr Connington and Mrs May. By the kindness of Providence, Mr Connington died one month after his benefactor's death, and did not live to receive the letter in which his brother-in-law's attorneys in Chicago informed him that no provision had been made for continuance of the annuity.

II

Stephen was seventeen when three friends came into his life and exercised much influence over him. One was a youth of his own age who had come to Nottingham in the employment of the Inland Revenue Department. Desmond Fawn was endowed with a personal grace of which he seemed quite unaware. When Stephen first encountered him he felt as if he had met a young god straight out of the pages of the *Odyssey*. Perfect in physique, his neat head was crowned with fair curls, and his features had a classical grace. To this physical beauty he added a quick mind and a warm nature that everywhere won him friends. Stephen immediately fell under his spell. Moreover, in an attractive friend he found also an excellent model. Fawn subjected himself with the greatest good nature to Stephen's demands. Often blue with cold in the attic bedroom, transformed into a studio, he posed in an endless rôle of classical figures. Now he was Achilles before the walls of Troy, the Discobolus of Myron, Ares the god of war, the Belvedere Apollo or Ajax defying the Lightning. They were members of the same Rowing Club, and every Saturday, in a crew of six, they rowed up the river past Wilford and its disfiguring colliery to Clifton Grove, at whose foot they beached their boat and clambered up between the dense beech and elm trees to the Grove and the village at the summit. There were peerless summer days when they stripped off their rowing kit and plunged into the swift river.

It was on one of these occasions that Stephen conceived a picture that brought him his first considerable success. He had just finished drying himself, and had thrown the towel over to Desmond, when he was suddenly aware of him, a young faun naked and glowing in a leafy frame. The swift consciousness of youth eternal dwelling in a lost Olympian world caught up Stephen in a moment of intense inspiration. " Don't move, stay there ! " he cried, and dashed for the sketch-book lying with his clothes. He worked feverishly while Desmond humoured him. It was a brief sketch, the work of a few minutes. A week later his picture, based on the sketch, was finished. " What a frightful pun ! " exclaimed Desmond, looking at the painting, for Stephen had called it " *L'Après-midi d'un faune.*" But he was pleased with it, and quoted a line of Yeats for whom he had a passion : " When I am old and grey and full of sleep, that's how a friend saw me once, I shall say, and no one will believe me ! "

III

Every Spring there was an exhibition of the work of Nottingham artists held in the Castle Museum and Art Gallery. The former residence of a Duke of Newcastle crowned the sheer rock that commanded the valley of the Trent, and adjoined the Park. It had been acquired by the municipality and converted into a museum and art gallery. This vast double-winged building, in line with the hill on which ill-fated Charles I had raised the Royal Standard of the Civil War on a windy day in 1642, contained a long gallery that was cleared once a year for the work of local artists. A friend, seeing Stephen's painting of the faun, suggested he should send it to the annual exhibition—an ambitious step Stephen would never have considered without the prompting of Miss Letty Formby. Stephen had met her through Miss Cust, who had studied with her. Miss Formby had once belonged to a prosperous family that still lived in The Park in a house that was much too large. Her father had been a lace manufacturer, but with the decline of the Nottingham lace industry, following the disuse of lace curtains and increased foreign competition, he had fallen upon lean years, and on his death had left the family in reduced circumstances. The staff of two maids, cook, chauffeur and gardener were reduced to the faithful old cook. One brother emigrated to South Africa, two daughters married.

There remained Miss Letty Formby, the faithful companion of an invalid mother. By way of increasing her income Miss Formby commercialised her art, and had established herself as a designer of Christmas cards and calendars. The presence in Nottingham of a firm of colour-printers was turned to good account. Prompt, pertinacious, pretty and practical, said one of their buyers, describing her. Dainty would perhaps have been a better word than pretty. She epitomised the alluring little ladies who smiled from her Christmas cards. Practical she was, in an impractical manner. She could achieve much for a friend, and little for herself, being gentle and modest. She could persist in an idea until she had achieved her aims. Romance was in her blood, but while she dreamed daringly, prudence always intervened. Her great and last opportunity came at thirty-two, when a very comely young man, ten years her junior, fell in love with her, believing she was twenty-two. Her formidable honesty compelled her to tell him the truth, and even this failing to check his ardour she pleaded her duty to an ailing mother.

From the first moment in which she met Stephen May she was convinced of his brilliant future. He became a welcome visitor to her studio over a warehouse in Castle Gate. Here they made tea and toast, talked art and discussed life. She stimulated his ambition and entranced him with stories of life at the art schools in London and Paris which she had attended. Even the articles in her studio were exciting—the bust of a Polish poet made by a French sculptor, an original drawing, in sepia, on faded paper, by the great Bernini, who made the splendid colonnade of St Peter's, and a small, precious water-colour of Dover by Richard Parkes Bonington. When Stephen showed her *L'Après-midi d'un faune*, she said at once that he must enter it for the Exhibition. She lent him a frame. Wrapped in brown paper, he carried it up to the Castle on the day for entries. His heart thumped with excitement.

Every day for ten days he waited for the fateful letter. Then one evening there was a long glossy envelope, bearing the City arms, awaiting him. His picture was accepted. In his excitement he almost knocked over the tea-things. Mr Connington was in his room, and was the first person, after his mother, to hear the news. " Ah, splendid—but not surprising. One day you will receive a similar letter from the Royal Academy. A matter of time, Stephen, a matter of time ! " observed Mr Connington, sitting in a basket chair with a plaid travelling rug over his knees.

A few minutes later Mr Cust received the news. " What price have you put on it ? " he asked.

" Price ? " echoed Stephen, surprised.

" Someone may want to buy it—you must give them a figure."

He had never thought about the sale of his work. That anyone should want to buy his picture had not occurred to him. He went to another new friend, wise and experienced, to whom he turned more and more, a source of never-failing kindness. He had met William Kiddier at an evening meeting of the local Society of Artists, to which he had been taken by Miss Formby, who knew everybody. He was an elderly man with a leonine head of grey hair and deep-set eyes. He had a prosperous brush shop in the Nottingham Market Place. High above it, on the top storey of the building he owned, he had a studio. Here he spent his days painting. The business below, well-established, served to support his life's ambition above. Painting was the alpha and omega of his existence. Passionate in everything, he made the cups and saucers dance on the table when he thumped it in emphasis of his views. At moments, his hair flying, his eyes blazing, he looked like an Old Testament prophet, or Savonarola denouncing the follies of the world. Yet no man was gentler or more generous. He was the devoted attendant of a delicate wife, he supported various relations, he had innumerable small private charities so that mendicant folk were always coming and going up the narrow stairs to his attic studio.

From the first moment of their contact he was a second father to Stephen. He taught him all he knew, he provided canvases, brushes and paint, with the most delicate tact, and, knowing that growing boys are always hungry, he would take him after a session of work, each busy at an easel, across to a restaurant, and press food upon him. " You must be strong to paint—it burns up energy," he would say, ordering a large steak. Such was the man to whom Stephen turned in the next momentous five years of his life, and never in vain. " Twenty pounds! Not a penny less!" said Kiddier when consulted on the price for *L'Après-midi d'un faune*.

" But won't twenty frighten them?—it's an awful lot of money," replied Stephen.

" How should they know you're not another Michelangelo or Raphael? You are a better risk now than you will be in twenty years when your value's fixed. Twenty pounds, my boy. Twenty pounds or nothing! You can never afford to be cheap. No, never!" declared Kiddier, bringing his fist down on the café table.

So twenty pounds was the price. And the miracle happened. Two days before the exhibition closed someone asked the price of No. 128 in the catalogue. The picture was sold to a Mr Gerald Wright of Plumtree, Notts. Years passed, and Stephen's incomparable friend had been long in his grave when he discovered that no such person as Mr Wright of Plumtree had ever existed. William Kiddier had bought the picture.

It was in this hour of triumph that Fate turned Stephen's rejoicing into the bitterest sorrow. The light of day went out of his world when, after an illness of only one month, young Desmond Fawn was struck down in the flower of his youth. A mysterious illness, beginning with a great weariness, developed into lukæmia, and like a retreating tide the young god of Stephen's adoration drew away from life. For the second time the Dark Invader had crossed the confident path of youth.

IV

Stephen stopped having Latin lessons when he was sixteen. Art absorbed all his spare time, but he was always welcome at the Custs. The Reverend William Carter had departed, in the custom of the Methodist Connexion, that moved its ministers every three years. Mrs May, for old-time sake, retained the pew at the chapel, but little by little she lapsed. She did not find the new minister, a well-dressed, pushing fellow, with a wife who was reserved, and a parlour-maid who wore a cap, at all sympathetic. The church began to see her more frequently, and the habits of her girlhood reasserted themselves. Mr Cust was a poor preacher, but a good fellow.

When he was seventeen Stephen began to attend the evening classes at the School of Art. It was a well-lighted building, with a tower, adjacent to the Arboretum Park, overlooking the General Cemetery. Kiddier paid his fees. He was well in advance of all the pupils there, but he endured the discipline of drawing from plaster casts and an occasional life model. The school was conscious of a fine tradition. Nottingham had produced the Sandbys, Edwin Ellis, Richard Parkes Bonington, and among the moderns Arnesby Brown, and Harold and Laura Knight. It was here that he learned of the British School at Rome Scholarship that procured for its fortunate owner the means of spending two years in Italy. At once it became his ambition to obtain it.

The intensity of his studies had an adverse effect upon his office duties, which became increasingly distasteful. The head clerk, a little raspy-voiced fellow, delighted in pouncing on Stephen. He thwarted every attempt on the part of the office-boy to get to the drawing-desk, and a long, steady war between them ensued. Stephen was rapidly approaching a nervous breakdown, which resulted in a lessened efficiency in his almost menial work. One day he was called upstairs by Mr Dane.

"May, I feel I must speak to you about your work. Mr Brown is repeatedly complaining that you seem to show very little interest in your duties. I feel I must tell you that from what I have seen he seems to have some justice in his complaints. You are now seventeen, and you have some gifts as an artist, but these are not what an architect's office requires. I am speaking to you in this manner because, believe me, I have your interests at heart. I had it in mind that we might contrive to give you your articles here, but my partner thinks, and in this I concur, that you haven't got the singleness of mind to apply yourself with any success to the necessary studies. You should, I feel, seriously consider your future, and ask yourself if you're not wasting your time here."

There was a silence. Mr Dane, uneasy, looked out of the window at the plane tree. Stephen, his heart pounding, heard the quiet ticking of the clock on the mantelpiece.

"You mean, sir, you want me to go?" he asked.

Mr Dane looked at the sensitive young face before him. "I didn't say that, May," he replied. "But the present state of affairs is not satisfactory to either of us, is it? Give it a little thought. I know how you are placed. I realise you have ambitions to be something more than a clerk. If I felt you had any real interest in your work, and could give less to your own, I would see if we could set you on the way to qualifying. Anyhow, think it over, and meanwhile try to give Brown— whose faults I am well aware of—a little more satisfaction."

"Thank you, sir, I will," answered Stephen. "You have always been very kind."

Mr Dane smiled at him, and Stephen withdrew.

As he went down the stairs he knew he had been warned,

not unjustly. He would there and then have thrown a gage to Fate, but he had his mother to think of, and an essential sixteen shillings a week in wages.

V

In winter the Society of Artists met once a month and held a small exhibition in their rooms. Stephen, now a member, regularly contributed, and on one occasion he ventured to speak in an art discussion. He spoke well, the charm of his youth and his sincerity compensating for his lack of experience. He was being congratulated at the buffet afterwards when a voice beside him said, " Stephen, you haven't any idea who I am, have you ? "

He turned to find a very pretty girl about his own age addressing him. She had a mass of blonde hair, clear blue eyes and vivid colouring in her round, smiling face, but more than anything else he was aware of the music of her voice. Though she had addressed him, he saw she was embarrassed by her own eagerness.

" I'm sorry—I wish I had," he replied, smiling.

" I'm Helen Watmough—remember ? "

He could not remember, to his own embarrassment. The poor girl was almost crimson now.

" Please tell me where we met—you make me wretched," he said, offering her a cup of coffee.

" I sat next to you at the Misses Woodward's painting class, years and years ago ! "

In a flash he knew. His face suddenly lit with joy. That she should remember him ! That he should not remember her, though he could still recall the last words she had said to him !

" Helen Watmough ! Of course ! " said Stephen. " Do let's go and talk, over there."

He led the way to two chairs by the wall and they sat down. He looked at her again, and saw how very beautiful she was in her virginal freshness.

" I'm going to ask you something if you'll forgive me," he said, with a twinkle in his eye.

" Yes ? "

" I confess I had forgotten you—but can you remember what was the last thing you said to me ? "

" No—what ? " she asked.

" ' You are a horrid, common boy ' ! "

" How awful ! How could I ? "

" Perhaps I was. I got into a brawl with your brother and another boy who threw my prize over the wall."

Helen looked at him, suddenly very serious.

" I remember it all now," she said. " Mother made us promise to apologise to you when she heard what had happened —but you never came again, so we didn't have to apologise, much to our relief."

They laughed together, and a momentary embarrassment followed, during which they drank their coffee.

" The freckled boy who started the trouble—who said, when he knew my father was a miner, that I'd come out of a coal-hole—what's happened to him ? " asked Stephen, breaking silence.

" He's at Oxford—still freckled and horrid ! Is your father really a miner ? "

" He was—he died in a coal-hole," replied Stephen, quietly.

" Forgive me—I'm terribly sorry. It doesn't make a bit of difference—or does that sound very snobbish ? I think it all the more wonderful that you—that you—— " She stopped, unable to express what she wished.

" Should have come out of a coal-hole so clean ! " he added, with a laugh.

They looked at each other with a liking reflected in their eyes.

" I hope I shan't have to wait ten more years to see you ? " he asked.

" You must come to see me—and my brother. He's at Oxford too," said Helen Watmough. " Then we can both apologise in the presence of mother."

The members had left the buffet and were gathering for the second half of the programme. Stephen saw Miss Formby keeping a chair for him. They rose reluctantly and said goodbye. Stephen went back to Miss Formby, who smiled at him.

" She's pretty, isn't she ? " she asked.

" Yes—you know her ? "

"Helen Watmough? Of course, and all the family. I didn't know you knew her."

"I didn't either. At least, I'd forgotten her—we met long ago at the Misses Woodward's painting class," said Stephen.

"What! You went there? But you've never told me!"

"No—it was rather a painful episode, at the time."

She was about to ask him what the episode was, but the chairman of the Society had begun to speak.

Helen Watmough was in his mind all the way home that evening. He could not forget her face and voice. She seemed a quite different person from the little girl who had called him a horrid boy, and he could hardly believe his good fortune in knowing her. No one in the whole meeting had anything like her beauty, and to talk with her had been heaven. He regretted that in the excitement of the moment he had forgotten to ask whether she had an exhibit in the show. He would have liked her to see the little portrait of Miss Florence Pearson he had sent in. It was a commission from one of the sisters for which he had received ten pounds. Miss Mary was delighted with it, Miss Florence pretended that it might have been less flattering of herself, and enjoyed everyone saying, " Oh no, it doesn't flatter you at all, dear Miss Florence; you look exactly like that!" The doyen of all the local portrait-painters, Denholm Davis, put his finger on Stephen's characteristic touch ten years before the world recognised it : the quality of lighting that gave such vitality to his portraits.

It was half-past ten when he reached home, and his mother was still up, ironing a shirt she had washed for Mr Connington. The tail was torn, and the neckband frayed.

"It's really time he had some new ones; he can't be that poor," she said, as she put it over the clothes-horse to air. " I'm saying nothing against Mr Connington, he's a gentleman in every sense of the word, but if I was as short as he is, I'd go out and work."

"And who'd employ him? He's been out of the habit for thirty years," said Stephen, going into the larder and returning with a large piece of cake. " That gentleman-stuff has no market today."

Mrs May began to mix a cup of cocoa for her son.

'Perhaps so, but the world would be a nicer place with

more like him in it!" replied Mrs May, feeling she had been a little disloyal to her lodger. She looked at her son critically. "You look very pleased with yourself. Had a nice evening?"

"Wonderful! Denholm Davis liked my picture," replied Stephen, his mouth full of cake. "Oh, Mom, I wish you'd go one evening. Miss Formby would be glad to take you."

Mrs May put back the kettle on the hob after mixing the cocoa, and rested a hand on the mantelpiece gazing at the old Post Office money-box that had fallen out of use since Stephen's childhood.

"That's very nice of her—but what should I be doing there? No, Stephen, you'll make your own friends, and if you're wise, don't try to mix them. I wouldn't be comfortable, and they wouldn't."

She sat down and looked at her son, aware of his youth and attraction. He would gladden any girl's heart, and the day could not be far off when he would be aware of other things beside canvases and tubes of paint.

"Stephen," she said, quietly, "I've got some sad news for you—Miss Hooley died this afternoon. Poor soul! she's spared any more suffering."

Miss Hooley, his music teacher. He put down his cup and stopped eating. When his father died she had come to his mother and told her that she would not want any payment for the music lessons and she hoped Stephen would continue. So for two more years they had continued. Then he had found that the practising took his scanty leisure hours from his art studies. His master passion was art, not music. But the three sisters had continued their interest in him, and the landscape he had given them had the place of honour in their ornament-littered parlour. He felt very stricken now, for only a few weeks ago he had drawn a caricature of Julia, Millie and Mabel, with their black bodices and skirts, their lace frills and high boots. No more would they hurry down the street, two abreast and one behind, chapel-bound. Six months ago Miss Millie had been operated on. She seemed better, and they saw her going about again to the pupils' houses. Then one day she was missing, and now she was dead of cancer of the lung.

"I'm sorry to hear that," said Stephen. "Why is it the nice people who have such awful deaths?"

" We must accept the ways of Providence—or try to," replied Mrs May, not quite sure of her own acceptance.

VI

A week had almost passed when on a Friday a postcard came from Miss Formby asking him to go to tea at the studio on Saturday afternoon. Did she know it was his eighteenth birthday, or was her choice simply fortuitous? He had great news to impart to her. Only that evening he had breathlessly raced up the stairs to William Kiddier's studio, to give stupendous news to his faithful ally. "Nothing succeeds like audacity," his friend often said, and now here was the proof.

Day after day on his way to the office in Wheeler Gate, Stephen had beheld, proceeding in a contrary direction, the high limousine car in which sat the great Sir Jesse Boot. All Nottingham knew the famous white-haired figure who, from a small shop in Goose Gate, had built up the great business of Boots Cash Chemists, with its multiple shops throughout the kingdom. A millionaire, lavish in benefactions to his native town, he was familiar to all as he drove daily to his office where he directed his business despite the fact he was crippled by rheumatoid arthritis. He sat in an invalid's chair, rather like a throne, that ran up into a specially built automobile. Beside the chauffeur sat a small, sturdy man in a black jacket, Sir Jesse's attendant. Sir Jesse rode godlike through the traffic towards his headquarters in Station Street, a long building from which he directed his vast organisation.

Nottingham, in that day, boasted of a number of business magnates, lesser Medicis of the Midlands. There was Sir Thomas Birkin, founder of a dynasty of Birkins, whose fortune had been made in the era of the city's supremacy in the world of lace. There was Sir Frank Bowden, whose fame and fortune marched with the popularity of the bicycle, for which he had invented a brake that perpetuated his name. The small cycle-dealer's store in Raleigh Street through the years had expanded into the acreage of the great Raleigh Cycle Company. With these, co-equal, ranked Sir Jesse Boot. The three big B's, they were called, who from dominions of lace, bicycles and chemicals, employing thousands of the city's inhabitants, progressed to millions and baronetcies. One other colossus, more austere and reticent, built up from tobacco a realm as solid and prosperous. What had been achieved by the thread, the steel pinion and the pill, John D. Player created from the tobacco leaf. He took for the trade-mark of his business the Nottingham Castle on its rock, and the bearded Jack Tar who ruled Britannia's waves.

Older in origin than these were the Morleys, whose domain was hosiery. Samuel Hope Morley was the son of Samuel, one time member of Parliament for Nottingham, whose statue, somewhat odd for a philanthropist, stood, frock-coated, holding out its hand on a pedestal in front of the Theatre Royal. The second Samuel, like Jesse Boot, eventually ascended to the peerage as Lord Hollenden.

No Nottingham boy could live unaware of these outstanding examples of success achieved by men of humble origin who raised themselves by their own ability to positions of power. Model employers of labour, the city's prosperity grew with them, and those who were received into their establishments assumed a certain superiority of caste; they were not here to-day and gone tomorrow. Their positions were generally life tenures.

Among these remarkable men of local fame, Sir Jesse Boot held pre-eminence, due in part to the heroic figure he made in his fight against physical infirmity. Nonconformist and Liberal, he received at his house *St Helier's* in The Park, the great champions of reform when they came to address the electorate—Burns, Churchill, Lloyd George, Asquith. The crowd broke off its singing of " God gave the land to the people " when Sir Jesse's chair was wheeled on the platform, attended by the political deity of the day, to give their gallant townsman a rousing cheer. He assumed in the public eye something of the character of the castle on its bold rock, a symbol of fortitude and permanence.

In the eyes of young Stephen May, the figure borne along in the high chair had a Jove-like majesty, and like Jove it was well known that Sir Jesse could thunder. His eye missed nothing, and through every ramification of the vast organisation there was a consciousness of personal control at the centre. He had time for the smallest matters as well as the greatest, and he never lost the human touch.

One day, on the suggestion of Kiddier, Stephen had called

on the manager of the Art Department, carrying some land-scapes that might be used for Christmas calendars. To Stephen's amazement, two were accepted at once, at a price of fifteen pounds each. The manager requested him to leave four more paintings for further consideration. Stephen left a portfolio of ten. Three weeks elapsed, and he began to lose hope of any further sales, when he was asked to call at the office in Station Street. He felt shaken when the manager told him that Sir Jesse Boot wanted to see him. Everyone knew the room with the curved window over the office entrance where, like the bridge of a ship, the captain held command. Every day the limousine arrived at the corner doors, whereupon the high chair with its occupant moved down a short gangway, across the hall and, in a lift, up to the chairman's room. Jove enthroned had not a more impressive seat, and it seemed to those ushered into the presence that if the voice that greeted them was harsh, the manner was genial, and cloaked a long habit of courage. Most men of experience found their first interview something of an ordeal; for the very young, like Stephen May, it was almost an unnerving experience.

The Art manager led him in, after a long wait in an outer office, and introduced him. Sir Jesse sat in his high chair behind a large desk, his back to the window. He greeted Stephen with a " Good evening, young man!" and without any preliminaries, glancing at the portfolio the manager opened in front of him, said :

" I like your paintings. They seem very suitable for our calendars. Of course this five-colour process is expensive. It would be better if you could keep to three colours. How long does it take you to paint them ? "

" It varies, sir—about a week to two weeks each."

Sir Jesse looked surprised.

" Well, I'm not an artist—it seems a long time to me," he said.

" We've had some artists who take over a month, Sir Jesse," said the manager, turning over the paintings.

" And some who can't do them in a blue moon," retorted Sir Jesse. " Well now, Mr May—that's your name, isn't it ? "

" Yes, sir, Stephen May."

" How old are you ? "

"Eighteen, sir."

"And where did you learn to paint?"

"I didn't learn. I just started, at six."

"Six—why, that beats me! I started at thirteen. Well, as you're so young and untrained, I don't suppose your price is very high," he said. He turned to the manager. "What did you say you're paying?"

"Fifteen pounds, sir. We've taken two."

"H'm. Well now, Mr May, if we take four more—what about a flat price of forty pounds, eh?"

He peered at the young man before him, his twisted hands resting on his chest.

Stephen hesitated, then, recalling that a bargainer respects a bargainer, he summoned up his courage.

"Well, my price is fifteen pounds each, sir. If they were manufactured goods, sir, I might consider a flat rate, but they are individual works of art."

"That's a good argument. Very well, fifteen pounds," said Sir Jesse.

The manager smiled and began to close the portfolio.

"A minute—show me that one with the river," said Sir Jesse.

The manager took it out of Stephen's portfolio.

"I like this—it's cheerful and a good picture. Have you seen my *Plaisaunce* on the Trent? I enjoy sitting there when I've time. Now, Mr May, I'm buying this for myself. You'll get no publicity with it, like the calendars. It'll hang in my house. So I think I should give you more. What do you say to twenty-five guineas?"

Stephen drew his breath, and then he said steadily, "I should be very satisfied with that, sir, and very proud that you want it for yourself."

Sir Jesse turned to the manager. "Tell them twenty-five guineas on my private account, and send it to *St Helier's*."

"Very good, sir," he said, picking up the portfolio.

"Goodbye," said Sir Jesse. "Are you a Nottingham boy?"

"Yes, sir—my father worked at the Clifton Colliery."

"Doesn't he now?"

"No, sir. He died when I was nearly thirteen."

"H'm. So did mine," said Sir Jesse. Then he smiled.

" You'll find the earlier you stand on your own feet the farther they'll take you. Good luck to you ! "

Stephen was dismissed. He went out of the room with his heart singing, and a mist in his eyes.

It was fitting that William Kiddier should be the first to hear his stupendous news, for he had suggested the approach to Boots. Kiddier smiled at him and nodded his magnificent old head. " Well, that's a start—but take warning. Don't commercialise yourself, or you'll be lost. Offer them what you think's suitable, but don't paint for them, or they'll turn you into a mould-maker. All my life I've done just what I've wanted to do as an artist, up here, because I've made my shop downstairs bring me independence. You haven't that foundation—but you've all your youth and faith, and I believe in you. Now, I suggest we go and have a good meal—good news is exhausting ! "

Stephen's mother was up when he got home. She knew now that when he did not come in to supper his old friend Mr Kiddier had taken him out. Stephen's manner the moment he entered made her aware of something unusual. He poured out his story. Then he seized her by the arm and marched her to and fro across the kitchen.

" We are now entering the Royal Academy. This is Private View Day. What a crush ! Who is that ? That ? Why that's the most fashionable portrait-painter of the day, Stephen May ! The lady at his side is Mrs May, his mother, a familiar figure at his studio in Chelsea. Mr May's striking portrait of Sir Jesse Boot is likely to be one of the successes of the year."

" Stephen—don't be ridiculous ! You're not painting Sir Jesse's portrait ! " protested Mrs May, a little breathless.

" Not yet—but I shall, you'll see ! I shall paint all the big Bs—Boot, Bowden, Birkin—but the picture that will get me the A.R.A. will be ' Portrait of the Artist's Mother in the Kitchen '. Whistler won't be in it, Mom ! "

He shook his head until his hair, grown a little long these days, despite Mrs May's protests, fell over his eyes.

" Stephen, you mustn't get too cocksure," she said, the old fear asserting itself.

" Mr Kiddier says *De l'audace et toujours de l'audace*."

" And what's that ? "

" Boldness and always boldness. That's how the Duke of

Marlborough won his battles. That's how I'll get into the Royal Academy. Mom, if you can't believe anything's possible at eighteen, you'll never believe it!"

"Your father believed in his dog-collars," said Mrs May. "Poor Richard!" she added, as she sat down.

Stephen stooped and kissed her on the cheek. In that moment, as at other odd moments, he was aware that she had been a beautiful woman, lost in a backstreet. Her profile was flawless, and the sweep of her greying locks over a perfect ear caught the artist in him.

"Perhaps he would have been successful with a little more audacity, but he never had a chance," said Stephen.

"No, he never had a chance," echoed Mrs May. "Well, it's time for our cocoa. Be a good boy and fetch me some coal in."

Stephen picked up the scuttle and went to the back door.

"Mr Stephen May, R.A., is about to return to his native place, the coal-hole!" he announced, opening the door.

As he went across the yard he suddenly realised why the phrase had a familiar ring. "I thought you'd come out of a coal-hole!" The words of the freckled boy at the painting class had burnt into him like a branding-iron nearly ten years ago. And now Helen Watmough had deliberately spoken to him and hoped to see him again.

He lay awake that night, for an intoxicating idea had lodged itself in his stimulated brain. Four pictures at fifteen pounds, one picture at twenty-five guineas, made eighty-six pounds. He had two pounds left of the twenty brought in by *L'Après-midi d'un faune*, and ten pounds from Miss Pearson's portrait. Altogether he had amassed a fortune of ninety-eight pounds! His head swam with the realisation of his wealth. For a mere forty pounds a year he was in bondage in a job that, it had been hinted, he might have to leave, not having his heart in his work. A heartfelt absorption in a job that brought in sixteen shillings a week was difficult for the poorest-spirited creature. For an ambitious artist whose motto was now *De l'audace et toujours de l'audace* the sum was ludicrous. Mr Dane he liked, but all else—the whistling gas stove for tea-making in the basement, the idiotic letter-press, the stacks of rolled-up tracings, and above all that blotchy-faced bullying clerk—lay heavy on his soul; and his conscience was troubled, for Mr Dane was quite right, his heart wasn't in his work. He now possessed the sum of two years' wages. Why should he not show a little more audacity and resign the office job? He would work at home. He might—and his heart thumped at the thought—go later, if things prospered, to the Slade School, or to Paris, or to——

He turned over in bed, but he was too excited for sleep. When his father died they had had to face life on a total capital of thirty pounds. He had been too young to realise fully what a challenge that had been to his mother. For five years they had lived, and never for a day had he been conscious of real want. Who was he to shout *De l'audace* when in the bedroom below lay a warrior who had fought and won a battle Marlborough had never known? Tomorrow he would go and buy the fur stole he knew her heart coveted. In all her life she had never been able to possess one unnecessary thing. Griffin and Spalding's in Long Row had good furs, and since he knew nothing about them, he would ask Miss Formby to go with him. Ten pounds? He thought he had seen them marked at that price. Rabbit, fox, beaver? Whatever price it was, his mother should have one.

VII

Miss Formby looked around her studio and thought it was the brightest and cosiest place in the world. A fire burned in the grate, there were flowers in the vases, and a copper kettle shone and sang on the gas-ring. She was pleased with her new cushions made from some hand-woven material she had bought on a stall in Florence last year—woven sunshine, she called it. On a Chelsea china plate were a dozen fancy cakes, and she was particularly proud of her success in cutting a plateful of thin bread-and-butter. For she was not domesticated and never would be.

Punctually at four-thirty she heard young Stephen come bounding up the stairs. She had a pleasant surprise for him, which would give her as much pleasure as it would him. The door burst open, and at a glance she saw that he was excited, his rosy cheeks and dark eyes more brilliant than usual. In a spate she heard of yesterday's session with the great man. He had still more astonishing news. He had come straight

F

from a conference with William Kiddier, who wholly agreed with him. He was going to leave the office and become a professional artist!

"But, Stephen—are you quite sure that——" began Miss Formby.

"Now don't discourage me! The die is cast. Listen— what do I lose? Sixteen shillings a week and misery and frustration. What is the worst that can happen? I can, after two or three years, starve. Have artists never starved before? If not, is *Bohème* all rubbish? Letty dear, if I starve I shall at least know I've tried. But I shan't starve! One day I shall ask two thousand pounds for a portrait——"

"But will you get it?" interjected Miss Formby, twinkling.

"No—but I shall ask it," he replied, bursting with laughter. "Oh, Letty, the studio does look nice—who's coming?"

"You."

"Yes—but I'm always here. Miss Cust?"

"No—at least I haven't asked her—but I'm expecting a friend."

"Who?"

"You must wait and see. I want to show you something I sketched yesterday," said Miss Formby, turning over a canvas. She found the one she wanted and carried it to the easel. They were engrossed in technical details when there was a gentle tap on the door. Miss Formby went and greeted her guest.

Stephen could not see who it was, the easel blocking the view, but at the sound of a voice his heart gave a bound, and he stood rooted to the floor. It was Helen Watmough who followed her hostess into the studio. Stephen turned and took the outstretched hand. For the first time in his life he found himself tongue-tied, and he made a fool of himself by turning crimson in the face.

After they had drunk many cups of tea and consumed all the cakes, he found himself talking not only freely, but with animation. Eager, bright, youth exulting in youth, Miss Formby watched them, and knew they were in heaven.

Helen Watmough was the first to go. When the door closed Miss Formby began to clear the tea-table. Stephen carried the cups into the little kitchen.

" She's nice, isn't she ? " asked his hostess, running the water in the sink.

" She's—I think she's—— " he began, and then stopped.

Looking at him she saw his young mouth was trembling, and knew then that it was first love that held him in bondage. But she was wise enough to disguise her discovery.

" I thought you'd like her—she does really lovely water-colours, and belongs to quite a clever family. I wanted them to send her to the Slade, but she's going to Girton. They're quite well-to-do, but she says she wants a profession."

The next day Letty Formby went with him to buy the fur stole. It was a fox fur, and cost seven pounds. Stephen carried it home himself. Mrs May was out when he arrived, but came in half an hour later with Mrs Popperwell, who had just closed her shop and come to borrow an extra hot-water bottle for Mr Popperwell, stricken with sciatica, his old enemy. Stephen had written his mother's name on the box, which he gave to her, saying, " This has come for you."

Mrs May looked at the box. " I haven't bought anything at Griffin and Spalding's," she exclaimed, reading the label. " It must be a mistake."

" Well, open it—we can always put it back. You never know—it might be from an admirer ! " exclaimed Mrs Popper-well, ever ready for a little bit of romance.

" Why, if it isn't a fur ! " exclaimed Mrs May, when the cover was off and the tissue paper pushed back.

" Then it's from an admirer ! " said Stephen.

Mrs May looked at it in the box, but made no attempt to lift it out. Mrs Popperwell had no such reluctance. She seized the fur and draped it over her friend's shoulder.

" My—it's lovely, and not rabbit, either ! It's real fox," she said, stroking it.

" It's beautiful," agreed Mrs May, " but however did it get here ! "

Stephen held up a piece of cardboard. " Ah, here's a clue," he said, reading aloud, " ' Sir Edward Poynter, President of the Royal Academy, presents his compliments to Mrs Richard May and asks her acceptance of the enclosed token of esteem for her son, Mr Stephen May, the newly-elected Academician '."

" Stephen—you don't mean you've bought it for me, you've—— "

Mrs May did not finish her words. She looked down at the fur and touched it with a half-frightened gesture. " Oh Stephen—what did it cost you ? "

" Mom, that's very rude. You never ask what a present costs ! "

" Accept and be thankful, says I," exclaimed Mrs Popperwell, stroking the fur. " And, if I know anything, this isn't the last thing you're going to have from this boy of yours— until some other girl's in the running," she added, with a chuckle.

Mrs May kissed her son. " God has been very good to us," she said quietly, taking off the fur and replacing it gently in the box.

He waited until Sunday evening, when she came back from church, wearing her fur, to break the news to her. As he expected, she was frightened by his decision. But she saw he was determined and that his happiness depended upon his new venture, and after expressing her fears, she acquiesced, saying, " It's your life, and I won't be a burden to you—and God has never failed us in our need. You aren't down the pit, and I'm spared that risk."

When Mr Dane came into the office the next morning Stephen immediately went up and told him of his decision. His employer could not have been more pleasant. " I wish you every success, my boy. And I have great confidence in you. This is not your proper place. An artist's life is always full of chance, and you may have a severe struggle ahead of you—but when you're young and full of faith, what does it matter ? Well, you don't want a sermon. I hope you won't forget this little hole in a corner when you're hanging in the galleries of Europe."

On the morning he left, Mr Dane called him into the office and gave Stephen a small box. " It's a little memento, a wrist-watch. I know artists aren't very good in the matter of keeping time," he said, smiling.

Stephen thanked him, and in a way was sorry to go down the stairs for the last time. He had crossed the Rubicon.

CHAPTER IX

VISTA OF FAME

I

A FRIEND of Kiddier's was the director of the local School of Art, and Stephen was now enrolled as a full-time student. He had a definite goal before him: the travelling scholarship that would take him to Italy. Perhaps it was the early Cust influence, the first sight of that water-colour of the villa at Fiesole with its terrace in the sun, of the Canaletto painting and the Piranesi engravings that had planted in Stephen May's heart the deep yearning for Italy. Miss Formby tried in vain to wean him from this loyalty to a scene he had never visited; Rome, Venice and Florence were an artist's paradise, but the true school of all art students was surely Paris, she insisted. During a six-months holiday fifteen years ago she had studied in a Paris *atelier*, and with every passing year the aura of that enchanted hour of her life glowed brighter and brighter. It had inculcated in her not only a passion for Degas' frilled ballerinas, for Manet and Renoir, but peppered her talk with snatches of French. When painting she wore a blue smock with a collar that made her look like a character in *Bohème*. The presence of Miss Cust turned the little studio into a department of the Académie des Beaux-Arts, for they chatted in French.

Two weeks after the tea-party in her studio, Stephen was invited with Letty Formby to tea at the Watmoughs', so after nearly ten years he entered the door of the house in The Park for which he had searched when a small boy. Mr Watmough was a director of a big engineering firm, Mrs Watmough was a good-looking but reserved woman of fifty. They had tea in a long drawing-room crowded with sofa, chairs, a grand piano, bronze statues, ivory figures under glass domes, and carpets so thick that it was like walking on a sponge. Three large windows looked over a wide terrace and a sunken garden towards the amphitheatre of The Park and the Castle on the rock. Eric Watmough was home from Oxford for the Easter vacation, a chubby youth who wore a vivid yellow sports waistcoat with brass buttons, affecting a horsiness in the first flush of his membership of a college hunt.

After tea, which was a little stiff, for Mrs Watmough seemed unable to unbend, giving Stephen a feeling that he was there on approval, they left the drawing-room and went up to the top of the house, the former schoolroom, now Helen's den. It was cosy and interesting in its chaotic state, Eric's belongings being still retained. Every minute was enchanted for Stephen, and the one thought in his mind was how he could see more of Helen. Fate sent him an inspiration when she showed him a self-portrait that she had attempted. " It's rather awful," she said.

" You can never do justice to yourself. Won't you let me try ? " asked Stephen, eagerly.

She looked at him, with surprise in her lovely eyes.

" Would you really like to ? I should love it ! " she said, simply.

" You can use my studio," said Miss Formby, tactfully.

Thus it was arranged. Helen Watmough sat twice a week throughout a month. He would not hurry the portrait. Every stroke of the brush was a labour of love. He came to know her, both of them losing their shyness, and he discovered in her character a singular directness. Their relationship became almost that of boy to boy. She told him he must cut his hair and not affect ' arty ' ties. " It upset Mother—not that that matters, for she is a bit of a stick, but you're too much the real thing to look like a stage artist." He laughed, demurred, but cut his hair so severely that he looked like Donatello's *St George*, she told him. Miss Formby observed that he was developing into a dandy. The floppy ties disappeared, his trousers were carefully creased in Mr Connington's press while he was away.

One June day Stephen asked Helen if he might take her in a boat to tea at Clifton Grove. She readily assented. He got the best boat at his club, with the newest cushions, and rowed Helen, enchanting in a flowered muslin frock and a large amber straw hat decorated with violets, from Trent Bridge, past Wilford, up to the Clifton Woods. As they passed the colliery, with its winding wheels crowning the derricks, he said, " That was where my father worked when freckle-face said I looked as if I'd come out of a coal-hole."

" You'll never forget that, will you ? " asked Helen. " Please, Stephen, don't be bitter. He was only a silly little boy. When you're famous you'll remember it almost with affection, by contrast."

" Do you think I shall be famous ? " he asked, pulling hard against the current above Wilford Church.

" Yes. We all do. Why do you think Sir Jesse bought your painting ? "

" Oh—I suppose he liked it."

" It was something more than that. Men like Jesse Boot are intuitive, they've made their success because of it. He saw at once you had something unusual," said Helen.

Stephen smiled at her as she sat before him, the tiller-rope in her pretty hands.

" You know—when people talk like that, I get scared in case I let 'em down. I've got a gift, I know that—it would be humbug to pretend I haven't—but how good is it, and is it the kind of gift the world wants ? " he asked.

" Yes, of course it is. If you can write a song, or a poem, or paint a picture, or carve a statue, the world will want it if it is really good. Beyond its necessities it finds such things are its essentials," declared Helen.

" Helen, how old are you ? "

" Twenty in September—why ? "

" You're very wise—you make me feel an infant."

" I must be honest. I borrowed a bit of that from Ruskin ! "

They laughed together at her confession. He was perspiring now, and he pulled off his club sweater, rowing in his short-sleeved vest. She saw how good was his figure, with its firm muscular mould, and how fair was his skin. She wondered if he inherited his strength from his father, and his fineness from his mother.

Stephen beached the boat at the bottom of the steep woods and then clambered up to the Grove. He took her hand and pulled her up. After a short walk along the crest, on the wide grass under the overhanging trees they came to a stile that led to the village. They paused here for a time, and heard the screaming of the peacocks in the gardens of Clifton Hall.

"Have you ever read Henry Kirke White, born in the butcher's shop behind the Exchange about a hundred and thirty years ago? a melancholy youth who got himself to Cambridge and died of over-work?" asked Stephen. "Poor stuff, much of it, but Byron had a good word for him. He wrote—

> The worm it shall riot on heavenly diet
> When Death hath deflowered the eye.

How they loved that sort of morbidity, but he did better than that, in a poem about this place—

> Dear native grove, where'er my devious track,
> To thee will memory lead the wanderer back.
> Still, still to thee where'er my footsteps roam,
> My heart shall point, and lead the wanderer home."

"I can never remember poetry," said Helen, when he had finished. "I've only one quotation. My mother was taken to tea with old "Festus" Bailey, who lived on the Ropewalk. He only wrote one poem, and it made him world-famous. He did very well out of it, for he got a Civil List Pension when quite young and spent the rest of his long life burying his poem with additions. The day Mother went there he'd received a huge plum cake from some admirer in America! She remembers how good it was and what a large slice he cut her. Mother once gave me sixpence to learn some of his lines, when I was quite young. Funny how you never forget the things you first learn—

> We live in deeds, not years; in thoughts, not breaths;
> In feelings, not in figures on a dial.
> We should count time by heart-throbs: he most lives
> Who thinks most, feels the noblest, acts the best."

She finished quoting, and there was silence over all the woods. His hand covered hers on the stile. We are young lovers in Clifton Grove, such as Kirke White wrote about over a hundred years ago, and we in turn will be less than shadows or last year's leaves. We should count time by heart-throbs, he thought, echoing the lines she had quoted.

"Stephen, don't be so serious!" cried Helen, withdrawing her hand after a silence.

He smiled at her. "Let's go and have tea. I want to find old Mrs Brown's, if she's living. My Mom and Dad used to bring me here. We paid twopence for hot water and sat out under an apple tree. I remember when I was almost a baby that she had a gander, and it got hold of my sash and pulled me until I screamed."

They found the old cottage, but Mrs Brown had long been dead. Full teas were one shilling; with two eggs, eighteen-pence. They sat in an outhouse and had tea with two eggs. It was there he kissed Helen, so shyly that she caught his face in her hands and kissed him soundly on the mouth. They were oblivious in one another's arms when the old woman came for the tea-things, and coughed discreetly.

II

Stephen May was soon twenty, and scarcely aware of it, so intense were his days. He studied hard, he shut himself up in his attic room, he went into the woods and fields with his paint-box hung over his shoulder. He had passed through the long-haired, corduroy-trousers stage, under the sharp eye of Helen Watmough. His manners had always been good, and now, with the added attraction of oncoming manhood, he found himself invited out. But the real life was still in his own home, in the familiar circle of the Custs, of Mr Connington with his pinched face and dignified air, of lively little Mrs Popperwell, and even Mrs Pieman.

In his twentieth year he made a bold gesture: he sent a picture to the Royal Academy's Summer Exhibition. William Kiddier gave Stephen the frame and paid the agent's fee in London. After some weeks of anxious waiting he heard that the picture had been rejected. The fact that it had been kept so long before rejection was taken as a good sign. "They hold some in abeyance until they know how much space their members have monopolised," explained his friend. "Go on sending. I know one fellow who's sent for twenty years and won't give up hope. But if you're determined to be hung regularly then you must get elected somehow. As an Associate or as a full Academician you are entitled to exhibit six pictures, and no one can throw you out. You can put up your fee for portraits, as your sitters are assured of being seen."

That summer Stephen took his mother to Skegness. They went as boarders this time. The Drummond Road was still a gay bazaar, the wind from the Fens still blew briskly across the level landscape. But the fatal auction room, scene of that early disaster, had vanished. So almost had the painting purchased on that occasion. It had settled into a muddy, blackened landscape, all its early lustre vanished.

It was the last week in July when they went to Skegness, and two major events made that holiday with his mother forever memorable. On the third morning after their arrival he received a letter from the Principal of the School of Art that sent him into the seventh heaven of happiness. He had been awarded the Travelling Scholarship, which enabled its recipient to pursue two years of study in Italy. It would be tenable from October next.

The prize brought a new problem of ways and means. While he was abroad it was unlikely that he would be able to pick up the odd commissions that came his way. Last month Mr Watmough had given him twenty pounds for his portrait of Helen. His reserve funds were down to eighty pounds, and with characteristic optimism he had refused to believe a crisis was approaching. But now the question of his mother's support became acute. He allowed her from his funds one pound a week, and only the strictest economy on both their parts enabled them to survive.

He was pondering over the problem that had arisen from his success when another event fell like a thunder-clap. A few sinister rumbles in the distant political landscape had begun to cloud the local scene. Ever since a wild young man in one of those Balkan countries had shot an Austrian archduke driving over a bridge, the armies of Europe had been indulging in precautionary mobilisation. " Grave crisis," proclaimed the poster boards outside the newsagents' shop. A special session of the Cabinet had sat late into the night.

" It's trouble all right," said Mrs Marsh, the landlady, clearing the breakfast cloth. " Folks are beginning to leave. We've had a shock this morning. Mrs Allcock's two sons, in the Naval Reserve, have been called up. What's to become of us, I'd like to know ? That Kaiser's asking for it until he'll get it in the neck all right, but at what a price ! "

Mrs May suggested returning to Nottingham, but Stephen, having planned for two weeks' holiday, and being engrossed in a Fen landscape, was in favour of staying. They went to bed on the night of the third of August in a land of peace. At midnight on the fourth England was at war. Great block letters proclaimed the fact from every news-bill and across every heading. It was a catastrophe—how great a catastrophe no one living on the earth that morning could foresee.

They stayed for four more days while Skegness emptied itself and the East Coast knew that its season was ended. Across the sea lay Germany, and every day there was a rumour that gun-fire had been heard beyond the Wash and a naval battle had been fought. On Wednesday the Mays realised it was no use ignoring the fact of war. They went back to Nottingham. One consequence was now clear. The Rome Scholarship was useless and all Stephen's bright dreams of life in Italy were swept away. Young men could no longer dream dreams or follow private ambitions. They left the universities, offices, factories, and shops and were soon bellowed at, marched and counter-marched across Britain's drilling-grounds. They were crowded into makeshift barracks where at the first snap of winter hundreds died of pneumonia. A country with only a small professional army, soon decimated at Mons, made desperate efforts to train its volunteers.

Stephen May, caught in the maelstrom, decided to join the quickly expanded Officers' Training Corps attached to the local University College. Nobody was less fitted for war, mentally or physically. An individualist, he felt an intense loathing for a system that reduced the human factor to the lowest common denominator. Without being able to define his rebellion, he found something revolting in the spectacle of hundreds of thousands of men being reduced to automatons, stiff-backed, mechanical in movement, mindless in servility, moved about in platoons, squadrons and regiments with the sole purpose of mass-murder, glossed over in the name of patriotism. The animals in the field and the birds of the air had not reduced themselves to this insensate regimentation. What had gone wrong with the soul of man that he must redress the lapse of reason and the eclipse of God? For although both sides confidently asserted His patronage, how could He become a part of a microscopic brawl in the face of Eternity? Deep within him, as within the souls of thousands of his fellows, Stephen May, inarticulate and trampled under by the herd instinct, heard the small voice of reason. But like millions across the face of Europe, taken from their homes and marched to the charnel-pit, he was helpless, crushed by a colossus that strode the earth, trafficking in the noblest instincts and trumpeting the age-old shibboleths. If you would not fight, your country was vanquished and you were subject to the tyranny of a triumphant enemy. An empire won by enterprise, blood and sacrifice, and held together by a great tradition, would dissolve, bringing ruin and tribulation to millions.

Stephen listened to all the arguments on either side and joined in them. The pacifist's case seemed unanswerable, except for one fact that invalidated all its logic. Unless the pacifists were in the majority on both sides the whole theory collapsed. It seemed to Stephen that the agony of the world was not due to the folly of Man, but to a basic deficiency in his composition. He was a faulty design, and Creation, somehow, had overlooked the compensator in the balance of his faculties. He listened to reverend gentlemen waxing eloquent on the nobility of the sacrifice by which men succeeded in butchering each other, and, as a footnote on Christian duty, heard the drill-sergeant at bayonet practice instruct the young Galahads to " give the bayonet a twist so as it pulls their guts out ". Posters of these gut-rippers, with a shadowy form of Christ blessing them, under the catch-phrase " For God, King and Country ", seemed to Stephen nauseating blasphemy. The spectacle of millions of nominal Christians, possessing no more land than was contained in the flower-boxes of the homes they had been snatched from, locked in a death-grapple in the sacred name of freedom, seemed to him a travesty of sense. " The War to End War ", the political orators called it. Did one, then, make a bonfire of civilisation to preserve civilisation ?

In the School of Art one of his colleagues, little Philip Gee, was a Conscientious Objector. He was hounded by his neighbours and browbeaten by a Tribunal, comfortably safe inquisitors of the public conscience. There was iron in the youth's frail constitution. He resolutely went to gaol, an ineffective witness to freedom of conscience and the penalties of independent thought. Stephen marvelled at this lonely and deliberate form of courage. When, two years later, his neighbours in Adelaide Row wished to celebrate the award to him of the Military Cross, he knew who was the braver spirit. He grieved for gentle Philip Gee, with all the promise of genius in him, born to create beauty in an ugly world. He had died, fatally chilled in a gaol and, later, segregated in a camp. There were no red poppies for him, no name on a memorial cross. All that remained were a few canvases, a dozen delicate water-colours, destined twenty years later to become collectors' pieces, and, ironically, a growing posthumous fame that survived a second World War and the mouldering memorials to the heroes of the first.

Stephen's friend, Lieutenant Alan Forbes, who shared with him the life of a rat in a subterranean hovel, fifty yards removed from the festering corpses of No Man's Land, had a pretty though perturbing wit. When he heard that Stephen came from Nottingham, he exclaimed, " What, the home of old ' Festus ' Bailey ! At my prep. school we used to rant those noble lines. If he'd lived here now he'd change 'em some-what—

> We live in mud, not human ; in stinks, not breaths,
> In frostbite, ghostly figures on a duckboard ;
> We count our leave by heart-throbs ; he most lives
> Who thinks least, feels the dumbest, scrounges best."

Dear gallant, cynical Alan ! He died in a night-wiring party bringing in a wounded sergeant. The vagaries of Fate ! For this exploit, in which they were engaged together, Stephen was given the Military Cross. He was quite surprised to find he was a hero. In the desperation of the hour, men gave no thought to their behaviour. Stephen felt it was invidious that he should have been selected when every man in the regiment was equally qualified.

He was on leave, breakfasting in the kitchen, when he read in a local newspaper that Sir Thomas Birkin's grandson had been killed in action, making a gap in the line of succession of one of the big B's. It recalled the occasion when, at one of those early O.T.C. drills in the Nottingham Guildhall yard, he had been clumsy in drawing a bayonet and had jabbed it in his neighbour's thigh. Thus he, a collier's brat, had drawn the blood of the Birkins. The wounded youth took it in good part, and they became quite friendly. Poor lad ! gone with so much to lose.

It was at this time that Stephen experienced one of those violent turns of the wheel of Fortune, so prevalent in war-time, which brings ruin to some and riches to others. An officer in his regiment was a partner in a London art dealer's gallery. He saw some of Stephen's war-time sketches, and was so enthusiastic about them that he arranged for a small one-man show. It was an immediate success, which left Stephen with a sum of money that stunned him. In addition to a degree of fame and the possession of capital, there was a consequence that changed his life. He did not go back to the regiment. After an interview at the War Office, with a Royal Academician transformed into a colonel with the task of organising an official art record of the war, Stephen found himself sent off to make portraits and sketches on the Western Front. Overwhelmed by his good fortune, he set to work with furious industry, maintained until, standing one misty morning on November 11th, 1918, in the cobbled market-place of Mons, he heard the trumpets proclaim the armistice that ended a victorious war. Amid a flare of Verey lights, the singing of *La Brabançonne* and *God Save the King*, and a general *kermesse* in which everyone kissed everyone, the curtain came down on the War to End Wars.

III

Back in Adelaide Row, Captain Stephen May, M.C., reviewed the position. For him it had been a good war. He had crossed, with many other thousands of nondescripts, the social line, almost obliterated in the ruthless shake-up, and he had become an officer and a gentleman, decorated. From a more practical viewpoint, he possessed five hundred pounds capital, and had a Rome Scholarship tenable for two years.

After his arrival home, on a chill January morning in 1919, he walked over the familiar wasteland of the colliery to the Trent side. He had just left Cologne, in the wake of the Allied march to the Rhine. Standing by his native river, cold and glassy as it swept round the curve by Clifton Church, he thought of the other river, of the Hohenzollern Bridge with its statue of the proud emperor at whose base Field-Marshal Haig had taken the salute as the victorious army passed on into defeated Germany. Between his first sight of the Trent and of the Rhine, through what vicissitudes his own life had passed! Here, on summer days, he had learned to swim among a shouting, naked brood of colliers' brats. Here he had seen little grimy pit-boys of thirteen thrown into the river in rough punishment for some underground misdemeanour. He recalled how on half-holidays the miners had come here to wash before hurrying off to the cricket match. Up this stream, on a lovely summer's day, he had taken Helen Watmough to Clifton Grove. He had not seen Helen for four years. He heard that she had been a volunteer nurse in France. Eric, her brother, had been killed on Vimy Ridge. What memories of the past came down upon the silver flood! Across the river there was a meadowland fronting the old *Ferry Inn* where he had flown his first kite, made by his father.

In March he was leaving for Italy to take up his scholarship. It was a little late, but all his life he would be a student, and Italy still beckoned him. That was to be the next adventure, perhaps the greatest. His whole life had to be replanned now. He had many problems. One of these had been finally settled by his mother. He had wished to take her out of Adelaide Row if possible, but she would not hear of it.

"In the first place, there's nowhere to go, everybody's desperate for houses, and I've been lucky to have this roof over my head. And what should I do or be, anywhere else? I'm not going to be a burden to you, Stephen, not more than I can help," she said. "I've passed most of my life here, I know the people and they know me, and it's too late to alter one's mode of life at sixty. You have another world to live in, and I've enough sense to know it can never be mine. After Italy you won't come back here; you'll be wanting a home of your own."

The plain sense of it left him without an answer. On one thing he insisted. Mr Connington had left for war work in Leeds, and had died there. A noisy young couple occupied the two front-rooms, their gramophone and a baby screamed at all hours. Stephen got rid of them, moved down from his beloved attic room, keeping it as a studio, into the front bedroom, and insisted on getting in outside help for the housework. Mrs Pieman was still active, but no longer 'living in sin', her partner having died. She now came in every morning for three hours, an arrangement to which Mrs May reluctantly agreed. It was the first time in twelve years that she had had a house wholly her own.

Musing over the changes, Stephen walked the whole length

of Victoria Embankment, from Wilford Bridge to Trent Bridge, and took a tram to the Market Place. He made a call at a solicitor's office, then once again he climbed the familiar stairs to the top-floor studio of his infallible old friend, consulted at every momentous stage of his life. The door opened and the leonine old patriarch stood before him.

"I'm interrupting you," said Stephen, smelling oil-paint.

"You never interrupt me. Come in!" said William Kiddier.

He had changed, Stephen saw at a glance. Fate had dealt him a harsh blow, taking his only son, inheritor of the business downstairs. His features were thinner, his hair snow-white, but the eagle-eye retained all its old fire. He had a crony with him, another son of the brush, Arthur Spooner, from the studio below. Sturdy, downright, he gave an air of the Latin Quarter to the place with the blue painting smock he wore.

Stephen looked round the studio. For nearly four years it had been his second home. Here he had come with all his problems, here he had first splashed on a four-foot canvas, here he had never failed to receive encouragement and sound advice from this generous-souled champion who had been a second father to him in those early years of struggle.

He took a seat by the stove. After a few minutes Spooner withdrew, aware a conference was impending.

"Well, you're looking fine. Tell me all about yourself," said Kiddier, rubbing his hands on his brown overall.

Stephen gave him an account. The old man nodded.

"No—after Rome you'll not come back here. Your mother's right," said Kiddier. "You're out of the cocoon now."

"I've something else—Alderman Huntsman asked me to call. I've just seen him," said Stephen. "Some friends want to give a portrait to Sir Jesse Boot on his seventieth birthday. I'd like to do it, but I'm worried by the idea."

"Why?"

"The doyen of all portrait-painters here is Denholm Davis. I wouldn't like to hurt his feelings. He's been kind to me. What would you do?"

"Go and see him. I've no doubt what his advice will be. He's the most generous fellow alive, and he's more work than he can do," said Kiddier. "After that come back. I'll have finished my varnishing, and we'll have some lunch."

Stephen crossed the Market Place, and climbed to another studio he knew well. Davis greeted him warmly. He showed not the slightest resentment when Stephen told him of his commission; indeed, he was quite enthusiastic.

"I've painted him, so it's sensible to have another artist. I warn you, he's not easy. He's a determined old fellow, and you must stand up to him," said Davis.

Back at Kiddier's studio, Stephen reported the result of his visit. "It's really very generous of him," commented Stephen. "He didn't seem at all hurt or surprised."

There was a twinkle in the eagle's eyes as Stephen told him this.

"It's just what I expected. Well, now that you've behaved so nicely I'll tell you something. Huntsman came to us. He wanted a fellow with a big name—an R.A., a two-thousand-pound photographic job, hung on the line. Denholm Davis said to him, 'Why not give young May the job? He's a local lad, but don't let that damn him. You'll go down to posterity for your discernment, and you'll get the portrait for a third the price.' He couldn't resist that!"

"So that's the story," said Stephen. "You and Denholm Davis——"

"And Spooner. So don't let us down, lad. Put Sir Jesse among the immortals; you'll never have a better chance!"

Kiddier took off his brown overall, and reached for the old felt hat he carried but never wore, being gloriously crowned.

"I suppose you've still a good appetite? I'm hungry, I've just done four hours on that canvas," he said, closing the studio door.

Going down the stairs Stephen reflected that a sovereign given to him by his old friend for a Christmas-box eight years ago had seemed enormous riches. Today he had five hundred pounds in the bank, a Travel Scholarship worth two-hundred-and-fifty a year, and a commission worth eight hundred guineas. Six years ago he had taken his life in his hands and brought his apprehensive mother to the verge of tears when he had walked out of Mr Dane's office sacrificing sixteen shillings a week. *De l'audace et toujours de l'audace.* Had he not prophesied that one day he would paint Sir Jesse's portrait? And now his chance had come. He had passed through the

jaws of Hell, Death his familiar.   Now Life smiled before him.
He felt awed, but determined.

Sir Jesse Boot had a domain at St Helier, Jersey, to which he
retreated at times.   When he bought a house in The Park he
called it *St Helier's*.   It was a modest establishment at first
but, fulfilling necessities, it grew into a mansion.   From a
glassed-in terrace above a large garden there was a fine view of
the Castle on its precipitous rock.

Sir Jesse gave Stephen sittings at *St Helier's* while he transacted business with his secretaries.   To Stephen's surprise, he
remembered him at once.

" I've got one picture of yours—I paid you twenty-five
guineas for it.   I don't suppose you're doing this one for the
same figure—and as I'm not paying for it, I hope you're getting
a nice big fee."

Sir Jesse laughed at his joke.   Stephen noticed how crippled
he was, his hands in an advanced stage of ulnar deviation.
But there was no lessening of mental vitality.   He had daily
consultations with his son, now taking direction of the business.
Stephen was amused to see how he kept his secretaries on the
jump, and how shrewd he was in dealing with all the various
schemes for which he was invited to part with his money.   A
millionaire addicted to public benevolence knows no respite,
as Stephen saw.   Just now he was engrossed in his plan
to build a local university.   In Morley Horder, an eccentric
architect of genius, he met a man as obstinate as himself.
They wrangled over the blue-prints for the lay-out, each
enjoying the battle.   All the time Stephen steadily worked,
wondering how he could capture the old Titan.   Sir Jesse
did not worry him after the first proclamation.

" You understand you're not to flatter me.   I'm no beauty.
I want you to paint me exactly as you see me, hoping you can see
straight—and don't be too long about it," said Sir Jesse,
bluntly.

Exactly as you see me.   How exactly, wondered Stephen
when he came to those hands, so cruelly racked by his pitiless
disease.   What a crucifix for any man, however heroic or
large-hearted.   If such a calamity ever came to him, thought
Stephen, he knew he would never have the courage to support it.

The attendant wheeled Sir Jesse away to his meals.   Every

movement required assistance, but without a complaint or a scintilla of self-pity business was attended to, the long list of public benefactions was meticulously planned. Alternating with wayward determination, and little gusts of passion, through which his tactful and devoted wife skilfully negotiated a path, he had his jocular moods. He recited to Stephen, with a chuckle, rhymes from his boyhood.

" I've always supported the arts, you know. I once employed a poet who got a living writing advertisement rhymes for a boot-polish firm, until he ran out of inspiration! " He proceeded to recite one of them. " Not bad, eh ? " asked Sir Jesse.

Stephen was sorry when the portrait was finished. He sometimes stayed to lunch with Lady Boot and her sister. Sir Jesse ate in his room. When he saw the portrait, before Stephen prepared to take it away and finish it, the old man looked long in silence at it. Stephen nervously awaited his verdict.

" How old are you, exactly ? " he asked, at last.

" Twenty-four, Sir Jesse."

" H'm. You'll go a long way. You've got the truth in you."

" Thank you, Sir Jesse. I hope you'll live to see it," replied Stephen.

" No man knows how long he's going to live, May. If he did he'd be a terrible menace. I hope your life'll be as happy as mine. Goodbye."

He was dismissed, and he went away very proud to have had such a man for his subject.

IV

During his work on the portrait he saw Helen Watmough twice. She came home from France, and after a short spell in London returned to Nottingham. She had seriously taken up nursing, and was now considering studying for a medical degree. He found her more serious and, he thought, a little determined, but he attributed it to her work and the things she had experienced. She greeted him again with real pleasure, and they had soon resumed their easy intimacy. She was delighted with his success and had eagerly followed every detail of his life in the past four years. Their former meeting-place existed no more. Letty Formby, on the death of her mother, had moved to London and, settled in a studio in Chelsea, was enjoying a new world. Helen invited Stephen to her home. Mr Watmough seemed always away on business. Mrs Watmough was more frigid than before. One afternoon, when the maid had cleared away the tea things and Mrs Watmough had retired, Helen suddenly said to him, " I suppose you've got to know, so hold on to your chair. My father and mother are separating."

" What ? " exclaimed Stephen, startled.

" They've never got on together ; we've known that as kids. Dad's amorous and Mother's an iceberg. He's picked up with his war-time secretary, a pretty little naval officer's widow who makes him feel a Romeo. He took me out to lunch last week in London to meet her. I didn't want to go, but at the same time I was dying to see her. She's pretty and has a trick of looking at Dad when he talks as if he were wisdom incarnate. So she's got him."

" But how long have your parents been married ? " asked Stephen, quite stunned by the news.

" Thirty-one years. It seems it's never too late to change," answered Helen. " But that's not the worst. My mother's taking it out of him by refusing to divorce him. She's going to make them live ' in sin ', as the saying goes. Pretty awful, isn't it ? I've argued with Mother. You could move the Castle rock first. So this home's going. My mother's taking a flat in London, Father's shifting his office there, and Nottingham'll know us no more."

" And you—what are you going to do, Helen ? "

" Father's given me a small allowance, enough to take me through Girton or King's College, London. You see, there's every reason now why I must stand on my own feet."

Stephen walked to the window and looked out. It was a grim March day, and already the light was fading over the leafless garden. He was leaving for Rome next week to begin a new life in Italy. Helen's news greatly distressed him. In her account he detected a fateful acceptance of the facts that almost bordered on cynicism.

He left the window, walked over to the lounge and sat down beside her, taking her hands between his own.

" Helen, my dear, I'm terribly sorry about this—I don't like it, I don't like what's happening to you. It's a serious thing to lose your parents—worse still to lose them like this, and to have no home."

" Home ? I haven't lost a home, Stephen. We've never had a home. Why, when we were kids we knew they could hardly tolerate each other. They used to talk at one another through us. When we went away to school we used to wonder how they could manage to sit at the same table."

" Who was to blame ? "

" I find it difficult to say. Mother's always been virtue enthroned, and Father's frailty imperilled by flattery. Funny, isn't it ? There must have been a time when they were locked in one another's arms. Stephen, that's why I've envied you."

" Me—envied me ? Why ? " asked Stephen, amazed.

" From what you've said from time to time, you must have had a happy home as a child. Your mother and your father were devoted to each other—you must have felt it, otherwise you wouldn't talk of them as you have. Do you realise how much that means to a child ? "

" I realise more now," said Stephen. " Yes, it has been something in my life. Helen, you mustn't be bitter about it ; don't let it hurt you too much. I'm going to say something to you, and you mustn't imagine I'm saying it because I'm sorry for you. It's something I've wanted to say, but have always hesitated to. If I give up the scholarship, and stay in England, will you make a home for me ? I love you. I can offer you so little at present, but I'm pretty confident—I'm confident enough to—to—— "

He faltered, and she looked at him, so gentle as he tried to express himself that she felt that he was the same little boy who had sat beside her in the painting-class years ago.

" Stephen darling," she said, as he looked at her, inarticulate with emotion, " you mustn't give up your scholarship. You've lived all your life for what's come to you now—freedom, Italy. You can't turn back now."

" What's a silly little scholarship compared with our happiness ? " he protested.

" It's not a silly little scholarship. You have a great gift, you are very ambitious, and travel will give you something you must have—experience and tradition. Besides, I, too, must work. We should frustrate one another."

"How could we? We should help one another!"

"No. I should always feel I had robbed you of something. Besides, there is something else. Stephen dear, don't be hurt; but just now I don't feel I want to marry. I'm too confused, I've been through so much, seen so much these last four years, that I'm not sure that I know what I want just now."

He released her hands, stood up and walked across to the high mantelpiece, leaning his hands on it, his brow pressed against them. After a few moments he turned and spoke to her as she looked up to him.

"Helen, I'm sorry if I have upset you. Can I ask you one question?"

"Yes."

"Do you love me enough to marry me, if not now—later?"

Helen did not answer at once. She sat for a while gazing down at her feet. After a long pause she looked up at Stephen and smiled.

"I can say that I love you more than anyone I know, but I can't say that I am ready to marry you—whether I would wish to marry you later, should you still want me, that is something you must ask me later. Stephen dear, I'm desperately trying to be honest; be patient with me!"

He walked towards her, took her hands and pulled her up to her feet, until they stood looking into each other's eyes.

"I shall go to Italy. When I return in two years I shall ask you to marry me," he said, quietly, and holding her to him, kissed her, seeing she was near to tears.

CHAPTER X

ITALY AT LAST

I

THE portrait of Sir Jesse gave great satisfaction. Stephen received his fee of eight hundred guineas and put it in the bank. Then in the third week of March he set off for Italy. At long last the dream of his boyhood was to come true. He feared, now that the moment had come, that reality would be less than imagination. The journey was difficult, as the railroads had not been restored fully after the devastation of war. He stayed in Paris only two nights. He had visited it twice in war-time, and it was for him still a city not yet restored to its normal civilian life. It was the gathering place of a great horde of delegates from all the nations, the victorious and the defeated, preparing for a new war of diplomatic moves provoking bitter clashes of opinion. He was afraid, too, that Paris might lure him from his first loyalty, Italy. Later, he would see what Paris had to offer and what its true life might be when all the uniforms had gone and the politicians were at rest.

He went on to Marseilles and thence along the Riviera to Genoa. For the first time he looked on a sparkling blue sky and sea, an unbelievable deep unbroken blue, lit with the brilliant Mediterranean light such as he had found only in paintings. Already Spring had trailed her floral robes along this enchanted coast. The almond trees were in blossom, clouds of pink petals delicate against the intense blue. The olive trees shone silver along the stepped terraces that looked down to the sea. Now, as the train threaded the tunnels of the rocky indented coast beyond Nice, he began to see the pattern of the Italy that had obsessed him for so long, the vines trained from tree to tree and along the pergolas, the marble terraces in gardens where the palm, the eucalyptus, the dark cypress, the giant cactus and the shining magnolia trees graced the smiling landscape. Most of all he saw the villas, with green shutters folded back on white walls, shining in their sleepy retreats. Here a fountain of nymphs and naiads, or dolphins and satyrs, threw a silver jet into the sparkling air. And over all, at intervals, as the train hugged the steep rocky shore, came the fragrant odour of orange blossom. The golden day lay on the mountains and his first adventure had begun.

He had planned to arrive in Rome at midnight, risking the finding of accommodation in some modest hotel. Later, he would search for a permanent lodging. It was one of the great merits of his Rome scholarship that he was free, with the Academy in Rome ready to give him advice and to make his path easy. He was tied to no classes, no set hours, no prescribed professors. All Rome was his to use and enjoy. He had set out well supplied with letters of introduction. His old colonel was attached to the British Embassy, a connection that might be valuable and was certainly pleasant. He had in hand a commission to paint him.

He had proposed arriving in Rome on the night of March the twenty-sixth, but Fate in the person of a young woman in the train intervened. He encountered her at Genoa, where he had to change trains. A general ignorance concerning the connection to Rome had resulted in some pantomime with a native porter who claimed to speak English. It was of a kind that proved more incomprehensible than Italian. It had been learned in Detroit twenty years earlier and with time and distance it had suffered a fearful transformation.

" This is the train for Rome—if it gets as far," said a pleasant voice, from the carriage window above them as they haggled on the platform.

Stephen looked up and saw a snub-nosed young woman of about his own age smiling at him. Before he could say anything she entered into a fluent argument with the porter. Then she turned to Stephen again, standing on the platform.

" This train should have gone an hour ago—it may not go for an hour yet, it may not go at all. If it does go it will probably stop at Pisa. Do you expect to get to Rome tonight ? " asked the young woman at the carriage window.

"Yes—won't it get there ? "

" No—we shall be lucky if we get to Pisa—there's trouble on the line."

" A breakdown ? "

" No—a flare-up. It's political. Three days ago a louse in Milan called Mussolini started to raise a guerrilla group to smash the Bolsheviks. He's a renegade Socialist, and naturally we're not taking it lying down. So trouble's broken out in the railway sheds at Empoli and elsewhere along the line. We shall stop all the trains if he doesn't fold up."

" We ? " asked Stephen, looking at his informant.

" We, members of the Italian Bolshevik Party." The train gave a lurch. " You'd better get in. It might decide to go. Have you any food ? "

" No."

" Any drink ? "

" No."

" You're an optimist. But get in. Luckily I have. I'm not an optimist," said the snub-nosed young woman with the tumbling red hair.

Stephen got in. There were three other people in the compartment, which was third-class ; a fat man with a bluish bristly growth on his triple chins, a peasant woman with two ducks in a basket, and a hefty boy of about fifteen bursting out of his incredibly short pants.

Stephen put his heavy bags up on the rack. He had a second-class ticket. There was no second-class. He sat down opposite the young woman.

" You're English ? " she asked.

" Yes."

" Then you're probably decent. That horrible boy has suggested we retire to the lavatory together, and Bluebeard has twice put his hairy paw on my knee. The woman or the ducks smell, which of them I don't know. It's a little like Gruyère, or perhaps I should say Gorgonzola, to be nationally correct. My name's Lolly Fellowes. What's yours ? "

" Stephen May—then you're English too ? "

" Hybrid. My mother was American, my father's Australian. He had a sheep ranch. Now he's rearing cattle in Texas. What are you ? "

" An artist."

" Good—you're one of us."

" I'm not a Bolshevik, if that's what you mean," said Stephen.

" You're a member of the intelligentsia ; the intelligentsia and the proletariat are united against the bourgeoisie," said Lolly Fellowes decisively.

" I wouldn't go as far as that—but I'm not politically minded."

" Do you see old Bluebeard's foot's up against my ankle ? I shall sock him in a minute. As I was saying—— "

The train gave a terrific lurch, then moved slowly.

" *Dio mio*—we're going," said Miss Fellowes. " Why are you going to Rome ? "

" To study art. I've got a scholarship."

" If you want to study art you go to Paris or Florence, you don't go to Rome. That's where they train priests."

" There were painters called Raphael, Michelangelo, and Pinturicchio who went to Rome," replied Stephen, smiling.

Miss Fellowes moved a leg quickly. The man winced.

" *Scusi !* " he said, trying to smile.

" *Prego*," retorted Miss Fellowes, glaring. Turning with a grin to Stephen, " I got the old buzzard then," she said. Suddenly her smile froze. The bare-thighed boy ogled her and eased himself in his shorts. The ducks started to quack, whereupon the old woman raised the lid of her basket and gave them a bang on the head.

" I maintain Florence is the place for you," said Miss Fellowes, resuming the conversation. " You may find yourself there anyhow. Pisa's a hole ; you can't spend the night there. If we can get on to Florence I'll take you to my *pension*, excellent food, and a view overlooking the Arno."

The train had drawn out of Genoa, and they saw the sea again. A mountainous wall rose before them. Miss Fellowes pulled down a bag, and out of it took a bottle of Chianti, half a cold chicken and two rolls of bread with *salami* between them. It was odd that a person of the Bolshevik faith should have such fine rings. They had large diamonds, which drew attention to her pretty hands. Apart from her snub nose and untidy red hair, everything else in her appearance was commendable. She had slender legs and dainty ankles, with tiny, expensively shod feet. Perhaps her breasts were a little over-developed or over-emphasised by a tight thin jersey, pointed by her nipples. She wore over the jersey a loose tweed coat, well cut, and unless they were remarkable imitations, a double rope of fine pearls. Her complexion was vivid, her skin creamy and well-kept and she had a beautiful neck and pretty rosy ears. The mouth, even more than the saucy snub nose, was her most notable feature. It was exquisitely curved, caught up at the corners, giving her a puckish smile. If she was a Bolshevik, she must be a parlour Bolshevik, for much about her suggested money. Her eyes were dark and lustrous. But for that nose she might have been a really beautiful young woman. Her vivacity made one forget the comic little nose. In the course of their conversation he came to the conclusion that, politics apart, she was a shrewd young woman. Who was she, what did she do, why was she in Italy? Her directness invited a rebuff at times, but there was something in her curiosity that was engaging, and it was impossible to show resentment.

" Are you single or married—single, I'd say ? " she asked, taking a knife and fork out of a leather case and starting to dismember the chicken on the grease-paper.

" You guessed right—single like you," said Stephen.

" I'm not single. I've got a husband somewhere."

" But you told me you were Miss Fellowes."

" Quite right. When I got rid of Tom I reverted to my maiden name. I always liked it better. Could you go through life being Mrs Quizzell ? "

She severed the chicken, put half on a piece of paper, with a roll, and offered it to him.

" Oh no, thank you, I couldn't—I—— " protested Stephen.

" Don't be silly. I'll bet you're hungry. I always carry enough for two. It makes an excellent introduction on a tiresome journey—if you want one," she added, smiling.

He took the chicken. She had beautiful teeth when she smiled.

" The name is a little peculiar," said Stephen, in reference to her question.

" A little ! It wasn't the only peculiar thing about Tom. Can you get out that cork ? "

She passed a bottle to him and watched him pull out the cork. It had been well jammed down.

" You've got strong hands—a man's hands. You look as if you'd do better in the ring than on the easel. How old are you—twenty-six ? "

" Almost twenty-five."

" I'm twenty-six and experienced."

"You don't think I'm experienced?" asked Stephen, laughing.

She was pouring the wine into a cup and stopped, looking at him hard. Then after a pause she said, quietly, "I should guess you're a virgin."

He blushed at her frankness, more embarrassed than annoyed. She caught his eye and laughed at him.

"Now I know you are! How wise! Curiosity killed me at twenty. I got out of school like a cat seeking mice, and I found one disguised in trousers. My husband had a passion for me, and a bigger passion for birds."

"Birds?"

"Real birds. He is one of the world's greatest ornithologists. He's rich, so he goes all over the world to look at birds. Do you know Holyhead?"

"In Wales?"

"Yes. We were married in Paris. I went to Baylor University in Texas and we had a professor mad on Browning, so he brought fifty of us in his Browning class on a tour of Italy, the country of *The Ring and the Book*—'O Lyric Love, half-angel and half-bird, and all a wonder and a wild desire'—good stuff, isn't it? That's how I came to be in Paris, and met Tom and jacked the Professor. Well, about Holyhead. Tom suggested we go there for the honeymoon. Beautiful cliffs, he said. What he meant was beautiful birds. On our honeymoon he got up at dawn—just when you most want to snuggle—and went out with field-glasses on to the veranda to look at seagulls. He went out in his nightshirt. He wore one of those ridiculous things right down to his skinny ankles. That's how I came to know about Holyhead—it's the most famous place in the world for seagulls. Ornithologists dream of it on their honeymoon, if they don't have it there."

She laughed, lifted up her Chianti glass and drank.

"Your quotation is very apposite," said Stephen.

"Apposite?"

"'O Lyric Love, half-angel and half-bird'—it suits an ornithologist."

"I say—you're smart! It was quite unintentional."

The blue-chinned man turned and smiled at Stephen.

"An old buzzard, too, if such I am, is not out of place, I might assure the *signorina*."

Miss Fellowes' eyes nearly popped out of her head.

" *Dio mio*, you know English ! " she exclaimed.

" I should.   I was born in Boston of Italian parents.   And I do not wish to be offensive, *signorina*.   I merely offer you admiration," said the blue-chinned man.

" I'll accept your admiration, at a distance, *signore*," replied Miss Fellowes.   " I wonder if that passionate tadpole in the corner also understands English—do you, tight-pants ? " she asked the boy.

His mouth expanded in a smile from ear to ear.   He stiffened his thick young neck like a gander.

" *Si, signorina !* " he said delightedly, grinning.

" You are a worm—not a tadpole ? " asked Miss Fellowes.

" *Si, signorina.   Vado a Pisa !* "

" Going to Pisa, eh ?   Well, when you get there I hope Mamma will meet her *bimbo*.   I shall ask her to spank that tight bottom of yours.   You'd make any tower lean in horror."

" *Come si chiama ?* " asked the boy, overjoyed.

Miss Fellowes threw him a scornful glare, then turned to Stephen.

" You should spend at least six months in Florence and then go to Venice—there's a paradise for artists ! "

Miss Fellowes proceeded to tell him about Venice.   She had lived there in a palace on the Grand Canal.   In the course of their journey he learned she had lived in Paris, Vienna, New York and Florence.   It was astonishing where she had lived in her brief twenty-six years with or without Tom.   The mystery of her education in Texas was explained.   Her father, having made a fortune, had bought a ranch in Texas and had sent her to Baylor University.   " I loved it, and they loved me.   Of course I wasn't a Bolshevik then," she explained.   " That's where I met Tom, and we fell for each other.   He couldn't bear Browning, but he followed us to Paris—which shows he really was in love with me, it meant leaving his birds.   His father's a millionaire—Texas oil, you know."

The blue-chinned Italian opened a smelly packet.   The odour of garlic filled the carriage.   He offered his food to everyone around.   Only the boy accepted.

" It is very interesting what you say," said the Italian, addressing Miss Fellowes, who had changed sides and was now sitting by Stephen.

" What did I say ? " asked Miss Fellowes.

" That the *signore* is a virgin. I am sure he is. The English are a remarkable race. I am told all the males are virgins until they marry quite late. It is admirable. It is not possible here."

" It certainly isn't, you should know ! " said Miss Fellowes emphatically. " If you could find an Italian male who's a virgin after twenty you should canonise him. A woman's chased here like a hen in a farmyard. You can tell me something, *signore*—with every Italian youth a rooster at twenty, how comes it there are any virgins left ? They can't all take refuge in convents ! "

The Italian smiled. He had childlike eyes and beautiful teeth, but his nails were dirty and his coat carried the dust of years.

" Our women have a beautiful example—Our Lady," he replied, crossing himself.

" Well, I'd say they need a lot of resistance with all these young Romeos prowling around. They're much too good-looking for human frailty. Do you mind if we open the window ? " She turned to Stephen. " This down-draught of garlic ! "

Stephen laughed to cover his embarrassment at the turn in conversation and lowered the window. What a terrifying young woman ! Somehow he must get rid of her if they were stuck in Pisa.

The train crawled along. At Viareggio they were two hours late. The light began to fail. Miss Fellowes' gloomy prophecy about the improbability of reaching Rome that night seemed likely to be fulfilled. They were stationary half an hour outside Pisa. Darkness fell. Someone walking down the line halted under the windows and had an animated conversation. Miss Fellowes, hanging out of the window, joined in. Presently she turned and announced, jubilantly, " There's a strike all down the line. No trains are running ! Now what will Mussolini's *Fascio di Combattimento* do ? We've called their bluff."

The Italian shook his head. " It is the beginning of much trouble, *signorina*," he said. " And we have trouble enough. *È vero !* "

Miss Fellowes began a rabid attack on the politicians and an animated debate was waged in Italian, in which the Bolshevik party member was both fluent and passionate. She was obviously delighted that the train service had come to a halt; despite her own discomfort. Presently all the lights went out. A chorus of harsh Italian voices began to vibrate all down the train, the sound of passionate argument filled the night. After a long time the train began to move. In about ten minutes it came into Pisa station. There was a crowd of stranded passengers on the platform. The only light came from some candles flickering over the station offices. Everyone had to dismount.

In the darkness and confusion Stephen was compelled to seek aid from Lolly Fellowes. She was obviously competent and energetic. She physically took hold of a reluctant porter and galvanised him into action. When their baggage had been piled up on a truck she informed Stephen that no train would proceed that night to Rome. They were making up a train for Florence, which might attempt the journey there. The line via Empoli was dead. There might be a connection via Pistoia. " We may be stuck here all night ! " said his companion, almost joyfully. The Italian, the woman with the ducks, and the boy in the bursting shorts had disappeared in the darkness. " You'll like Florence, if we get there," she said to Stephen, as they sat on the luggage truck. She seemed quite determined that he was going to Florence. There was nothing else for him to do but accompany this odd young woman. Against his will he found himself liking her despite her preposterous political views and her unrestrained conversation. She had vitality and good nature.

An hour passed. Then an empty train, bound for Florence, came in. There was a rush of passengers, and in the wild scrimmage, ruthlessly waged by shouting Italians, Stephen lost Miss Fellowes and his baggage. He ran up and down the dark platform in a medley of bodies, when an unmistakable voice screamed, " Stevie ! "

He resented being called Stevie anywhere, by anybody, but in his situation it was like a lifebuoy cast to a drowning man. He halted and saw a dishevelled red head projecting from a window, wedged forcibly among other heads, all screaming at people on the platforms.

" Stevie, come in ! The baggage's here ! " shouted Lolly Fellowes.

The train began to move.   Stephen jumped on with half-a-
dozen desperate passengers.   It took him five minutes to fight
his way down the dark corridor to the compartment where his
companion sat.   She had already established relations with
everybody, and under her directions they suffered one more
body to be wedged in.

"I love these people.   An Italian will kill you to get what he
wants, and then share it with you *per cortesia*," she said, breaking off an animated conversation.   "So you're going to
Florence, after all, Stevie—I think it's Fate."

"Don't call me Stevie, please," said Stephen, too irritated to
acquiesce in her familiarity, indebted though he was.

"I don't mind what you call me—but if you prefer to be Mr
May, very well.   My, aren't you English!"

He was about to retort.   "My, aren't you Australian!"
but although he had never been to Australia or known anybody
from there, he felt it would be a libellous remark.   He made
no reply.   For the next hour she rode triumphantly over a
torrent of Italian conversation.   When at last, towards midnight, tired, in an odour of compressed bodies, they crawled
into the station, Lolly Fellowes had hypnotised them.   They
competed for the honour of handling her luggage, to which she
added Stephen's.   A man whose brother had waited two hours
with an automobile insisted on giving them a lift to the address
supplied by the triumphant young woman.   Stephen, exhausted
and bewildered, late at night in a strange foreign city, let himself
be carried on the current of her goodwill.   But he wondered
where he was being taken by Comrade Fellowes and whether
the price of all this commanding kindness would be an expec-
tancy that he would make love to her.

"Just where are we?" asked Stephen as they stood in a dark
well with a caged-in shaft.

'The *Pensione Biancamano*.   I live here; you'll like it," she
replied, ringing for the lift.

It descended slowly.   They got in, piling up their luggage.
It was a tight squeeze.   The cage began its upward journey
reluctantly.

"This is an old palace.   The *pensione*'s on the third floor—
a warren of spinsters; but don't be frightened," explained
Lolly Fellowes.

A black-headed youth greeted them. He had obviously been awakened from his sleep. A single light feebly lit a large high room into which they passed. It was a strange introduction to Italy. The next development was even stranger. The half-dressed youth, according to Lolly, informed them that there were no vacant rooms.

" Then you will sleep in my room," said Lolly Fellowes, " and we'll arrange something in the morning."

" But I can't ! Really, I—— "

" Don't be silly. I shan't rape you. There's a divan and a screen. If you like I'll give you a handbell to summon aid."

She turned to the youth and gave him instructions. In no way astonished, he followed them with their portmanteaux. They went down a corridor, up three steps, across a large salon, along a passage, round a corner, up six steps and across another hall. The pension was a maze.

Lolly threw open a door and switched on a great Venetian glass chandelier. It was a vast room with four tall Gothic windows, two on each side. There was a double bed with a canopy and white muslin mosquito nets looped up over the head. In one corner near a washbowl, covered by a screen, there was a divan. The room was sparsely furnished. A large rack of shelves was packed untidily with paper-covered books, the table was piled high with magazines, papers, three pots of cyclamen, writing and drawing materials. The general impression was one of homely confusion. It lacked a single feminine note.

The youth went out for the other luggage.

" Have you been here long ? " asked Stephen.

" Off and on for three years."

" Three years—but the war only ended five months ago ! "

" I was in the war—on the Italian front. I retreated here at intervals. My bed, you see, is large enough for two. You may be Sir Galahad, but I've no sword—so that's out of the question. If you like I'll take the divan ; it's very comfortable."

She took off her hat and coat. It was a silly little hat and its absence greatly improved her. She looked less pert.

" Hang up your things," she said, pulling back a curtain over an alcove.

Stephen hung up his coat and hat. " What do you mean

G

about a sword ? " he asked, looking at a picture by Bronzino on the wall.

" Isn't there some story about a knight who went to bed with a maiden, and put his sword between them ? I always wondered what she thought about it ! " laughed Lolly, pulling back her hair.

" I'll take the divan—and it's your funeral," he said.

" Funeral ? "

" What they'll think in the morning."

" I can bear that," replied Lolly.

The youth came in with the luggage, looked round and smiled. " *Buona notte*," he said, going out.

Lolly went to a cupboard, took out a bottle of Cinzano, and filled two glasses, giving him one.

" Here's to your first night in Italy," she said.

They drank. She looked much nicer with her hair pulled back. Her brow was wide and white. There was a wave in her long hair.

" Not to embarrass you I shall undress in the bathroom, and by the time I've finished you'll be in bed," she said, taking things out of the wardrobe.

In a few moments she left the room. Putting the screen across the divan, he undressed. He was in bed when she returned. He heard her walk about the room. His heart thumped a little. The situation was perturbing. After a while she called to him.

" Do you know the Italian for Goodnight ? " she said.

" *Buona notte !* "

" *Buona notte e dormire bene*," she said, and switched out the light.

He did not sleep for a time. He heard her turn over in her bed, and the sense of her there troubled him. Should he . . . did she expect. . . . There was not a sound, or rather there was a sound, coming in from the window—the sound of falling water. This was his first night in Italy—in Florence, and not in Rome. He had dreamed of this since he had seen, at Mr Cust's, the water-colour of a terrace in the sun. It was of a villa at Fiesole, near Florence. How strange ! Never in all his boyhood's dreams had he imagined an introduction to Italy like this. It would astonish Mr Cust. Meditating on his singular situation, he fell asleep at last.

When Stephen awoke in the morning he was a few seconds recollecting the situation. A goddess attended by heroic youths covered his ceiling. The sun streamed into the high room, but a screen blocked his view. Then he knew he was in Miss Lolly Fellowes' room in the *Pensione Biancamano*. He coughed discreetly and said, " Good morning ! " There was no response. Rising quietly, he looked over the top of the screen. The bed was empty, the bedclothes were thrown back. There was no sign of his hostess. But what he did see sent his heart leaping. Through the open window there was a green hillside terraced with villas and gardens dotted with cypresses, dark and pointed, cutting the blue sky. He went across the room and leaned out. Beneath him lay the Arno tumbling over a weir just below a bridge. Lower down there was another bridge with arches in its centre, open to the light, with buildings on it, running from bank to bank, small windows in the upper structure. It needed no one to tell him that this was the Ponte Vecchio, famous through the centuries in art and literature. It was like turning a page in the book of Time to see it there, spanning the wide river, backed by the wooded hills, villa-crowned, that took the golden light of morning.

But nearer lay equal enchantment. The gleaming marble façade of San Miniato rose on the crest of a forested hill, and as his eyes travelled towards it, he saw, like a familiar friend, the unmistakable heroic form of Michelangelo's *David* silhouetted against the sky. Below the window ran the long boulevard of the embankment retaining the torrential river that swept, tawny and fierce, under the bridges. Across the river a long line of palaces caught the morning sun, backed by a hill where lay, as he learned later, the Boboli Gardens and the Pitti Palace, home of the Medici.

Breathless with wonder, he did not hear the entrance of Lolly Fellowes until she spoke to him.

" Quite a view, isn't it ? " she asked.

He started and turned. She stood before him in a scarlet silk dressing-gown, her auburn hair down her back. Her eyes laughed at him and she made such a youthful picture with her puckish little face that the artist in him saw a subject rather than a human being. She, in turn, observed an attractive young man, pyjama-clad, and starry-eyed with excitement.

"It's—it's unbelievable! Isn't that *David*?" he asked, pointing to the statue on the skyline.

"One of them—that's on the Piazza Michelangelo, in bronze. There's a marble one in front of the Palazzo Vecchio, which all the photographers think is the real one."

"Isn't it?"

"No—they put the real one in the *Accademia* to save it from the weather."

"What fun this is!" exclaimed Stephen.

"Seeing *David* or me?" she asked impishly.

"Everything—may I say you look very pretty this morning?"

"May I say you look very handsome? You see what Florence does for one. To come down to earth—the bathroom's free, and while you're in it I shall dress. Do you want coffee or tea? I shall order it. We breakfast in our rooms."

"Coffee, please—in here?"

"Here—we shall keep up the honeymoon rôle, if you don't mind," she said, smiling at him.

"Oh—of course," he said, and taking the large towel she gave him out of a cupboard, he left the room.

II

March passed into April, and April into May before he left Florence. In all the after years that first experience of Italian days was never dimmed. Day after day Lolly Fellowes showed him the splendours and delights in ways where the poet Dante, Giotto, Michelangelo, young Raphael, da Vinci, Cellini and Donatello had trod. There was an open loggia at the *pensione* in which they breakfasted in the warm spring mornings. It framed, between its columns, the bold machicolated tower of the Palazzo Vecchio. Stephen stayed on at the friendly *Pensione Biancamano*. They found him a room the next day, and he discovered he was under no cloud following his nocturnal introduction. After three weeks the progressively incredible Lolly Fellowes went away for some days. Trouble was brewing in Bologna, where the battle between Communism and Fascism was reaching a climax. Stephen missed her more than he cared to admit. Closer acquaintance only increased the bizarre fascination she excited over him.

Little by little he learned her history. Her passionate

advocacy of the Bolshevik faith he found more comic than distasteful. It was the only disharmony in their friendship, and he refused to be drawn into her circle. She spent much of her time with a horde of passionate young men, mad Socialists, spoiling for a fight in the maelstrom of politics sweeping through Italy. He laughed at her, which she accepted good-naturedly. But with his laughter went admiration. She had spent two years nursing with the Italian army. Through all the rigours of the winter campaign in the Dolomites, and later, in the disaster on the Piave, her courage had spread abroad her fame. Three times cited in despatches, twice decorated, to her personal service she added her money. Two ambulances had been financed and directed by her. She was wealthy, he learned, yet her daily life was passed in the utmost simplicity. She had no regard for comfort. From dawn to darkness she lived in a whirl of committees, public meetings, and propaganda tours.

"I believe that, like Joan of Arc, you'll get burnt in a public square—and like it," he told her one day, on her return.

"You think I'm a notoriety hunter, don't you?" she asked.

"No—I think you're just plain mad."

She looked at him in silence for a moment before she answered.

"If I am mad, Stephen, then Jesus Christ was mad. He hated arrogance and loved the poor. He would not let people go hungry. He lived possessing nothing and died possessing nothing. He took no thought for the morrow, but much care for today. I am revolted by the inequality of life."

"Do I understand you are the daughter of a millionaire and the wife of a millionaire—how do you reconcile that?"

"My dear, good, simple Stephen, I don't. I didn't choose my father. I married a man I thought I loved. What they are has nothing to do with me."

"But their money?"

"I take as much of it as I can get, to help as many as I can. You've told me you came out of a coal-hole in a horrible little mining slum—you've got out because you've a gift. What about a million little kids without a gift, thrust down in the dark for a few shillings a week?"

She was fierce and adept in argument. In her private life she reserved nothing for herself. When he challenged her about her diamonds and pearls, suggesting inconsistency, she flared.

"You brute! You silly, stupid little boy! So obvious a point in your justification, isn't it? It is inconsistent, I know. It's weak sentiment. They were my mother's. She left them to me. One day I may be big enough and strong enough to get rid of them. I'm a woman, and they please me!"

She was near to tears, he saw, and felt he was the brute she had called him. He put his arm round her, which was a stupid thing to do, for she sobbed on his shoulder and he held her in mute embarrassment.

"There are some times I hate you so, and sometimes I love you," she said, mopping her eyes. "You can kiss me, Stephen."

He kissed her with more passion than he intended.

She pushed him away and stroked back her hair. Then, with the puckish smile on her face, said, "I am human, Stephen, however mad I may be."

All this had happened one evening, as they leaned out of her window watching the sunset light falling down the Arno valley, with the Ponte Vecchio cut in black cardboard against the crimson west.

Two mornings later there was a note waiting for him when he came in for dinner. It was from Lolly.

> "I am leaving this afternoon for Milan. I did not feel I could say goodbye. I am not much different, after all, from any other silly young woman who lets a man get under her skin. When I return you will be in Rome. Good luck, Stephen. Your Bolshie friend, Lolly."

Yes, she had gone, they told him in the *pensione*. She often went like that, and returned just as abruptly.

He stayed on in Florence one more week. It was not the same place without her, and somewhat perturbed at this discovery, and trying to believe it was because he had stayed too long and the place was getting stale, he packed his bags and left for Rome.

CHAPTER XI

A ROMAN STUDIO

I

THE warmth of Spring was giving place to the heat of summer when Stephen May arrived in Rome. Instantly he took it to his heart. Its roaring activity, its mixture of the ancient and the modern, its silent courts, its deserted ruins, broken and lovely with the patina of Time, its medieval and Renaissance lustfulness, with Popes tearing it asunder that men of genius, Bramante, Raphael, Michelangelo, Sangallo, Sansovini, Bernini, might build it anew, its leafiness along the boulevards above the lazy Tiber, its mellowness of tufa and travertine, where the great baths of Caracalla and Diocletian, and the timeless castle of St Angelo rose mountainous under the tranquil azure of noon and the starry velvet of night—Rome in a thousand phases of glory, ruin, exultation, anguish and somnolence, crept into his heart. He loved the umbrella-shaded stalls with their tumbling cascades of flowers at the foot of the heaven-ascending stairs of Trinitá dei Monti. The deep ilex woods, the long avenues of pincushion pines in the Villa Borghese, with its statue-haunted vistas, its ornamental lakes, its emerald glens, its chestnut and orange-tree promenades, cast an enchantment over him. Time, a deep strong current, carried him lazily through the days : days of bright mornings under a luminous sky, of silent, siesta-smitten afternoons in the shuttered city. And came the night, following the swallow-haunted crimson sunset, warm and convivial, vocal in every nook, along every pavement where the diners and loungers sat in the shadow of immense churches and palaces magnified by the moon.

He found a small studio in the Via Margutta, a street inhabited chiefly by artists and antique dealers. The street was cobbled and hidden away between the thoroughfare of the Via Babuino and the steep hill on whose crest stood the superb

Villa Medici, with its twin towers, on a tree-shaded terrace overlooking Rome. Built for a cardinal of the great Florentine family, it had housed Galileo during his trial by the Inquisition and Velasquez during his visit to Rome. The fortunate winners of the *Prix de Rome* lived there, in the *Académie de France*. Friendship with a young French artist, living in a studio apartment built into the ancient Aurelian Wall surrounding the grounds, gave Stephen access to the classical porticoes and avenues of this elysium.

His own studio was an eyrie at the top of a yard, reached by an open stone staircase. The door opened off a small, pergola-shaded terrace. From his studio room with its long, glassed window a door gave access to a garden on the slope of the Pincio hill. He was high enough, in the upper part of the garden, to overlook the roofs of Rome and the Tiber valley. A large magnolia tree and a slender cypress gave him shade and dramatic decoration. It was a very great stroke of luck to acquire a studio so soon and so wonderfully situated. A predecessor who had completed his two years had vacated it, and the British School gave him possession. He furnished it with odds and ends that he picked up in the second-hand markets. Their acquisition was part of the entertainment of Rome.

Within two months he had acquired a little Italian. He took art lessons from Professor Casani, a renowned teacher, but he learned more on the streets of Rome, and he had no trouble in finding models. He should have been completely happy, but he was not. Since he had come to Rome he thought much of his days in Florence, and in this recollection Lolly Fellowes took a foremost place. He missed her vitality and her possessive nature. She was unlike any other human being he had ever encountered. She had had the dual quality of stimulating him mentally and physically, and now, in this surging capital, so fecund and physical for all its patina of dead generations, he experienced a vacuum in his own daily existence. He knew well he could not live with such a woman, she challenged and provoked him in a dozen ways, but living without her made him conscious of the incompleteness of his existence. She had awakened something in him, undefined, and her absence had left a void he knew not how to fill. All that summer he worked intensely.

II

In October, when the Romans returned from their holidays, and the month of gold touched the city with inexpressible glory, he began his portrait of Colonel Tabley. Slender, white-haired, he was a handsome man in the early sixties, aggrieved because he had not obtained a post with the British Delegation to the Peace Conference for which, as a fine linguist, he considered himself particularly suited. His wife was a vivacious Frenchwoman, whose exuberance sharply contrasted with the Colonel's taciturn manner. She made herself very agreeable to Stephen and he was much at their apartment in Parioli, the fashionable modern quarter growing up on the outskirts of Rome, beyond the Villa Borghese.

Italy was now rocked from end to end by intense political quarrels. The Peace Conference at Paris, bringing bitter disillusionment, had fanned the flames of unrest. Lolly's ' louse ', Mussolini, came more and more into the headlines. Following the November elections the Prime Minister, Nitti, had made the false move of arresting him on a charge of armed plotting against the security of the State, but Nitti subsequently lost his nerve and released him. The flamboyant d'Annunzio, part prophet, poet, mountebank and patriot, marched into Fiume and seized it in defiance of the grave elder statesmen in Paris. The flame of Italian discontent became a bonfire. " A corpse to be buried in a ditch," the Socialist *Avanti* had screamed at Mussolini. But the corpse began to walk. The Socialists had raised a formidable adversary from their own ranks.

In the opening months of 1920 there were nothing but strikes accompanied by violence. Even Stephen's mother in far-away Nottingham began to be alarmed. He assured her he was in no way involved in the political turmoil. Helen, to whom he wrote every week, also reflected the current alarm. " I expect you will be coming home soon—you cannot work much in such an atmosphere," she wrote. Her letter surprised him. His mother had no reason for understanding the political situation, but Helen should be better informed. Meanwhile he worked incessantly.

In his second year he stayed in Rome until the heat of July drove him up into the mountains. He joined a sketching party at Sulmona, in the Abruzzi. At the end of September he returned to Rome with a portfolio of sketches to be worked upon in the studio.

It was about this time that he found a new subject for his brush. Colonel Tabley, a devout Catholic, had an Italian friend, Cardinal Vanotti. When the Colonel suggested bringing the Cardinal to the studio to look at his portrait, returned for varnishing, Stephen readily agreed. He had never met a Cardinal, and the great figures in the vast Catholic hierarchy spread all over Rome were unknown to him. On the day of the visit of this distinguished prelate he filled his studio with flowers. He smiled to think what the sidesmen at the Wesleyan Chapel, his father's old colleagues, would say to his contact with the abhorred Papacy. Even Mr Cust, a low Churchman, might feel a little perturbed.

At five o'clock on a bright October afternoon a limousine entered the old stable yard below his studio. Stephen wondered whether it would be proper for him to go down and greet His Eminence. He decided to wait in his studio. To his surprise, he saw that a lady accompanied Colonel Tabley and the Cardinal.

Stephen opened the door as the party arrived at the threshold. The Colonel presented him to the Cardinal, then, turning to the lady, " Mr Stephen May—Princess Pordenino," he said.

He knew her instantly. She was one of the great hostesses of Rome, the wife of a prince of the fabulous Pordenino family that traced its line back to the days of the Roman Empire. In their vast palace were housed great treasures of Italian art. Its hospitality was of a regal order, and the entrée to its entertainments set the seal on a social aspirant.

The Princess was a woman of about fifty, tall, slender and of arresting beauty. Her pallor was emphasised by the absence of all cosmetics. The whiteness of her face and throat enhanced the dark beauty of her flashing eyes. She spoke English without an accent. Distinction and a quiet assurance marked every movement as she walked across the studio. Stephen had a swift and ludicrous thought as he watched her. She was the epitome of everything Lolly Fellowes sought to abolish. He could almost wish her present.

Within ten minutes, as they talked and looked at Stephen's portrait of Colonel Tabley, it was the Cardinal who dominated the room. He was utterly unlike the cardinals of the imagination, as created in novels and films. He was a little man with upright wire hair crowning the face of a monkey. He had tiny eyes that darted and sparkled as he talked, his funny little shrivelled face puckering into a thousand wrinkles. His large thin ears flattened against his head were almost transparent and his skin was a piece of time-weathered vellum. This grotesque head was fitted on to a small, rotund body. He looked, except for two features, like a little old woman behind any market stall, good-natured and shrewd. The two features that gave him immediate distinction and transformed him from an insignificant little man into a commanding personality were his voice and an air of effortless command. He spoke English fluently with an oddness that enhanced its attraction. He had been for two years the Apostolic Delegate at Washington, bringing back from his post a few Americanisms that surprised the ear. He spoke rapidly, his whole body in animation, assisted by the use of his beautiful frail hands.

" It's good, sure it's good," he commented, examining the canvas closely, as if near-sighted. " How much time you take, *signore*, to make so ? " he asked.

" A month, *Eminenza*," answered Stephen.

" A lot of paint, a lot of patience and a lot of talent," commented the Cardinal, with a smile. " How old are you, *figlio mio* ? "

" Twenty-six."

" Our Raphael died at thirty-seven. That's not to frighten you but to encourage you—think what he accomplished in eleven more years," said the Cardinal. He turned to the Princess. " If he can do this with *il Colonnello*, what might he not do with you ? "

" If you mean by that, *Eminenza*, that after me all things are possible, I do not feel you've paid the Princess a compliment," said the Colonel. " Looking at our young friend's work, it is obvious that he can make the wise beautiful—but what kind of a transformation can he effect with someone already beautiful and wise ? "

" Very pretty, indeed ! " laughed the Princess, who had seated herself in the property chair. " You should have been a diplomat, Colonel, not a soldier ! " She turned to Stephen. " You like Rome ? "

" I still feel like a schoolboy on holiday. I stare and stare—it is the most wonderful pageant on earth!" said Stephen, eagerly.

The Princess looked at him. How young and enthusiastic he was in this old capital full of sophisticated people!

" Mr May, when you are fifty you will know that, at half that age, every day is a pageant," she said, smiling.

" And when you are sixty, which is twice the Princess's age, you will know, *figlio mio*, that every pageant is filled with puppets like myself, caught in the web of circumstance. But don't let our wisdom intimidate you. The portrait does you and *il Colonnello* much credit," said the Cardinal and added, slyly, " Now can we turn from artifice to nature? I have a weakness for landscape—do you paint landscape?"

" I've done about a dozen, *Eminenza*, but they are all around Rome," replied Stephen, carrying round a tray of drinks.

" *Va bene*. Let me see them, if you so please. I collect Vanvitellis."

Stephen brought some canvases by the wall and placed them on the easel.

" They are beautiful!" exclaimed the Princess.

The Cardinal was silent until the last canvas had appeared on the easel.

" *Grazie, molto interessante*—most beautiful!" said the Cardinal, rubbing a hand through his hair and knocking off the little scarlet cap balanced on the back of it.

Stephen picked up the cap and gave it to him, and for the first time, as the hand with the large ring reached out towards him, he was aware of its arresting beauty. With the face of a monkey he combined the hands of an archangel. The Cardinal's sharp little eyes detected his surprise and recognition. He smiled at him and seemed to say with a look, " So I have my points!"

After an hour his guests rose to go. The Cardinal thanked him gravely. Stephen escorted them down to the Princess Pordenino's car. She paused before entering and said to Stephen—

" I have a small party for lunch on Tuesday—I should be very glad if you could come?"

" I should be most happy to do so, Princess," he replied.

" Tuesday at two, then. *A rivederci!*"

She gave him a dazzling smile.   He bowed as the car drew away.   Then he bounded up the steps into the studio and went straight up to the portrait of Colonel Tabley.

" Thanks, *mio Colonnello* ! " he cried, jubilantly.   " We've made it, we've made it !   ' I have a small party for lunch on Tuesday.   I should be very glad if you could come.'   ' Alas, Princess, on Tuesday I'm lunching with the Duchess of Montecalini.   I'm so sorry.'   ' Mr. May, I will ask His Holiness to give you a sitting at the Vatican.'   Mr Stephen May, you brat out of a coal-hole, Rome's gone from your heart to your head !   Be careful, my boy, be careful, you're not President of the Royal Academy yet—but you're on the way ! "

If at that moment anyone had looked in at the studio door they would have seen a usually serious young Englishman waltzing with his canvases as he carried them back to the wall.

On Tuesday he lunched at the Palazzo Pordenino.   The small party consisted of twenty guests.   They lunched in a room hung with splendid tapestries and were waited on by footmen in the Pordenino liveries of buff and crimson with gold cords looped on the shoulder, white gloves on their hands.   The names of the guests made a fanfare of Roman history.   The Cardinal, two monsignores, an admiral and the Secretary for Foreign Affairs were in the party of men.   Stephen sat by the Duchess of Cavalcante, who invited him to come and see her Leonardo da Vinci—" Reputed, of course, but really beautiful." She confided that she painted in water-colours.   He smiled at this, and when she asked him the reason he told her the story of a little boy who went with his father and mother on the tour of an English castle, and how the Duchess of Rutland, who owned it, had passed by and he had made a sketch of her from memory and sent it to her, and she had sent him a letter saying she painted also, and wrote to him ' as one artist to another '.

" You are my second duchess—and you paint also, so I had to smile—but I am no longer twelve," said Stephen.

" How charming ! " exclaimed the Duchess.   " Gloria, Gloria ! " she called down the table to her hostess.   " You simply must hear Mr May's story about your friend the Duchess of Rutland—it's delightful ! "

So he had to tell the story, and it was a great success, for he told it well, with a nervous simplicity, but not without a sense of drama, and they listened, and being young and good-looking, and a foreign young man, they were very courteous. When they rose from the table they all knew his name, and those who knew little about him assured those who knew nothing about him that he was one of England's most brilliant young artists.

Before Stephen left he had six invitations to famous palaces in Rome. When he said Goodbye to the Princess she detained him a moment, taking him to a small salon to show him the wall decorations by Mantegna. On leaving she told him that she received on Tuesdays and Fridays at seven, and would he come to see her? She was so beautiful and gracious in her splendid setting that he went down the great staircase with its classical statues a little dizzily. He paused for a few moments in the colonnaded courtyard with its fountain and marble group of Diana and Actaeon, feeling it was all a dream far beyond those wild fancies when he had waited for Mr Cust and looked at the Canaletto, the marble nymphs of the mantelpiece and the water-colour of the villa at Fiesole. Back in his studio in the Via Margutta he wrote three letters home, one to his mother, one to Helen, and one to William Kiddier.

III

It was always in the early morning, as he lay in bed, day-dreaming, that his best ideas came to him, and learning how elusive they were unless captured at once, he kept a pencil and pad by his bedside. The morning after the party at Princess Pordenino's, as the dawn broke over the hillside and the first rays of sunlight struck the magnolia and cypress trees in his climbing garden, he had a sudden idea. Of all the new faces he had seen in an eventful week it was the Cardinal's that was most clearly etched in his memory. That lined monkey countenance had an attraction with which no man, however handsome, could compete. 'Puppets like myself caught in the web of circumstance,' said the Cardinal. One thing was certain, no puppet had ever exuded so much force of character. Here was a prince of the Church, experienced, wise, and certainly adroit, who, aware of the great historical tradition in which he fulfilled his rôle, was also aware of the transient nature of human affairs. If it were possible to convey the transitory vanity of high office, as epitomised by the Cardinal, what a portrait he might make! The idea came to him with compelling force. On the bedside pad he wrote, " Portrait of Cardinal V—— not caricature—revelation of consciousness of human vanity— ' dressed in a little brief authority '—' I charge thee fling away ambition, by that sin fell the angels.' "

At eight o'clock, as he was shaving, his daily help, a gnomish little old woman called Teresa, appeared. She was a great gossip, and although he could understand not a quarter of what she narrated in dialect, he was kept well-informed of events in the Via Margutta, where she had passed her life serving a long procession of artists. Romances, grim poverty, comedy, suicide, murder and success had visited the colony dwelling along this cobbled alley of bohemians. Her store of stories was inexhaustible. An old spinster, romance had not passed her by. Once a week there came with her a little bare-legged boy, a lustrous-eyed, black-curled cherub, whose angelic smile extracted *lire* from Stephen. It was not until Stephen had gained sufficient Italian to know that *nonna* was Italian for grandmother that a query was propounded. " Teresa," he said, one day, " why does Mario call you his *nonna*? " Teresa raised her eyes to heaven. " Ah, *signore*, I was a girl in love. *Com'era bello!* but I was *tradita*. I have a son, Mario's father."

The betrayed Teresa, consumed by irresistible curiosity, endeavoured to read all his letters. She cultivated a deep personal interest in Stephen's mother. " I pray for her and bless the Santa Maria for giving her such a good son." The regularity of Helen Watmough's letters soon encouraged her to bless a romance that must unite two happy lovers. Her vision went beyond the altar. " *Signore*, when your little son cries for his *babbo* you must go home." Repeatedly he insisted that, being neither engaged nor married, a son did not exist.

This morning Teresa, who lived in a hole in the wall with two cats and a duck, all sleeping in the same room, arrived with one of the duck's eggs which she boiled for the *signore*. He ate the egg with some trepidation, wondering how sound it could be, propagated in such surroundings. When he had finished breakfast, and while Teresa cleaned the studio, he went over to a shop across the way and telephoned to Colonel Tabley. Would it be possible, asked Stephen, to get the Cardinal to sit for his portrait in full regalia?

"You would do better with the Princess. The Cardinal eats out of her hand," said the Colonel. "Of course I'll support the idea. Ask her."

A week later Princess Pordenino had arranged everything. She asked Stephen if she might commission it, as she would like to present it to the Cardinal on his seventieth birthday next July. Two mornings later the Cardinal's secretary sent word that His Eminence could receive Mr May for the first sitting at the Palazzo Bonaparte on Friday at eleven. But the Cardinal would be compelled to transact business during the sittings.

On the eleventh of November the Cardinal gave him the first sitting. As Stephen set up his canvas and began sketching, he thought how singular it was that exactly two years ago he had stood in the Grande Place at Mons, and now he stood by a window overlooking the Piazza Venezia, in a palace where Napoleon's mother had lived and died. On the other side of the Piazza rose the 'marble wedding cake', Italy's much-abused colonnaded memorial to King Victor Emanuel II. Stephen most resented it because it masked the Capitol hill and the Forum, the very heart of ancient Rome.

In odd moments when he was not busy with his secretaries, the Cardinal poured forth the treasures of his mind. Born in a noble Roman family, he was a repository of extraordinary lore concerning this fabulous city. What astonished Stephen was the amount of mundane business the Cardinal had to transact every day. Painter and subject were now on the friendliest terms, otherwise Stephen would not have presumed to ask him, jokingly, when he found time to pray. "I rise at six, my son, and I enter the world at seven," he replied. It was singular how the personality of the Cardinal grew on Stephen. He had started, frankly, with the intention of painting a portrait that was to be a thinly veiled study of human vanity. In the course of his work the portrait had changed in character, and a man, physically insignificant, but in personality a giant, began to emerge from the canvas.

Twice a week Stephen called on the Princess Pordenino. He met at the *palazzo* all the leading figures in public and ecclesiastical life, and she seemed to find pleasure in seeing that he met influential and useful people. For her part, she liked this good-looking, simple young man. His eager appreciation of everything was refreshing in this complacent capital, where every sensation had long been exhausted. Bursting with energy, he overcame her reluctance to sit. " I am painting Rome's greatest man, please let me paint Rome's greatest lady," he pleaded. " I would like to make you a present of the portrait after you have allowed me to exhibit it." She consented after a time, but insisted that it should be a commission. He named a price so low that she exclaimed, " Neither you nor I could survive so small a fee. Let's treble it."

To his great regret he finished the sittings for the Cardinal's portrait before Christmas and carried it to his study for the final touches. The portrait of the Princess was a much slower work. She was so late rising that morning sittings were almost impossible, and the light in the afternoon had gone by four o'clock. It was a month before it was completed.

In the first week of February, the Cardinal's portrait finished, he held a small private view in the studio. The guests were limited to fifty, but owing to the Princess and the Cardinal the leading personalities of Rome appeared to be crammed in the studio at the top of the courtyard. Never had there been seen such a coming and going of cars. Stephen put a crimson drugget down by the steps of his studio and hired a butler and a footman to serve the drinks. He had only one regret. He had sent out cards to Mrs Richard May, the Rev. Stuart Cust, Miss Cust, Miss Formby, Miss Watmough and Mr William Kiddier, but he knew they could not be present. From this private view sprang a startling suggestion. Why not try *The Cardinal* for the Royal Academy's Summer Exhibition, asked the Director of the British School. He thought it in every way worthy, and although Stephen felt he had made a great advance he was not so confident. But one idea supplied another. He planned to go home next June. It would be good to have this portrait and the one of the Princess to show in London after his Roman sojourn. The Cardinal and the Princess readily agreed. A week after the private view *The Cardinal* was sent to the Royal Academy. It was a wild hope, felt Stephen.

His days were now very full. Twice a week a model came to the studio. She was a girl of about twenty, with a full, ripe figure and sleepy eyes. He had had no intention of employing her, but she made it plain that she had a prescriptive claim to him. She had posed for the former tenant of the studio. One morning, hearing a tap on his door, he went to it and found her leaning against the balcony at the top of the steps. She wore a black shawl, and the great mass of her raven hair was held up by a large tortoiseshell comb, which gave her a Spanish air. She wore black stockings and backless slippers on very small feet.

"*Buon' giorno, signore,*" she said, smiling, with two rows of pearly teeth behind her crimson full lips. "You are Signor May."

"Yes?"

"I came here often, for Signor Stanton."

"Ah, yes."

"May I come in?" she asked, her sultry dark eyes surveying him with the utmost self-possession.

He moved aside. She walked into the studio, and, standing in the centre, surveyed the room. Her eyes fell on the canvases.

"You paint portraits? Men—no women?" she asked.

"As it happens—men chiefly. But I am painting a lady now."

"Figure?"

"No—a portrait."

"You should paint the figure, *signore*. I have the best figure in Rome. I am not expensive."

"Thank you, but just now I am not painting the figure."

She smiled at him. Then she took off her shawl and threw it on a chair. "*Signore*, you have not seen me," she said, pulling off her white blouse.

"No—no!" protested Stephen. "I tell you I do not want you."

She took no notice of him. There was a screen covering a wash-basin in the corner of the studio. She went behind it, and on the top of it began to cast her garments as she unrobed. Stephen shut the studio door. What could he do? He could not physically eject this determined creature, and already she was in a state that made such an act impossible. He waited by the easel. The black stockings appeared over the screen. A few moments later she emerged, totally naked and completely unembarrassed. She had removed her comb, and the thick black tresses fell to her waist.

"*Mi guardi! Come sono bella!*" she cried, raising her slender white arms above her head.

She was beautiful. The perfection of youth was in every

line. She was of a virginal ripeness, nurtured in the sun, warm as the fecund earth, knowing one luscious hour. The smooth alabaster shoulders bore a throat and head proudly poised. Her breasts, full and firm, were as the grape whose time has come for the vintage. The swelling line of her belly, with the amphora-like stomach curving to the firm thighs, had suppleness and strength. She had the legs of Diana, taut, strong, as though the meadows with the bounding fawn had lured them tirelessly in the swift chase. Confident, smiling, she turned on her delicate feet that he might see the sinuous curve of her back, the shapely buttocks of a young Callipygean Venus.

His annoyance and embarrassment gave place to reluctant admiration. He had had little experience in the life-classes, but he knew that he was looking upon a perfection he had never seen before and might never see again. Here was the living classic, Galatea, warm and breathing within sight and touch.

As she turned her glance fell on the large studio divan. " *Mi guardi, signore !* " she cried, and ran towards it, throwing herself on it so that her shoulders and head hung down over the edge, her hair falling in black pools on the floor, one rounded leg poised over the other. The whiteness of her flesh lit the dark divan with the radiance of her youth. For a few moments she was static, then she sat up and looked at him, her great eyes regarding him in silence.

" You have certainly a good figure."

" Fifty *lire* an hour," she said, breaking silence.

" But I do not want a model."

" Forty-five *lire* an hour, *signore*. When Signor Stanton——"

" You must get dressed, at once," he said, turning away. He took a cigarette from a box, and lit it with a trembling hand.

The model stood up, walked towards him and put out a hand. " Please ! " she said, smiling.

He took the cigarette out of his mouth and put it in her own. She walked across to a canvas on the chest of drawers. " ' The Appian Way '—*bellissimo* ! " she said.

" Will you please get dressed ? " repeated Stephen.

She drew at the cigarette, and handed it back to him.

" *Va bene*," she said, demurely, and went behind the screen. She dressed slowly. When she emerged she sought the mirror and began to comb her hair.

" Are you single ? " asked Stephen, touching the canvas on the easel and not looking at her.

" Yes—I am a virgin."

" Have you parents ? "

" A mother."

" She knows you go modelling ? "

" Yes, *signore*, but my mother is a bad woman. She wants me to sleep with men."

She made a gesture, rubbing finger and thumb together, the Latin indication of money.

" Do you ? " asked Stephen.

She did not answer for a moment. Then she put her head on one side and made a little mouth at him, like a petulant child, her large eyes serious and unflinching.

" A little. Some men expect it as well," she said, quietly.

" For fifty *lire* an hour ? " retorted Stephen, brutally.

He regretted it the moment he had spoken. She looked at him as a trusting dog looks at one who has struck it over the nose, puzzled, unprotesting. Her mouth trembled, but her glance did not flinch from his own.

" I am a truthful girl, *signore*. I tell you, for nothing— because I am young and I like them."

She picked up her shawl. There was a bowl of fruit on the sideboard. She walked towards it and carefully selected a ripe banana.

" *Scusi*," she said, putting it under her shawl, as she walked to the door. " *Addio, signore*."

" Wait ! I did not wish to be unkind. What really made you come here ? Do you want money ? Are you hungry ? " asked Stephen.

Again she looked at him with her beautiful black eyes. They had the luminous softness of a doe's.

" A little, but I came because I have seen you go up and down the Via. I like you."

She said it quite simply, truth in every word, he knew.

" Are you really a model ? How old are you ? "

" Seventeen."

" Seventeen ! " he exclaimed.

She did not move, nor show any reaction to his surprise. Stephen put down his brush and went towards her.

" What is your name ? " he asked.

" Isabella Tasinati."

" I will employ you—but you understand, there is no nonsense, no love-making."

" *Sì, signore.*"

" Very well. Come on Friday at ten o'clock, for two hours," he said, opening the door.

" *Sì, grazie. A rivederci, signore.*"

" *A rivederci.*"

When he heard she had reached the bottom of the steps he lit another cigarette, and poured himself a vermouth. Glass in hand, he paced the studio. What could he do with her ? The figure was so superb he could not let her go. Every line of her was sheer poetry. Seventeen, on the borderline of adolescence and maturity. Ten more years, no, five or even three, and perfection would have vanished as inexorably as the richest sunset.

He put down his glass, but his throat was still dry. He went over to the mirror and brushed his hair, recalling words he did not know he had remembered, the words of the blue-chinned Italian in the train to Pisa. " The English are a remarkable race. I am told all the males are virgins until they marry quite late. It is admirable. It is not possible here."

Stephen looked at himself in the mirror. " You are playing with fire," a voice within him said. Aloud, to the mirror— " It is possible here, Bluebeard," he said, fiercely.

IV

It was possible, but only just. At the end of a month when he had only half completed *Nymph and Roman Fountain*, for which Isabella came to pose, he felt he must abandon the picture. Isabella made no demands on him, but her naked body in every pose or movement perturbed him and he could never attain the detached evaluation of the single-minded artist. He grew fond of her. She had the directness of a child and the impishness of a monkey. She stole his soap, she never failed to use the lavatory because, she told him, it had *tanto acqua*, lots of water. He always kept a bowl of fruit from which she filled her pocket. If she had a new article of clothing she always produced it for his inspection on undressing, telling him the price. Otherwise they were artist and model, but only because of a silent battle tensely fought between them. Once when he went over to shift her leg to a required pose, she playfully trapped his hand between her warm silken thighs. He slapped her face playfully, but a flame consumed him, and for five minutes behind the easel, where he took cover, he could not paint at all. Every time as she was departing he wished to tell her not to come again, but instead he named the day and hour.

By the beginning of April Stephen had almost finished *Nymph and Roman Fountain*. He felt it was a success, and the most ambitious work in the nude he had ever accomplished. The sensuous figure of the young nymph dreaming, with one hand dabbling in the fountain, had a human warmth. It was the living Isabella of a modern day, despite the classical treatment. It had been a difficult picture, since the model had dominated him, instead of himself dominating the model. There was still war between them.

One evening, while he was cleaning his palette, the bell in the small iron gate of the loggia was rung violently. He was expecting no one. He put down his palette and went out, still in his painting jacket.

" Stephen ! " cried a woman's voice.

He saw a young woman, carrying a small valise. He recognized her at once.

" Lolly—well, what a surprise ! I thought I should never see you again. When did you get here, you vagabond ? "

He opened the gate, and she flung her arms around his neck and hugged him. He picked up the valise.

" Come in ! " he said, leading her into the studio.

She stood still, looked around, and then exclaimed, " I'm here ! I've just arrived—half an hour ago. How nice this is ! "

" Sit down—tell me about yourself," said Stephen.

She had not changed in any way. Her hair was untidy, she was as snub-nosed, as puckish as he remembered her two years ago. It was as if they had got off the train from Pisa and arrived at the *Pensione Biancamano* only last night.

Lolly did not sit down. She removed her hat, and sniffed.

" Stephen—I'm dreadfully hungry. What do I smell ? "

" Chicken stew on the gas-ring."

" Is there enough for two ? Let's eat here. I'll wash up afterwards. I'm domesticated."

He laughed derisively and forced her down into a chair.

" Lolly, you're as mad as ever ! Yes, you can eat here. Now, where have you come from ? "

" Vienna—it's in a shocking state. Stephen, they're starving, literally starving ! I can't begin to tell you. Look ! " She held out her hands. They were rough and red. " I've worked like a black in a Friends' Canteen."

" A Friends'—not a Communist one ? "

" Oh, I'm through with that nonsense. Don't laugh, Stephen, I'm serious."

" And now what ? "

" I sail from Naples tomorrow. Have you heard of Professor Jung, the great psychoanalyst ? I'm one of his pupils. I'm going to New York to found a Jung School of Psychiatry. So I've found you," she said, breaking off. " I thought you might still be in Rome, so I wired the British School. Oh, Stephen, I am glad to see you ! "

" Glad I'm not forgotten. Have you come to psycho-analyse me ? I'm in a bad state," he said. " An artist on the verge of a mental breakdown."

" You look fine. And you mustn't tease. While we eat I'll give you my history."

They ate on a little table by the window looking into the garden. It was nine o'clock when they had washed up in the kitchen.

" And now—where shall we go ? " asked Stephen.

" Nowhere. It's lovely here, with you, in this studio. I want to see your pictures."

" We won't bother with them."

" Please ! I've not seen much of your work."

He showed her some portraits, landscapes and sketches. He did not show her the long canvas *Nymph and Roman Fountain*. She was enthusiastic over his work. While he replaced the canvases she went out into the moonlit garden. He followed her up the terraces to the little lawn between the magnolia and the cypress. The lights of Rome shone below. The night was warm, summer warmth, without a movement in the trees, immense and black in the moonlight.

" What a lovely corner, Stephen ! " she said, slipping her arm in his. " You must be very happy here."

"Yes and no. Rome's been very kind to me. In June I go back home. I shall miss it, but I'm an Englishman."

Somewhere in the night a clock struck the hour.

"Eleven! It's not possible!" exclaimed Lolly. He, too, had been unconscious of the flight of time. They went indoors.

"I'll take you to your hotel, Lolly," he said.

"I haven't got one yet. I came straight here in a taxi, hoping to catch you."

"Your baggage?"

"It's gone to Naples. I've only that valise for tonight," she replied, going to the mirror to put on her hat. It was halfway to her head when she turned.

"Stephen, I may never see you again," she said, simply.

"What on earth do you mean?"

"Just that."

"What rubbish you talk," he said, laughing at her.

"Please, Stephen, I know!" she replied, coming towards him. "Two years ago you slept in my room, and I said something about a sword between us. Tonight I would like to sleep in your room, with no sword between us."

She lifted her face up to his. For a moment he thought she was being dramatic, but her eyes told him this was no make-believe mood.

He took the hat from her hands. "Very well, you shall stay, Lolly," he said.

Her arms were around his neck instantly. He caught her up, kissing her passionately, the pent-up emotion of months consuming him, all restraint gone.

It was dawn when he woke, and was astonished to find she was not beside him. He sat up, scanning the room in the half-light. Then he saw that the door leading to the garden was wide open. He got out of bed and put on the jacket of his pyjamas. Lolly's clothes lay on a chair. He went out on to the terrace, and then he saw her, a slim figure in cream silk, her auburn hair down her back. She was standing quite still, under the magnolia tree, statue-like in the dim light. He went out to her.

"Lolly!" he called.

She turned as he came up to her.

" It is so beautiful ! Look, dawn over Rome—the mist, the light, the birds chirping—as the Caesars knew it, as the Legions dreamed of it in exile. Rome the Eternal ! "

He made no reply, but stood behind her, enfolding her, his mouth touching the soft crown of her head. The light grew as they watched. Suddenly there was a glint of gold far across the valley. It sparkled aloft, solitary, above a dove-grey dome. The sun's ray had struck the Cross crowning the great cupola of St Peter's. Gradually the pearl of early morning lapsed into tides of rose and pale azure. A dark line loomed along the horizon. It was the pinewood on the crest of the Janiculum.

He felt Lolly shiver in his arms.

" Come in," he said, " you are cold."

She lifted her face upwards, her eyes searching his in silence. Then she spoke, softly. " Never, never shall I forget this moment, the dawn, the flame on St Peter's, the magnolia tree, you, Stephen."

Raising a white arm, she broke a small glossy leaf off a branch above them. She put it to her lips and then held it for him to kiss, tucking it away in the channel of her breasts.

They went down the path back into the studio. He looked at his watch on the side table. It was half-past six. In the bed he tucked the covers around her and pushed back the rebellious hair from her face as she eased herself into his arms, sighing contentedly like a child. They slept again as the light grew and the noises of awakening Rome rose in the morning air.

V

On a morning in the last week of May, Stephen stood in his dismantled studio. His bags had gone down to the waiting taxi, and the last minute had come in this place he loved. His pictures, crated and labelled, awaited the export agent. He closed the garden door, taking one last look at the little garden on the steep hillside, the cypress, the magnolia now in creamy bloom, the mauve wistaria and the fresh green vine hanging along the rustic pergola. Roses bloomed, and the banana tree had broken anew from its sheath with great blades of green against the azure sky. His heart was heavy at leaving paradise, but ambition beckoned. In London, it seemed, he was famous. *The Cardinal*, hung on the line at the Summer

Exhibition of the Royal Academy, was among the pictures of the year. Kiddier had sent him an illustration from *The Times* with *The Cardinal* in a group of five selected pictures. Helen sent him a bundle of cuttings from the Press. It had been a wonderful close to his Roman period. There had been the excitement of the letter of acceptance, the news that he was hung on the line, the burst of recognition. He thought of the phrase that told how, on the publication of his poem, *Childe Harold*, Byron awoke to find himself famous. The story of Byron marched through his growing years. At the top of old St James Street in Nottingham there was a plaque on a house stating Byron had once lived there. There a quack had tortured the lame boy with a contrivance for his foot. A few miles out of the city, on the edge of the Sherwood Forest, lay Newstead Abbey, the ancestral seat where the undergraduate had roystered with his college friends in the ruinous rooms, and drunk libations from a cup made from a monk's skull. At Colwick Park his Mary Chaworth had lived and been mortally affrighted by the Reform Bill rioters. Stephen remembered how at school they had ranted the heroic verses—

> Of the three hundred grant but three
> To make a new Thermopylae!

And now he awoke to find himself perhaps not famous, but certainly in the public eye. Twelve years ago he was an office-boy, an unsatisfactory office-boy, at eight shillings a week. Today he had almost three thousand pounds in the bank. It was wealth beyond his dreams; and the future was even brighter. "We must find a nice little London studio. I've heard of one at Campden Hill, and we will look at it next week," wrote Helen. We. So Helen had accepted him.

Old Teresa came in. She was almost in tears. He put his arm round her. "I shall come back to Rome, Teresa," he said.

"They all say that, *signore*—but they forget the Via Margutta and me—most of them."

She went with him down the steps to the taxi. As it turned into the street he saw her standing in the yard, waving, a little black figure against the old fountain and the silver water dripping over the emerald moss.

CHAPTER XII

SHIPWRECK

I

A PHILOSOPHER once said that we are hurried out of youth into manhood like sailors on board their ship, in a state of intoxication. The film of life flowed past Stephen in the next five years. He had progressed through various phases, each marking a new stage of prosperity and ambition. He would have stayed contentedly in the little studio house on Campden Hill that Helen had found on his return from Rome, and where they set up housekeeping and Richard was born. But Helen never ceased in her ambitious plans for Stephen. He had to be a figure, to keep in the public eye, to obtain new commissions. To achieve this she uprooted him three times in five years. Their social circle was always widening, and Helen, fashionably dressed, became a popular hostess. Their small house in Montpelier Square was crowded with a bright young set, journalists, gossip-writers and rising politicians.

The pace alarmed Stephen, who wanted to shut the studio door and get on with his work, but Helen made him appear. She selected his tailor with as much care as she selected her cook and parlourmaid. However much he grumbled about the continuous whirl of people in and out of the house, her method seemed successful in the matter of securing commissions. He was now charging a fee of a thousand guineas and had four or five clients a year. They were invited down to the country, to fashionable house-parties—a loss of four days, complained Stephen, for Friday was consumed in getting ready and Monday in recovery. But again Helen was right. They came up from Wilton with a commission to paint a brilliant Under-Secretary of State, and from Chatsworth with another for the portrait of Lady Venetia Moredon, the reigning beauty of the season. Lady Venetia, who did not confine her interest to the portrait, found herself outpointed by the alert wife of the artist. She was consoled by the *réclame* of the portrait in the Royal Academy Exhibition, which brought her a Hollywood film offer, gratefully accepted because of the young Moredons' taste for living utterly beyond their means.

Stephen worked so hard that he scarcely knew whether he was happy or unhappy. Certainly as an artist Fortune smiled on him. At thirty-two his first one-man show had been a social event. There was a galaxy of the famous and beautiful, as well as the ugly and the clever, at the Private View, and the flashes of the Press cameras played over the Gallery like summer lightning. There was a whole page in *The Tatler* with Mrs May, *svelte* in a Molyneux gown, laughing with the handsome young heir of the Duke of Porchester, whose mother's portrait, heavy with pearls among billowy tulle and guardian borzoi dogs, dominated the end of the Gallery.

Stephen escaped the next day to go up to Nottingham to see his mother, a fidelity to the ancient scene that annoyed Helen. " You've got rid of all that; why must you clank your discarded chain ? " protested Helen. She refused to go with him on these " slumming expeditions ", as she called them. But in this instance, Stephen, accommodating in all others, was adamant.

He smiled as he seated himself in a third-class compartment in the train to Nottingham, knowing how Helen would rail at his economy, legacy of a penurious youth. " Comfort apart, it's not good business. You don't know whom you might meet in a first-class carriage. You do know you can't meet anybody worth while in a third."

" I'm travelling up with Letty in a third," he had retorted on a former occasion.

" Letty Formby—what has she done for herself, scratching along in a back bed-sitting-room ? " cried Helen.

" Letty has done a lot for herself. Left on her own, she has established herself in London, where she enjoys life and asks no one for anything. She adds a note of cheer and courage to the landscape," he said, digging a spoon into his breakfast egg.

" There's no need to be angry about it, darling."

" I'm not angry, my dear. But all these smart people we give drinks to aren't worth Letty's shoe-lace," he retorted.

He never liked losing old friends. Helen craved new faces,

smart people, drawing-rooms, theatres, night clubs. She called it good business. They gave enormous cocktail parties, forty and fifty at a time, crammed into his studio, with, of course, the important person he was painting prominent on the easel. He once caught Helen shuffling the card-tray on the hall table, bringing the titles and bigwigs to the top. When he laughed, she retorted that it was foolish not to have the best goods in the window. When he replied that they did not keep a shop, she said, "Oh, yes, we do! I sell my husband's portraits." It was true, he had to confess. Her efficiency was frightening.

He was thinking of Helen as he sat in the train going to Nottingham. There was a fat old woman with a moustache and wisps of white hair opposite to him. Obviously she had had a long battle with life, and he wondered what her history was. Her experience lay in the kitchen and the small parlour with the snippet rug. He would rather paint her than the Lord Lieutenant of the County he was now labouring with. Those peacocks in uniform! Better than a General's, the uniform of a Lord Lieutenant was the best value for show. It included a plumed hat, a sword and lots of gold lace. Dark blue was kind to a big belly and set off the medals. " Increase the decorations and reduce the wrinkles," said old Thomas Maxwell, R.A., one varnishing day, as he looked at his latest portrait.

Stephen began to talk to the old woman. He was soon in possession of her history. She had buried two children and reared five. One son had a drapery business in London. She had been to visit him.

"Doing well, he is. There's nothing like a good trade. I've allus told me 'usband that—he's a night watchman at Players. What's your trade, may I be asking ? "

" I'm a painter."

" That's a good trade too—that and plumbing," said the old lady.

Stephen agreed. She produced a bag of fruit and offered him a banana. He peeled it and ate it. He impishly wished Helen could see him. She was at this precise moment playing bridge at Lady Crassington's.

When he arrived at Nottingham he walked all the way home, down Queen's Walk, across the end of Wilford Road to

Adelaide Row.   He went in the back way, and his mother was in his arms immediately.   Her hair was snow-white, but she was as straight as ever, for all her sixty-five years.   The kitchen shone, nothing had changed in it.   He had offered to re-furnish the house, but she clung to the old things.

" I like to keep it as your father knew it," she said.

It was seven o'clock, and there was a high tea awaiting him on the white table-cloth, exactly as when his father came in from the mine.   As he ate, pouring tea from the old brown pot, she gave him the local news.   Mrs Pieman had given up ' doing ' for her, her rheumatism was too bad, but Ethel, Mrs Popperwell's daughter-in-law, came in every day.

" You won't forget to go and see Mrs Popperwell—she always asks after you ; you were always her favourite."

" No, Mother—and Mr Cust ? "

" Very feeble—never been the same since his wife died. She was a burden, poor soul, but you can miss a burden sadly," said Mrs May.   " I've news for you ; hold on to your chair, Stephen.   Miss Cust's married—at forty-four ! A naval officer.   She's gone to live at Malta.   She'll have plenty of blue sky now.   You and she were always talking about blue skies."

He rose, picked up his bag to take it up to his room.

" I've put a bottle in your bed, and there's a towel on the washstand.   It's very different from your room in London, Stephen."

" And how should you know that, since we've never been able to get you to visit us ? " asked Stephen.

" There's an illustrated article in *Homes* called ' An Artist's Home '.   Helen said you were very particular about colour schemes in domestic decoration."

He laughed.   It was so like Helen.   She knew well he never cared a button what the decoration was.

It was the old room, with the washstand and ewer and basin. Mr Connington's wicker chair was still there.   He knew the exact number of brass nobs on the bed—ten at each end, and one that always rattled as one got into bed.   As he looked at the mantelpiece, his eye fell on a childhood's friend.   The old red pillar-box savings bank stood there.   He picked it up and shook it.   There was not a rattle.   He put a penny in for old time's sake.

When he had washed and put out his things he went down-stairs and told his mother he was going out.

"To Mr Kiddier's, of course?" she said, smiling.

He nodded. "Do you take a morning paper?" he asked.

"Yes—the *Daily Mail*."

"There'll be something in it tomorrow that'll interest you, Mother."

"What?"

"Just wait and see," he replied, and kissed her.

She looked at him closely as he picked up his hat.

"That's a nice suit you're wearing, Stephen."

"Yes—Helen dresses me."

"She's a good wife to you. And Richard?"

"He's just achieved a governess, and he talks your head off."

"So did you—you were never a silent child. I shan't sit up for you, Stephen. I expect you'll be late. I'll cover the cocoa down on the hob."

"Ah, the cocoa!" he said. Then with a hug he left her.

As he walked down the grey, mean street he thought how tiny the houses were. Each time he came back they seemed to have shrunk, like the people in them. He caught a tram to the Market Place, and bounded up the long stairs as in former days. He had warned his old friend, and he seemed to be at the door waiting. How white-headed and venerable he was, growing more and more like an Old Testament prophet. In some ways he resembled another Nottingham figure, old General William Booth, founder of the Salvation Army.

"Ah—well, you look fine!" said William Kiddier, perching on his painting-stool. "Now give me all the news—then we'll go out and eat."

"I've just eaten."

"Then we'll eat again!" declared Kiddier, straightening some brushes in a pot.

Stephen gave him his news. Towards the end he paused and then said, quietly, "I've a surprise for you. Tomorrow I shall be listed among the new A.R.A.s."

William Kiddier brought his hand down on his thigh with a resounding smack. "I knew it! You don't surprise me a bit. The first time you threw paint on a canvas in this studio I went in to Spooner and said, 'We've a future R.A. in there.' 1926, A.R.A. I should say you'll be R.A. in 1940. I'll not live to see it, but I'll bet my tombstone on it, unless you play the fool.   Now we'll go and eat—and a bottle of wine on this ! ''

II

They moved again early in twenty-nine to a large house in Bruton Street, with a bigger but less satisfactory studio for working purposes.   Stephen put up a fight against the move. They were spending three thousand pounds a year.   There was now a butler and two parlourmaids.   Stephen's market was still rising.   He showed every year at the Summer Exhibition of the Royal Academy.   He asked fifteen hundred pounds for a full-length and a thousand for a half-length portrait, and had a waiting list.   In 1928 he went to Washington to paint Andrew Mellon, the statesman-financier, for which he got his expenses and three thousand pounds.   On his way home he picked up another thousand for a five-days' study of Mrs Cornelius Vanderbilt.   He could have stayed on and earned a large sum, but despite Helen's protest, he insisted on getting home.   '' I want to see Dickie at Christmas—and my mother's not too well.''   So they came home.   It was their first serious quarrel. Back home the rout in Bruton Street was more hectic than ever. The house was filled with a rather raffish crowd.   The net now embraced the theatre and finance.   Even so, Stephen's painting grew in quality and force.

In the April of 1929 they received an irresistible invitation. Princess Pordenino had a villa at Serbelloni on Lake Como. She invited them to join her house-party.   The villa was high above the blue lake.   A series of terraces with statuary and a flight of stone steps, bordered by sixty cypresses, led ceremoniously down to the water.   The villa was embowered in roses, carnations and almond blossom.   Nightingales sang in the dark ilex woods.   The snow-capped mountains swam around them in a sea bluer than the lake.

When the Princess greeted them, she said to Stephen, '' I have an old friend of yours staying with me.   She is delighted to see you.''

'' Who ? '' asked Stephen.

'' The Duchess of Rutland.   She tells me she has one of your earliest portraits ! ''

Stephen laughed, and was touched to think that after some

twenty-three years she should have remembered him and kept his sketch of her at Belvoir Castle.

The house-party was large and international in character. The place seemed to ooze nobility. There was a grandee of Spain, the picturesque Duke of Altavara, and his French wife, a Bourbon. There was the Duke of Stornaway, an amiable, insignificant little man with his wife, Georgie, a great beauty, affable and charming, plucked from a famous bevy of beauties at the Gaiety Theatre who were infusing with their vivacity the tired blood of England's aristocracy. There was a penniless Russian Grand Duke, a formidable bridge-player who existed on his earnings. He lived mostly in New York, well entertained, where, as he put it, with a wink in his reptilian eye, "They don't play as well as they should, or they tactfully won't."

Helen was in the seventh heaven in this welter of nobility. Somehow she knew all their pedigrees. She delighted the men, with a reserve that did not perturb their women. Stephen's Roman portrait of his hostess hung in the great entrance hall under a Giulio Romano ceiling, and opposite an Arras tapestry—fierce competition in which he was gratified to see it held its force and colour. But he longed to repaint the left hand, having learned much since those early days in Rome. It was this portrait, perhaps assisted by Helen's flattering remark to the Duke of Altavara that he had a head worthy of Velasquez, that resulted in an invitation to Madrid, to paint his portrait, when he returned from polo-playing in the Argentine. Stephen discovered that the Dowager Duchess of Rutland was every bit the Duchess of his boyhood and the wonderful letter. They went out in a boat on the lake, halting by little quays and terraced gardens to make sketches. She made him promise to call on her in her house in Arlington Street.

"And, of course, you must come to Belvoir, though how long my son can keep it going the Lord and My Lords of the Treasury only know."

The weather was halcyon. Stephen put up his easel at the end of the terrace and began to paint the long façade, ablaze with bougainvillea and azaleas. On the fourth day the house-party went by launch up the lake to lunch at the Villa d'Este. He pleaded a desire to finish his painting, a gift for his hostess. They did not return until dusk. A little before the party

H

arrived he was standing by the lily-pool, in the scented gloom by the orange trees, when in the deep silence he heard distinctly a voice say, " Stephen ! "   He recognised it instantly.   It was his mother's voice.   He stood transfixed.   Then he rapidly walked into the house and sought the butler.   The Milan–St Gothard express called at Como the next morning at ten-thirty.   It was the only possible train to London.   To catch it he would have to go to Como soon after eight o'clock in the morning.

He went to his room and began to pack.   It was there Helen found him on her return.

" What are you doing, Stephen ? " she cried.

He told her of the voice by the pool.

" You don't mean to say you propose jumping out of here because of an imaginary voice ? "

" It wasn't imaginary.   My mother called me, unmistakably."

" But surely you'll wait and see if you get a telegram—it's probably a complete hallucination."

" Whether it is or it isn't, I'm going by the first train.   I may be too late now," he said, decisively.

" However will you explain it to the Princess ?   They'll think you're mad.   Stephen, you can't behave like this ! "

He stood up over the bag he was packing and looked at his wife's hard face.

" I don't care what they think.   I am going at eight in the morning.   If you don't wish to come, stay ! " he said.

" Very well, I will.   I won't have any part in your outrageous behaviour ! " she replied, going over to the mirror and patting her hair.   " At least you can say it is an important business call —that has some sense."

" And like you, no feeling.   I shall tell the simple truth. Helen, can't you—— "

She turned on him, her eyes blazing, an ugly flush on her face.

" You are impossible !   I've spent my life trying to make a gentleman of you.   I've given—— "

" Helen," he said, very quietly, with a tone that checked her, " I find that unforgivable.   The mistake is yours.   You can't do anything with a brat out of a coal-hole.   You should have chosen better."

He closed down his bag, then he left the room in search of his hostess.

III

It was Mrs Popperwell who opened the door two nights later at the sound of his taxi in Adelaide Row.

" What is it ?   How is she ? " he asked, instantly.

" A stroke, Stephen.   By the mercy of Providence she seems to know nothing since Wednesday, but ten minutes ago she asked where she was and if you had brought the coal in.   She doesn't seem to know you've been away."

They went through into the kitchen.   There she told him all she knew.   Old Dr Bentley came twice a day ; there was nothing to be done.   He thought it was a blood-clot on the brain.   Her right side was paralysed.

" Is there any hope ? " asked Stephen.

" I'm afraid not, Stephen.   Poor soul ! you wouldn't wish her to linger."

" Can I go up ? "

" Yes, she's awake."

He went up the narrow wooden stairs.   The gas was burning low in the small back room where his mother lay, for she would never go into the front room, saying it was his, and keeping it always ready for him.

How small she was in the dim light !   He stooped over her and kissed her, then seated himself by the bed.

" Have you had your supper—you're late at the office again, Stephen," she said in a low voice.

" Yes—we've a lot of work in just now," he replied.

" I can't move—am I ill ? " she asked.   " I want to get up, but I can't."

" No, you must rest.   You do too much, Mother," he said, his hand moving down to take hers.   There was something closed in it.   " What have you got there ? " he asked.

She made no answer, but smiled at him.   From her hand he took a cracked piece of glossy paper.   It was a photograph of a small boy in an Eton suit.   He put it back in her hand.

Presently a Popperwell relation came in, to sit all night with her.   Stephen went downstairs.

He was in and out of the bedroom all the next day. Sometimes she knew he was there, sometimes she wandered, but about seven o'clock in the evening, as the mail plane flew over the house, she said, " I shan't hear that tomorrow. I shall be gone. Your father came a little while ago. He stood at the foot of the bed, very plain. He's waiting for me."

Stephen made no reply. How much do the dying know? The next morning, just before dawn, she was gone.

It was strange how small a family they were; in fact, there was no family. Mrs Popperwell, his mother's oldest friend, sat with him in the first carriage, together with Mr Cust, who offered to conduct the service, despite his frailty. Some of his father's old friends from the Chapel and the colliery, white-headed all of them, also followed. It was a raw, bitter day. The hearse climbed the Derby Road to the sprawling cemetery on the hill, with its pseudo-classical entrance. In the grim funeral chapel Stephen was moved to see William Kiddier and the two old Misses Pearson and Letty Formby, who somehow had got the news and had hurried up from London. At the graveside he was suddenly aware of familiar surroundings. Just over the wall was the house in Clarendon Street where he had gone for his first painting lessons. It must have been here his enemy had thrown the prize pencil-box over the wall. Across the road by the lower gates stood the scene of his early triumph, the heavy, arcaded School of Art, with its open tower. He saw the big windows of the rooms in which he had studied and where he had made the picture that brought him the Travelling Scholarship. The trees were breaking into leaf and birds twittered in the cold afternoon as Mr Cust dropped soil on the lowered coffin and pronounced the Christian formula, " Ashes to ashes, dust to dust." No one there knew that within a month the solemn words would be repeated over him.

IV

Back in Bruton Street, he found Helen had arrived that morning, not knowing the news until she had entered the house. She met him in the hall.

" Stephen, I'm dreadfully sorry. Unhappily you were right.

I was so wretched I simply couldn't stay on. The Princess was very sweet. She thought you were quite right to go."

He kissed her, and she went with him upstairs to unpack. When he took out a tin savings-bank she exclaimed, " Why, whatever's that?" He explained. "There's a chair, my mother's, and a marble clock coming. That's all I've kept. Oh, and this," he said, taking a cardboard box out of his portmanteau. It bore a label, with a dog's head on it: *The Mayway Slip Collar*, it said. "When we buy Dickie a dog we can use it."

A few days later Stephen left for Cannes to paint a portrait of the Maharajah of Caputhala. While there he spent a weekend at *Springland*, the villa slightly above the town where Sir Jesse Boot, now ennobled as Lord Trent, paralysed from neck to foot, spent his winters. He was nearing eighty, but despite the fact that a second affliction made every movement perilous, the indomitable old lion journeyed once a year from his home in Jersey to the south of France. One degree from the horizontal position in which his life was now passed would have proved fatal. The male nurse by his bed watched a spirit-level like an engineer engaged on a work of precision. The journey was made, a promulgation to a wondering world of an edict of the spirit defying the flesh.

Lord Trent had lived to see many of his dreams come true. The vast business he had built enabled him to follow the rôle of Maecenas. He had conceived a university in his native city of Nottingham. He planned it, contested every official frustration, and, from the turning of the first sod to the completion of its tower, he had watched over each phase of this child of his fancy. On the laying of the foundation stone he wrote, with an air of triumph, a cheque for an endowment of one hundred thousand pounds. Previous to this, on receiving, at the age of seventy, the Freedom of his native city, he had poured out his wealth, giving to Nottingham the University site, a great swimming-pool, a boulevard, playing-fields with cricket pavilions, tennis-courts and bowling-greens; all this "in commemoration of a long and happy life", as the old warrior phrased it.

Lord Trent now lay in an upper room of *Springland*, the blinds drawn against the fierce sunlight, his long wispy white hair falling over the pillow, from which his head never rose.

Below, in the large reception-rooms, his guests enjoyed them-selves in a house where great wealth catered for every pleasure. His wife came to his room twice daily, devoted, infallible, and she related the events of the day that, for him, had neither beginning nor end as he lay there in the semi-darkness. All the doors were closing in his prison-house, and he was now so deaf that she told her story through an ear-trumpet while he made difficult responses. But the brain somehow retained its power, sight going, speech going, all physical movement impossible.

The second evening, just before dinner, Lady Trent said her husband would like to see Stephen for a few minutes. She took him upstairs, along a corridor into the darkened room. The large windows looked seawards. Lord Trent lay prone on his bed, dressed wholly in white, his hands motionless on his breast.

" Here's Mr May to see you," shouted Lady Trent, and, turning to Stephen, added, " Speak up, he's very deaf now."

Stephen bent over him. The sharp eyes scanned his face.

" Oh, May, nice to see you ! How are you ? "

" Very well, thank you, Sir Jesse," said Stephen, the old name slipping out.

" I've been thinking. It's ten years since you did my por-trait. You've come a long way since then. Glad to hear of it. And it's about seventeen years since I bought that painting of yours, of the Trent. I paid you twenty-five guineas, I believe. I suppose it would be four hundred now ? You were just a lad then. I was always a good picker ! " He gave a little chuckle.

" You've a marvellous memory, Sir Jesse."

" Yes, about all I have got now, I'm seventy-nine, you know. But I'm not complaining. I've had a long and happy life. Do you go back to the old town much ? "

Stephen gave him some news. They talked for a few minutes. Then the male nurse came in with food. Lady Trent made a sign. Stephen said Goodbye.

" Goodbye ! Glad to see you. Hope you're enjoying your-self," said the prone figure, alive only in voice and eyes.

Outside, as they went along the passage bright with potted hydrangeas and azaleas, Lady Trent said, " He likes to see his friends, but we mustn't tire him."

Stephen made no reply. He could not. Soldiers got V.C.'s

in battle for hot courage.   Here was a long battle being waged
in cold courage.   There should be the Order of the In-
extinguishable Spirit for such warriors as this.

V

He was a month in Cannes, and two weeks in Paris.   In all
this time he had had only two letters, although he had written
to Helen every week.   In the gossip columns he saw she was
entertaining more riotously than ever.   She had organised a
Society Paper Chase for charity that had disorganised London's
traffic and caused questions to be raised in the House of
Commons.   When Stephen got back at the end of June, Helen
was not at home.

"When do you expect Mrs May?" asked Stephen, as the
butler carried up his bags.

"Mrs May went away last week, sir."

"Away, where?"

"There's a letter for you on your desk, sir," said the butler,
evasively.

In the study Stephen found the letter.   He opened it and
read it.   He read it a second time, and then he sat very still.
She had slammed a door on his life.

Dear Stephen,
    You ask why I don't write.   I can't write.   It is not
easy for a woman to tell her husband she wishes no longer
to be his wife.   That is my case.   I have tried my best,
but whatever I do does not seem to suit.   I cost you
too much, I break in on your work.   How much work and
how much money you would have had without me does
not seem to have occurred to you.   There are others who
appreciate me, and I know you will not miss me much.
Sir John Golberry will marry me as soon as you free me.
I hope you will let me divorce you, for Richard's sake.   I
feel I have a right to him, but I do not wish to be un-
generous, so I am willing that at vacations, until he comes
of age, he should spend half with you, if you desire, and
half with me.   John is willing to see that he has everything he requires.   I have left things as straight as possible.
There is no money at the bank, as usual, for the quarterly

bills, and there are bills outstanding for about £1200. As you will no longer have me to support and you can now work uninterruptedly, this will not trouble you. I am sorry it has ended this way, but things have been impossible between us for a long time. I am going away now to friends in Dinant for the summer. My solicitors will do everything that is necessary. Please act as quickly as possible; it is only fair to John, who is very kind to me.

Yours,
Helen.

He picked up the letter and read it a third time. That pip-squeak Sir John Golberry, with his watery eyes and his tremendous appreciation of his own jokes, and, more important, his twenty thousand pounds a year and his estate in Warwickshire. How well she arranged everything. Richard, her Richard, generously for half-vacations, himself muddied in the divorce court. She was a fool to write such a letter; he could use it as proof of collusion. He would not do so. He would give her her freedom. He had wondered often if she had ever really loved him, and to be fair, if he had ever whole-heartedly loved her. He was aware now how, after his proposal, she had put him on probation for two years to see how he succeeded and how, immediately following his success with *The Cardinal*, she had taken him for granted, found a studio and married him. She had been a wonderful organiser, she had manoeuvred many commissions for him. But what commissions! Dreary dowagers holding up their sagging throats with diamonds; swollen-bellied stock-market sharks; a pompous judge; a simpering peer. How often he had longed to go out and fetch in a barrow-boy and a stall-woman exuding vigour and good humour. He was aware also of the spiritual and physical failure in their relationship. She weighed him down with a quiet assertion of superiority. He could not suppress a sense of physical incompletion. He had had to dismiss forcibly an invidious comparison of all his marital relations with that one memorable night of ecstasy and total well-being when Lolly Fellowes lay in his arms. Try as he would, he had never quite succeeded, and something that should have faded into triviality, a folly of youth, remained vivid and possessive.

He walked upstairs, and on his way looked in at the long

drawing-room. Helen had infallible taste. This had been her campaign ground, and it had been excellently laid out. He could not feel the same about the cocktail bar in the back room. A feeble imitator of Picasso had decorated the walls at a preposterous figure. *A nous la folie* said a scroll over a halfstripped trull. *A nous la folie.* Poor Helen, poor Stephen, and above all, poor Dickie, now sleeping blissfully in his dormitory.

At nine o'clock he went out and dined at the Athenæum Club. He might meet Rupert Clover, K.C., who could tell him how to go about things.

CHAPTER XIII

SUNSET

I

STEPHEN MAY put up the house in Bruton Street for sale and removed all the furniture to storage. Before the divorce proceedings he gave Helen everything she wanted. Perhaps he gave her more than she wanted, for he offered to relinquish any claim to young Richard and to pay all the expenses of his education. He would not subject the boy to the tragedy of divided homes; either he came entirely to him or went entirely to her. She replied that in that case the boy would make his home with her—" since he seems so little in your life ". So, with a dagger thrust, she took everything.

In October the divorce—a twenty-four hours' wonder—was published and forgotten. On a day of unforgettable anguish he went to a house in Wimbledon where the boy was living with his governess's family. He was relieved to find it was a cheerful home with a large garden. It was arranged that Helen should not call that day. He had tea with Richard and the family. After a time they tactfully withdrew. He had brought with him a large box of mechanical toys that filled young Richard with joy. He was a sturdy, fair-haired little boy, taking his eyes and colouring from Stephen's mother. Very gently the fact that his father was going on a long journey was conveyed to him.

" Very long—a hundred miles ? "

" Well, longer than that, I think."

" A thousand miles, Daddy ? "

" Perhaps more. It will take me quite a long time. While I am away I want you to be a good boy."

Richard stopped playing with a mechanical toy and looked at his father.

" I won't die while you're away, Daddy. You mustn't look

234

so sad. Woodie said I'll live to be ninety-nine, like her grandmother."

The word of Woodie, the Scotch governess, was incontestable. Stephen did not challenge the prophecy. What could he say to the child, the victim of their domestic tragedy? Whatever their differences, he knew Helen was an excellent mother and the boy would lack nothing.

The last moment came and he summoned desperate courage, holding up the little fellow to kiss him Goodbye when Miss Woodson came into the room at a pre-arranged signal. They went to the door to watch him get into a taxi, and his last sight was of Richard, standing by his governess, waving and shouting " Goodbye, Daddy! Goodbye!"

In the cover of the taxi it was another child who huddled in a corner while the tears filled his eyes.

Stephen set out for India and Nepal. He was there six months, and painted five portraits. Then he came home via the Suez Canal. At Alexandria the Duke of Altavara joined the boat. He insisted on Stephen fulfilling his promised visit to him, and painting his portrait. No time could have been better. They would leave the ship at Gibraltar, where his car would meet them and go to his palace in Seville in time for the celebrated *Feria*. Fatigued by India, Stephen accepted the invitation. He was suddenly stale and dispirited. At thirty-five he began to wonder what life was about.

Spain is perhaps the last land of the European pageant. Its sun smiles as fiercely, its upland plains are as deserted, its people as reticent and proud as in the great days when Velasquez's King Philip was prodigal with the wealth drawn from his empire in the West. In her vast cathedrals the spirit bows to the dark mystery of Creation, her anguished saints, depicted by the genius of Zurbarán and El Greco, glow in divine ecstasy above the heads of the famished poor. In the burning light of the arena the bull falls to the gleaming sword-thrust of the slim matador, multitudinously acclaimed. Still rides the Grandee breasting the flood that threatens his long tradition, while in the torrid south somnolent Africa, though the Moors have long departed, enchains the hours in gardens that listen for the *muezzin* from the crumbling towers.

It was a new world for Stephen. The splendour of April

had smitten the plains and the ravines of the south as they drove through the *vegas* of petalled flame, of mauve and purple and gold, in that spring glory of the fecund earth. They went via Ronda, above the deep gorge and the rainbow bridge, whence they looked on the parti-coloured plains of Andalucia far below. To Stephen's eyes there was almost violence in this light-smitten land, and a sense of ruthless Time, for the Romans had come and gone, the Moors had come and gone, and their dominion had been as the passing of a cloud over the eternal landscape.

The palace of the Duke of Altavara lay behind high walls, but through the great iron grille the world might look in on the *patio*, where the old fountain threw a silver jet, guarded by giant palms and myrtles, and where the goldfish hovered in limpid water in the blue-and-gold faience basin. The palace, once inhabited by Moorish rulers, arcaded, with a deep loggia on the upper floor, was dominated by the old crenellated tower. Within, the vast walls and high cedar ceilings kept cool the scented air, for thus early the heat of summer could be foretold.

The *Feria*—the great festival of Spring, following Holy Week with its processions of gorgeously arrayed Madonnas and cowled penitents—had begun in this mid-April. The roses were in bloom, the scent of orange-blossom pervaded the warm, narrow streets. They drove out to the Fair in a low carriage drawn by a mule-team, the grooms wearing the Duke's livery of yellow and corded blue, with cockades, hammercloths and harness decorated with yellow rosettes. Pretty girls in flounced frocks rode pillion-wise behind their short-jacketed swains in flat-brimmed Cordova hats. By horseback, by carriage, by foot, a gay company thronged the lanterned avenues.

Some twenty guests composed the Duke's house-party during a delirious six days of horse shows, bull-fights, dancing and banqueting in a city that was a bower of roses, camellias and orange-blossom. All through the night the air vibrated with the strumming of guitars, the sharp rattle of castanets, the rhythmic stamp of feet to the staccato music, or, by contrast, the subtle movement of the *seguidilla* when the feet hardly move and raised hands and sinuous wrists sway like reeds in a stream of music.

The guests were mostly Spanish, but Stephen was delighted

to see again the Duchess of Stornaway. He asked if the Duke had come with her.

" No, nor his duchess," she replied, with a ripple of laughter. " So you haven't heard ? I divorced Stornaway, who is quite happy having already found young consolation, and I married ' Pony ' Thirkell only last week, so this is really our honey-moon."

She was more beautiful than ever, and just as light-headed, thought Stephen. Colonel Thirkell was a polo-playing col-league of Altavara's. He was tall, thin, and built to wear the longest riding-boots on the slimmest legs. He had a tired voice, and it seemed as if at any moment, like a run-down clock, he would stop dead. He was a transformed creature on a horse, and Stephen, seeing him ride, wondered where the man ended and the animal began, so perfect in unison was their action.

Stephen stayed on for a few days after the *Feria* and finished Altavara's portrait. He spent the summer wandering slowly northwards, making sketches, until he reached San Sebastian, where he painted portraits of the Villamonte children. After a few weeks in Paris, he crossed to England in the late autumn. He visited young Richard at his preparatory school in Surrey, and then he found a retreat in a small Somerset village, bowered in great elm trees, where he took a furnished Georgian house. There he worked on his Spanish sketches, preparing them for a show at the Leicester Galleries. He exhibited two of his Spanish portraits in the next Summer Exhibition of the Royal Academy, and one of them, of the Duke of Altavara, in polo kit, attracted much attention. Stephen remained on in Somerset until the following October, then he went to London, where he took a small house and studio on Campden Hill.

So he was back from where he had started. This time he knew a quiet content. He was his own master, he worked in seclusion, his expenses were low. He had had a diet of rich clients too long. He selected his subjects now, instead of his subjects selecting him. The next year he sent in to the Summer Exhibition no generals, no magnates, no Society ladies. He exhibited a portrait of his charwoman sitting in her Kensing-ton kitchen, and a view of the Clifton Colliery seen from the churchyard across the River Trent. That year he was elected a Royal Academician. Helen sent him a telegram of congratulation. Another came—" So I have lived to see it. Bravo! Your prophetic old friend William Kiddier." Of all the messages he received, the one he most treasured came from young Richard at his preparatory school. "Mr Fletcher, my form master, showed me your picture in the paper today. I am very proud you now Royal Akadamitian. Your loving son Richard." He tucked the letter in the studio mirror, beside a photo of a bare-kneed boy, above the red tin pillar-box that stood on the mantelshelf.

II

The years fled on silver wings and but for a sense of loneliness he would have accounted himself happy. His painting absorbed him, and he made a new reputation in quite a different genre from that of society portraits. His character studies were less remunerative, but they gave him intense pleasure. One of these, painted from memory—a study in a grocer's shop, which he called "Mrs Popperwell's"—had much success when exhibited. Then one bitter February day in 1934 the news came of William Kiddier's death. He had just returned from America, and was in bed with a severe attack of rheumatism, but he got up in defiance of his doctor's orders and travelled to Nottingham. Memories flooded over him as he stood by the open grave. One by one the links with the past were snapping. His mother, Stuart Cust, Mrs Popperwell, William Kiddier, all gone. Among the remaining friends of his youth there was Letty Formby, still dainty and vivacious. She seemed happy in her Chelsea studio, where she pursued her career as an artist. She often came to tea with him, a most welcome visitor, and she brought him news of Nottingham via her relations still living there.

In the summer of 1938 he went to Bradfield College to see the school play, in which Richard, now a stripling of sixteen, had a part. The sylvan setting of the open-air theatre, with its green branches overhanging the hillside auditorium, was matched by the grace of these boys, whose clear voices gave music to noble words. Stephen's relationship with Richard had surmounted the difficulties of the divorce. Helen now seemed quite anxious that the boy should not lose contact with his father. He was not surprised, therefore, when, one day that summer, she made a proposal over the telephone. They were going off on a trip round the world. Would he not like to have Richard with him for all the summer holiday and the following Christmas? He readily agreed to this. Richard could go with him to Austria at the end of July. " You know, Stephen, despite our misunderstanding, I am very proud of you! " said Helen at the end of their conversation. He thanked her, reflecting that she could not be very proud of Sir John Golberry, a moneyed nit-wit.

Stephen had accepted an invitation to be the guest of Franz Czerny, an old polo-playing friend of Altavara's, at his schloss on Wolfgangsee. He had commissioned him to paint his wife and children. Stephen wrote to Czerny explaining that as he would have his boy with him he would go to one of the hotels on the lake. Czerny would not hear of it. They were to join his family. Thus it came about that Richard found himself in a noisy, happy nest of three boys and two girls, ranging from ten to twenty. They rode, played tennis, bathed in the lake, went on mountain excursions, and to these pleasures young Richard, in heaven, added German lessons and learned *schuhplatter*, the native Austrian folk-dance. Dressed in *lederhosen*, an embroidered jacket, a red-spotted shirt, with knitted half-stockings over his calves and a green felt hat with a *hirschbart* plume, he was a real Tiroler. Tall, graceful, with a smile that lit his dark brown eyes, he was a great favourite. Stephen painted him in costume. The following year the portrait hung on the line at the Royal Academy, called simply " My Son ". Spooner came down from Nottingham to see it, and said to Letty Formby, " You can see an adoring father in every brush stroke ! "

The year closed in tragedy. Sir John and Lady Golberry were killed in a plane-crash at Karachi two weeks before Christmas. So that holiday young Richard came to the studio at Campden Hill, now his home. Thus by a devious path of Fate father and son were together.

There followed the happiest months of Stephen's life. At Easter he took Richard to Florence. They visited the galleries, and he poured out all his knowledge for the eager ears of his son. He rejoiced in his quick intelligence, his physical grace, and his heart leapt with pride when strangers recognised them as father and son, though in their relationship they were more like two boys together.

When the summer holidays came round they abandoned their plan for an extensive tour of Italy and France. The European situation was mounting to a crisis. Hitler seemed bent on war. They were hurriedly constructing shelters all over Great Britain. Richard made a suggestion that surprised while it pleased his father.

"Dad, let's go to Nottingham and visit all the places you knew as a boy. I want to see everything—Clifton Colliery, Adelaide Row, the place where you walloped the kid who called you a miner's brat."

"I wouldn't say I walloped him," interrupted Stephen.

"Well, that's Letty Formby's story. And I want to row up to Clifton Grove, where you first took mother for tea, and see the Vicarage, where you learned Latin, and William Kiddier's studio. And above all I want to go to Skegness and look at the place where Grandpa ruined the family."

So in August, en route for the Westmorland lakes, they set off in a car to Nottingham. They stayed with a friend in The Park, viewed Adelaide Row, and after a few days made a side excursion to Skegness. The place had grown into a prosperous East Coast resort, but Drummond Road and the Memorial Clock Tower had not changed, except that the auction-room, where Signor del Sole had displayed his gift as a lightning artist, had long vanished.

"Wonderful sands!" cried Richard, exuberantly, as they rode their hired horses along the great level beach. At one point, by the Marine Gardens, Stephen halted his horse and stood looking at something.

"What are you looking at, Dad?" asked Richard, coming up to him.

"There used to be a phrenologist's booth just here. My mother one day was very rash and spent sixpence to have my bumps read. The old Professor told her that I was 'a child of abnormal artistic perception'. She didn't like the word 'abnormal', and told him there was no insanity on either side of the family."

"Well, he was a pretty good guesser, wasn't he, Dad? He must have felt your R.A. bump!" laughed Richard. "I'll have to have my head felt. I wonder what on earth I'm going to be."

" Oh, we won't worry about that yet. I've no fears," said Stephen, looking with pride in his eyes at the handsome lad on the horse beside him.

These were very wonderful days for him, warmed by his boy's affection and admiration.

The war-clouds darkened. They returned home from the Lakes three days before Hitler marched into Poland. Richard went back to Bradfield for his last year before going up to Cambridge. They both knew there would be no Cambridge. Moloch had conscripted the young.

Stephen stayed on in his studio, and did duty with the Home Guard. He was troubled that winter with a pain in the shoulder that was diagnosed as fibrositis. Then it shifted into his hands, making work painful. He was alarmed by this development, but in the Spring it vanished. Summer came. It was the strange period of the war that was not a war, until Dunkirk crashed down the false curtain and the enemy stood at the gates. Suddenly young Richard appeared. He was joining the Royal Air Force at once. He departed, high-spirited. The studio was unbearably silent when he had gone.

That winter the fires of Hell consumed London. Letty Formby, bombed out, found refuge with Stephen. She was full of spirit, in no way dismayed. She had hot coffee ready for him when he came in from chilling spells of fire-watching, but after six months he was compelled to relinquish his duties, the rheumatism in his shoulders and arms had returned. He had days of excruciating pain and was wrapped up in thermogene. Fortunately, he had no commissions. He began to use his capital.

On May 22nd, 1943, the light of day was blotted out for him. Richard was missing after a reconnaisance flight in North Africa. Letty came back from a shopping excursion and found him sitting crumpled up before his painting of a lad in *lederhosen* and a flowered jacket. . . .

EPILOGUE

STEPHEN MAY had never finished *The Portrait*, which he read through, until late in the evening. Even had he had the desire, writing had become a physical torment. And since those days of which he had written the world had fallen into ruin.

He put down the manuscript and lay quiet, thinking. It was nearly eleven, and the faithful Groves, after making him comfortable for the night, had retired. He had been to Nottingham only once after Richard's death, this last summer, in a vain pilgrimage to the scenes of his youth. He had visited a former client and his wife, a hospitable pair who had bought a place in the Dukeries. The dukes had all departed from their sylvan haunts, though the memory of Robin Hood, Maid Marian, Friar Tuck and the Sheriff of Nottingham still abided in the deep oak forest. The Duke of Newcastle's house had been pulled down; Rufford Abbey, dismantled, was falling into ruin; Byron's seat, Newstead Abbey, had been divided into apartments; Welbeck Abbey, with its vast underworld of ballroom and passages built by an eccentric duke, was closed. The tall, beautiful Duchess of Portland who, with the Duchess of Rutland, had filled the background of his boyhood in Nottingham, had retreated in her widowed old age to a dower-house. Taxation and a changed era laid a withering touch on the ancient aristocratic splendour.

In the city itself the ravages were as great for one who looked for souvenirs of his boyhood. The booths and stalls had gone from the Market Place to a more practical but less picturesque covered market. The shops no longer knew the glare and pandemonium of the Goose Fair. It had been banished after many centuries to the Forest Recreation Park. The old flat-faced Exchange, with its clock, the beloved toyshop on the corner, and the interior Shambles, haunt of the butchers, had been swept away. In their place rose a grand

Council House, on the classical model, with a great dome and clock dominating the city. Little things Stephen missed. The statue of Samuel Morley, philanthropist, had been removed from opposite the Theatre Royal to make room for a traffic roundabout. The sturdy old reformer had collapsed during a lorry journey to a new site. The graceful marble statue of Richard Parkes Bonington, under a canopy before the School of Art, had vanished.

Stephen wandered up to the Castle on its steep rock dominating the Trent Valley. In the grounds he found the statue of a young airman, Captain Albert Ball, V.C., D.S.O., M.C., Legion d'Honneur, Freeman of the City, killed May, 1918. A boy of twenty-one, the greatest air ace of the first World War, Stephen had met him at the Front in those last weeks of his life. " Yes, paint me, before they get me," he said. " Get you ? You're invulnerable ! " replied Stephen. " Oh, no, my turn'll come—I get tired of always having to kill, one really begins to feel like a murderer ! " The portrait was never made.

The streets off the Wilford Road and around the colliery were as dismal as ever, but the *Crocus* had now a bright parlour and had been transformed by the interior decorator. The customers also had been changed out of all recognition. There were now no more midnight brawls outside the *Crocus* or the *Cremorne*. In Adelaide Row and the other streets the insanitary tub " privies " had been replaced by water-closets. The new prosperity of the miners, earning ten pounds for a forty-hour week as against twenty-five shillings for a fifty-hour week at the close of the century, was denoted by television aerials that rose above the slate roofs. No Popperwell served in the store on the corner. In place of dismal lighting there was electricity. The people looked well-dressed. No pinched children, in semi-rags, screamed in the back-yards.

But walking down these mean streets, their squat houses crushed together in a regimented life, he wondered how he had had the spirit to escape, or how his mother had never lost her neat individuality. Aware of the foolishness of raising ghosts, he could not resist going to the old home. He knocked on the back door, and a clean plump little woman opened it. He told her he had lived there as a boy. Might he look in ? She invited him into the kitchen. As of old, some potatoes were boiling in a saucepan on the oven fire. She wiped a wooden chair and asked him to sit down, while she dried her hands on her apron. Her husband worked at the pit. Owing to the housing shortage, seven people lived in the house : their married daughter with husband and baby, in the parlour, a young lodger in the front bedroom, and a sister, a waitress, in the attic. He asked if he might go up to the attic. " I began my career there," he explained.

" I don't suppose Nellie would mind," said the woman, leading the way.

How tiny it was, how dismal, yet there had been hours of ambitious work when he had felt in heaven here. Desmond Fawn had posed here, shivering, as *Ajax Defying the Lightning* ; here he had drawn his portrait of the Duchess of Rutland. He thanked the woman. No, she had never heard of anyone called May, or Cust, or Popperwell. He said Good morning and left, sad at heart for the forgotten past.

He motored from the Meadows to the new University Park, along a fine boulevard leading to the gates. There, on a pedestal, stood the bronze bust of Lord Trent. Beyond a long lake with an island, crossed by a balustraded bridge, rose the new University, with high columns in a fine classical façade. It was superbly conceived. He left his car and walked by the lake, along a border ablaze with rhododendrons. Then he mounted the hill to the central building and came to a long, broad terrace. Students were walking and sitting in the sun, youthfully animated in their talk. Below them, at the bottom of a green slope, lay the long lake, the crimson-and-white rhododendrons, the boulevard and playing-fields, with the Charnwood Hills rising mistily blue beyond the valley of the Trent. " A long and happy life," said the old warrior on his prison-couch. How gloriously he had crowned it here with his gift to the future !

Somewhere in Monte Carlo a clock struck the hour. Laying aside *The Portrait*, Stephen May switched off the bedside light, meditated a little longer on the past years, and fell asleep.

II

He was awakened the next morning by young Groves bearing a breakfast tray and on it some letters. One had an airmail stamp and the name Schwartz, Szabo and Hillman, with a Los Angeles postmark. It was the reply he awaited. He tore open the envelope.

My dear Mr May,

We thank you for your letter of January 2nd inst. and are glad to learn that we had correctly located you. Our client, Mrs Cyrus D. Pulmacher, who died on October 28th, 1949, by her Will, dated July 4th, 1945, left a number of legacies. Among the legatees is your name, and you are entitled to receive from her estate, free of tax, the sum of one hundred and fifty thousand dollars. Mrs Pulmacher was the widow of Mr Cyrus D. Pulmacher, a San Francisco stockbroker who died in 1938. Mrs Pulmacher was the former wife of the late Mr Thomas D. Quizzell of——

He stopped reading for a moment. Lolly Fellowes! Out of the past she came into his life again. His hand trembled, and he saw, as he had first seen, the little snub-nosed face leaning out of the carriage window as he changed trains at Genoa, over thirty years ago. He read on—

. . . Thomas D. Quizzell of Waco, Texas, who died in 1925, with one child of the marriage, John Denton Quizzell, who was killed at Okinawa in 1945. The late Mrs Pulmacher left a letter addressed to you, with the instruction that if possible it should be delivered to you personally. We have accordingly forwarded it to our Mr James P. Hillman, who is now in Paris. On receipt of a communication from you he will be pleased to call on you, when he will deliver the letter and inform you of the details of the Will and give you any further information you may desire. Mr Hillman will be writing to you in the next few days from the Hotel Crillon, Paris.

With the pleasure of being at your service, dear Mr May, we remain very cordially yours,

Schwartz, Szabo and Hillman.

There was another letter, from the Hotel Crillon, Paris. It was from Mr James P. Hillman, asking if Thursday,

January 19th, would be a convenient day for him to call. He was seeing a client in Cannes on the 17th.

Quick workers, these Americans, thought Stephen, picking up the first letter and re-reading it. Lolly Fellowes. It was as if she had stretched out a hand from the grave to help him, alas! too late. So she, too, had gone. He wondered what the years had given her. There had been a son of that unhappy first marriage. If already there had been a child of the union when he met her in Italy, no word of this had ever escaped her. She had always been unpredictable in her comings and goings, a woman of swift enthusiasm. He wondered what had happened to the School of Psychiatry she had said she would found. What quixotic generosity she had!

Groves came in and cast a reproving eye at May, whose breakfast was half-eaten. His employer looked solemn.

"Not bad news, sir?" he asked, seeing the open letters.

"On the contrary—very good news. I've been left a legacy by an American friend."

Groves opened wide his eyes. "There, sir, you see! You're lucky! I've never been left anything, and don't see how as it can ever happen to me—we're a hard-up lot. But I'd say money left you by the dead is the best money of all. They can't change their minds. You'll have your bath now, sir, and a little massage?"

May nodded.

Groves went into the bathroom to run the water.

Stephen May began to think of Lolly, recalling her youth, her impulsive, generous nature. One hundred and fifty thousand dollars. There was a lot one could do with such a sum, especially in dollars—one of the few free currencies these days. Yet it came to mock him, an almost paralysed hulk. He began to think of the persons to whom he could make legacies. How few they were! What a lonely man he was! But he had always been alone: as a small boy with his dreams, as a young man striving to make his name, and now as a useless cripple, his one passion denied him, his achievement useless.

III

On January 19th at eleven o'clock Mr Hillman arrived, a punctilious little man in a well-pressed suit, with rimless pince-nez and manicured nails. He could tell him very little more about Mrs Pulmacher except that she had left a very large estate, having been wealthy in her own right as well as having inherited a fortune from her second husband. Her son had been born in 1922, after her return to her first husband in 1921, later an invalid, whom she had nursed devotedly. After legacies to a sister and some cousins, she had left half a million dollars for the foundation of a museum to house Thomas D. Quizzell's collection of birds, and half a million to endow the School of Psychiatry she had founded in New York. Ornithology and psychiatry, she had been faithful to the thing she ridiculed and the thing she believed in, after the wayward fashion of the rich who can endow their foibles.

" I have to deliver to you this letter," said Mr Hillman, taking an envelope from his wallet. " It was the express wish of Mrs Pulmacher that you should receive it personally."

" Thank you," said May. Though filled with curiosity, he placed the envelope marked *Stephen May* in his wallet until Hillman had departed, promising to return for dinner that evening.

As soon as the door had closed on the lawyer, May took out the envelope. What message across the years did it contain from Lolly Fellowes?

He opened the envelope. It contained a folded sheet of blank paper with a dry leaf in it. On the back of the leaf was written *Rome, April* 5, 1921. That was all, but it was sufficient. He held the yellow magnolia leaf in his hand. Clearly, as if yesterday, he could see the studio garden on the hillside behind Via Margutta, and Lolly's white hand reaching up to pluck a magnolia leaf as he stood holding her, his lips on the crown of her hair, while the dawn came up over Rome.

When Groves came in he found May sitting in a chair on the balcony, looking out over the morning sea. The January sunshine lay on the blue mountains, resplendent where their snow-capped peaks caught the sunlight. Groves was carrying a mid-morning cup of coffee. He had over one arm an old pair of trousers. In three weeks of devoted service May had become attached to this cheerful youth. He was gentle, constant in attention, a good cook and a most excellent masseur, from whose ministrations he had already derived some relief of his pain.

"These trousers, sir, in your trunk. They've got oil all over them. Shall I send them to the cleaners?" asked Groves, displaying them.

May laughed. "Those were my favourite painting trousers. They're almost a palette, I wiped my knife on them. You can burn them; I shan't want them again."

"You never know what you'll want, sir. So I shan't burn 'em. One day you'll paint again, you'll see. And when you do I hope you'll paint me!"

May smiled at the youth. "I'll make you a promise, Groves. The first canvas I spoil shall have your face on it."

They both laughed. Groves stood by while May drank his coffee.

"It is beautiful here, sir, isn't it?" said Groves, looking out across the blue sea towards Cap Martin in the morning sunlight. "There doesn't seem much wrong with the world until you turn on the radio, or somebody sends you a letter."

"Or you lose your health," added May.

Groves looked at him. "The other day I found a book in your trunk, sir, given you by the author—*Achievement*, by Cecil Roberts," he said quietly.

"Oh yes, I know him. He wrote it for the Jubilee of Boots the Chemists, and gave me a copy, as we both knew Jesse Boot."

"You knew him?"

"Yes, I painted him. He bought some of my earliest things. Lord Trent, as he became later, was a very remarkable man."

Groves picked up the empty cup and paused.

"I liked the book," he said, "especially the part about Jesse Boot. And I couldn't help thinking something, if you don't mind me saying it, sir. There he was, poor man, paralysed for thirty years, and when he was seventy and couldn't move, he gave a big sum of money to his own town ' in commemoration of a long and happy life ', as he put it. And then he went on and gave the city a university. And flat on his back, and fed through a spout, he never complained, and lived to be over eighty. And I said to myself, ' There he was, cheerful and doing things for people, and here's Mr May, just as great in his line, and not nearly in such a bad way, and years younger. Why does he think he's finished? What's he complaining about?' P'r'raps you think I'm cheeky, but that's what I can't help thinking, sir."

May looked at the honest lad before him.

"I don't consider you at all cheeky, Groves," he said, after a pause. "Perhaps you're right. You make me feel rather ashamed of myself."

Groves smiled, showing his strong, gapped teeth. He picked up the trousers. "I'll have 'em cleaned, sir, though I expect you'll be wiping your palette knife on them again," he said, and left the room.

For a long time Stephen May sat in his chair examining himself.

IV

In March the tenancy of the apartment in the Avenue de Grande Bretagne came to an end. A friend living in Alassio, on the Italian border, told him of a small villa to let there. It had eight rooms, a long garden laid out in terraces on the mountain-side, with wide views over the little town and the pretty bay with its enfolding mountains. There was a long, sandy beach and quaint little arcaded streets with vistas of the blue shining sea through the arches.

May sent Groves to inspect the villa, since he would have the task of running it. He came back very enthusiastic. "It's a little gem, sir. Palm trees, roses along the arbour walk, orange trees with oranges on them, lemon trees with lemons on them, grapefruit trees, mimosa in blossom and purple bougainvillea climbing all over the house. And the views from the terrace, sir—it's just like a picture postcard!"

"The house itself, the rooms, the kitchen?"

"They seem all right, sir. There's a marble staircase out of the little hall, nice rooms with balconies and views, five bedrooms, bathroom, sitting-room, dining-room, kitchen, and one big room with lovely great windows looking north-east that might have been made for you, sir. Nicely furnished, and what's very odd, just like here, right next to the English church!"

"Then you think we should take it?"

"I do, sir. It's just right."

"Very well. Alassio it is," said May.

V

Two weeks later, as they made their preparations for moving, something was worrying Groves. His smile was not so quick, he had a preoccupied air. May, sensitive to the change and somewhat perturbed by it, as his life now depended on this good fellow, spoke to him, asking if anything was wrong.

" Yes, sir ; but nothing as you can help."

" Three things are usually the cause of worry to the young. Health, money, love," said May. " You're healthy enough, you tell me you're quite satisfied with your pay, so I assume it's love. Am I right ? "

" You're a wizard, sir. That's just what it is. You see, sir, I've got a girl at home—she's a very nice girl—no fancy stuff, real sensible. We're kind of engaged. She's not seen me now for close on five months, and she's beginning to wonder—natural-like—if I'm serious."

" Are you serious ? "

Groves looked at him with his clear young eyes. " I'll never love any other girl like her—she's one in a thousand."

" She'll marry you ? "

" I'm pretty hopeful of that, sir, when it's possible."

" Then why don't you marry her and bring her out here, and you can both look after me ? "

Groves looked at his employer in silence and wonder. " Do you really mean that, sir ? It's the kind of thing I've dreamed about."

" Nothing could be simpler. Get her to come out, have the parson in Alassio marry you, and take your honeymoon in the villa."

Groves smiled all over his pink face. " Why, it's like a fairy tale, sir, and there's old sourpusses tell you there aren't any fairy tales. I'll write Mary today," he said. " I'm sure she'll come. It's not seeing me that's worrying her."

VI

One morning there was a letter from Letty Formby giving May the latest news. Mrs Littler, formerly Sylvia Cust, now wife of a rear-admiral, would be in Villefranche at the end of April. She was coming out to meet her husband when the

Mediterranean Fleet called there on its Spring cruise. Letty wondered if there was any possibility of Sylvia's seeing her old friend Stephen.

There was, and as he thought about it, May had an idea. Letty Formby must be over seventy now. A holiday in the sun, in so paintable a place as Alassio, would do her good and give him great pleasure. She could come out with young Groves's Mary to look after her on the journey When he mentioned it to Groves, he thought the idea excellent. The next day Stephen wrote to Letty. He used a typewriter now, at Groves's suggestion, with two fingers, and it saved him much pain and was more legible. A week later Letty replied saying she would be delighted to come.

On the first of April they moved into the Villa Mimosa on a foothill above Alassio. Towards the middle of the month Letty Formby arrived, accompanied by a pink-cheeked girl, robust and sensible—Groves's future bride. Letty was quite incredible, a timeless wonder, still dainty, with hardly a wrinkle, and the same quiet eyes and romantic outlook. She was excited by the forthcoming marriage and was delighted to play the rôle of bridesmaid. "I do hope we shall have Sylvia her for the wedding," she said, as they sat after lunch on the terrace, under a gay awning.

"You were always incorrigibly romantic, Letty," said Stephen.

"And you never were?"

Stephen was silent for a few moments, then he said quietly, "My dear, do you see that magnolia tree in the garden below? It reminds me of a story I am going to tell you. It begins in a train along this coast and ends in Rome. No, that is not quite correct. In a way it begins in a vicar's study in Nottingham where I first saw a terrace in the sun, and ends here, where we are sitting on one."

Then he told her the story of the magnolia leaf.

THE END